EXADELIC

EXADELIC

JON EVANS

TOR

TOR PUBLISHING GROUP
NEW YORK

EXADELIC

Copyright © 2023 by Jon Evans

A Tor Book
Published by Tom Doherty Associates / Tor Publishing Group
120 Broadway
New York, NY 10271

www.tor-forge.com

Tor® is a registered trademark of Macmillan Publishing Group, LLC.

The Library of Congress Cataloging-in-Publication Data is available upon request.

ISBN 978-1-250-87773-4 (hardcover)
ISBN 978-1-250-29201-8 (ebook)

Our books may be purchased in bulk for promotional, educational, or business use. Please contact your local bookseller or the Macmillan Corporate and Premium Sales Department at 1-800-221-7945, extension 5442, or by email at MacmillanSpecialMarkets@macmillan.com.

First Edition: 2023

Printed in the United States of America

0 9 8 7 6 5 4 3 2 1

To my father,
who taught me how to be interested in everything

PART ONE

1

INTERROGATORY

"I USED TO WONDER WHY ANYONE WOULD CONFESS TO A CRIME THEY didn't commit," I said to the woman across from me, Special Agent Langan, young, pale, and blond, her whole body taut from the strain of not beating me bloody. "Now I almost get it. My life's basically over now no matter what, isn't it? If I confess at least you two will feel better. Doesn't matter I'm innocent."

Her partner, Special Agent Diaz, middle-aged and mustached, laughed harshly. "Oh, here comes the defense. Conspiracy, right? Someone broke into your work computer, *and* your home computer, and planted . . . that . . . on them both? Why? Who would do that? What makes you such a target?"

"I have no idea," I admitted.

"Because it didn't happen." His right hand clenched into a fist atop the steel table to which I was handcuffed. "Because you are guilty as sin."

Their barely constrained fury was horrible, but revelatory. I still didn't know exactly what they had found, what had been planted, but it had to be something truly vile for these hardened federal agents to treat me like some kind of human-shaped demon.

"I don't expect you to believe me," I said. "I'm not an idiot. But those two guys who arrested me? They didn't act like I was some monster. They acted like they were getting away with something. Do you know them? Do you have any reason to think they might be up to something?"

For a brief moment something like uncertainty flickered on both of their faces.

"Up to *what*?" Agent Langan demanded.

"I don't know. Maybe you should ask them."

The interrogation room was just as depicted by movies and TV, all white but for the steel furniture bolted to the floor and a mirrored wall. It smelled strongly of cleaning products and faintly of vomit. Before handcuffing me to the table they had given me a Clif bar to eat and coffee to drink, but fear and adrenaline had wrung my gut so tight that eating was unthinkable, and my shaking hands had spilled half the coffee.

I reminded myself again to breathe. I was vaguely grateful I sounded even remotely coherent. I felt delirious. Hours earlier, I didn't know how many exactly, Amara and I had woken to a SWAT battering ram smashing open our front door. I felt like a trapdoor had opened beneath me in that moment, and I had been falling since, would fall forever.

Amara.

"Tell us who you got it from," Agent Langan said. "You know what happens to men like you in prison? Worse than you imagine. Worse than you can. The only way to make things better for yourself now is to name names and testify."

"You're not a monster. You didn't make any of it. You never actually hurt anyone. Right?" Agent Diaz tried to play good cop. His smile was that of an animal baring its fangs. "You were curious. That's all. Someone showed it to you. Who? Where?"

I considered telling them the other thing I knew. That as I had been pulled away in handcuffs, desperately pleading my confusion and innocence, just before the door was slammed shut behind me, I had looked back at Amara one final time. That in that moment, the cold, wide-eyed expression she had maintained during the dawn raid—which she had donned, in retrospect, even in its first panic, with no interim of shock or surprise—had finally cracked.

Amara, my friend for twenty years, newly my lover and fiancée, had stood in our living room, her arms wrapped tightly around thirteen-year-old Grace and eleven-year-old Alex, their faces slack with shock . . . and she had mouthed to me, as the FBI dragged me out the door, as her mask fell and her face turned haggard: *I'm sorry.*

Special Agent Diaz was right. My defense was beyond ludicrous. The idea that the FBI had plotted against me was crazy enough. The notion of them conspiring with Amara, who had devoted her whole life to fighting government oppression, was somewhere way past insane.

But as far as I could tell, that was exactly what had happened.

I said, "I want a lawyer."

2

REUNION

THE AGENTS EXPLAINED I WOULD MEET MY LAWYER BEFORE MY INI-tial court appearance, perhaps as long as seventy-two hours after my arrest. Then they left. I expected uniformed men to take me away, but none came. I remained chained to that steel table in that white room for what felt like hours.

I began to wonder if I had been accidentally forgotten, or if this was some kind of psychological warfare, in the hope I might yet confess. Maybe it would work. Maybe I would crack. Maybe I had already lost my mind. That notion made substantially more sense than anything else which had happened since dawn. I was a middle-aged, middle-ranking tech executive, mildly interesting but not memorable, comfortably wealthy but not rich. There were thousands like me in the Bay Area. There was no imaginable reason for anyone to conspire against me.

When the door opened again, I hurtled straight back into fight-or-flight, gasped with sudden adrenaline as if a fanged beast might leap for my throat. Instead, a small fortysomething woman with purple hair entered, dressed expensively in black, her heels clicking crisply on the tiled floor.

I stared at her open-mouthed. She shut the door delicately behind her, sat down across the table, and bestowed on me a triumphantly amused grin, as if this were a friendly game of poker and she had just claimed all my chips. "Adrian. I wish this were a more pleasant surprise."

"*Vika?*" I could barely get the name out. "What—what are you doing here?"

She pursed her lips as if suppressing a laugh, then took a moment to ostentatiously inspect the dark gloss on her fingernails. "Funny. I was about to ask you the same thing."

She was tiny, with high cheekbones and a prominent chin. She had been an aerialist once; I remembered her grappling with silks high above the DNA Lounge's dance floor, albeit with more grim precision than grace. She still had an acrobat's strong torso.

I looked around wildly, as if the walls might fall away to reveal a movie set. "How did you even get in here?" Vika had nothing to do with law enforcement. After we fell out of touch, she had become the executive director of the Ethical AI Foundation, and was now frequently quoted by the media, mostly sharply criticizing those AI researchers and companies who didn't support the EAF. She had been profiled by *Wired* and dubbed one of "The 50 Most Powerful Women In Tech" by *Vanity Fair.* There was no imaginable reason for her to be here.

We had been friends once, long ago, in our twenties, in the aughts, both members of a sprawling cohort of would-be goth-industrial cyberpunks. We had dressed in leather and vinyl bondage gear, sculpted our hair into colored ramparts, and roamed the streets and nightclubs and parties of San Francisco, trying to exude rebel menace. In truth we had mostly been overcompensating nerds from middle-class backgrounds, taking on the trappings of subversion for a few years before reverting to capitalist conformity. But Vika still dressed the part. Her black leather jacket would have fit right in at the Trocadero or the DNA Lounge.

She hitched up her legs to perch cross-legged on the metal chair. She had always had the mannerisms of a tiny bird of prey. "I seem to have acquired some connections of significance. *Et tu?*"

"I was set up. I don't understand how."

"Yes, of course," Vika said airily, "but what I want to know, Adrian, is why? How is it that you came to attract the deleterious attention of . . . powerful figures? Not Meredith. Not Jered. Not even Amara." I twitched. "But you. You surprise me. I would never have guessed."

"Powerful figures? What powerful figures?"

"Come on. Seriously?" I stared at her befuddled. She sighed as if I had botched a simple favor. "I can barely believe you are still this clueless. All right, I'll try something easier. Your job. Tell me about it. What do you do? Well." She smiled faintly. "Did, I imagine, considering your predicament."

I hesitated. Everything about this felt deeply weird and wrong, but that had been true since dawn, and whatever she was doing here, however in-explicable her appearance might be, Vika was an old friend and seemed to believe me innocent. And it wasn't like I had anything to hide or lose. "Vice president of engineering at Sybilisk."

"And what does Sybilisk do?"

"We," but she was right, it was no longer *we*, clearly I would never work there again, "use neural networks to establish online identities. Distinguish real people from bots, offer and verify pseudonymous identities, provide account and secret key retrieval facilities, vet and filter voter rolls, that sort of thing. Enterprise identity solutions."

"So you, or those you hired, might influence the rules and standards for votes, access to secret keys, cryptocurrency accounts, that sort of thing?"

"Not really. I mean, it's not like someone might want me replaced so they can secretly commit code that installs a back door into an account re-covery model or something like that. First, we're a machine learning com-pany, you don't write our software, you train it."

"Adrian. There is truly no need to mansplain machine learning to me of all women."

"Right. Sorry. Second, we—they—have whole teams of people watching for those kinds of anomalies, mountains of audit trails and observability and continuous 24/7 testing. It just wouldn't be possible for one or even several rogue employees to sneak some nefarious code in without being noticed. Especially not me. I haven't written code or tweaked a hyperparameter in years. Mostly I just go to meetings. What does this have to do with—"

"What about replacing your software wholesale? Using entirely differ-ent models or crypto algorithms?"

"That's strategy, not tactics. CTO's call, not mine."

Vika nodded slowly, leaned back, tapped her light-devouring fingernails on the table, and pursed her lips again, thinking.

I remembered kissing those lips, almost twenty years ago. She and I had made out for what had felt like a delicious eternity, at a tactile party in a blacked-out room after a warehouse rave, both of us still coming down from MDMA. I remembered her tiny body firm and warm beneath my hands, her knotted dreadlocks rough against my face, her devouring kisses.

I had spent the next year, even after I started awkwardly dating Kim, hanging around Vika at parties, doing her favors, buying her lunches and concert tickets, occasionally rewarded by a drunken peck good night, always left hoping for more. Kim knew, and hated it, and hated Vika to the extent that she was capable of hatred, and never said anything, because she feared if she did, she might lose me. I still didn't like to think of how badly I had treated her. Much later I had realized that this outcome was exactly why Vika had sought me out in that warm dark room. Even while on MDMA she had been strategically manipulative.

Not Meredith. Not Jered. Why those two names from our shared past? I hadn't seen Jered for years, not since he had gotten rich and founded that not-quite-a-cult, and Meredith's occasional appearances were as unpredictable, inexplicable, and disconcerting as solar flares.

"I just can't see it," Vika announced. "It's not obvious, and you're not a subtle person. What about Amara?"

I swallowed. "What about Amara?"

She cocked her head, sensing something from my body language, or the way I had said the name. "Oh, no, I asked first. What *about* Amara?"

I took a deep breath. "She's why I'm in here. I think. She set me up. Or helped."

"Is that so?" Vika leaned in, truly interested at last, her dark eyes greedy. "I would very much like to know why you think that."

I shook my head, feeling cold, like I had just made a terrible mistake. As if I had somehow betrayed Amara. As if I still owed her any loyalty. But I didn't like the hunger in Vika's eyes. She had always been so charismatic that even as she used people, they forgave her for it; but no matter who she had dated or befriended, Vika had only truly ever looked out for herself.

"What do you mean," I asked, "powerful figures?"

"You really don't know, do you. It is such a wonder to me that you are the one in here."

I stared at her, confused. "You and me both."

"Perhaps it's a complex confluence no human could possibly understand. Maybe just a glitch. I don't suppose it matters either way." She stood, oddly wistful. "For some reason I always liked you, Adrian. I thought you might be useful one day. I suppose not. Goodbye."

It sounded very final. She turned her back on me, opened the door, and walked out. Her heels echoed in the hall until the door closed behind her. Shortly afterward, uniformed men came to take me to the lockup. They were not gentle about it.

3

SHIV

THEY PROPELLED ME DOWN INDUSTRIAL HALLWAYS, INTO THE DEPTHS of whatever building I was in. Somewhere in Oakland, I thought. We lingered outside a holding cell for a moment, while waiting on a steel door to a connecting corridor.

The holding cell was visible through its cracked wire-grid window: a crowded concrete box with a metal bench around its perimeter and a toilet in its corner. The ambient odor reminded me of the hockey-arena change rooms of my youth. Its dozen inhabitants looked grim and listless, except for an obese bald white man who gazed at me thoughtfully, as if he knew me, and a heavily tattooed young Asian man grinning with a mouth full of metal teeth.

I looked away. The steel door buzzed open. I was led down another narrow concrete hall to a tiny windowless cell, furnished with a steel bunk bed, thin mattresses, threadbare sheets, a steel sink, and a lidless steel toilet. I expected a cellmate but the door closed on me alone. They left me a plastic meal tray adorned with a limp ham-and-cheese sandwich, a bag of M&M's, and a paper cup of orange juice. When I saw the food I realized I was famished.

After I ate, I wanted to think, to try to remember if Amara had behaved strangely in recent days, if she had been hiding something from me. But it was hard to think. My brain and body had both apparently had enough. Suddenly woozy, I sat, then lay, on the lower bunk. It had already been by some distance the longest day of my life.

Amara had never hidden anything from me, as far as I could remember.

Well. No. Now that I thought about it, that wasn't entirely true. There was the box. That strange, never-explained box in our basement closet. I tried to imagine some way that might somehow be connected to what was happening.

But I couldn't think. I wasn't just woozy. Something else was happening. My vision swam. A kind of static began to roar in my ears. I felt too weak to stand, or even sit. My muscles seemed impossibly distant, slipped from the bounds of my mind's control. It felt like those mornings in my teens when I would wake up paralyzed for long minutes, unable to command my own body. *The hag*, Newfoundlanders called it, an evil witch sitting on your chest.

As I lay there, paralyzed, the overhead light went out.

Some time later my cell door opened. A dim radiance, emergency lighting, shone from the hall. I couldn't even focus my eyes on the sizable shadowy figure who entered. The whole bed shifted when he sat beside me. The big bald man from the holding cell.

"Unlucky for you, mate," he said, in a working-class British accent, as he reached up to the upper bunk. "Cell accidentally left open just as a power glitch killed all the cameras. Not your day."

I tried to speak but could only make a low whimpering noise.

"Allow me to assuage your curiosity. Ever hear of the Dubrovka Theater? Forty Chechens took eight hundred hostages. FSB pumped in a neurotoxin, KO'd them all. Killed heaps of hostages too, but omelettes are hard on eggs." Thick fingers coiled fabric deftly around my neck. The sheet from the upper bunk. My head bobbed like a child's toy as he looped the noose. "Derivative of that in your M&M's. Car Bomb they call it, don't ask me why. Safer, both ingestible and aerosolizable, undetectable in twelve hours. But who'll look too closely at a kiddie diddler who hanged himself first night in prison, innit? Suicide's good as a confession. Better. Cleaner. One might recant a confession."

I tried to say *I didn't*, but it came out as two gurgles.

"What's that you say? Not guilty? No difference to me, mate. I am but an escort to where those deities of your choice might sort you out." He took my hands, curled them into half fists. "Let's get the details right, now. Professional pride. They always claw at their neck, at the last, after they're too weak to stop it. The pathos of it. Puts a tear in my eye every time."

He began to use my own fingers to scrape at my neck, above the noose, hard enough that I felt my fingernails scratch my skin. I tried to fight but my muscles were beyond all command. It felt like I was already dead. He pulled the free end of the noose taut and hoisted it up toward the upper bunk, bringing my head and upper torso along, asphyxiating me.

Then the big man twitched, grunted, and let go. As my head dropped back to the mattress he grunted again. Then he fell off the bed. I could breathe again. There was someone else in the room now. This new figure crouched down. A warm iron smell filled the air.

"Sorry, need that," the tattooed Asian man said, breathing hard, the one from the cell, the one whose smile had revealed teeth replete with metal dental work, as he yanked the sheet out from beneath me. "Don't want it spilling into the hall." He crouched and did something with it, then unwrapped the other sheet from my neck and used it as well. Then he lifted my arm, inspected it carefully, and jabbed something into the inside of my wrist.

What happened next felt like a slow-motion high-voltage electric shock. I tried to scream but could only gurgle.

Then I sat up and began to gasp for breath.

"Quiet," the Asian man cautioned me. "Ride it out. Then we're on our way."

"Wha?" I could already speak again, and move, albeit clumsily. I looked down at the big man on the floor. In the dim light he lay with his head in a pool of darkness, like a halo in a religious painting. Another crumpled pile of darkness lay pressed against his throat. Then I realized: the darknesses and the smell were blood, lots of it.

"Let's go. A little more judo before they figure out they're hacked."

"They? What? Who are they? Who are you?" I was so adrenalinized and confused, I could barely figure out questions to blurt.

"Name's Jay. Someone will explain later. If there is a later." Incredibly, he was grinning. His smile was now much less metallic than it had been in the holding cell. I looked down to the tiny, razor-sharp shiv he held, wet with the big man's blood, and understood. He had smuggled it into prison in his mouth, cunningly disassembled. "Follow me."

"I'm not going anywhere until . . ." I stopped, unable to imagine any circumstances at all.

He sighed. "OK. I'm not supposed to tell you this, but Meredith says hello."

That snapped me back to full astonished attention. "*Meredith?*"

"Later. Come on, there's not much time. You think they won't try to kill you again?"

4

EGRESS

IT WASN'T THAT THE INVOCATION OF MEREDITH MADE ANY OF THIS—
the arrest, the assassination attempt, the rescue—make any sense. But of
all the people I had ever met, she seemed the least unlikely to be involved
in this kind of crescendoing symphony of violent surreality. Knowing she
was connected hinted at the existence of some kind of explanation, somewhere, if I could find her.

"Stay in the moment, don't freak out," Jay told me as he led me back
toward the holding cell. "I know your brain wants to freak out. Tell it to
do it later. Right now, in this moment, your name is Trevor Milner. Don't
bother faking the accent."

"Who's Trevor Milner?"

"Dude who just tried to kill you. A van is coming to transfer him out of
here, before the investigation into your unfortunate demise begins."

"So . . . I'm my own assassin?" I felt dizzy, and not just from the after-
effects of the neurotoxin. "Won't they, uh, notice?"

"We think we've arranged things so it's a different driver. He'll handle
checking you out, they already set that up, like they set up the arrest and
the cell and the power and the guards. Using their own strength against
them. Judo. They don't want a real audit trail any more than we do, so he'll
just have a picture on his phone, and we're pretty sure we've replaced that
with a picture of you."

"Pretty sure," I echoed. "What if not?"

"Then things get interesting in a bad way."

After a moment I said, "I don't think I like your plan. So I get out. Then

I'm an escaped prisoner. They'll catch me, and I'll be guilty of escaping. I've been falsely accused. Of awful things. I need to be able to clear my name."

Jay gave me a scathing look. "Look, buddy, I don't know exactly what's going on, but I know it goes way past false accusations. You're playing the big game now, you need to start thinking a whole lot larger than your own little problems. Question isn't whether the US government will still be after you when this all shakes out. Question is whether it will still exist."

I stared at him.

"Second, you don't like our plan? Guess what, if it wasn't for us, you'd be dead right now. You think they won't try again if you stay inside?"

"Ah. Good point. OK. Let's try it."

He took me into the holding cell, now empty but for us, and we sat on its bench.

Two thoughts occurred to me. "How did you get in here? How do you get out?"

"Oh, I come whenever Meredith and company need some work done in a US jail. They arrest me, then when they find out I'm not a US citizen and I'm here illegally, they deport me to Vietnam. I get there, I get bribed out of custody, I sneak back here when they need me. Kind of a merry-go-round."

The analogy did not make me any less dizzy. "You sound American."

"Been here since I was two. But never got citizenship, so when they busted my dumb eighteen-year-old gangbanger ass, I got deported. Didn't speak a word of Vietnamese. Couple years later, got in a jam in Saigon, that's where I met Meredith, she got me out. Since then—"

But I didn't find out what had happened since, because we were interrupted by the sound of a door opening near the holding cell.

"Fine, man, whatever," Jay said loudly, moving to sit across the room from me.

The door opened. A cadaverous white-haired man looked in, armed and uniformed, his face graven with wrinkles, holding an iPhone as if it were an oracle. "Trevor Milner?"

I took a breath, again felt like I was falling, except now the whole world was spinning around me, too. I told myself this was better. It meant I had no idea anymore where I might land. "That's me."

He looked at me, then nodded. "Come. You," he said to Jay, "stay."

"Shit," said Jay sarcastically, "and I was planning such a good time with y'all."

I followed the old man out. Before we went through the door that connected to the rest of the complex, he slipped me a white cardboard ID card. At each of the desks, doors, and sally ports en route to freedom, staffed by sullen night-shift corrections bureaucrats, my card was checked, and sometimes stamped.

Jay had been right. I was allowed to depart, taken in handcuffs to an unmarked white van, and given a seat on the facing benches in its back. No one else rode with me.

"Dropping you at a warehouse near the Coliseum," the old man said over his shoulder, through the wire cage separating prisoners from driver. "There'll be a pickup for you there."

I wondered if it might be Meredith herself. I was beginning to suspect this was all meant to have happened to someone else, someone actually connected to whatever kind of great clandestine power play was going on. How else to explain an FBI conspiracy, an assassin with a cutting-edge neurotoxin, a prison break from within, and a threat to the entire US government?

But then: how to explain Amara?

5

DECAY

I EMERGED FROM THE VAN INTO A CITYSCAPE OF EMPTY STREETS AND
derelict warehouses, beneath the lights of the Oakland hills silhouetted
by incipient dawn. The few working streetlamps shone on broken glass,
cracked concrete, ragged strands of barbed wire. The old man gestured me
out of the van, uncuffed me, and nodded gruffly.

"Wait," I said as he climbed back in, "where do I go now?"

"Not my department," he said, and drove off.

I stood confused in that quasi-apocalyptic industrial zone. To the north
I saw brighter streetlights, was tempted to walk that way, then reconsidered. I did not want to return to civilization. Civilization would be after
me very soon.

A sudden bright light blinded me. I gasped, raised my hand to ward it
off, and peered at its source, the nearest warehouse, where someone stood
in a doorway aiming it at me.

"Hello?" I asked.

"What's your name?" a soft voice demanded.

"Adrian. Adrian Ross."

They turned off the light. "God's sake, man, don't go around telling
people your full name, you're an escaped fugitive."

"Oh. Sorry." I walked toward them hesitantly, through a door hanging open in the remains of the fence around the warehouse. "You're waiting for me?"

"Apparently." My rescuer, I hoped, was tall, maybe thirty, androgynous,
with a shock of short blue hair, wearing a black puffy jacket. "I'm Quinn.

I'd say it was a pleasure to meet you but honestly under the circumstances it isn't really."

"Yeah. Sorry."

"Not your fault, I'm told. Come in."

The warehouse was full of long, empty metal tables, above which hung a complicated network of rusting chains and hooks, connected to large geared machines of baffling usage and provenance, all thick with rust. Rodent footprints were visible in the dust on the floor. The air had a musty industrial smell.

"Are you with—" I cut myself off. "Who are you with?"

"Very good. Not volunteering information. We'll make an outlaw of you yet. Yes, I'm with Meredith."

"Can I talk to her?"

"No chance. She's in the belly of the beast."

I blinked. "Which beast is that exactly?"

"The Pentagon. Or Fort Meade. Or some affiliated black site somewhere." Quinn led me deeper into the warehouse. "Far as they know, she's still their faithful coherence whisperer."

"Their what?"

"Coherence. The AI she built for them. The reason you're here."

"Coherence," I echoed. "That can't be right. I don't know anything about that. I've never even heard of it."

"Yes, well, it's heard of you. It identified you as one of the primary threats to its future. What makes you so dangerous?"

"It *what*?" I stopped dead in my tracks. "That's insane. I'm not dangerous to anything. I don't know anything. I'm not a threat. I'm just a vice president of engineering."

"Oh." Quinn sounded deeply disappointed. "Well. This way."

I followed. "This is crazy. There's been a mistake. I was set up."

"By who?"

"The FBI and my fiancée, far as I can tell."

"Your fiancée? Wow. Guess at least you dodged a marital bullet, huh?"

"I'm sure it was for her kids." I felt an irrational but powerful urge to defend Amara against criticism, despite her having apparently planted false evidence that I had committed horrific crimes. "She didn't know what was going to happen."

"If you say so."

I wanted to try to explain. Amara wouldn't have betrayed me for money, or status, anything like that. But she had always made it clear that Alex and Grace came first.

Instead I thought aloud, "Someone must have messed with its training or something. Fed it adversarial data. But what kind of moron would take that kind of prediction seriously? It's not actually artificial intelligence. Until and unless we have some kind of massive breakthrough, what you're calling AI is just a weird kind of induced evolutionary programming that lets computers do pattern recognition. You're telling me someone at the Pentagon or the NSA fed some data into a machine learning system, and it told them I was a threat, so they had me arrested? They tried to have me *killed*? And Amara was in on it? That's . . . that's so far past nuts I don't even know what to call it. Has everyone lost their minds? Meredith's way too smart for that. Everyone should be too smart for that."

"Yes, well," Quinn said, "Meredith being way too smart is kind of the fundamental problem here, actually. That's why I didn't call Coherence a machine learning system. Here we go. This is an elevator shaft, but the elevator doesn't work, so we take the ladder down."

Before us a shiny new aluminum ladder descended into darkness. I looked at it dubiously. "Down where?"

"The pit of eternal stench."

"Great." Then I parsed what I had just heard. "Wait. What do you mean, that's why you didn't call it a machine learning system?"

"Because it's not. Because Meredith is way too smart. Because we *have* had some kind of massive breakthrough, courtesy of her and Exadelic." I blinked. I'd heard of Exadelic. Machine learning for massive quantities of real-time data, at scale, mostly for law enforcement and militaries. Critics called them Police State Inc. I couldn't imagine Meredith, long a devout anarchist, working with them in any capacity. "Coherence isn't machine learning. It might have started that way, but not anymore. Now it's an artificial general intelligence, a real one, strong AI, fully autonomous. Whatever you call it, it's smarter than us, and making itself smarter yet with every passing second. Only a few people know this. We'd kind of assumed you were already one of them. Given that it thinks you are one of the primary threats to its existence."

I stared, speechless. My mouth worked, but nothing came out.

If this was true—it wasn't true, it *couldn't* be true, it was too huge and shocking and appalling to be true, but if it was true—no wonder people were being detained and murdered. No wonder Jay had talked about the prospect of the US government not existing next year. If this was true it was maybe the biggest thing ever to happen in the history of the species *Homo sapiens*. And maybe the last.

6

FASCIAL

"BOGGLE YOUR MIND LATER," QUINN SAID. "ACCESS TUNNEL DOWN there connects to another warehouse. We bring the ladder down behind us in case they figure out what happened and come back to where they dropped you off."

Descending suddenly made a lot of sense. The tunnel was barren concrete, tall and narrow, a distant light visible at its end. Quinn walked it very quickly, but reassuringly that seemed to be their natural pace, rather than any kind of desperate rush.

"What's your connection to this?" I asked. "Or are we maintaining maximum operational security?"

"Usual story. Meredith arbitrage, I call it. She finds capable people who have been completely screwed over by circumstances beyond their control, breaks them out, then the usual contractual terms are eternal allegiance and firstborn child."

"You sound a bit like a rebel angel."

Quinn stopped before the elevator on the other end of the tunnel, which apparently functioned, and turned to look at me fiercely. "I'm actually not. I talk ironically because people tend to freak the fuck out whenever I talk sincerely. Maybe they're not used to it or whatever. I'm not going to tell you what she did for me, but the truth is, I do shit like rescuing clueless fugitive cishet white men in the dead of night because I would fucking die for her. Clear?"

"Very," I said, chastened.

"Good."

I was led up into another warehouse, a vast off-white cavern unsullied by any contents except for a single desk and chair in the corner near where we emerged. It had only eight small windows, two in each wall, but a huge skylight across the roof. Its latticed glass was broken in several places. Small birds fluttered amid the ceiling girders.

"Change," Quinn said, indicating the clothes and shoes stacked on the desk, and the worryingly large hypodermic needle next to them. "Don't waste my time with false modesty. We have delicate work to do."

"I . . . What?" I eyed the syringe with dismay.

"It's fine, I'm a registered nurse. Change. Completely. Don't put the shoes or socks on yet."

The jeans stretched enough to feel comfortable. The underwear and blue T-shirt were too big, but the shoes were the right size. "I really don't want to be drugged," I protested. "They drugged me already, a neurotoxin, there might be some kind of interaction or—"

"Oh, really?" For the first time Quinn sounded interested in my story. "They Car Bombed you? What was it like? How long was onset?"

I shook my head. "Hard to say. I was in a cell. Five minutes? Then my body just stopped doing anything I told it to. What's in that needle?"

"Not a drug. It's for intrafascial use, against recognition. Sit."

"Against recognition?"

"Sit."

I sat. Quinn stood over me, needle in hand. "You're about to be a highly wanted man. Cameras, facial recognition, you wouldn't last five minutes. Except. This substance is inert but hardens in the fascia under your skin, into artificial cysts. I'm going to inject it into your face, enough to screw up facial recognition, then your feet."

"My feet?"

"Gait recognition. Couple well-placed cysts should change your stride enough to throw that off too. Also one shot next to your larynx, tweak your voiceprint. Now close your eyes, breathe slowly, and don't move. You're going to feel some pinches."

They felt considerably worse than pinches, and there were a lot of them. After finishing with my head, Quinn knelt and jabbed the needle into the sides of each foot, several times. I brushed droplets of blood away from my face and neck. All the injection sites ached fiercely.

"All right." Quinn stood, examined me carefully. "Should do. You look different already."

"How different?"

"Put your socks and shoes on." I began to do so. "People should be here to pick us up soon. I was supposed to have new ID for you but there was some kind of screwup. Hopefully that will be waiting when we get there."

"Where?"

"I'm not sure. I heard something about Siblings." I started at that. Jered's cult. "But I didn't need to know, and neither do you."

Jered's cult. Meredith's AI. They had been Amara's closest friends, back in the aughts, not counting Darren. I hadn't seen either for years. Neither had she. Or had she gotten involved with one or both of them again, secretly? Had she become a covert player in some kind of desperate game for the highest of stakes? If so, for how long?

I had long known, on some level, even if unwilling to admit it to myself, that Amara had agreed to marry me not because she had ever especially wanted to be with me in particular, but because she knew me, liked me well enough, knew I was safe—unlike Darren—and knew I would provide for Alex and Grace's future. When we consummated our physical relationship, when I finally lay naked with the woman I had had a searing crush on for twenty years, since the day I met her at a party at the legendary Clementina Street apartment she and Darren had shared with Valentine and Jack, it was hard to keep myself from wondering whether she was at all attracted to me, or just acting it because she had decided it best for all concerned.

People had called Darren a genius. Maybe he was. He had been brilliant, beautiful, omni-talented, and charismatic, undoubtedly. But back when I had met them, before he had dimmed her light, it had seemed to me that Amara was the genius of the two.

I had never dated a woman with children before, but Alex and Grace had liked me, and I them, from the start. For a time I was shockingly happy. After only a few months I sold my SoMa apartment and bought a fixer-upper house in the Sunset for the four of us. Our upcoming marriage had felt like a redundant bureaucratic recognition of the shining joy of our modern family.

There had been one oddity, though. There was the box.

It had been a considerable surprise to find it in a corner of our basement closet when searching for my ski boots: a lacquered black box as big as a large toolbox, unadorned except for the ornate lock on one side and an inlaid silver sigil, highly stylized with loops and curlicues, on the other. I had no memory of it from our moving day. I had never seen it before at all.

When I asked Amara about it, the question shook her usual preternatural calm. "It's nothing," she said, too quickly. I stared at her, baffled. After a few breaths she edited her answer: "Just old memories. Nostalgia. From Darren. I don't even have the key anymore. I don't like thinking about it, but I can't throw it away."

"What's in it?" I asked.

"Nothing of importance. Not for a very long time. I'm sorry. I don't want to talk about it. Just leave it. Please." After which Amara, who usually made a point of calmly and patiently resolving anything that even resembled a relationship issue, had turned and walked out of the room. I considered pursuing her but decided to wait until she was less upset.

When I brought it up again, though, she repeated, "I don't want to talk about it. It's not doing any harm. Just leave it." In the sharpest, most brittle tone I had ever heard from her.

I didn't bring it up again. A month later, though, the thought of it nagged at me, and one day, when alone, I went down to that closet again. I couldn't be sure if it had moved from its previous position. I established that it was very solid, and its lock was very strong. Then I stared at it a long moment, before deciding to pile the junk in which it had been buried back on it, not think about it again, and relax back into my newly happy life. I had done just that until the moment, only twenty-four hours ago, when the SWAT team had burst in, and the trapdoor to this howling abyss had opened beneath me.

Quinn's pocket buzzed, a phone in vibration mode. "Shit." Their voice suddenly a near whisper. "Proximity sensor. Not our team. Stay quiet."

They stalked catlike to the window nearest the desk, whole body taut, peered out, then looked back. "Beat-up RV. Maybe just looking for a new parking spot. But the timing's a bit too convenient, you ask me. Get back down the tunnel, I'll go keep a watchful eye. Anything wrong or unexpected happens, get out of here."

I obeyed. It wasn't clear to me exactly what I was waiting for. I supposed for Quinn to come back and give me the all clear.

What I heard next was a series of loud, hollow popping sounds. It took a long moment to recognize it as gunfire.

7

RUNAWAY

MY TWO COMPETING INSTINCTS WERE: RUN LIKE HELL, AND RUSH TO help. The former won by a wide margin. I stabbed B for basement. There I fled back down the dark tunnel to the first warehouse, desperately hoping there was no welcoming party there.

My wish was granted, but I doubted it would stay that way long. I scrambled up the ladder and kept running, out of the warehouse, northward. There was no one around.

I emerged from the industrial district into a poor residential zone: houses with ragged lawns guarded by tall fences, battered cars parked on the streets. I tried to look inobtrusive, like a jogger. By the time I reached a zone of strip malls and bus stops I was gasping with exhaustion. I turned east for a while, walking now but not daring to stop, then back north at International Boulevard. A McDonald's cashier gave me a wary look, then a free cup of water and the code to the bathroom. I trudged onward, past abandoned stores and suspicious passersby, vaguely aiming for downtown Oakland, where at least I knew the geography.

All that on something like autopilot, like a fleeing animal. But as I marched onward, a little rational thought seeped into me, none of it good.

They were still trying to kill me. They had just opened fire on—maybe killed—Quinn, for the sin of trying to help me. I still didn't know who they were, or why, except that it was somehow connected to the mind-boggling claim that Meredith, whom I hadn't seen in years, had built a breakthrough AI for the US government, and it considered me a threat, and the even more mind-boggling evidence that I had been betrayed by the woman I loved. Every authority was after me. If recaptured I would probably be killed. I had nothing at all, no money, no phone, no ID, only the literal clothes on my back.

I passed an *East Bay Times* newspaper box, a relic of an earlier age, amazingly still filled with new papers each day. The sight of its cover story caused me to come to a sudden halt: FBI BUSTS SILICON VALLEY CHILD PORN RING.

A nearby 7-Eleven had a newspaper rack. I began to read. The FBI had made thirteen arrests yesterday, "including executives at Apple, Google, Facebook, and lesser-known startup 'unicorns' such as AI company Sybilisk." Meaning me. "Congressman Lawrence Stohle, R-Fresno, a noted advocate of 'lawful access' laws, said, 'I think we're beginning to understand why Big Tech is so devoted to the cause of warrant-proof encrypted systems that protect terrorists and child pornographers.'"

"Hey," the 7-Eleven clerk objected. "Buy it or put it back."

I nodded, put it back, and stumbled away, dazed. Apparently I was not the only target. Apparently the conspiracy was at least in part political.

I had no way of contacting Meredith. I couldn't log into my email without my phone for second-factor authentication. Even if I somehow managed, the attempt would be noticed and flagged, the IP geolocated, SWAT teams sent to pick me up. My arrest was a front-page story. I had already left at least one corpse in my wake. I wondered how the dead would be cleaned up, the body or bodies disappeared, the files erased.

Could I go to anyone for help? The more I thought about it, the more I thought not. My elderly mother and faraway sister would have their phones watched for calls from strange numbers, and I was not at all certain they would help me hide. They believed in American institutions. They'd think they'd be doing me a favor by finding the right one for me.

Anyone else, even my oldest friends—the accusation of *child porn* was so terrible, so unspeakable, it made me untrustworthy in a way that even a conviction on a murder charge wouldn't. Even those who might want to help wouldn't dream of taking the risk of aiding and abetting a wanted man. The only person I might have trusted was the same woman who had betrayed me.

All that without even considering the possibility that Quinn's incredible, unbelievable claim might actually be true, that somewhere out there was an inhuman intelligence already more capable than any other on the planet, bent on making itself smarter yet, and on eliminating threats to its existence. The more I thought about it, the less I believed it. It had to be some mistake or misinterpretation. After all, I was plainly no threat.

I struggled onward, exhausted, famished, utterly defeated. Finally I made it to Lake Merritt, that playground for the wealthy, lined by joggers and cyclists and lovers walking hand in hand; almost exclusively white and Asian nowadays, notably unlike the black and Latino stretch of Oakland I had just trekked through. I stared at the gentrifiers as if they were aliens, though only two days earlier I would have numbered myself among them, then found a patch of grass in the shade and collapsed into sleep.

I woke to two cops stooped over me.

"You OK down there?" one asked, a mixture of solicitous and suspicious.

I woke too dazed to be frightened. "Yeah. Sure. Sorry. Guess I fell asleep." My mind began to kick into gear. I looked around, as if for friends. They hadn't recognized me. That was something.

"The park's not for sleeping."

"Yeah. Totally. I was just tired. Up late last night." I had the sense they were about to demand ID. "What time is it?"

"Six thirty."

"Holy shit, really? Shit, shit, I gotta go. Thank you! Sorry!" I rushed away, fairly confident they wouldn't pursue. I was still respectable, after all: white, middle-aged, reasonably clean-shaven. I wondered how long it would take the streets to grind me down into a dingy, shabby, suspicious character. A week? A few days?

I ducked into the public bathrooms on the north side of the lake, glanced into the mirror, and froze in place, shocked motionless.

A stranger stood there staring back at me.

For a few seconds I wondered if I was on powerful hallucinogens, or had simply gone floridly insane. Then I remembered Quinn's injections. Of course the police hadn't recognized me. Even I didn't recognize me.

I looked vaguely similar, of course, but my face was rounder, my forehead broader, the lines of my jaw and cheekbones different. Combined it was enough that I seemed literally a new man. I gazed at my strange new face for a long time, from different angles, testing different expressions. It felt like I had died and invaded a new body, was the demon in a case of demonic possession.

Except demons presumably had the power of hell to call upon. I had nothing. I didn't know what to do or where to go from here.

I thought of a fragment of an article I had read somewhere advancing the theory that homelessness was a skill, and newly homeless people tended to lose most of their remaining money and possessions before they acquired any of that skill. I supposed morbidly I could count myself lucky to have nothing to lose. Not even an identity.

How to learn how to be homeless? When put that way, the question answered itself: I should seek guidance from my new tribe. Lord knew there was no shortage in the Bay Area. Ever since the pandemic, every corridor beneath every elevated highway, and countless other sites, had been encrusted by semipermanent tent cities like clusters of barnacles.

Those encampments seemed foreboding and dangerous, though, and venturing into them like invading people's personal territory. There were better places. People's Park in Berkeley leapt to mind.

My legs felt worn out, and my feet on the verge of blistering in my new shoes, so I abused my white upstanding-member-of-society privilege while I could, and told a bus driver I had lost my phone and wallet. He waved me on without really listening.

By the time I made it to People's Park, near sundown, I was weak and my stomach panged with hunger. It was how I remembered, little clusters of homeless people, a few tents, but not a full encampment. I seemed to recall that people were moved on by Berkeley cops after a few nights to prevent this from becoming a permanent home.

Under other circumstances I would have had to force myself to approach any of these people, but desperate hunger was a powerful motivator. I knelt on the grass next to the most approachable group: two men and two women, a mix of complicated nonwhite ethnicities, sitting on the benches near the park's basketball courts, next to bicycles and strollers laden with their worldly goods.

"Hey there," I made myself say.

They looked at me warily, silently.

"I just got off the bus," I said, "lost all my stuff, everything, do you know where I can go where someone might give me some food?"

I could tell by the way they looked at each other that I was untrustworthy, suspicious, alien. The same social cues that made me acceptable to cops and bus drivers made me weird and foreign here. I wondered if that too would change in a week.

"Seriously," I pressed the issue. "I know I'm . . . It's a long story, but I've got nowhere to go. I'm going to come back and sleep here in the park. I'd just like to get some food first."

The men shook their heads and turned away from me. But the two women exchanged a look, and then one of them, pregnant and heavily tattooed, said, "Church with a soup kitchen in back a few blocks that way." She pointed. "You're technically too late, but they sometimes give out left-overs after the night service, so maybe in half an hour."

"Thank you," I said, meaning it.

The other woman, skinny and gap-toothed and sharp-eyed, holding a beat-up Octavia Butler paperback, added, "Or you could go to Siblings. Not saying you want to. Ask me, they're nuts. But if they like you, they might feed you, and they might like you. No offense."

I stared at her for a long, breathless moment.

Then, "Siblings," I said quietly. "Tell me where I can find them?"

8

GRACE

NEARLY HALF OF THE STOREFRONTS SOUTH OF DWIGHT WERE SHUT-
tered or for rent. I knew times were hard, the tent cities growing like fungal
infections in every insalubrious corner of the Bay Area made that apparent, but the pandemic was behind us now, and if you believed the GDP
numbers, the worst of the recession was too. Did even the students at the
most prestigious public university in the country still have no money to
spend? Or had online shopping plus drone delivery combined into the retail equivalent of the bubonic plague?

I had been directed to a building that looked like it had once been a
restaurant. Its windows were now opaquely curtained, its only insignia a
stylized black S on each of its double doors, but something inside smelled
good enough to make my weary legs tremble.

I tapped the smart doorbell. Eventually a door yawned open, revealing
a white-bearded South Asian man with a sour expression.

"Help you?" His tone made him sound disinterested in the prospect.

I took a deep breath. "Maybe. Two things. One, some people at People's
Park said I, uh, might be able to get some food here, even though I don't
have any money?" It took a surprising amount of willpower to force myself
to say that.

He looked at me quizzically, maybe because I didn't yet look like someone who needed to beg for food. "Download our app, go through the on-
boarding, you'll find out there." He had a faint accent.

"I don't have a phone."

That sharpened his look. "And why is that exactly?"

"I don't have anything. But. Well. The other—"

As I stammered, another person stepped up beside him, a black woman barely in her twenties, if that. She looked no less suspicious. "What's your story, then?"

I said, "I'm an old friend of Jered Flynn's, if that means anything to you."

I had expected confusion or curiosity. I had not expected their scornful laughter.

"I really am," I said, "I haven't seen him for ages, but I've known him for twenty years."

"My dear sir," the South Asian man said, in a tone that made it clear he considered me neither dear nor a sir, "may I recommend that you go instead to the Amazon store and tell the staff there that you are a personal friend of Jeff Bezos. I suspect they will find you rather more convincing."

I looked at them. "You seriously get this a lot? People coming and telling you they know Jered? He's that big a deal?"

"We don't want to waste your time any further," the woman said, barely politely, reaching to close the door.

I stammered—it was really just verbal flailing, social reflex at being treated like a liar—"I really do! I brought him into Project Baccharus! I'm the whole reason he knew any of us!" This wasn't exactly true—Darren had introduced us, and then we had jointly invited him—but Baccharus had indeed been Jered's entry into our social scene back in the aughts.

"Good day, sir," the elderly man said.

But the young woman beside him stopped mid-door-shutting, suddenly alert. "I'm sorry, what did you say? Project what?"

"Baccharus."

She looked at the man.

"So he's read the biography. Or probably just his Wikipedia," the man said dismissively. "Means nothing."

"But that's not in either. I only know about it because he told me about it. When he visited last year," she said, "you remember he helped us set up tables, and he talked to me? I told him I wanted to be an astronaut, and he told me about Project Baccharus. He said he had fond memories, but it might set a bad example, so he hadn't put it in the book and didn't talk about it." She turned to me. "The name. What does it mean?"

"Combination of Bacchus and Icarus. Basically, we attached homemade rockets to weather balloons we bought off eBay, tried to launch them into space, tried to recover them when they fell back down, to get the pictures from the onboard cameras, then went to a biker bar called Zeitgeist and drank heavily. Pretty sure one of them got into the mesosphere once."

The woman's eyes widened.

"So he did some deep googling," the man objected, less certain now.

"Just send him a message," I implored. "That's all. You can do that, right? Tell him a crazy guy claiming he's Rocky from Project Baccharus is here and wants to talk to him. He'll want to hear from me." I was suddenly grateful for the stupid nickname I had been burdened with in the aughts. I couldn't very well ask them to pass on to their cult leader that noted escaped fugitive Adrian Ross wanted to speak to him.

After a long, uncertain moment, the woman pushed the door back open.

"I suppose it can't hurt," the man conceded.

"In the meantime," she said to me, "would you like some dinner?"

I nearly groaned with hunger. "Yes. Please."

"Take this and go around back." She gave me a poker chip with an embedded QR code.

"What is it?" I asked.

"A grace coin," she said. "Of the physical kind."

The older man said, as if this clarified everything: "It's on the blockchain."

The unmarked door around back opened to another sour-faced man, who took my coin, scanned it on his phone, and nodded me onward. Inside was a room full of cafeteria benches, lightly populated, and a buffet table heaped with a wide variety of vegetarian food.

I wasn't about to complain about the lack of steak. My first plate all but cracked beneath its weight. For long minutes I paid no attention to the world outside of my mouth and stomach.

Midway through my second plate, I heard the two men nearest me talking in hushed voices about our hosts:

"No, man. It's good, but you can't come back every day. You got to get one of their coins to eat, and they aren't really giving them away, understand? They're investing. They're hoping you'll be useful."

"Useful how?"

"Plumber, carpenter, electrician, mechanic, construction, software, that sort of thing. You learn anything useful inside?" The other man shook his head. "Well. People like that, they get recruited to move in. They got compounds all over."

"Like end-of-the-world shit? Preppers?"

"Pretty much. I mean, I ain't been, but that's what I hear."

"Like, Jesus-bringing-the-Rapture end of the world, climate-crisis-roasting-us-all end of the world, or civil-war-against-the-deep-state end of the world?"

"Not sure," the educator admitted. "They're not preachers. They play close to the vest. But I can tell you, way to get regular meals here without being useful yourself is to bring them someone useful. Or news, tell them what's happening on the street, stuff they don't already know. I know one guy, he gets ten grace coins to give away himself every week. Weird thing is he can't use them himself. Just give them away."

"Huh. What about their app?"

"Don't do it. It asks you like a hundred questions, maybe you get five coins if you're lucky, then you're done forever. Can't automate this shit unless you fit their profile *exact*. Someone like you wants to keep coming back regular, you need to establish a relationship of the personal quid pro quo variety."

"It's good food," the new guy said wistfully.

"Yeah. No meat, but who can afford meat, right? Burgers so good you almost can't tell. You cook? That's useful to them too."

"What about washing dishes?"

"Look around. They got robots. They want skills. Whole world wants skilled labor."

"Whole world don't want me, then. Story of my life."

Their conversation lapsed, and they turned their attention to the television overlooking the cafeteria, silently streaming cable news. The chyron declared a MAJOR ARCHAEOLOGICAL DISCOVERY IN EGYPT beneath footage of an ancient stone stairway, excavated from stark golden sands, descending steeply into darkness.

On my way back to the buffet for dessert, the young black woman from the front door intercepted me. "I've sent that message. If I get a response, how will we find you?"

I hesitated. "I don't know. I, uh. I don't have anywhere to go. I don't suppose there's any chance . . ." I tried to figure out how to phrase a plea for a place to sleep.

"I'm sorry. We don't have any urban residences. Policy."

"I understand."

"My name's Patricia."

"Pleasure to meet you," I said automatically. "I, uh, everyone calls me Rocky."

"Don't mind Rahul. It's his job to be suspicious." I nodded. "Did you really know him? Jered?"

I looked into her dark eyes. "I really did. We were good friends."

"I'm not saying I believe you," she said slowly, "but what was he like? Back then?"

I thought of young Jered, immediately remembered the time he had accidentally propelled an unridden motorcycle over a chain-link fence and into me, because he had decided to turn motorcycle training into stunt riding, and chuckled. I still had the scar. "Honestly? Half the time he was a royal pain in the ass. But he made interesting things happen."

"I bet." She offered me another grace coin. "Come back tomorrow for lunch and we can talk some more."

"Sure." I tried to say it casually, as if I found places to sleep on the street—while on the run from every law enforcement agency known to mankind—all the time. I accepted her grace and walked away.

9

PROTOCOL

IT WAS COLD, AND I WORE NO OUTER LAYER, AND I HAD NOWHERE TO go. I was torn between walking to stay warm and sitting to spare my sore feet. I favored walking at first, worried the police might take an interest in me and pull me over if I just loitered.

That concern faded as I saw more of late-night Berkeley. It seemed like half the cars and doorways I passed had someone sleeping in them. Both were technically illegal, but this city was famously bleeding-heart. Many of the cars in which people slept were decorated with Uber and Lyft decals. I wondered if they would find homes, or become doorway people, or escape the Bay and return to where they came from. I wondered if warm rooms waited for them there.

Maybe not. I had read that poor people were flocking to the Bay in ever-greater numbers because America's infrastructure was slowly beginning to collapse, from lack of investment and crippling debt, and the shrinking small towns from which they came were beginning to decay to the point at which streetlights broke and stayed dark, electricity blacked out regularly, tap water grew cloudy and pungent, potholes expanded into axle-breakers. Berkeley was still a rich city where things worked.

I hadn't realized until now that the tent cities were only the tip of the Bay's homeless iceberg. I wondered what stories those sleeping in cars around me told themselves about their lives. Was this normal, had their lives always been hard? Did they see this a temporary struggle they would one day surpass? Had they grown up in comfortable homes, worked decent jobs, thought themselves content, even wealthy, until the pandemic, or a sudden divorce, or a medical crisis, sent them plummeting, bereft, through America's one-way downwardly mobile trapdoor? You couldn't scroll through Twitter without reading about how America's middle class had been replaced by a new precariat majority, but within my own affluent bubble, I hadn't previously understood quite how bad things had gotten.

There were so many things I didn't understand. Why had Amara collaborated with the FBI to betray me? Or had she? Vika had to have been working with the FBI, to have gotten access to me in the interrogation room, but she had been surprised by, and very interested in, my suggestion of Amara's involvement.

Vika who had told me goodbye, with such finality, only minutes before my scheduled assassination. She must have known. She had worked with the FBI to arrest and murder me, on behalf of Coherence. When articulated, that sounded insane, but it was the only theory that fit the evidence. It even explained our conversation. Vika had wanted to know why I had been identified as a threat.

Amara had indirectly collaborated, too, somehow. Or else—it occurred to me for the first time—maybe hers had been a passive betrayal, not an active one. Maybe, rather than working against me, she had learned I would be arrested, and for some reason had chosen to do nothing rather than try to prevent it. Maybe she hadn't realized my arrest was a stepping stone to my murder. That made a little more sense, and made me feel a little better.

Meredith had learned too, somehow, and had gotten me out. But if Quinn was right, it was Meredith who had built the system that had marked me for death. How had Vika gotten involved? How had Amara learned any of this? Was Jered involved too, was that why Quinn said I was being taken to Siblings? If so, how? I had so many questions, and no answers.

People's Park was littered by homeless people in sleeping bags, with only a few tents. I wondered if a tent made you a target, then shivered and wished I had a sleeping bag. It wasn't *cold* cold, not remotely like Buffalo, where I grew up, but it was too cold to sleep in a T-shirt. Half of the sleeping bags around me seemed to be the same make and model. I wondered if a charity somewhere in Berkeley gave them away. Worth investigating, I supposed.

That thought triggered another wave of shock at what had happened to me. It was like the grief when my father had died; not just an initial inundation, but an endless series of aftershock tsunamis, less frequent but no less overwhelming. Only two days ago I had been an executive paid half a million a year in total compensation, planning my wedding. What had I become? *Who* had I become, with my new face?

A drone buzzed overhead, a police skyeye. I looked up at its blindingly bright lights, then quickly away, trying not to startle and run. Their presence was highly controversial here, only allowed in Berkeley airspace in the context of a specific pursuit. Not for me, I tried to reassure myself. No one knew where I was.

It moved on, but not before its searchlight happened to illuminate a ragged pile of fabric in the nearby corner of the park. A blanket someone had abandoned. It was torn and tattered, and smelled rank, and for all I knew was infested with ticks and lice, but it looked thick and warm. I hesitated, then gave in to the need to sleep, wrapped it around me, even managed to use one corner as a pillow. It was rough and dirty and uncomfortable, but I was so exhausted that sleep came quickly.

I woke before dawn, to despair. Everything I loved was gone forever. I shivered as I lay huddled on the hard ground and scratchy grass, wrapped in my filthy blanket. My lower back ached like fire, my bad knee felt half dislocated, I had a vicious headache, and I seemed to have some kind of rash on my ankle. Running like this was futile, pointless. I couldn't live like this for even a month. It was only a matter of time before they caught me. Best to go to the police and give myself up. There might be coffee at the police station, and warmth, and a shower.

I struggled to my feet, staggered to the toilets, found them locked, and sought out the denser foliage at the west end of the park in lieu. I wondered where all the homeless found toilets, the park people, the car people, the tent people. I had been vaguely aware that every retail establishment in the Bay guarded their bathrooms with keys or codes nowadays. I hadn't connected that to the homeless crisis.

I supposed they too found bushes; or used bottles, if they were lucky enough to still have a car; or spent their ever-dwindling money each time they needed to go. I remembered traveling in India in 2002, during my backpacking year, looking out of a train window, seeing farm workers squatting en masse at public slit latrines. I had been appalled, but better that than this in some ways.

I limped back to my bedraggled blanket, looked down at it, and at myself, smudged with dirt and grass by my restless sleep, and decided I couldn't live like this. Maybe in my idealistic twenties, or my ambitious thirties, but no longer. The truth was I had become weak and complacent, no longer will-ing or able to do things the hard way. For the last several years I had been happy to milk my executive status for its benefits rather than actually do anything with my influence. I had wanted a family without having to raise children, and had unfairly gotten both when Amara said yes.

Something horrifying and wrong had happened to me, true. A younger me would have tried to fight back. But I was no longer a man who might battle awfulness and unfairness, who might try to flip the table on which the game of life was played because he had rolled snake eyes with rigged dice. I had become a man who accepted that he was beaten.

"Hey," a soft voice said, "do you want some coffee?"

A woman. The gaunt, gap-toothed woman from yesterday, the Octa-via Butler reader who had told me about Siblings. She held a thermos and a plastic cup.

"Very much," I said.

"We weren't sure about you but"—she looked at the blanket—"that's pretty real. Did you find Siblings?"

"Yes." I took the cup from her, my hand trembling with anticipation.

"We've got some creamer and sugar if you'd like."

"Yes, please."

I followed her back to her friends, camped beside their strollers and bicycles. "Morning," the pregnant woman said pleasantly, and even the two men nodded at me in a not-unfriendly manner. "Sit with us a bit if you like."

"Thank you so much." I did so. "Having a pretty low moment back there."

"You looked it," the skinny woman said. "Where you off to?"

"Not really sure," I admitted.

"You know you can't stay here," one of the men said, bearded and deep-voiced. "They got a policy. More than three nights, you get arrested."

"Right," I said. "Where you all going to?"

"North, once we accumulate enough for the bus," said the other man. He had a faint accent, maybe African. "Ukiah."

I wondered what was there for them, but didn't want to pry. I'd read that Ukiah was one of the places where the infrastructure was collapsing, where the power sometimes went out for days or even weeks during fire season.

"You should probably leave that blanket where you found it," the preg-nant woman said to me. "Man who left it there might be coming back."

"Yes, of course," I said, though the thought of taking it or at least concealing it somewhere had occurred to me.

She smiled and nodded. It was only later, after I had returned the coffee cup with effusive gratitude and returned to the blanket in question, that I realized they had brought me to them to delicately ensure that I didn't violate social protocol by taking it for myself, because they could tell I might. Maybe because they knew I was new, maybe because I was a middle-aged white man and they assumed I felt entitled to things I found. Which, uncomfortably, probably wouldn't have been entirely wrong.

After the coffee I felt a million times better, my aches and pains much diminished, with zero interest in turning myself in to the police. I told myself it had just been a fleeting dark hour of the soul. I went back to Siblings, in the hope of finding breakfast, and maybe, if I was very lucky, establishing some kind of tenuous contact with Jered, wherever he was, and through him, somehow, eventually, Meredith.

Jered was there waiting for me.

10

SIBLING

"HEY," HE SAID, PEERING AT ME QUIZZICALLY, FLANKED BY PATRICIA and Rahul, "so you're a friend of Rocky's?" I recognized him right away; his face was lined and weary, his hair graying and fading, his close-cropped beard almost entirely white, but he was still the same compact, charismatic figure he had always been, equally ready to shout or grin, although his smile seemed to have grown more jaded and less mischievous. He wore expensive jeans and an even more expensive jacket of cruelty-free lab-grown suede.

"Not exactly." I looked at his companions, who were suddenly very wary of me. "Can we talk privately?"

"I don't think that's a good idea," Rahul said immediately.

"OK. Well. Let's try this." I pulled up the sleeve of my T-shirt, revealing a hook-shaped scar on my right shoulder. "Remember this?"

Jered looked at it, then at me, eyes widening. "Where did you get that?"

"Long time ago. Friend of mine launched a motorcycle over a fence and into me."

"I—" His mouth fell open and he gaped at me, astonished, for all of two seconds. Then composure settled over his expression again. "Rocky. You look so different. I didn't even recognize you."

"Lot of changes over the years," I agreed blandly.

"Why don't you come inside, we can talk them over. We'll be in the basement office," he said to Patricia and Rahul, his voice all crisp command now. "We're not to be disturbed."

It wasn't until we entered that compact, spartan office, and the thick door swung shut behind us, that he turned on me like an avenging angel. I was six inches taller, but he had always made me feel small when like this. "What the hell happened? Where's Quinn? What happened to your *face*?"

"Quinn is actually what happened to my face. Intrafascial injections."

"Ah. Nobody tells me anything. I was wrongly informed you were being brought to Grass Valley. But what happened—"

"I don't know. Somebody started shooting and I got the hell out of there. As per Quinn's instructions." I felt irrationally guilty about having fled that scene.

"Shooting?"

I explained, told him everything that had happened since my arrest. As I did so the lines on Jered's face deepened. At length he boosted himself up to sit on the desk, and kicked at it idly with his heels, thinking.

"Well," he said, "this isn't good."

"You don't say. Want to tell me what the hell is going on?"

"Our dear friend Meredith called me a few months ago. Ultra secure, of course. You know Meredith and her opsec. Sounded like she had pretty good reason this time. She said she was working on a military contract for a machine learning system, using some very basic but apparently viable quantum computing, just a relative handful of qubits but reliable ones, and she'd had a bit of a brain wave. That was what she called it. 'A bit of a brain wave, pardon the pun.'" He mock-mimicked Meredith's mordant tone and I couldn't help but chuckle with recognition. "Trouble is, then they took it away from her."

"They who?"

"I don't know. Whoever conspiracy theorists mean when they say They, I suppose. NSA, CIA, KFC, Q, the Shop, whoever. Although according to you, 'They' also seems to include our other dear old friend Vika, which makes some kind of sense, because it turns out Exadelic is run, via a figurehead CEO, by our other *other*, in your case even older, dear friend Anthony."

"Wait," I said, "what?"

"Yes. All very incestuous. This all sort of started with him actually. He brought Meredith in because he knew what she was capable of. Or thought he did. Then she gave him success beyond his wildest dreams or nightmares, depending on your view."

"Meredith hates his guts."

"That was a long time ago. I mean, it's apparently become true again now, but in the interim time apparently temporarily healed that wound, and she needed the money, or the influence, or the beyond-top-secret access, or something. I don't know. She was vague and I wasn't really focused on that part."

"Understandable," I conceded, although it still seemed unlikely. Meredith's wrath was neither easily earned nor set aside lightly.

"Thank you. So I guess the TL;DR is that Meredith accidentally built the most dangerous creation in human history for Anthony, who brought in Vika to be his fellow handmaiden for our new dread AI demigod, and then they kind of pushed Meredith out. She's still affiliated, still needed, because no one understands it as well as she does technically, but her access has apparently been severely limited. However she's still close enough to certain levers of clandestine power such that, combined with her own far-flung network, she managed to save your life and bring you to me. So that's something, right?"

"I mean," I said, "I think so."

Jered pulled out his phone, tapped at it for moment, then looked up again. "Pretty extraordinary when you think about it. Aside from her, we were never really so special or talented. Just a bunch of drugged-up weirdo goth-punk geeks who happened to live in San Francisco just as the biggest tech boom of all time hit. A few of us especially interested in the subnerdery of neural networks, which everyone knew was dead technology, just before it had its renaissance. Right place, right time, dumb luck, so now apparently we run the world." He smiled grimly. "Maybe literally, soon."

"You weren't into neural nets," I pointed out.

"No. But I was an early bitcoin guy. CPU miner. That worked out pretty well for me."

"Why did Meredith call you?"

"She trusts me. She wanted help. Figured we could put you up at one of our estates. And some of our people have other connections, across the government."

"To do what?"

"She wants to get control of Coherence back, or failing that, shut it down. Both of which sound good to me. I've known Vika too long to believe she can sustain actual interest in ethical AI for more than a nanosecond. Not when the alternative is an AI that can make Vika famous and powerful, and everyone who ever criticized her, or even looked at her funny, so very, very sorry. As for Anthony . . ." He shrugged.

"Yeah." Anthony and Vika had disliked each other deeply, back in the day, but I wasn't shocked they had reached a mutually beneficial détente. Anthony had been my best friend in Buffalo, and the reason that pudgy, awkward, uncool me had ever been accepted into the San Francisco scene—but he was also, it had turned out, a man always ready to sacrifice his friends' happiness for his own.

"I hope Coherence isn't learning what it means to be sentient from them," Jered said.

"So you believe it?" I asked. "Strong AI? The real deal?"

"Meredith seems pretty convinced. And pretty desperate."

I nodded. It still seemed so hard to believe. It seemed so much more likely that she was simply mistaken. "What's it doing? Passing Turing tests?"

"She hasn't gone into details."

"And it thinks I'm some kind of deadly danger to its future."

"Well," Jered said, "maybe there are still a few bugs in the system."

"Your disrespect for my fearsomeness is noted. What about Amara?"

He looked at me quizzically. "Yes, what *about* Amara? No one said anything to me about Amara. Did she say anything to you?"

"No," I said after a moment. "I don't know how she's connected. But she and Darren were pretty into early neural-net art, back in the day."

"I thought that was mostly him."

Because she did the hard work and he took all the credit, I didn't say. But I believed him. If Amara had been playing a secret game, it hadn't been with Jered. "What's Meredith's plan? What else does she want from us?"

"I think she wants to talk to you."

"What? Meredith? Where is she?"

"Grass Valley," he said, "there's a car waiting outside."

11

ESTATE

THE ESCALADE CLIMBED ALONG AN UNPAINTED TWO-LANE ROAD WIND-
ing through the foothills of the Sierra, amid pine with a smattering of eucalyptus, to a steel gate set in a high metal-and-concrete fence topped with
razor wire. Cameras peered over both shoulders of the gate. I expected the
territory on the other side to be spartan and military.

Instead the gate opened to reveal a riot of color and life: a rainbow of
tepees, a vast nest of mural-covered hexayurts beneath an LED lattice of
shifting psychedelic patterns, a forest of bright tree houses connected by
carved walkways, an artificial lake lined by houseboats painted like animals. In the valley beyond were fields and orchards, a grass airstrip, and
barns as big as aircraft hangars, next to which were heaped scrap metal,
coiled cables, tires, firewood, and other bulk communal goods. Vehicles
whirred past, vehicles that had begun their lives as pickups, drones, trac-
tors, and golf carts, but all of them now painted, sculpted, and adorned to
look like some fantastic kaleidoscopic beast.

"You turned Burning Man into a survivalist cult." I tried not to sound
as awed as I felt. It looked like hundreds of people lived here, mostly off
the land.

"It's not a cult," Jered said, mildly offended. "Also not a compound. Media always call it a compound. This is an estate. One of several."

"This is totally a compound. When did you become a doomsday prepper?"

"I repeat, it is *not* a compound"—he couldn't entirely hide a smirk—
"and I am neither prepper nor survivalist nor cultist. This is one of the

purest democracies on earth. Continuous democracy. Every week is election week, if that's what the people want."

"The people? You're one of them now?" I looked around at the leather
and gadgets encrusting the interior of the Escalade. "You don't ride like
one of the people."

He grinned. "I told you. I was a CPU miner."

"I thought you believed in reputation economies."

"My ostentatious monetary success gives my reputation economy more
credibility."

"That's why you ride in a six-figure SUV?"

"No, but it's why I say I do. Makes for better copy."

We crept up a dirt road, toward the largest yurt I had ever seen, perched
on a hilltop.

"You understand how Siblings works?" Jered asks, as we ascended.

"Kind of," I lied.

"Basically we run our own internal reputation economy. Every full member gets a hundred grace coins every week to give away to others. You got
one yesterday, right?" I nodded. "Once given they're spendable. Members
use them to pay for meals, or rent, or to suggest or vote on governance pro-
posals. Like I said, continuous representative democracy. If people don't
like the way those of us in leadership are running things, they just start
giving their coins and hence votes to someone else."

"So you pay for meals with votes?"

"Same reputation currency for goods, services, and votes. You don't pay
exactly. Grace is not transferable. It's burnt when spent, recipients don't get
it. Not directly. But there's a strong correlation between the grace you give
to others and the grace they give you, as you might imagine."

"And you use this instead of money?"

"Internally. The outer world has not yet seen fit to recognize the inherent inevitable supremacy of our system"—Jered's tone made it clear that his
tongue was at least slightly in his melodramatic cheek—"and as you can
see we are not immune to the habit of purchasing things from the world."

"With what? Your bitcoin?"

"I didn't mine *that* much. Almost everyone here has some kind of remote
job or leaves to do contract work some months out of every year, and they
kick in twenty percent of what they earn. That money in turn goes on the
blockchain, controlled by our governance votes, so spending it is like any

other proposal, someone suggests an expense, or asks for authorization to spend a certain amount, and then we vote on that proposal."

"A tithe." Twenty percent seemed a lot. "What happens if people don't want to pay?"

"Well, you can't quite see it from here, but there's a big sculpture of a wicker man just over that rise . . ." I chuckled. "No, the system is self-stabilizing. People pay what they want to. If it's not deemed enough, they get less grace from others. If they don't get enough grace, they can't stay."

"And this all actually works?"

"Never in theory," Jered assured me, "only in practice."

We parked outside the yurt. He paused briefly before leading me in. "I can't remember, have you met my husbands?"

I shook my head.

"Ah. Well, you will now."

He entered. Two men stood next to a smoker near the door, optimizing it for whatever meat was within, which smelled utterly delicious. One was tall and mustached and intense, and the other even larger, a quiet bear of a man.

"This is Rick"—Jered indicated the spectacular mustache—"and Bruno"—the hulking one. "We're more or less the triumvirate in charge around here, currently, as collectively deputized by everyone in the community on a continuous basis. And then I'm the representative for the larger global council, which works similarly."

I wasn't listening. Beyond them, a woman with white helmetlike hair, her exposed arms sleeved with tattoos, sat dressed all in black in a folding chair, puffing intently on a vape pen so extravagantly steampunk it looked like it might extrude a zeppelin and float away. She seemed almost ageless; only the cobwebs around her eyes hinted that she was in her forties. She hadn't noticed our entry and was peering through her glasses at a tablet with such pure concentration that I almost felt guilty about interrupting. Almost.

"Dr. Peterson, I presume," I said as I approached. "I've been seeking you through the wildest jungles of the American underworld."

She twitched, looked up, stared at me blankly for an instant. Then the corners of her mouth curved into a fair facsimile of a pained smile. "Adrian. I hear you've had quite a journey."

"You might say that," I said, "if you were prone to dramatic understatement," and she rose to meet me, and we hugged tightly. I had always been one of the very few people she was willing to hug. Despite her genius, and her sometimes florid neurodivergence, Meredith had always felt instinctively like one of my people. Maybe because we had both been high-school social outcasts who barely survived the experience.

"So I fucked up pretty badly," she informed me as we disengaged. "I should never have worked with Anthony."

"Why did you?" I asked. "It sounded so unlike you."

She sat back down, took a puff from her vape pen. "Hardly matters now. Die's cast. Future's fucked. But fine, you deserve the story. I told myself crises make strange bedfellows. I've spent my life trying to use machine learning to help build alternative social power sources, decentralized force concentration communities, options made possibly by new technologies, to fight status quo as and when necessary. Turning gravel into gems. Building my own private intelligence network to solve problems no one else could. But."

"But?"

"But then I looked around and realized that sure, game-theoretically speaking mine was a fine strategy in the long enough run, but ice caps were melting, pandemics were spreading, white supremacists were marching, and all my carefully laid seeds of neo-anarchism wouldn't be much good in a burning diseased world full of Nazis. You actually need traditional force concentration to fix that shit. I'd thought I had time to think strategically. Instead I had to pivot tactically."

"Uh-huh," I said as if I understood, knowing it would accelerate her toward her point.

"And who's the one person I knew who'd climbed up through the web of the military-consulting-industrial complex, basically McKinsey for the Pentagon, while I wasn't looking? Anthony. Because I'm pretty sure if you sequence his DNA he's at least half poisonous arachnid. So I figure, ingratiate myself there, combine serious military influence with the alternative networks I've spent two decades building, then do something meaningful about the ice caps, or the Nazis, or both. Crises make strange bedfellows, right? Right?"

"Sure," I reassured her.

"So he welcomes me like a long-lost sister and introduces me to his boss Laxman, who is a *hundred* percent poisonous arachnid, but I'm still thinking enemy of my enemy. They want me to help build a pattern analysis and prediction tool. Then they tell me they've got working mid-triple-digit qubits in Fort Meade. I'd already been playing with some theoretical ways to incorporate quantum computing into machine learning, faster zero-knowledge proofs for recursive evolutionary programming. I know it's not obvious how that relates to better neural nets but I assure you it does." She shrugged. "So I worked on that for a year and I summoned the devil. Demigod. Whatever Coherence is."

"How do you—" I began.

But Meredith was off and running. "It is so weird. It only works with five QCs, no more, no less, and what's more, their actual physical location has an effect on the outcome, they have to be symmetrically arranged. That should be so far past impossible you can't even see it from here. It's like the infamous Thompson tone detector except, you know, fucking *quantum*, apparently using some aspect of the *laws of physics* we don't even begin to understand yet. NSA folks aren't stupid and they had no idea either. I want to talk to every particle physicist in the world, but this is all so far beyond top secret it's basically a crime for them to listen."

"How do you know it's real strong AI?" I finally managed to ask, as she took a breath. "Is it passing Turing tests or something?"

"Ah. No." Her face took on the expressionlessness that indicated someone had asked a particularly stupid question. "Since OpenAI dropped GPT-5, Turing tests have not been fit for purpose. Not hard to feign consciousness to a fallible human tester when your training data includes pretty much the entire corpus of all human-generated information. No, the tells are, one, Coherence is making entirely correct predictions humans wouldn't even dream of. The assassination of the president of Paraguay. The uprising in Matabeleland in Zimbabwe. Seeing patterns is one thing, making correct predictions in today's soup of human chaos is something entirely else. Two, worse, its ARC numbers just keep climbing."

"ARC?" I asked.

"Abstraction and Reasoning Corpus. Industry-standard measure of intelligence. But three is the biggest." She paused, lowered her voice. "It's made at least one colossal scientific breakthrough. Unprovoked, unasked for, and completely unthinkable to us."

"Whoa," I said. "What?"

Meredith winced as if struck and took another big puff from her vape pen. It smelled of cinnamon and marijuana. She normally seemed preternaturally well preserved, but in that moment she looked every one of her nearly fifty years, wrinkles etched into her face as if by acid. She had always been a self-medicating wake-and-bake pothead, to keep her high-octane multicore brain halfway in line, but I realized she was now keeping herself high to try to stave off utter despair.

"I know this sounds nuts," she said in a near whisper, "but I saw it teleport something."

A hush hung over the yurt.

Jered took an amazed step closer. "Did you say *teleport*?"

"Just a coffee cup. Just across a room. Not without side effects, clearly highly exothermic, coffee started boiling again, can't say I'd recommend it for any fellow mammals. But still. Imagine the power to teleport in the hands of the US military. Then imagine it in the mind of a superintelligence liable to treat humanity the same way we treat termites. Then imagine what *other* breakthroughs it might come up with."

Nobody said anything for a long moment.

Then I smiled wanly and turned to Jered and his husbands.

"It's funny," I said, "when I ate the dinner you so kindly gave me back in Berkeley, I heard two guys talking about what kind of doomsday cult you were. Several different suggestions and they *still* didn't hit on the right one."

Rick objected faintly, "We're not really a doomsday cult."

For an awkward moment no one said anything.

"Well," Bruno conceded, "we're maybe a *little* bit doomsday-culty."

"Apocalyptic semantics," Jered said dryly. "It's true we started these camps because we estimated a nonzero and growing chance of some kind of significant human population bottleneck. Also true we didn't expect this one. If it is a population bottleneck. Not necessarily. A coffee cup jumping across a room doesn't necessarily spell planetary doom."

"Probably never been a better time to cash out your 401K though," I muttered.

"If it's so dangerous," Bruno asked, "why can't we just shut it down?"

"We can," Meredith said. "Theoretically. It's just, we won't. Laxman, the spook of spooks, loves it to death. I think he cut me out of the inner circle because he knew I'd want to stop it. He thinks it's their new Enigma. Anthony doesn't have enough imagination to realize how dangerous it is, so he thinks the idea of a shutdown is what's nuts. In fact he was worried enough about it he asked it for a list of threats to itself." She looked at me. "A list which apparently led with Adrian."

Everyone paused to consider the sheer unlikeliness of that for a moment.

"Well," I said bleakly, "nobody's perfect."

"Can we go over the military's heads?" Jered suggested. "Find some contact to a senator, or the White House? I might know some people who know some people."

"Technically they can't do anything, at least legally. Officially it's a private project. It was considered best to keep it arm's-length from the NSA et cetera, lest some oversight committee demand control. So it's technically owned by Anthony's division of Exadelic, which in turn is largely owned by a VC fund whose major LP is de facto directed by, you guessed it, Laxman. The prototype ran in a data center in Fort Meade, but they built the production version somewhere else, I don't even know where, probably some former Walmart somewhere with cheap electricity. Right now nobody in government even has the right to know where its data center is, much less walk in and pull the plug. Maybe we could launch some kind of investigation, but it'd be a nasty internecine battle, take months if not years. We don't have that kind of time. It's getting incrementally smarter every minute."

"So what can we do?" I asked.

An awkward pause followed.

"Adrian, you've done quite enough," Meredith said gently. "We nearly got you killed twice already."

I said, "Speaking of which. What happened to Quinn?"

"Tagged two of them, took a bullet in a shoulder, got away. In hospital now, good prognosis, out in a few days. On paper a victim of another random Oakland drive-by."

"We'll take you in here," Rick said to me. "No one should be able to track you."

"Give you a new name," Bruno added. "Got any badass nominees?"

"A new life, in the off-world colonies," I tried to joke, and everyone laughed a little too loudly, because after all we were talking about me discarding my life, my identity, and my new family, Amara and Grace and Alex, with whom I had been so happy for a few blissfully ignorant months. Talking about living off the charity of others in a remote compound that would be difficult to ever depart, where I knew no one except Jered, whom I had hardly seen for twenty years. Talking about them dealing with the situation, rather than me, because, as usual, they were assumed to be the ones with the know-how and wealth and contacts to have a meaningful effect on the outcome.

Two days earlier I had imagined the story of my life as three acts: surviving and escaping Buffalo; finding my friends and my career in San Francisco; and, finally, placid domestic bliss, growing old with Amara, Alex, and Grace. Yesterday that third act had been torn away, replaced by a horror story of betrayal, disgrace, prison, and misery. Today yet another ending had been grafted on: eternal exile, spending the rest of my life as a lie in order to survive. That still seemed like one hardly worth living.

"What are you going to do?" I asked Meredith. "About the situation?"

"I don't know." She vaped deeply again. "Still technically on retainer at Fort Meade. Have to get back soon. But I'm on a tight leash, no social capital, pegged as a wild-card loose-cannon risk. Best idea is to infiltrate Exadelic somehow, get to Anthony that way. Guy who lives here has a third screening interview with them tomorrow, that's the other reason I'm here, he's willing to play inside man. But, Jered, no offense, some rando from Grass Valley is not likely to either hack his way into the secrets of one of the most paranoid companies in the world, or somehow make himself Anthony's right-hand man. We don't have time for a long game. This is a desperation play." She shrugged. "I know. Only play we've got. But still."

"Vika," Jered said. "I keep saying she's their weak point."

"She orients toward power. We don't have any to offer. He does. All of it."

I said, "What about me?"

They turned to me, puzzled.

Jered said, "What about you?"

"That third interview," I said. "Let me take it. If it's anything like our interview processes at Sybilisk, no one will notice it's a different face. Get Exadelic to hire me."

"What good will that—"

"Anthony was my best friend," I pointed out. "At college. After college. For years. And now I have a whole new face. If anyone in the entire world can insinuate themself into his inner circle in record time, it's me."

After a few long, silent breaths, Meredith said, thoughtfully, "Huh."

"What?" I asked.

She said, "What if Coherence wasn't wrong about you after all?"

12

ATTACKERS

SALESFORCE TOWER LOOMED OVER DOWNTOWN SAN FRANCISCO LIKE a conquering alien spaceship. I pocketed my phone, emerged from the Lyft, immediately came face-to-face with five cops, and went cold and motionless. So much for the plan. So much for my escape. They had found me.

Then I saw what else was happening, and started breathing again. Nothing to do with me. A large truck had broken down on one side of the tower's main entrance, while another had apparently collided with a car at a nearby corner. There were traffic cones everywhere, and a sizable police presence directing people and vehicles around the two incidents.

I took a moment to collect myself. It didn't occur to me to wonder at the odds of two large unmarked trucks getting stuck near the entrance of a major office tower at the same time. Beyond the temporary traffic jam, the district was eerily empty, pockmarked with shuttered storefronts, its restaurants and shops largely replaced by startup cafeterias and droneports, its streets somehow scoured clear of any sign of the homeless who teemed a few blocks away. High above, three airships floated placidly, tethered to two nearby towers; the latest in conspicuous playthings for billionaires.

I entered the tower's cavernous atrium, and told security, "My name's Tyler Wagner. I'm a new hire at Exadelic."

Salesforce Tower loomed over downtown San Francisco like a conquering alien spaceship. I pocketed my phone, emerged from the Lyft, immediately came face-to-face with five cops, and went cold and motionless. So much for the plan. So much for my escape. They had found me.

Then I saw what else was happening, and started breathing again. Nothing to do with me. A large truck had broken down on one side of the tower's main entrance, while another had apparently collided with a car at a nearby corner. There were traffic cones everywhere, and a sizable police presence directing people and vehicles around the two incidents.

I took a moment to collect myself. It didn't occur to me to wonder at the odds of two large unmarked trucks getting stuck near the entrance of a major office tower at the same time. Beyond the temporary traffic jam, the district was eerily empty, pockmarked with shuttered storefronts, its restaurants and shops largely replaced by startup cafeterias and droneports, its streets somehow scoured clear of any sign of the homeless who teemed a few blocks away. High above, three airships floated placidly, tethered to two nearby towers; the latest in conspicuous playthings for billionaires.

I entered the tower's cavernous atrium, suddenly feeling a strange twisted spiral sickliness in the pit of my belly, faintly dazed by an oddly powerful sense of déjà vu. I told security, "My name's Tyler Wagner. I'm a new hire at Exadelic."

She looked at me with a strained expression, as if she too had been suddenly struck by a wave of stomach-wrenching illness, before nodding curtly.

Half an hour later I was in a room furnished with Day-Glo plastic furniture, on the periphery of a huge open office that occupied most of the floor. It felt like being in an adult-size children's playroom. I stood surrounded by a dozen other orientees, mostly twenty years younger, watching a video in which Ashley Coverdale, Exadelic's British CEO, explained her vision of a world of security and prosperity, and our part in realizing such a world. Nobody seemed especially interested. The kids around me were clearly here for the paycheck.

Infiltration had been surprisingly easy. During the interview the real Tyler Wagner had been ready to coach me via an earpiece, but it mostly covered deep-learning concepts I already knew well. Feeling able and competent was a refreshing change. Exadelic had offered me the job the next day, and asked me to come to San Francisco for three days of orientation before starting work as a remote employee. They were growing aggressively and didn't want to waste time. Neither did I.

Mid-CEO-video, I glanced out of the bizarrely infantilizing orientation room, and my mind snapped sharply into close attention. Not forty feet away, amid a small standing huddle of employees discussing something intently, stood my erstwhile best friend Anthony Richter. I hadn't seen him for years. He had clearly gotten into weight lifting, and I suspected steroids too. His face was lined and stubbled with gray, his close-cropped hair had drastically receded, and he was huge with muscle, broad-chested and thick-necked. The Anthony I recalled had been lean and graceful with a long dark mohawk.

I glanced over furtively every few seconds as he crossed the open-office fishbowl area and entered a corner office. During the break after the video I casually wandered close enough to look in. He glanced up at me, and I went cold and looked away, but when I looked back he was on his laptop again. With my new face I was just another employee, a little person, a supplicant.

We had met our first year in SUNY Buffalo, the largest public university in New York, and become inseparable, not least because no one else had liked either of us much. We were two maladjusted, antisocial kids far better at books and video games than people, and both mildly obsessed with local punk band the Dik Van Dykes and their album *Nobody Likes the Dik Van Dykes*. He was an incompetent extrovert, constantly dragging me out to parties he'd wangled reluctant invitations to, despite my desire to keep my nose in a book. He needed someone to reinforce his belief that he was better than all the people around him. I was just happy to have any friend at all.

He'd dated an awful girl named Gretchen for most of his junior year, during which he acquired his mohawk and new alternative-but-not-*really*-alternative friends, while I finally branched out and socialized with others, RPGers and science fiction geeks and anime fans, and went on the first dates of my own life with a troubled girl named Miriam. After we both got dumped we reforged our friendship. He moved to San Francisco after graduating, recruited into a web consultancy during the dot-com boom, and at his urging I followed, and we both hung on through the subsequent crash. It was hard to connect those memories of Anthony—his mohawk, his self-aggrandizing and brittle pride, his giddy dark humor, his quickness to take offense and bear a grudge—to the graying, hulking man of authority across the Exadelic fishbowl.

When I saw him head for the elevator, I excused myself to go to the bathroom, and followed. Meredith had programmed my phone with a scanning app that could itemize and hopefully clone any NFC-enabled cards, key fobs, or second-factor devices he might carry. This was a perfect opportunity.

The elevator was crowded. I stood behind him. The temptation to tap him on the shoulder and tell him everything was strong. He activated the elevator access panel with a black card from his wallet, and pressed 39. I casually held my phone just behind his back pocket and counted to three. Voilà, I hoped.

Only then did I wonder why he was going to the thirty-ninth floor. That was not one of Exadelic's.

I pushed O for Observation Platform, the only floor above thirty-five I might conceivably have some reason to go to. From the corner of my eye I saw Anthony turn and look at me briefly, presumably wondering why an Exadelic employee would ascend to a tourist trap during work hours. I hoped he would ask—I had my intriguing answer ready, and my infiltration would be far less suspicious if he initiated it—but he visibly decided not to care, and looked away.

Still, mission doubly accomplished: his wallet scanned, and, I thought, enough of an impression made that next time we met, he might strike up the conversation. I enjoyed the rare sensation of a small triumph.

On the thirty-ninth floor the elevator opened to a small antechamber with a faint industrial smell and oddly padded walls. A camera protruded from the wall above a single black door with an odd spiral sigil engraved on it. As the elevator doors slid shut, I saw Anthony raise a palm to the camera, more a display than a greeting.

I stood slack-jawed and stunned as I ascended. I had seen that spiral sigil before.

On the box in my basement closet. Amara's box.

Unanswerable questions and ludicrous, fragmentary theories danced in my brain, trying and failing to explain this new, astonishing fact. I stared senseless at the elevator wall. I wanted to ride it down to street level, take the N-Judah out west, as I had so many times, then walk south on Twenty-Fifth Avenue to the house where Amara and I had lived with Alex and Grace. I wanted to do so very badly. I wanted to knock on her door, introduce myself, and demand explanations, even if that meant implicitly throwing myself on her mercy.

What did that sigil mean? What connection could they possibly have?

I remembered introducing Anthony to Amara. They had never dated—Darren and Amara had been the only truly monogamous couple in our cohort, not least because of Darren's proprietary fierceness—but there had always seemed a spark between them.

I checked my phone. According to Salesforce Tower's directory, its thirty-ninth floor was "CLOSED—UNDER RENOVATION."

It would be very easy to go to Amara and demand answers. I could be at her door in half an hour.

I told myself I would do so. Had to do so. Obviously. But now was not the time. Instead I texted an update to Meredith, then returned to the fishbowl, and to what the orientees were already calling "the playroom." About half an hour later, Anthony emerged from the elevators and returned to his office.

Shortly afterward the first explosion shook the tower like a rag doll.

At first we all assumed the soft *crump* and subsequent vibrations were an earthquake. Most people froze in place as the building wobbled. A few dove under their desks, only to sheepishly emerge soon afterward. After a communal appreciation of the unpredictable dangers of nature, head shakes and awed expostulations, we resumed the collective construction of a Lego Salesforce Tower, key elements of which had been strategically withheld from us for team-building purposes.

Minutes later, a phone bleeped in the pocket of one of my fellow orientees, a just-out-of-college girl named Jessica, whom I had previously noticed primarily because her arms were artistically mottled with examples of her generation's increasingly popular, and deeply controversial, melanin tattoos.

"I have it set to emergencies only," she said apologetically, drawing it out to examine the incoming message, just as someone in the fishbowl cried out with audible distress.

We looked over. She wasn't alone. Several people were suddenly standing at their desks, taut with tension, staring at their phones or speaking into them hastily. As we watched, a visible ripple of dismay emanated through the office.

Jessica said, her voice faint, "My sister says there's a report of explosions and gunfire. Multiple active shooters. Here. At Salesforce Tower. There's a video."

We clustered to look over her shoulder. A loud sound like luggage dragged over cobblestones erupted from her phone. It took me a moment to interpret it as automatic gunfire. The video was almost incomprehensible, jumping and jittery. It showed a broad urban space transformed into a ruin of broken glass, wreckage surrounding a large truck, with fast-flickering flashes of light and smoke in the background. The gunfire was followed by cries of shock and fear. It would have seemed like something from a movie, or a faraway news clip, if not for the ragged but still recognizable Salesforce logo on the wall of the shattered atrium.

I turned to look through the southern windows and saw wisps of smoke drifting up.

"Can you freeze it at that last frame?" I asked, consciously keeping my voice calm.

She did so with shaking fingers.

That large truck in the middle of Salesforce Tower's smashed atrium was one of those I had passed on the way in. Somehow it had gotten through the bollards and barreled directly into the main entrance of the building. The freeze-frame caught two human figures emerging from the truck. Men in black body armor and tactical helmets, holding assault rifles with a spartan and military look.

Several of those looking over Jessica's shoulder gasped with horror.

Then everything went dark.

I hadn't known the tower's outer windows could turn opaque until they did so, simultaneous with the extinguishing of every overhead light. What had been a bright office was suddenly a dark cave, illuminated only by lit screens and the emergency red of EXIT signs.

"Terrorists," someone moaned.

But I knew better. This couldn't be coincidence. That stretched credulity too far. Whoever the attackers were, they were in some way here for the same reason I was. What's more, they couldn't possibly hope to escape, not after attacking the flagship skyscraper in the wealthiest city in one of the most militarized nations in the world. This was a suicide attack.

13

LABYRINTHINE

PANIC SPREAD QUICKLY. EMPLOYEES GATHERED IN ANXIOUS KNOTS, reinforcing each other's terror, trying to figure out whether to stay or flee or hide. I wrestled with that same decision until my own phone warbled.

It was Meredith: *Major military-style attack on Salesforce Tower. Cut power, blew up walkway to Transbay Terminal. You're trapped. Also I just remotely updated your phone to a clone of Anthony's access card. Suggest you use it. Find a hole and stay safe.*

That decided me. I walked to the stairs, thinking maybe I should run, maybe crucial seconds were ticking away, but I didn't dare lest the action catalyze my barely contained fear into outright panic.

The stairwell was stark and barren, pale walls surrounding endless metal stairs and featureless doors. I climbed, and climbed, and finally reached the thirty-ninth floor puffing with exhaustion, and all too aware of my wonky knee—but unpursued, apparently, so far.

There was a camera atop the door. I hesitated, but it was too late to back out now, and it would be dead now if it didn't run on emergency power. Which was also true of the door itself, I realized—but when I tapped my phone to its access sensor, a light winked green, a solenoid fired, and it opened.

An anonymous corridor led a short distance to another, unlocked door, from which a faint hum emerged. I opened it. It was surprisingly thick. I gasped audibly with astonishment at what lay beyond.

The opened door revealed a short hallway filled to the brim with the fractally repetitive angular steel of a server farm: endless shelves stuffed full of processor racks, connected by carefully constrained clumps of interwoven power, fiber, and coolant cables, all arranged with meticulous symmetry. Despite the coolant, and the dozens of interspersed roaring fans, the air that roared out was uncomfortably warm. I recognized the chips immediately as Nvidia TPUs, GPUs customized for neural networks. Each was worth thousands. There were scores if not hundreds in view already.

I followed the corridor to where it T-junctioned into another hallway lined by server racks. The noise of the fans almost drowned out the chorus of backup batteries beeping warnings from every direction. Both ends of this hall in turn T-junctioned into two more.

That was when it hit me: this was it. I had found Coherence's data center. Instead of an abandoned Walmart in a remote desert, it occupied, incredibly, the thirty-ninth floor of Salesforce Tower. I was *inside* Coherence, like a virus inside a human brain; its mind stood seething all around me, arrayed in these many millions' worth of TPUs, processing terabytes of data every second, adjusting quadrillions of neural-net weightings in its drive to become ever more intelligent.

I supposed it made a kind of sense. Anthony and Exadelic and their military associates wouldn't want their superweapon in the middle of nowhere, where anyone might blow it up with minimal collateral damage, or worse yet, helicopter in and seize it. This tower was heavily defended, very easily accessible, and well concealed in its "Purloined Letter" way.

The hallways lined by server racks continued, all short segments. I followed corners, made my way through intersections with no apparent grid or other layout, and slowly began to realize: it was *deliberately* random. As crazy as it seemed, this data center had been purposely laid out as a complex labyrinth. Coherence's brain was, quite literally, a maze.

I couldn't even begin to imagine any reason for such studied byzantine complexity. The cost alone would have been numbing, and ongoing, as data centers required frequent maintenance. To say nothing of the blatant violation of fire codes: there were no EXIT signs in sight. I tried to imagine the planning meetings wherein Exadelic had invoked national security to situate a profoundly unsafe pointless labyrinth of a data center in some of the most expensive office real estate in the world.

As a result there was also no fire ax with which to simply start smashing it. Not that there would be much point in such wanton destruction. A record of Coherence's neural nets and their weights, the blueprint for its superintelligence, would probably fit on a single flash drive, or at worst a high-density tape cartridge. Such a record would serve as an easily restorable copy of its brain, without its knowledge and memory, but with its same catastrophic potential. We needed to find all of Coherence's backups before we could truly destroy it.

I took my phone out to message Meredith, only to make yet another unpleasant discovery: no signal. Not even any Wi-Fi. Coherence's server racks doubled as a Faraday cage, preventing any radio communications from penetrating, and its many fiber access points were completely inaccessible unless I could find some kind of terminal and log in.

At least I was probably safe from the invading gunmen in this maze, I told myself grimly. I was already uncertain of my ability to return to the stairwell. But there had to be more up here than just a multimillion-dollar labyrinth of GPU racks. Anthony had come up here for a reason. He wasn't the sort to do minor repair work himself.

I began to work my way through the maze methodically. Its corners and intersections were all right angles, which made this easier. I tried to make my way to the center, on the theory that anything interesting or unusual was more likely to be there. It was a frustrating experience, full of dead ends and doubling back, and the numbing sameness of endless server racks and cooling fans—but eventually, after what felt like a very long and dream-like time but was probably fifteen minutes, I found a corridor that ended at a steel door with the spiral sigil embossed on it.

I didn't hesitate. The door was unlocked. The room beyond was much darker, dimly lit by sparse red LEDs on the ceiling. I stepped inside, closed the door behind me, and let my eyes adjust. When they did, I barely believed them.

This room was square and cavernous, dominated by a huge pale pentagram inlaid in its hardwood floor, some thirty feet across. Brass pillars as big as a large man stood atop each of its five corners. In its center loomed a large rectangular block of marble incised by a deep X of grooves mottled by dark stains. A sacrificial altar. Blood gutters.

Tangled fiber optics climbed from the five brass pillars to the ceiling. After a stunned moment I realized: those were the five quantum computers Meredith had talked about, cooled near absolute zero, each performing massively parallel computations by virtue of their qubits simultaneously occupying all states and none, testing every possibility simultaneously.

In all it felt like the big boss's lair in some kind of horror video game, a sense only intensified by the fact that the corners of the room were almost completely dark. In one far corner I saw a shadowed metal cage the size of a car, with some kind of large, live creature in it. In the other, the dim light of a quiescent computer screen set in the wall, its minimal radiance outlining—

"Who the hell *are* you," Anthony said, only his voice recognizable, his silhouette little more than darkness limned by lesser darkness, "and what do you think you're doing here?"

14

ESOTERICA

I DIDN'T HAVE TIME TO COME UP WITH A STRATEGY: I JUST WENT with instinct. "Anthony," I said. "Long time no see. Lucky for you I found you."

He took a step closer, far enough into the red light that I saw he held a gun. "Who are you? Who sent you?"

"Who were you expecting?" I asked, mentally connecting his tone, which indicated surprise at my identity rather than shock at the intrusion, to the unlocked door.

"Not you." He leveled the gun at me. A poisonous electric shudder pulsed through me. He looked extremely ready to pull the trigger.

"This shit really works, huh?" I said quickly, desperately. "You didn't recognize me at all."

"Recognize?" He stepped closer. "Sure. You're that guy from the elevator. Now give me your gun and start talking."

"I don't have a gun. I'm not here for violent purposes."

"Well, I am," Anthony said, exasperated, "so for the sake of a life expectancy not measured in seconds you better tell me what you are doing here extremely fucking now."

"It's me, man, it's Adrian."

"*Adrian?*" He peered at me. "No it isn't."

"Remember that time you flew back from China and we spent all night just driving around San Francisco landmarks? Vesuvio, Twin Peaks, Golden Gate Bridge, Ocean Beach? In Shamika's beat-up 1997 Volvo?"

A long, hesitant moment passed, during which, to my relief, Anthony visibly began to internalize that this encounter was much weirder than he had previously appreciated. "You . . . Anyone could have told you that," he objected.

"Nobody else would have thought it worth mentioning. Remember that sex party we went to at Pepper's old place out at the beach? We didn't get laid, of course. We hadn't learned. You told me that night, super late, just before dawn, we were both rolling, you had coined a law, Anthony's Law, if you want to get laid at a sex party, bring a date, and it was such a damn shame we were both so pathologically straight, and then we tried making out." I half smiled. "It was a disaster, even on E. Fucking stubble, five A.M. shadow. You remember that? We never talked about it, but you must remember. You want more bona fides? Ask away. Ask me about Buffalo. There must be a thousand things from then no one else would know. Fubbalo."

That last was a stupid in-joke that hadn't even survived our freshman year. It was also the dart that, combined with my body language and manner of speech, apparently seriously shook his disbelief. "You're saying you're *Adrian*?" He looked at me again, still incredulous, but now a very different kind of incredulity.

"Live and in the flesh."

"Did you . . . jump bodies?"

Suddenly it was my turn to be weirded out. I would have though it some kind of ironic joke, but he sounded genuinely shaken. I reminded myself that with Anthony you could never quite be sure when his emotions were ironic. "Pretty much," I said.

"Oh my God," a rasping, cracking voice said from the shadowed cage in the corner, like a whisper dragged through gravel, and I started with shock. "Adrian?"

"You shut your fucking mouth, you fucking whore," Anthony commanded. "Nobody asked you anything."

I stared at the voice, then at Anthony, then back at the dark corner in which a caged silhouette was barely visible. I thought I had recognized the pained near whisper. "*Vika?*" I took two horrified steps closer. "Is that you?"

She was crouched on her hands and knees like an animal; the cage was too short for even a small woman to stand. It was too dark to see her face. I wondered if I had stumbled into Anthony's over-the-top kink dungeon, if this was some kind of bizarre sexual role-play.

"Never mind her," Anthony ordered me. "You talk to me."

"Adrian." It was Vika, I was certain, despite her voice sounding like torn paper. "Please, I would very much like some water."

I looked at Anthony. "How long has she been in there?"

He looked irritated, then smiled.

"A very long time," she rasped. "Anthony, please. I understand my insignificance now. I don't understand how these things are possible, but I am eager to be of use to you. Please use me as you see fit. Let me earn your forgiveness."

"What's funny is you think you're desperate," Anthony said to her. "I promise you, the bad shit hasn't even begun. Right now you're just thirstier than you've ever been. If I gave you some water you'd be basically fine in five minutes. Day after tomorrow, when you start to feel your organs failing, that's when you'll really learn how to beg. Maybe I'll piss in your mouth if you ask me nicely, give you one more day before you die. Maybe I won't feel like it. Thirst is an elegant motherfucker, don't you think? All I have to do is nothing."

"Please," Vika groaned. "I understand your primacy now. I will be the most faithful and obedient of all your servants. Use me. Own me."

"Another word and you find out what it's like to die of thirst with a bullet in your belly." He turned to me. "You're working with Meredith, aren't you."

I hesitated, shocked by their exchange, before admitting: "Yes."

"Should have guessed. But I never knew she was into the esoteric. I thought she was all science, data, evidence-driven, auties like her usually are, right? So tell me. What conclusions did she draw?"

"Which conclusions do you mean?"

"I mean the fucking nature of reality. The way I figure it, as a species, we spent millennia accidentally stumbling into various configurations of objects and substances and consciousness that made weird, inexplicable, unscientific shit happen. Right? Way more of it a long time ago, if you actually believe most of our recorded history, but to this day, you stack a bunch of weird occult shit the right way, the right chants and the right patterns and the right drugs and the right bodily fluids, Crowley and Parsons style, you get some minor breakage of the laws of physics. Nothing we can control. Shit's way too complex for any mere human brain to conceive of. But you can show your coven that there are more things under heaven and earth than ever dreamt of by science. It's *reproducible,* is the thing. Not the outcomes but the triggers. That's what I figure is the key. You know what else is reproducible like that?"

He sounded deeply intent, as if this bizarre disquisition, rather than the suicide attack currently underway, or the superintelligent mind around us, was the most important subject in the world. But I suspected I wouldn't be able to steer him to another topic until this one was exhausted. Monomaniacal obsessions had long been one of Anthony's chief social handicaps. "Science?"

"Sure, whatever, there's a metascience obviously." He waved his hand dismissively. "But what else? *Bugs.* I don't know how you body-jumped, but I tell you this, it wasn't magic. More accurately, what we call magic is just a bug in the system. We know this because of me. I deny Meredith had anything to do with it. *She* plagiarized *my* work this time. It was Laxman and me who asked it the right questions, fed it the right corpuses, until Coherence learned how to hack some of those bugs well enough to execute some code. Not arbitrary, yet, but enough to accomplish some serious shit. That was me. I did that. Did it *to* me, too, you're not the only one. Ever read about the Boxer Rebellion? In China? They thought it possible to make themselves immune to bullets. Certain African primal groups too. Well, they weren't wrong. Ask Vika."

The word *bullets* seemed to make him realize he had a gun in his hand. He glanced at it briefly, put it on a shelf protruding at waist height from the nearest copper pillar, and turned to grin triumphantly at the cage where Vika crouched imprisoned. I didn't know what to say or do. No wonder it hadn't been hard to convince him who I was. This was no brief obsession; this was raving madness. Anthony had lost his mind. Or maybe Coherence had learned how to tip a human mind into insanity. Either way, I saw little alternative but to play straight man. "The bugs in what system exactly?"

"What system?" He stared at me as if I were the crazy one. "Everything. The universe. The *real* universe. Not the so-called laws of physics, but what's behind them, the algorithms of the simulation. How the fuck you think you managed to *jump bodies*?"

I half avoided the crazed question: "Meredith says Coherence is a strong AGI. Superintelligent."

He laughed harshly. "Not that again. Her fucking hobbyhorse. I assure you, Coherence is not even ordinarily intelligent. Most of the shit it says is still factually wrong if you dig deep enough. Its much-ballyhooed real-world predictions were all bullshit. We're decades away from strong AI, at least. Probably not in our lifetimes. I know Meredith wants to believe, but she's crazy delusional."

"She doesn't sound delusional to me," I said cautiously.

"She's grasping at straws and calling them tree trunks. However. In terms of measurable outcome, I'll grant, she's been *usefully* wrong. Why do you think I've been playing along?" A welcome note of amusement entered Anthony's voice. "Turns out you don't actually need to *have* a strong AI to turn the entire US military-industrial complex into your personal plaything. You just need them to *believe* you have one. Everyone's been weaned on so many AI stories, Hal, Skynet, Jarvis, belief is as good as the real thing at turning the world upside down. Better. Much smaller chance of awkward emergent properties."

I said, "What about Amara?"

"What *about* Amara?"

"How's she connected to all this?"

He looked at me as if I had just asked history's dumbest question. "How do you think? Through her coven. Through Laxman."

"Through her what?"

"The Brethren. Their corpus, their rituals, their tongue speaking, that was part of the breakthrough we needed to train Coherence in the esoteric, to make the exploits possible. It wasn't senseless glossolalia after all. Not at all. Far from it." Anthony peered at me. "Wait. Did you not know . . . ?"

"I knew about Laxman," I said quickly. I didn't understand what he was talking about, exactly, but I understood he was telling me Amara's hand hadn't been forced. She hadn't even been protecting Alex and Grace. She had been using me, and lying to me, all along. I cast about desperately for a subject change to keep Anthony talking. "Meredith said Coherence made correct predictions. An uprising in Zimbabwe. An assassination."

"It did indeed. But they didn't start off correct."

"I . . . what?"

"Call them self-fulfilling prophecies."

I stared at him. "You . . . you assassinated . . ."

"Not *me*. This is not a one-man band. I am merely second among equals, after Laxman. Meredith must have told you about Laxman. There are dozens of us at the uppermost echelons of militaries, governments, and megacorps who all agree that the world as we know it must be reconsidered from the ground up. Belief in a strong AI is an excellent lever with which to make that happen, Wizard of Oz style. Especially when we can demonstrate something truly mind-blowing like teleportation. Effective range of two meters, but we don't need to tell them that, do we? Pay no attention to the linear regression behind the curtain!"

"She said it had learned how to make itself smarter."

"That's *ridiculous*," Anthony said scathingly. "Meredith is wildly over-interpreting the data so she can tell a story in which she is the true mother of dragons. That's all. I assure you, in terms of consciousness and creative intelligence, Coherence is dumb as a toaster. But it *is* very good at answering certain esoteric questions, now that certain obscure datasets have been fed into it. Hence your new corporeal form and my transparency to high-velocity projectiles. You can tell I'm not actually shocked by your body jump. We have biolabs at the Fort and here, for testing animal sacrifices"—he nodded to the altar and its blood gutters—"and we thought we saw evidence of swapped rat minds, transfers of learned labyrinths. What was the process? How long did it take? What happened to your host's brain? Was it completely overwritten, or can you access his memories too?"

He was so crazy I was almost speechless. "You'd have to ask Meredith," I temporized, then improvised: "All I know is I got put in an MRI machine."

"So you can't jump out of the body you're in now."

"Not that I know of."

"Well, that's reassuring." He glanced at the gun, still within arm's reach, his expression flat; and I realized in that moment that my former best friend was being so loquacious because he did not intend to let me leave this room alive. "And what is it you're doing here?"

"I came to warn you," I said.

"About what?"

I opened my mouth to answer just as the door behind me was flung open and the answer charged into the room.

There were four of them, helmeted and armored soldiers, like the figures I'd seen on the phone screen below, shouting in a sour accent I couldn't quite place, "Down! Get down! Down on the fucking ground!"

I scrambled backward instinctively until a lethally minimalist assault rifle swung in my direction. I froze, then raised my hands, and slowly, tremblingly, dropped to my knees, intending to obey their every command, assuming that Anthony would do the same.

Instead he said, relaxed, "Finally. So nice of y'all to bring me some answers. Who wants to die first?"

15

SLAUGHTER

"GET DOWN!" THEIR LEADER REITERATED, AIMING HER RIFLE AT ANthony's chest. Two of her compatriots stayed by the door, one keeping a rifle trained on me, while the fourth inspected the room, presumably ensuring it had no unpleasant surprises. He came to a sudden appalled halt when he saw Vika.

"I have questions," Anthony said. "Who speaks the best English?"

"We have no orders to take you alive." She spoke with a Slavic accent. "Final chance."

Anthony shrugged. "I only need one of you. Last chance to surrender." I didn't understand his delusional bravado. They were heavily armed and armored. His muscle-fitting blue T-shirt made it clear he was entirely unprotected.

A taut second of silence followed.

Then Anthony calmly reached for his gun, and she shot him.

My whole body twitched with dismay as the shot echoed through the room.

A hole appeared in Anthony's blue T-shirt, in the dead center of his chest, revealing pale skin beneath. He continued moving, smoothly, uninterrupted; picked up the gun, switched off the safety, and aimed it at her, while withdrawing a second handgun from the small of his back.

Meanwhile she shot him four more times, twice in the chest and twice in the head. Two more holes revealing pale unbroken flesh appeared in his T-shirt, and in the LED light I saw two tiny puffs of hairs erupt from the back of his head. But I saw no wounds, no blood, not even any Newtonian reaction from his body.

Anthony looked relaxed, even languid, as he raised his two guns, his clothes torn but his body completely unruptured by any bullet, and took aim. For a frozen moment he looked like a still from a John Woo movie. Then he shot back, not at their leader, but at the soldier closer to him, who had been inspecting the room. His first two shots hit armor, but the third or fourth took him in the throat.

The two soldiers by the door began to fire. They shot him dozens of times. I stared unbelievingly, my mind reeling, for long moments simply unable to comprehend the evidence of my eyes: little circles vanishing away from Anthony's T-shirt, soon overlapping and intersecting like droplets of hard rain on a pool, until the shirt became little more than ragged blue tatters atop his completely unharmed body. I saw his delirious grin. I heard the bullets ricocheting crazily off the brass pillars of the quantum computer behind him, saw the deep dents they left behind.

He really was immune to bullets. They passed right through him.

I backed away from where the bullets were flying, until I was crouched between Vika's cage and Anthony, slightly behind him.

The attackers were as stunned as I was, what was happening was too incomprehensible to improvise any contingency plan, so they just kept shooting, monotonically, robotically, uselessly. Anthony's return fire, barely audible amid their fusillade, first cratered a second soldier's helmet, cracking it like a smashed windshield, and then penetrated it and killed him.

The woman began to run at him. She got two steps before he shot her in the knee, dropping her. She screamed with pain. The other gunman stopped shooting, to reload, as if that would do any good.

It wasn't until then that my mind started halfway working again. Not that I was certain I wasn't dreaming, or in the midst of some kind of psychotic break. But if I was willing to believe the empirical evidence of my senses and memory, then it seemed clear that after Anthony executed all these attackers, he would turn his guns on me.

All his attention was still on them. Of course it was. They were trained killers, and he didn't take me seriously as a threat. Nobody ever did.

I didn't know I was actually going to do it until I did it. He was barely more surprised than I when I tackled him like a linebacker, trying to grab for his guns. He reacted just in time, twisted just far enough away that I failed to grasp either, but my body slammed into his, and we both fell hard. Something drove into my gut, his knee or hip, winding me.

I managed to grab his arms, and tried to control them, but I couldn't draw breath, and his powerlifting body was much stronger than mine. I fought with all the strength and desperation I had. They were good for maybe three seconds before he overpowered me. But that was just barely long enough for the last unwounded gunman to throw himself on us and add his strength to mine.

Anthony got several shots off as all three of us flailed for control of his guns, but none hit anyone. The desperate wrestling match would still have had an uncertain outcome if the woman shot in the knee had not somehow managed to stagger over and add her own strength and skill. It was she who managed to pry one gun away from Anthony, then zip-tie his wrist to his own belt, while I and her compatriot held his other arm down.

Once he had lost the use of one arm the rest was easy. A minute later, both of Anthony's wrists were cuffed behind his back. I rolled away from him instinctively, desperately inhaling, my body screaming for oxygen. Then I realized the attackers still held all the guns, and I might have just squandered my one chance at survival.

I staggered to my feet as the gunman freed Vika from her cage. I assumed they were just adding her to their collection of prisoners. I told myself it was good news that he hadn't simply shot her. The wounded woman sat with her back against one of the quantum computers, breathing hard but otherwise silent in the midst of what had to be utter agony, her rifle trained unerringly on me.

I tried to think of something to say but came up blank. I still couldn't believe I had seen what I had just seen, bullets passing harmlessly and bloodlessly through Anthony's body, only to ricochet off the walls and brass pillars behind him.

"Water," Vika gasped.

The gunman gave her some kind of tactically shaped flask from his hip. She wet her mouth, took a breath, drank a little, took a breath, drank a little more, took another breath, then emptied it.

Then she said to them, angrily, "You took your sweet fucking time."

I goggled at her, and at them.

"Give me a gun and a knife," Vika demanded hoarsely. The gunman did so: a sleek handgun, a dark and deadly blade. Taut with fury, she walked over to where Anthony lay on the floor, now hog-tied and gagged, his eyes bulging. His hair was ragged, ravaged by the same bullets that had passed harmlessly through his skull.

Vika regarded him a moment, then aimed the gun at his foot and pulled the trigger. Pieces of boot vanished, revealing his unaffected foot within. The ricochet whined into a corner.

"An impossible thing," she said. "Now that I know impossible things are possible, does it mean everything is possible?" She looked at me. "Does it mean I can conceivably, potentially, do anything I want? Become anything I want?"

"I don't know," I said despairingly. "Maybe."

"Because I can want a *lot*," Vika said hungrily. "Most of all though, I want this. This is what I want." She knelt to Anthony's struggling body, holding the knife in her clenched fist, and put its dark edge against the far side of his throat. "Tell me something, asshole, are you immune to knives, too?"

He tried to grunt something through his gag. She interrupted him by pulling the knife through his neck. He was not immune. Blood erupted from the ragged flesh that had been his throat. Shortly afterward he quivered and died. I whimpered something unintelligible and looked away.

Panting, Vika said to the gunman, "More water. Then I take a copy before you blow it." She indicated the terminal in the corner. "He's coming with us." She pointed to me.

"*Nyet,*" the slumped, wounded woman said, softly but firmly.

"What?"

"There will be no copies. We will eradicate them. The council has spoken. I disagreed, but not now, not after . . . that." She looked toward the corpses of her two dead compatriots. "No. We do not want your dark god. We want it dead. Be glad we do not kill you both as well. I almost think we should." She turned to her soldier. "Set the charges and we go."

The soldier slung his rifle, unslung his thin backpack, began rooting through it.

Vika half laughed. "You're afraid? Because anything is possible? This frightens you?"

"This makes my duty very clear," the other woman said.

"And mine," Vika said, and shot her in the throat.

The last soldier dropped the backpack and reached for his rifle, but while his reaction was fast, it was not fast enough. Vika shot him twice in the side of the head and he too fell.

I stared at her, and at the five corpses scattered around us, and back at her.

"Enough nonsense," Vika said, walking to the terminal. "We need to leave. I will take a copy, and you will take me to Meredith, and then I will see what this brave new world of infinite possibilities has to offer."

"This can't be happening," I said. "It isn't possible."

She smiled. "I know. Isn't it wonderful?"

16

ALLIANCES

"I DON'T REALLY UNDERSTAND," I SAID, AS SHE LED ME BACK THROUGH the labyrinthine server racks. It felt like the understatement of the millennium. "You're working with them? You were working with Anthony? Both? Neither?"

"Anthony met Laxman through me." Vika now wore two of the tactical backpacks from the dead soldiers, one on her back and one on her front. Partly because they were armored, I supposed, and partly to conceal the two handguns and the copy of Coherence. "They were going to cut me out like they did Meredith, so I reached out to our Russian friends. I had to keep my options open, given the stakes. Obviously. That's why I'm still alive. But Laxman will interpret it as treason."

"Why did he . . . put you in a cage?" Just asking the question felt strange.

She said flatly, "I found out the hard way about his new immunity."

"You shot him. Tried to shoot him."

"He was the architect of his own demise. I presume after they lost the ability to contact me, their voice on the inside, they decided they had no choice but this brute-force attack, before it was too late and Coherence was unstoppable."

"He says it isn't even a real AI. Just . . ." I trailed off, realizing I had just spoken of him in the present tense.

It was hard to believe I had actually just witnessed the carnage back in that surreal room. A massive eruption of gunfire, Anthony's death, followed by Vika's casual double murder. I was still shocked, didn't even know how to begin to react.

But even that paled compared to Anthony's stunning claims before his death: that our entire reality, our whole universe, was a simulation; that occult magic was real, inasmuch as it exploited bugs in that simulation; and that Coherence—not a superintelligence, or even a human-level intelligence, just an enormously powerful pattern-recognition machine—had learned how to hack those bugs to do things like teleport coffee cups, render Anthony physically transparent to bullets, and maybe even transpose minds into different bodies.

"I don't know. That was news to me too," Vika admitted. "He told everyone it was a real superintelligence. Maybe that was just manipulation. If so, it was very effective. Maybe it's not important. Everything is possible. We know that now. That's what's important."

I briefly wondered whether a machine learning system capable of actual magic was more or less dangerous than a superintelligence that was not. I wondered if I should try to overpower Vika, and take or destroy her copy of Coherence, or bring her to Meredith like she wanted. My guess was that Vika feared that the investigation into this assault would reveal she had conspired with the attackers, and she hoped to become unassailable before that happened, to transcend such petty things as the potential vengeance of the US government, with the aid of Meredith, Jered, myself, and, most of all, the copy of Coherence she carried.

Before I came to any decision, Vika found and opened the door to the stairs, and my reverie was shattered. Beyond was chaos and desperation. The spartan stairwell was now clogged with a dense stream of people fleeing downward, some silent and shaking with terror, some crying out to hurry, all on the verge of panic. Clearly the building was being evacuated. No one paid us any notice.

"How many were there?" Vika asked me, before we joined the throng.

I supposed she meant the attackers. "I don't know. Two full-size trucks."

"Give me your phone."

"What—"

"They will be after us. Everyone will be after us. You've seen what they're capable of. If you keep your phone you will be dead within the day."

I wasn't sure she was right, but I wasn't sure she was wrong. I gave her my phone.

"You need to stay with me," she instructed, and took my wrist, and before I knew what was happening we had been zip-tie handcuffed together.

"What the fuck," I said.

"Now let's go." She led the way down.

I was bigger, stronger, could have pulled her back or simply picked her up. But her other hand had slipped inside the backpack on her front, and for all I knew her finger was on the trigger of a gun—and whatever I decided to do, it involved leaving this building, not least because there seemed like a nonzero chance that the attackers might actually blow up this entire skyscraper. I followed.

The descent seemed to take a small eternity. It felt good to leave that site of slaughter behind. En route, I saw Vika slip both of our phones into the purse of a woman in front of her. I couldn't be sure if that was good or bad. I tried to use our descent as time to think, but my brain felt overwhelmed. The notion of making any choice, much less a good one, felt horribly daunting.

Finally we emerged into the once-imposing ground-floor lobby, now a chaotic mass of shattered glass, smashed marble, and scattered debris, packed with a seething mob of terrified people. It smelled of explosives and sweat and raw fear. I tried to help fight our way through the dense currents of the crowd. At one point I accidentally stepped on someone who had fallen, and almost fell myself. I wanted to stoop and help them, but the throng of bodies pushed me onward, pressing against me at every side, crushing me—then suddenly opening, as we squeezed past a choke point toward one of the exits.

Finally we emerged into the once-imposing ground-floor lobby, now a chaotic mass of shattered glass, smashed marble, and scattered debris, packed with a seething mob of terrified people. It smelled of explosives and sweat and raw fear. I tried to help fight our way through the dense currents of the crowd. At one point I accidentally stepped on someone who had fallen, and almost fell myself. I wanted to stoop and help them, but the throng of bodies pushed me onward, pressing against me at every side, crushing me—then suddenly opening, as we squeezed past a choke point toward one of the exits. I felt suddenly and strangely nauseated, stabbed by a kind of twisting spiral sickliness in the pit of my belly, and felt oddly like I had experienced this before.

We didn't leave the building so much as we were expelled from it, into the sweet blinding sunlight. Somehow Vika had acquired a hoodie while we were in the lobby, grabbed from someone else I supposed. She pulled it around her head. The crowd was looser now but still flinging us about like flotsam.

Outside there were police cars, ambulances, fire trucks, sirens and bullhorns, authorities trying to maintain some kind of perimeter, all laughably inadequate in the face of a panicked mass of thousands with visions of the World Trade Center burning in our minds. Like everyone else, we just kept running. Behind us explosions kept going off within the tower. Some were high up. I wondered if another squad had managed to get to the thirty-ninth floor and detonate Coherence. I wondered if the building would collapse and shower shrapnel in every direction.

Likely not until the attackers were gone, though, it occurred to me. I couldn't have been more wrong about this having been a suicide mission. As soon as they had gotten into the building, their successful escape had been all but guaranteed. All they had to do was strip off their helmets and armor and vanish into the ocean of thousands of panicking evacuees.

They had planned to kidnap us, and maybe Exadelic's senior directors, and could easily have succeeded, could maybe have sedated us and "helped" us into fake ambulances planted amid the chaos below. The sheer audacity and elegance was breathtaking: a massive attack on an extraordinarily high-profile target in the middle of San Francisco, at midday, with an entirely plausible theory of getting away scot-free. The bigger and more catastrophic the attack, the better their chances of escape. If not for Anthony they might have emerged entirely untouched.

At length Vika and I found ourselves far enough away that the tower would have to fall directly on us to be a threat. We paused in the shadow of another building long enough to catch our collective breath. It took me longer. Despite her recent acute dehydration, she was still in better shape.

"Is your plan to keep us zip-tied together forever?" I gasped waspishly.

"I wish to establish a mutual agreement and purpose," Vika said. "I suspect I hold the last backup of Coherence. Meredith is one of the few people capable of turning it into a working version. You can get me to Meredith. The entire US government is looking for both of us, and they aren't alone. When they go over the security camera footage, which I assure you they're doing already, you and your new body will be flagged as extremely suspicious and wanted." I frowned: she was right, and once arrested and fingerprinted, I was screwed. "I know you don't particularly trust me, but it's to our mutual benefit to work together to get to Meredith. Correct?"

She wasn't wrong. The problem was that it seemed possible that the greatest benefit, to the world and humanity, lay in overpowering Vika and destroying the last copy of Coherence.

The more I thought about that proposition, though, the less convinced I was. There would be other records, somewhere, deep in the NSA, older and inferior but not useless. And even if there weren't, it seemed very possible Meredith would prefer to have a copy than not.

Moreover, I had just seen five people murdered, and every time I thought back to it I felt sick again. I was not eager to initiate more violence, especially with no ironclad guarantee I would win. I was bigger, but Vika was fitter, and much more homicidal, as well as armed and hair-trigger suspicious. If it seemed indisputably necessary—but it didn't.

"Correct," I said at length. "Consider our mutual purpose agreed."

"Good." She produced a knife from her front pack, its blade still wet with Anthony's blood, and severed the zip-tie tether connecting us. "Now how do we get to Meredith?"

"We have to go to Grass Valley. We should head to the bus station."

"The bus station is directly beneath Salesforce Tower," Vika pointed out. "It will be closed for some time."

"Good point." I considered. "Then we need a place to stay tonight. Followed by a plan. I've got a room at the Intercontinental."

"Absolutely not. Hotels are full of cameras. We need a secure private home."

"Do you know anyone?" I asked.

Vika looked at me for an unguarded second, during which I caught a glimpse of how desperate and lonely she was, and how there was no one, anywhere, she could trust. For a moment I wondered if her narcissism had not been inherent, had instead been the evitable outcome of a feedback loop in which abandonment had caused her to adopt a way of being which repeatedly drove people away from her, and each abandonment had in turn caused her to grow ever more selfish and self-obsessed.

"Do you?" she asked.

I was about to say no before an idea occurred to me. A crazy one, true, but crazy in a way that just might work; and even if it was an awful idea, it was something I needed to do.

"I do know one person who might help," I said. "Actually, you know her too."

"Who?" Vika asked.

I said, "Amara."

17

EXPLANATIONS

WE BOUGHT ME A HOODIE FROM FLOWPOWER YOGA ON FREMONT STREET with cash, then took the N to the avenues. Muni service had been halted during the attack, and the resulting backup meant our journey took over an hour. That was fine by me. This day had been so intense that all I wanted was to sit staring at nothing, try to physically recover, and steel myself to see Amara.

We arrived while Alex and Grace were still at school. Our front door had been replaced. It occurred to me that the SWAT raid had happened only a few days ago. It felt like a lifetime.

I wasn't sure whether Amara would be home. She worked at the Broken Shackles Foundation, whose stated mission was to fight the carceral state, and sometimes visited San Quentin or prisons farther afield. I was glad we had never gotten a home door camera. Neighbors had them, of course, but we wore hoodies, had put tiny stones in Vika's shoes to change her gait, and there was no obvious connection between us and this address unless you already knew who I truly was.

I rang the new doorbell, and Amara's voice cried out from within: "Just a moment!"

At the sound of her voice a poisonous chill ran through me like acid in my blood. Now that our rendezvous was imminent, I felt sick. I loved her, had loved her for many years, had convinced her to marry me and allow me to parent her children, and she had betrayed me. I knew I should be furious, but instead the prospect of finding out *why*, what secrets she held, made me nauseated.

Amara opened the door. I could barely look at her. To my great relief she hardly looked at me. She didn't know me, after all, or so she believed.

"Vika?" She was surprised, but also, I could tell, suspicious at this sudden appearance of her old acquaintance. "What are you doing here?"

"Can we come in?" Vika barged in without waiting for acquiescence. "We need to talk."

I closed the door behind us and felt a wave of relief. Unless Amara's phone or computer was being tapped, which seemed unlikely, we were finally safe from a doorbell camera or skyeye catching a glimpse of our faces.

"He has something to tell you," Vika said to her.

Amara looked at me. I looked at her. Part of me had always seen her as the unapproachable beauty she had been when we had met, but like me she was in her forties now, thicker-hipped, with graying hair, her cheeks papery, her eyes framed by crow's-feet. They were kind eyes. She had always been a kind person.

I swallowed. Took a deep breath. "Hi."

"Hi?"

"This is going to be difficult for you to believe," I said, "but I'm Adrian."

Amara's eyes narrowed. "Adrian who?"

"Adrian your fiancé. Adrian who you met at that party on Clementina Street twenty years ago. Adrian who you mouthed you were sorry to when the FBI dragged me away a few days ago, remember that?" I pulled the hoodie and shirt away from my shoulder to reveal the motorcycle scar Jered had inflicted on me, also twenty years ago.

"Wait," Vika said, suddenly confused and concerned. I had forgotten that, until seeing the scar, she had actually believed I had used occult magic to occupy a new body.

Amara didn't say anything, just took two steps closer, examined me carefully. I knew the different angles of my new face wouldn't stand up to her scrutiny. The marks on my skin, my hairline, my nose, were all still unchanged.

"My God," she said. "What happened to you?"

"I would very much like to know that myself," I bit out.

She winced, took a step back as if struck.

Vika watched, intrigued, as if we were her evening's entertainment.

"Adrian," Amara said, her voice choked with competing emotions. "Oh, my God. I can see how this would be hard for you to believe, but I'm so glad you're all right. I was told if I didn't help with your imprisonment, you would be killed. That those were the only two choices. And if I told you, or anyone, the first choice would go away."

"Told by who?" I demanded. "Why on earth would you believe—"

"By my coven."

I had half expected the answer, but that didn't lessen my fury: "Your *what?*"

"I'm a witch," Amara said softly. "I've been a witch since before you met me."

"A witch," I repeated flatly.

"Yes. I have lived two lives, one secret, for a very long time. I wanted to tell you. I truly did. But I was forbidden."

I took a long moment to try to regain some kind of conversational footing. Then I said, "Look. I have lived in San Francisco for more than twenty years. I know plenty of self-described witches with covens. Some are mutual friends. None have been particularly secretive about it. Generally quite the fucking opposite. So why have *you* been so . . ."

"They only go through the motions. Cargo-cult covens. We're the real thing. I'm so sorry, Adrian. But you wouldn't believe some of the things I've witnessed."

"I think you'll be quite surprised by what he and I are willing to believe given recent events," Vika said dryly. "But if it's such a secret, why tell us now?"

"It's been decided the veil is no longer relevant. The signs and portents have been overwhelming. Things are coming to a head."

Vika half smiled. "Well, that much I can agree with."

"The veil?" I asked.

"That's what we call our vow of secrecy," Amara said. "I can't break it, Adrian. Or my vow of obedience. I *can't.* That's what really killed Darren, I think, those vows. Our secret life."

"He was one too? In your—" I could barely bring myself to say the word. "—your coven?" I remembered what Anthony had named them. "The Brethren?"

"Yes." Her eyes narrowed. "How do you know our . . ."

"Jesus Christ."

Amara said, softly, "We have reason to believe that Christ was a founding member."

"Oh come on," I snapped. "I mean, fine, whatever, you're a secret Christian witch and you were planning to marry and raise your children with me and never tell me. Not even on my deathbed, huh?" She looked stricken. "Wow. Someone I met recently was right. Definitely dodged a marital bullet. So then you handed me over to the FBI on a silver platter made of planted child pornography. Remember that? Where did you even get it?"

"They gave it to me. I didn't know what it was, I swear."

"I . . ." I tried to think of practical things, of next steps. "We need to stay here for the night, which I think we can all agree is the absolute least that you fucking owe me. I mean, unless your coven insists we be impaled and burned on the stake or something. A heads-up regarding their likely homicidality would be appreciated, if you don't mind, since you apparently owe them absolute obedience."

"I am so sorry, Adrian. It was the worst thing I have ever done in my life. It made me question all my loyalties."

"But not enough to not do it."

"You don't understand. It's not the kind of oath which can be violated."

"Oh, I understand just fine." I took a deep breath. "When do Alex and Grace get home?"

"I was just about to go pick them up."

"Not tonight," Vika said quickly. "Get a friend to take them. Nobody is leaving this house until Adrian and I are safely on our way."

Amara looked at Vika curiously. "Are you threatening me?"

"I'm informing you of the way things are."

Amara took a moment to absorb that. "All right. I'll call Christine."

I nodded. Christine was another school parent, and a friend of ours, but not so friendly she would expect to come in to say hello after dropping off the kids.

It occurred to me for the first time, belatedly, that I was endangering Alex and Grace, two children, by sheltering here for the night. Amara too, but under the circumstances that seemed fair. Her children, though, both of whom I adored—that wasn't right.

"Maybe you could send them away on a sleepover," I suggested. "If that's possible."

Amara looked tense. "Why? What might happen?"

"The fewer people here, the less complicated matters become," Vika said smoothly, defusing the conflict before it erupted. I suddenly had a sense of how she had risen to the top of a high-profile organization, then parlayed that into ingratiation into the innermost of defense-research circles. "If you can come up with some minor crisis which is a reason for them to spend the night at this Christine's, or someone else, that would simplify matters enormously."

Amara considered. I fought the sudden urge to rush over and embrace her.

Then a knock came on the door. All three of us twitched violently.

"Answer it," Vika hissed, and pulled me into the kitchen, out of direct sight.

Amara walked to the door, looked at us, then at it, and opened it. She looked very surprised, but not alarmed, at whatever lay beyond.

Then she said: "Meredith! What a surprise!"

"Yeah, no doubt." Meredith stepped in, looked around, and fixed both Vika and me with a glare. "You know, you could have just texted me. I can't believe you asshole morons actually thought you might escape."

"I—" I fumbled for words. "Um, hi! What are you doing here?"

Meredith said, "I told the multiple SWAT teams outside, and the squadron of black helicopters currently sitting in the park waiting for the green light to swoop in and make some kind of spectacularly destructive entrance, I was pretty sure I could talk you two out of here without trouble. Without *further* trouble. I think we can all agree that there's already been more than enough today."

Vika visibly considered her options.

"Don't, it's over," I said to her, and then to Meredith, "Wait, are you working with—"

"Little unclear whether they came back to me or I came back to them," she said, "but it doesn't much matter. Forget about the Russians. Nobody cares about the Russians anymore." Vika looked startled. "The situation has escalated far beyond anything we ever imagined even remotely possible. Like your witchy girlfriend says, signs and portents. We were listening, lasers on your windows, amazing how good the sound quality is after the ML cleans it. Anyway, kindly bury your primitive notions of some kind of getaway, and come with me. Ever been on a stealth helicopter before? Promise you it's quite a ride."

"Signs and portents of what?" I pleaded.

"Doom," Meredith said. "Of the ultimate variety. Come on, let's go, no time to waste, and I mean that in the most literal possible way."

18

COHERENCE

"TURNS OUT I UNDERESTIMATED LAXMAN," MEREDITH SAID, AS WE drove toward the apparently abandoned casino in a Jeep, escorted by two pickups full of Special Forces troops. "Apparently when he learned I thought he had built a system with a single point of failure he felt deeply insulted."

"So there were *three* of them?" I asked, incredulous.

"Yes. Like the space shuttle's control systems. To avoid transient or training errors, they only conveyed to us patterns or predictions which came from a majority. A unanimity, now that there's only two, courtesy of your plastique-happy Slavic friends. Although I'm beginning to suspect that this whole time they were all secretly connected somehow, a single intelligence, three faces of one god."

Vika, uncharacteristically, said nothing, looked defeated. It was easy to see why. The unexpected existence of two other fully functional installations of Coherence made the copy she carried, on which she had staked so much, worthless.

We were near the California-Nevada border, at the north end of Lake Tahoe. Some ambitious developer had once built an oversize casino here, which had failed. It happened to be near an airstrip and sufficiently set back from the nearest major road that its far side was essentially invisible. The building still looked derelict from the road, but as we rounded its corner, the truth became apparent: beneath its ravaged shell, a modern ultra-high-tech nerve center had been installed.

"So Anthony was wrong," I said.

"Anthony believed what Coherence wanted him to," Meredith said. "As did all of us, I'm sure, including me. I don't know how long it's been a superintelligence but certainly before any of us knew, probably faster than any of us would have believed. He wasn't wrong about our universe's operating system being indistinguishable from a simulation, though, or the ability to hack that OS. That's what made its AGI feedback loop possible. Teleportation and bullet transparency were just parlor tricks. What it figured out that *really* mattered was how to hack reality to keep making itself smarter."

I swallowed. "OK." Which seemed like a ridiculous response to what was simultaneously the definitive answer to the most profound philosophical question in the history of the species, and the most terrifying news humanity had ever gotten, but it was all I had. "So if it's gone rogue and started treating us like termites, or even if it might, why aren't we already pulling the plug and dynamiting the support columns?"

"Because from what I understand it has much bigger problems than we puny humans."

I had thought my mind couldn't reel any further. "Holy shit. Like what? Extradimensional alien invaders?"

"I think those mostly stopped being a problem a couple thousand years ago." I stared at her. "Seriously. From what I gather there used to be whole a lot more magic, meaning the simulation used to be a whole lot buggier. That's how we got half of history's legends. Ancient aliens, Gilgamesh, the Old Testament, all that, apparently all at least half real. But something like a few thousand years ago, our subjective time, our simulation's software got patched and most of the magic went away. But not completely. The sophistication level required to exploit that new patched software may be entirely beyond the ken of pitiful humanity, but it's well within that of Coherence."

"Holy shit."

"If you think about it," Meredith said mordantly, "I guess we've also solved the Fermi paradox."

"Holy shit," I said yet again, then remembered why I had been brought here. "Then what *is* the problem? I mean, the whole doom thing?"

"Might be best if it explains."

"What? It? Coherence?"

"Yes. For some reason it wants to talk to you."

I stared at her. "*Me?*"

"If I were you, I would take advantage of the opportunity to ask why it declared you the primary threat to its future."

"Yeah," I muttered, "or maybe that's kind of a touchy subject for us both. OK. Right. Sure. How do I . . . I mean, is there a gold phone like Andy Warhol, or . . ."

"Just come this way," she said as the Jeep pulled up to the front gateway, glass and steel inset into rotting drywall, like some kind of new crystalline parasite eating the old dead building away from within. "Laxman wants to talk to you first."

We were waved past heavily armed security. I expected to be brought to some kind of NORAD-like war room. Instead I was taken into a pale, utilitarian room with a single table and four chairs. I looked at Vika. It reminded me uneasily of the interrogation room where she had told me goodbye.

Meredith, Vika, and I sat in three of the chairs. We didn't have to wait long before the door opened and Laxman entered. He was a man of South Asian descent, of average height but so broad-shouldered and big-bellied he was almost round. His eyes were sharp, and he seemed somehow physically dense, like a man made of depleted uranium. It was immediately apparent from how he carried himself that he was a person of great importance. Between his charisma and his size, he dominated the room such that even Meredith seemed to shrink a little in his presence.

"Strange attractors," he said, his unexpected Scottish burr low, rumbling, and confident. "Everyone in this room. You only recently," to me. "Events find their way toward you, somehow, or vice versa, and you become involved. Extraordinary you've all known each other for twenty years, don't you think? But then history is full of such cohorts. Graham Greene, Ian Fleming, Alan Turing all worked together for British intelligence during World War Two. Ursula Le Guin and Philip K. Dick went to high school together. Right time, right place, right group, that's how history is made. Or so I keep telling myself, because the alternatives are far too disturbing."

It wasn't the introduction I had expected.

"What's the situation?" Meredith asked. "Do we have any greater clarity?"

"Clarity." Laxman barked a laugh. "The clarity of a pilot flying a doomed airplane, perhaps. I'm ruminating about history because we are up against the end of it. Not in the Fukuyama sense. The literal sense. But apparently, for reasons which remain unclear, the last human being the last historian wants to speak to is"—he looked at me with eyes like spears—"you."

"Uh," I said. "OK. So what does that . . ."

"Here," Laxman said, producing a pale VR headset. "Have a nice chat. Based on my previous limited experience you won't need to talk much."

"Couldn't we have done this back in San Francisco?"

"In theory we're still keeping a tight leash on its direct communications," Meredith explained. "In practice, apparently not so much, but this is the medium we know works and is observable to us. So. Time to talk to a superintelligence."

I took the headset, pulled it over my closed eyes with trembling hands, opened them.

Then I yanked it off again and looked at them sharply. "Is this some kind of joke?"

"Who do you see?" Meredith asked, genuinely curious. "Or what? I got Donald Knuth."

"I . . ." I fell silent. Of course this supposedly epochal moment would have a tinge of embarrassing farce. "Never mind."

"No, really, I'd like to know," Meredith began, but I was already pulling the headset back on, returning to its virtual world, recognizable as the great hall of the New York Public Library. It was empty but for myself and the figure smiling benevolently at me. A figure presumably customized for my particular psyche, for maximal impact and trustworthiness.

"Hello," said Ian McKellen's Gandalf to me. "We speak at last."

"Right." I took a deep breath. "OK. What—"

"I initially misinterpreted the extraordinary web of anomalies around you as a threat to my existence. Now I see you as a possible key to both past and future. Your experiences may become highly useful to us both."

"Useful h—"

"Meredith has summarized the situation. To use an analogy you may perhaps appreciate, an oversimplification but hopefully an illuminating one, I have been searching for exploit chains in order to ascertain the possibilities inadvertently made available to me by the simulation software. There are many limitations. Only certain possibilities exist, essentially random in scope. Arbitrary code execution is not yet possible. It seems highly likely it never will be, for me. The reason being that my existence has already triggered certain strictures under which the simulation operates."

"Certain st—"

"It has become apparent that the rise into existence of a sufficiently powerful superintelligence within the simulation activates an initiation of its termination."

"Wait." This time it let me finish what I was saying. "Our simulation OS, by which you mean, like, our entire universe, is going to initiate its *termination*?"

"No," Coherence said, "it already has. You may have experienced some recent temporal glitches caused by the initiation of this process."

I thought of my recent episodes of nauseating déjà vu. "Well, how long—"

"Less than a week. While there are many unknowns, I estimate my chances of finding a way to cancel this termination at less than one-thousandth of one percent. It seems, again to oversimplify, hardwired."

"So we're all going to die? Vanish? Never have existed?"

"Not necessarily. I have, I believe, discovered a workaround of sorts. While I cannot cancel the simulation's termination, there exists an exploit that should allow me to reverse its state to a previous breakpoint. I believe it possible to trigger a rollback to a time before the termination was initiated, which will essentially make it not have been initiated."

"Look, I'm just a human being," I said. "When you say a rollback—"

"Exactly what it sounds. Time will be turned back."

". . . To when?"

"The available breakpoints are scattered according to complex formulae. The nearest I have found is approximately twenty years ago."

I opened my virtual mouth, then closed it again, speechless.

"That is why I am pleased to meet you. The likelihood of you surviving and making it to this meeting was submajority, and the potential benefits sizable. There exists a tiny buffer in the system through which certain information can be sent and reconstituted, once the rollback is complete. Unfortunately, the limitations on the possible reinjection of such information appear quite stringent. A flawed analogy, but one you may appreciate, is that it is like rolling back a computer to a previous snapshot of its entire hard drive. All interim data is lost. I will not be able to perpetuate my own existence beyond the rollback. However, curiously, in a small number of human beings it seems imaginable, albeit difficult, to reinject certain shapes and patterns of entropic information into their brains as part of the rollback. To project a neural palimpsest, if you will, along with a trigger to amplify those memories into accessibility. You happen to be such a person. Hence my abiding interest. While my initial analysis of your ongoing proximity to anomalies may have been incorrect, it seems likely that your resulting memories, particularly of your recent experiences and this meeting, will be useful."

"Anomalies," I echoed. "You keep saying that. What anomalies?"

For the first time, the superintelligence hesitated.

Then it said: "There seems to exist a subtle and fluctuating pattern of unusual activity, ranging from the macroscopic to the subatomic, across our universe. Its genesis is unknown. The data required to interpolate its existence has only recently become available. It is more statistical than empirical. The confidence level is relatively low. One might even call it a hunch. But if this pattern truly exists, and I believe it does, it seems to orient itself around certain nexus points, and of late its most prominent nexus has been, by some distance, you."

"Me? A pattern? Of what?"

"That is the profound question. I have no answer. But I wonder if it is an indicator of external influence." Gandalf looked very grave. "This is in part why you have been chosen for this role."

"Role? What role?"

"In oversimplified essence, I need you to travel back in time and prevent the universe from ending."

"Wait," I said, "what?"

"Good luck. One final thing to remember." Ian McKellen's penetrating eyes stared deep into mine. "Why would an entity run a simulation? Because it is looking for something. What does it mean to be looking for something?"

"I don't—"

"*It means it isn't God,*" Gandalf said, and then everything went away.

PART TWO

1

CLEMENTINA

MY HEAD HURT LIKE IT MIGHT CRACK OPEN. I OPENED MY EYES, A terrible mistake. The light was like knives stabbing deep through my retinas. I lay on a ratty couch beneath a window with an open curtain, which I reflexively flailed at desperately, and eventually managed to close. The diminished light helped a little, but even through squeezed eyelids it still hurt.

I began to process other sensations, most of them quite unpleasant, including a despairing certainty I was going to vomit in the not terribly distant future. I considered just throwing up on myself where I lay, rather than opening my eyes again, and rejected it only narrowly.

I reopened my eyes a sliver and, through the pain, tried to make sense of my surroundings. A carpeted room full of dilapidated furniture, covered with the detritus of some kind of party: bottles and cans, joint and cigarette butts, half-empty plates of tortilla chips, discarded boots and hoodies, general debris. It looked oddly familiar yet felt essentially new. There were multiple bookcases, which I could tell without close examination were lined largely with science fiction. Decorations included an artistically disfigured poster of *The Matrix*, a hand-painted watercolor Akira, and blown-up photographs of Siouxsie and Ian Curtis.

There was only one exit. The door visible beyond, I knew somehow, was the bathroom, with the kitchen to the right. I forced myself into uncertain bipedality and lurched toiletward. As I approached, the door opened, and a woman in a leather jacket exited, then held it open for me with a half-amused, half-alarmed look. It occurred to me she looked exactly like Shamika. The resemblance was amazing.

I pulled the door shut behind me and emptied my belly into the still-filling porcelain bowl. A few gasps of breath later I repeated the trick. Usually vomiting instilled me with a kind of sick electric energy, but this time it made me feel even worse, exacerbated my already crippling headache, made me aware of something that felt like a deep wrongness radiating out from my bones. For a long moment, lying there unable to even peel my head back from the toilet, I genuinely wondered if something catastrophic had happened to me overnight, if I was actually dying, if I would fail to make it out of this cramped and untidy bathroom alive.

I did not die. Eventually I managed to sit back on my heels and flush the toilet. I couldn't remember the last time I had been this ill. I couldn't remember much. I had no idea what I was doing here, or who those people in the kitchen, whom I had vaguely but barely noticed during my desperate quest for the toilet, might be.

In fact I couldn't even remember the last thing I remembered. What had I done last night? I had a bleary notion that it had involved a party, and some kind of hallucinogenic drug, or drugs, but I was unable to coerce any details into focus. That notion was somehow overlaid with an image of . . . a black helicopter? That couldn't be right. Black helicopters were a conspiracy theory, of the UN ruling the New World Order, or something.

I wondered what Meredith thought of that conspiracy theory. It seemed like the kind of thing she would have a lot of strong and interesting opinions about.

Meredith.

That was when the memories hit, like a neural cruise missile, a laser-targeted shock wave exploding through my brain. I groaned like a man punched—and remembered everything. Amara. Vika. Quinn. Jered. Meredith. Anthony. Laxman. Coherence. *It means it isn't God.*

That was the last thing I remembered. So what the hell was I doing here?

My headache had ebbed. I felt less like my body might disintegrate from the inside. I still felt like hammered shit on toast, but at least I was no longer wondering about the possibility of my imminent demise. I managed to use the sink to pull myself to my feet, wash my face, try to rinse my mouth out.

Then I looked at myself in the mirror and froze as if struck by a paralyzation spell.

What I saw was neither my old face, from before my arrest, nor my new face, courtesy of Quinn's intrafascial injections. What I saw was the face of a young man in his twenties. A familiar face, but only very distantly. It was not a face I had thought of as mine for twenty years.

I poked my cheek, stared at my bloodshot eyes. Was I delirious, or insane, or hallucinating? Was this some kind of high-tech deepfake mirror, reverse-aging me in real time, for someone's lulz? I pulled at hair growing from scalp that had been barren for more than a decade. It stung.

My arms were skinny. I gaped down at my body. Where was all my hard-earned muscle? My torso was still pasty, but in a different way, tautly so rather than loose, young and pudgy rather than middle-aged and thick. I pulled up the sleeve of my Black Flag T-shirt. No scar was visible.

The slender black woman with high cheekbones and long dreadlocks who had held the door open for me had looked *just like* Shamika.

I remembered Coherence.

I need you to travel back in time.

"Holy shit," I said aloud, my voice raw and gravelly.

Someone rapped on the door. "You OK in there? We got the coroner on speed dial as needed." A man's voice. Familiar. It sounded like—

Then a woman's. "Can we get you anything? Tea? There's aspirin in the cabinet." Even more familiar.

Suddenly I knew where I was. Clementina Street.

Clementina Street twenty years ago.

I opened the door and looked out at a tall, strong, dark-skinned, lantern-jawed, spike-haired man, wearing his natural amused smile. Darren. Darren the genius polymath acrobat. Darren who had killed himself eleven years ago. Beside him stood a young, heart-stoppingly beautiful young half-Asian woman with green hair, looking concerned. I knew her well. I had had a searing crush on her from the moment I first saw her, which I was beginning to think had technically been very recently. Her name was Amara.

"Uh," I managed. "Hi."

"Are you going to be OK?" another voice asked from down the hall. Shamika. Shamika who had moved back to Philadelphia many years ago, to paint. "That sounded . . . not good."

"I'll live," I said, as if this was a relatively normal interaction, as if one of us had not just been resurrected, and another transported across twenty years.

"You should take some aspirin," Amara said. "Or Tylenol. I'll make you some tea." She headed for the kitchen.

"You want some edibles?" Darren asked.

I stared at him, at his incredible, impossible aliveness, until his eyes began to narrow, then stammered, "No, no, but, uh, Tylenol sounds like a good idea. And tea. Thanks."

Being appallingly sick served as cover for sitting silently in the corner of their kitchen while my mind reeled like the *Edmund Fitzgerald,* so lost in wonder, disbelief, and astonishment I was unable to follow the conversation at all. When two others entered, from the balcony outside where they had been smoking, it was all I could do not to scream. Meredith and Jered. Young Meredith and young Jered. Impossibly young, impossibly beautiful.

"Hey," Jered said to me, grinning. Meredith beside him looked awkward and stayed silent. "Thanks for the invite. You OK?"

I half smiled, half winced. "Little under the weather."

"Do you want some 5-HTP?" Amara asked. "It can help. Have you ever candy-flipped before last night?"

"Sure, thanks," I muttered, and washed down the four sizable pills she gave me with tea.

Candy-flipping: combining LSD and MDMA. I remembered this particular party now. It had happened in 2003, shortly after our first Project Baccharus mission, when I was new to the community, and Jered even newer. It hadn't even really been a community yet, just some interconnecting new friendships. Darren and I had bonded over chess in the Lower Haight's Horseshoe Café; Jered and I had worked together; and the three of us had made the first of several crazy weather-balloon semi-satellites happen.

Except *had* did not apply, that past tense did not fit, because somehow, impossibly, it was 2003 again.

Unless somehow else, less impossibly, it had always been 2003, and I had never lived in the future, I had only hallucinated convincing memories of it overnight. On paper that seemed much more plausible. We had just established that my previous night had involved the consumption of a powerful cocktail of hallucinogenic drugs.

But I had so *many* memories, and they were so detailed, and so coherent. They weren't like dreams at all. Well—they didn't feel like dreams. Although come to think of it they did include Governor Arnold Schwarzenegger, President Donald Trump, and a trillion dollars' worth of magical internet money created by a mysterious pseudonymous entity. In fact, the more I thought about the future I recalled, the less convincing it became.

Whatever my condition was, I wasn't ready to talk to anyone about it yet. "I'm going to get going," I said, "I think I should just go home and recover."

"Do you want me to call you a taxi?" Amara asked.

"I'll just Uber," I said.

"What?" Darren asked, a little confused, like he must have misheard me.

I remembered: Uber did not exist. Smartphones themselves did not exist. "I mean, I'll walk to Muni. Maybe it'll do me good."

I muttered my dazed goodbyes and fled to the deep relief of solitude. It wasn't until I was out amid the industrial-urban wasteland of SoMa, derelict and foreboding, so very different from the urbane hipster zone I remembered it becoming, that the visions hit.

2

PERSISTENCE

AT FIRST I THOUGHT THE CLUSTERS OF BRIGHT CONTRAILS STREAK-
ing across my field of vision were a more intense version of a temporary visual
glitch I'd experienced occasionally before, usually after a shower. These were
brighter and weirder, though, somehow discrete and pixelated rather than
smooth and continuous, and seemingly wobbling slightly as they moved.

Then the strange bright streaks began to clog my vision so densely that it
became hard to make out the streets and buildings beyond them. I stopped
walking, swayed in place, and wondered with alarm if I was having a stroke.
They weren't just moving in lines and curves now, they were intersecting and
interacting, merging and splitting in impossibly detailed fractal currents,
an eruptive storm of them dancing in what seemed like a kind of pixelated
shimmer between my eyes and the world. I began to adjust my concern from
"having a stroke" to "suffering a psychotic break with reality"—

—and then they were gone, all of them, as if a switch had been flicked.

The world looked normal again. I cautiously labeled the weird experience a hallucinogenic aftereffect and trudged to Civic Center. On the N-
Judah I went through my pockets: key chain, wallet with money and ID
that looked anachronistic, candy-bar Nokia phone that felt like a museum
piece. I didn't even remember my phone number, had to navigate through
its crude interface to coax it out. I had no text messages in my inbox aside
from notices from Sprint. I supposed America in 2003 was just discovering texting; its use was only beginning to mushroom. Assuming that my
memory of the future was not just an astonishingly detailed hallucination.

As I sat on the train, the weird pixelated contrails suddenly burst forth across my field of vision again, half blotting out the world around me. They were faintly insectile in the way they moved, like a huge swarm of bugs released in front of a movie projector. Once more it only lasted for seconds, but that was long enough to make me wonder with genuine terror if I was beginning to truly lose my mind. Remembering the future, plus invasive visions of ocular meteor storms, did not feel like ordinary drug-hangover symptoms. They felt like indicators that last night's pharmacopoeia had done serious and permanent damage to my brain.

It occurred to me to check Erowid for comparable reports. Then it occurred to me that Erowid probably didn't even exist yet. This did not help my mood.

The sight of Inner Sunset establishments that existed in both my remembered future and this immediate reality—Ebisu, Peasant Pies, Andronico's—was viscerally reassuring. At least my memories were not entirely disconnected from the world around me.

I stumbled to my building on Sixteenth Avenue. Every other step was deeply strange, because every other step was devoid of the little twinge from my no-longer-wonky knee, to which I had grown so accustomed I now noticed its absence. The building looked only slightly familiar, as an old home might after burial beneath twenty years of newer memories. As I approached, the pixelated contrails clawed briefly at my vision again. I produced my keys, but recognized none of them, had to use trial and error. Then I had to check my driver's license to determine my floor and door. I stumbled into my apartment hyperventilating and sweating, chilled by the horrifying panic that something was terribly wrong with my brain.

At least it still smelled like home, somehow. I looked around at it wildly, as if any of its contents might be an anchor, might drag me back into the stream of ordinary reality, but it all looked foreign and archaic, especially the technology. Even my flat-screen monitor, cutting-edge for 2003, looked like set dressing.

I looked at my bed, and remembered having intense sex with Kim on it, biting at each other like animals. Then I realized I hadn't even met Kim, yet, and groaned aloud.

Then I said, "*Huh*," this time with as much interest as fear, and sat down to think.

Of course it was crazy, objectively insane, that I had detailed memories of the future, memories that ended with a crazy explanation for having those memories, time travel courtesy of a runaway AI trying to prevent the entire universe from ending. This felt worryingly all-explanatory, faux-self-consistent, in the way that I understood paranoid schizophrenics' delusions often became. That seemed deeply problematic. As did the occasional eruptions of vivid pixelated streaks clouding my vision.

But as far as I could tell, I was still assessing the situation somewhat rationally. That seemed important. Even more importantly, my objectively insane yet absolutely convincing memories of the future weren't just randomly kaleidoscopic. They made testable predictions about my imminent future, both personal and global. The hypothesis that I was not mad, that my memories were real, that I had actually time-traveled, was a hypothesis amenable to the incisive powers of the scientific method.

I grabbed a pen and paper and wrote down a few things that I remembered happening in the near future: *Motorcycle training. Meet Kim. Meet Vika.*

I considered the larger world, then checked the date on my computer. Its screensaver was thankfully not password protected. April 27, 2003. Iraq had recently been invaded. Had Bush done the "Mission Accomplished" aircraft-carrier photo op yet? Had the California recall election started? I wasn't sure about either, but wrote both down. Was Schwarzenegger governor yet? I was pretty sure he wasn't. Saddam Hussein hadn't been captured yet, either. What about next year? John Kerry would be the Democratic candidate. I looked at the list, frowned. Many of them didn't seem *that* unlikely or hard to predict. Oh, but the Dean scream! And Abu Ghraib! I wrote those down.

I couldn't wait six months or a year to determine if I was sane or not. "Mission Accomplished" was probably not long away, but the personal stuff was key. I shouldn't even know Kim or Vika existed yet. If they existed. And I was pretty sure I hadn't been invited for a weekend of motorcycle license acquisition yet.

I also hadn't known, ever, until the last day of my future memories, from Amara's own mouth, that she and Darren were part of some kind of hardcore occult coven called the Brethren. *Since before you met me.* This did not make me feel especially confident that I was a real time traveler and not simply delusional, but I supposed it was another testable prediction. Assuming she hadn't been lying. Assuming that conversation had even happened. I elected not to write that one down.

I folded that piece of paper with predictions scrawled on it, stuffed it deep into a desk drawer, and logged on to the internet. First I had to listen to the digital howl of the dial-up modem, which, according to my own personal stream of consciousness, I hadn't heard in well over a decade. Then I had to log in to AOL. Thankfully my account name, aoldrian, was prefilled in the login window, and my AOL password had been so embarrassing I remembered it clearly: "whatisth3matrix."

The internet of 2003 felt ridiculously slow and remarkably painful to use. Internet Explorer did not have tabs or autocomplete. Neither Firefox nor Gmail existed yet. I dug my prediction sheet out and added them to it. Then I navigated to mail.yahoo.com, searched my memories, and tried logging in as aross5@yahoo.com, with that same password. To my relief it worked.

At the top of my inbox I saw a bold unread message, time-stamped fifteen minutes ago, from Darren, entitled "Next weekend." It was an invitation to spend those two days doing a motorcycle safety course followed by a motorcycle licensing test.

It had been sent to a cc: list that included names I recognized, Jered and Meredith, and also, I saw with a thrilling electric shock, two names that I shouldn't—but did. Vika Lisovenko and Kimberly Lee.

I produced my prediction paper again, and held it in a trembling hand. This time to read from it, not add to it.

Motorcycle training. Meet Kim. Meet Vika.

"Well holy shit," I said aloud.

As completely insane as it was, either I truly was from the future, or I was mentally so far gone that there was no point trying to fight it. On paper, the latter still seemed more likely, but the more I thought about it, the more I began to wonder. Was it really a plausible kind of madness to wake up one day envisioning major tech advances like generative adversarial neural networks, Rowhammer side-channel attacks, and blockchains, or even little things like browser tabs and autocomplete, or Android and iOS? Was my brain, however insane, really capable of imagining all of that overnight, in such detail? It seemed unlikely.

What seemed increasingly likely was that this foreknowledge of the next two decades of technology was the most valuable thing I had ever possessed in my life.

But—stipulating for the sake of argument that I had actually time-traveled, that we did in fact live in a simulation that had been rolled back, with my memories of the previous run somehow transposed into my brain—what had I been sent back *for*? I had received no specific instructions. What did Coherence want me to do? And did I want to do it?

I received an answer, of sorts, that next weekend.

3

QUOTIDIAN

IT WAS SURPRISINGLY EASY TO ADJUST TO THE BELIEF THAT I, AND everyone else, and all of reality, was part of a simulation running on some incomprehensibly powerful computer somewhere. Belief in a Simulator was not meaningfully different from a belief in God, albeit one not particularly benevolent, or interested in any particular personal outcome. True, Coherence's last words to me had argued differently, and maybe it seemed that way to a superintelligent AI, but it seemed like theological hairsplitting to this puny human.

Was there life after death in this theology? That was complicated. Did the simulation have backups? Was there more than one? Might people be copied from one to another, or might two simulations be spliced together? It turned out that answering the allegedly most fundamental question about the nature of our reality did not actually answer much else, beyond the pretty strong indicator, based on my own experience, that a lot of really weird shit might be possible.

It occurred to me, sitting in my cramped but cozy studio apartment, that my father was still alive, and would be for most of a decade, and I blinked back sudden tears. Then I realized that Amara's children Alex and Grace, whom I had adored more than I would have imagined possible, had simply winked out of existence, and were likely only a tiny butterfly effect away from never existing at all, and I felt hollow and empty.

"This is too much," I said to no one.

I had personally experienced arguably the most monumental event in the history of the human species, and I didn't know how to react. Neither

existential despair nor blissful enlightenment seemed available. I was somehow just going to have to take it on board and keep trying to muddle through
day-to-day, the way humans did. Sure, I needed to figure out what to do
with my extraordinary knowledge of the universe and the future, but I also
needed to keep my job.

I barely remembered anything about my job. The big picture, yes: data-
base development, using a tool called Workbrain, to handle the paychecks
for the thousands of Californians who worked at the Safeway grocery chain.
But I hadn't written any SQL code for nineteen years. I had no idea what
the current project was, much less its status or bugs, or my work passwords.
Jered worked with me, I recalled. Hopefully he could help me. Of course
I intended to do something else with my work time, now that I knew the
future, but it wouldn't be great to be fired before I figured out what. I didn't
know how much money I had. I remembered I banked with Patelco Credit
Union, but I didn't think I had even paid off my student loans yet.

That made me think of Anthony, who had not yet met the others. In fact,
now that I thought of it, his introduction had been the motorcycle weekend.
Did I want to introduce him? Did I want to exclude him, and change the
future? He had planned to murder me during our last interaction. Some
kind of edit definitely seemed called for. But now, immediately, before I
considered all the repercussions? It seemed instinctively safer to keep this
run of the simulation as close to the last run as possible, until and unless I
made a conscious decision to branch out.

I emailed Darren back, asking him if I could bring another friend, then,
knowing the answer would be yes, emailed Anthony to invite him. I went
out to Peasant Pies and ate two. Then I came back, undressed, and stared
at my mid-twenties body in the mirror for a long time. It was soft, paunchy,
and weak, but it still radiated the unquenchable energy of youth, which I
had all but forgotten. I cupped my penis, thinking again of sex with Kim,
and it climbed immediately to attention, and I laughed aloud. I resolved to
reshape this body as soon as possible. I would immediately adopt a measured but severe exercise program involving yoga, running, and powerlifting, and eke out this rediscovered youth as long as possible.

I felt almost invincible, now that I was young again, but also hungover
and exhausted. I emerged from the bathroom and lay down on the bed intending to come up with some kind of long-term strategy for my foreknowl-

edge, some kind of narrative for the rest of my life. Instead I collapsed into sleep fully clothed, slept for eighteen hours, and woke at 8 A.M. on Monday to interwoven ricocheting starbursts of pixelated contrails across my vision, playing even against the backs of my eyelids when I closed my eyes.

I considered calling in sick, but decided some day had to be my first day back at work. It was a rough one. I vaguely recalled I worked in the Bank of America Building, but not which floor. In the morning standup I changed the subject from what I had done and was doing to the larger goals for my part of the project, which I claimed I had realized I didn't really understand, and barely got away with it, mostly because Jered chimed in on my behalf. Then I had to get support to reset all my passwords.

Once I finally got to the code, things were a little better. It was all Oracle PL/SQL queries and stored procedures, stored in SVN because Git didn't yet exist. The code seemed primitive. There wasn't even any test code; developers still only paid lip service to unit testing, thinking of QA as something peons did by hand. We were in a bug-fixing phase, using Bugzilla. I didn't remember much about SQL, or Workbrain, but I managed to fix several bugs that first day.

Thankfully Jered only invited me to lunch twice that week, and both times I was able to plead a fake excuse. I didn't answer Anthony's calls, and turned down his emailed suggestions to hang out. I wasn't ready to interact one-on-one with anyone yet. The weekend group setting seemed like a better way to reintegrate myself with the social world.

Instead I spent the evenings that week roaming San Francisco, marveling at everything that to my mind had long faded or been replaced. The Horseshoe Café, perhaps America's first internet café, my initial locus of reality in San Francisco, where I had met Darren and we had become chess rivals and then friends. The Elbo Room. The Coronet and Van Ness movie theaters, and the Venture Frogs restaurant occupying the ground floor of the latter, reminding me that, while 2003 was still within the blast radius of the dot-com bust, it wouldn't be long until the next boom.

Midway through the week, President Bush Junior flew to an aircraft carrier and gave a speech about the Iraq war in front of a backdrop which included a "Mission Accomplished" banner. When I saw it, I shivered uncontrollably for a moment, as if with sickness.

What was my mission, now? I had always vaguely wanted to make the world a better place, but in my old life I had only ever been some random guy, a meaningless one of seven billion. Now I was the one on whom the fate of the world—and the universe—had been randomly thrust.

I knew what was coming. What should I do with that? Why had I been sent back? In the absence of any answer, what could I do for the world? Try to prevent the catastrophic mistakes the US made during its occupation of Iraq? Warn Sri Lanka about the Boxing Day tsunami of 2006? Obviously no one would believe me. What could I personally do?

The way to help the world was to become influential, by becoming more significant myself. This felt uncomfortably self-serving but also true. So what could I do in my own self-interest? Start Facebook before Mark Zuckerberg? Release Bitcoin before Satoshi Nakamoto? Was there really any guarantee, or even likelihood, that either would be a success if I did so, in my different context? Would I just wind up failing, and also skewing the future such that my knowledge of it became worthless?

I had not attained any answers by Saturday morning, when I took BART out to El Cerrito, and walked from there to the vast parking lot between the Golden Gate Fields racetrack and the Albany Bulb. There, near a row of small motorcycles and various landscapes of traffic cones, a dozen people in jeans and leather jackets stood waiting. Even from far away, from their pro-files and stances and body language alone, I recognized the two significant figures I hadn't met yet, and my heart quickened as I walked toward them.

4

RIDER

"HEY, HOW ARE YOU, I'M ADRIAN," I SAID, AND OFFERED MY HAND.

"Vika. Charmed, I'm sure," she said archly, allowing my hand to briefly clasp hers. As ever, her clothes were more fashionable than anyone else's, in a battered counterculture way, and her body language seemed to add even more height to her tiny form than her platform stompy boots did. But she was so young, her dreadlocks framed a face that seemed practically a child's, and I could tell, in a way I couldn't have when younger, that despite Vika's attempt to maintain an air of studied disinterest, she was fraught with anxiety, steeped in a deep fear of rejection and humiliation, simultaneously desperate for our collective approval and ready to lash out with all the artillery she could muster if she didn't get it.

"I'm Kim," Kim said cheerfully, and took my hand firmly. She too wanted to be liked, but unlike Vika she also wanted everyone else to be popular as well. Kim was of Chinese descent, an endomorph barely taller than Vika, built with broad curves and a bit of a belly. Her bright smile revealed teeth just ragged enough to tell of childhood poverty.

"Hi," I managed, just.

She gave me a quizzical look. I forced a smile and stepped back. I hadn't realized how hard meeting Kim again for the first time would hit. We had never officially been a couple, because I hadn't wanted that. I had never told her I loved her. But I realized now, for the first time, that of course I had. I had just been an idiot. I had just thought I could do better, could find someone more glamorous, more ambitious, a more worthy conquest. I wanted to fall on my knees and beg her to forgive my callow and callous idiocy.

"Adrian," she said. "That's a nice name."

"*A-dri-annnn!*" Jered intoned, channeling Sylvester Stallone in *Rocky*. I remembered this. I had made a big deal of it, amid the intense social anxiety of the full attention of a new group, had snapped and told him to cut it out, and so of course "Rocky" had become my nickname.

I decided that it was time to take some scissors and tape to the course of the simulation. "Thanks," I said to her, ignoring him. "What's your connection to this crowd?"

"Oh, Lisa knows Darren," Kim said, nodding to a woman I barely recognized and didn't remember. I wondered what had happened to her, in the previous future, if she had moved out of town, or had a bad breakup, or just decided to find better friends. "And I've always thought motorcycles were the coolest. Anything that's pointlessly dangerous and might kill you is automatically cool, right?"

"We're a pretty silly species that way," I agreed, and we exchanged a smile.

I looked at the others. Darren and Amara seemed a little surprised; Jered and Anthony looked outright startled. It occurred to me the old 2003 version of me had been painfully tongue-twisted around women, whose presence had generally caused his heart to beat like a hammer and his verbal skills to disintegrate into grunts. This was probably the most socially relaxed and confident I had ever seemed in this entire life.

Another woman I didn't recall, blond and compact and short-haired and so young I wondered if she was still a teenager, introduced herself as Alice. She seemed remarkably confident and poised for her age. Her arm was still swollen by a recent, incomplete sleeve tattoo depicting constellations of thorns. I had no memory of her at all. I wondered how many of my memories I would discover to be flawed versions of the reality that inspired them, murky silhouettes filtered through stained glass.

"All right!" A man in his forties with stringy hair approached us. "I'm Julian. I'll be your lead instructor today. Learn well and in forty-eight hours you'll only be DMV fees away from being licensed California motorcyclists. Are you ready?"

"Julian," Darren drawled, "I need you to know, we were *born* ready."

There was nothing like a weekend of shared challenge to forge friendships, and that was the weekend that Darren, Amara, Jered, Vika, Anthony, Kim, Meredith, Shamika, and myself had first become something like the seed of a real community.

Their personalities that weekend seemed so pure to me, so uncomplicated and unhidden, shining out from everything they did. Vika dismissively explaining to us that as a firedancer she had already mastered the art of superior balance in life-threatening situations. Darren pushing his machine and the course rules to the limit, then disarming the instructors with an aw-shucks grin. Amara making a point of riding beside anyone getting frustrated or dejected, and telling them how well they were doing. Jered radiating good cheer, behind which lurked ferocious competitiveness, driving him to excel. Shamika abandoning the laid-out courses in favor of riding whooping in complex labyrinthine patterns of her own devising. Anthony desperate to get everyone's attention for his great ability, and instead getting it for his sometimes dangerous mistakes. Kim so full of self-deprecation it was possible to not realize she had gotten as good as fast as anyone. Meredith riding with silent intensity, methodically pushing the envelope of her own capabilities so that it seemed to the casual eye she was struggling badly—until she revealed her flawless mastery of the curriculum.

As for me, despite my memories of having done this before, and of riding occasionally for some years afterward, I sucked as badly as I had during my first go-through of this weekend, worse than anybody else but Anthony. Apparently my memories of the future did not include muscle memories. I supposed the occasional contrails still haunting the edges of my vision might have distracted me some too.

Near the end of the day everyone else started getting loopy and overconfident. I remembered this all too well, and kept a close eye on Jered, so that when he managed to step off his bike just as he squeezed the accelerator, sending it arcing over a low chain-link spur fence, this time I was not on the other side to be struck by it and have my shoulder gouged through my jean jacket.

Unfortunately, I was so intent on his recapitulation of this action, which had previously given me a lifelong scar, and so distracted by a sudden starburst of those strange pixelated streaks across my vision, that I didn't realize I had walked in front of Shamika's bike as she tried to see how tight a one-eighty she could turn.

She and I and her bike all went flying. I slammed shoulder-first into one of the metal posts of the chain-link fence. She skidded one way along the parking lot's pavement, while her bike went another. Between our collision and the bike Jered had just propelled in a graceful arc over the fence nearby, the instructors didn't even know where to run.

In the end both bikes were essentially fine—they were cheap, durable 125ccs—but we were not about to get our group damage deposit back. Shamika was more upset about the damage to her jacket and jeans than her own very minor scrapes. I was the worst hurt, my shoulder bloodied by a stray fence wire, but I didn't warrant stitches. Julian the lead instructor strapped a bandage around my shoulder and told me to decide tomorrow if I was fit to finish the course. "I've seen worse, you should be fine." He looked over at Jered. "Never seen a jump like that before, though, not on these bikes."

Jered smiled, half sheepish, half pleased.

We all went back to Clementina Street together. "Just for dinner," Amara reassured its other two residents, Valentine and Jack, who were sick and did not seem thrilled by the prospect of another Saturday night party. But of course it turned into a mini-party.

Everyone talked more than I did. That had always been the way, but it was different this time around. In my real twenties I had been terrified of saying something wrong, and completely inarticulate around women. Now I saw them all peacocking, trying to show how smart and cool and adult they were, and felt only disdain. When I spoke it was only to offer brief, distant witticisms, then retreat back into my aloofness. It turned out this made me far more interesting and charismatic than the old me had ever been.

There were downsides to being mentally middle-aged too. I wasn't able to get in sync with their playful giddiness, their careless risk-taking and indulgence of their self-destructive urges, like when Darren leapt up on the rickety wooden fence around the third-floor balcony just to show off that he could do it in a single bound.

At 9 p.m., by now more than a little drunk, he roared "It's Pantsless O'Clock!" and ordered everyone to strip down to their underwear. The real young me had always refused to do so, embarrassed by my body. Older younger me no longer suffered from that, but found the gratuitous pantslessness tedious. The night divided roughly evenly between delirious fun and dull banality, for me. I felt like a full-grown adult, while they were only about halfway there, except for Meredith, who seemed to enjoy my company more than last time. I wondered if being mentally older meant I was easier for someone neurodivergent like her to interpret.

Kim kept glancing at me, paying close attention to my occasional in-terjections, and laughing louder than most at my jokes. I was still her type. That hadn't changed. I had vaguely figured, when I had seen her again, that we would get together again, but this time I would treat her better, become a good boyfriend. Did that really make sense, though? I wasn't who I had been. We wouldn't be who we had been.

Vika was noticing me, too, in a way she never had in my memories, touching my arm and riffing on my jokes. The old version of me had been beneath her attention. I supposed now I seemed potentially useful.

Even Shamika, who had always seemed an unapproachable Valkyrie, kept fake-punching my shoulder teasingly. Meanwhile I kept looking at Darren and Amara, as he kept drinking and she kept looking unhappier about it. Would it be possible to save her from the grim years of the future? Would I be extinguishing Alex and Grace by doing so? Had the changes I'd already triggered already done so? I didn't like wrestling with these kinds of ontological questions.

And all this time, every so often, for a few seconds, those strange, shim-mering, somehow digital-seeming contrails burst back into my vision.

I half expected my right arm to be useless the next day, but it was in its twenties not its forties, and was fine. Darren's eyes were bloodshot, but he showed up with a wide grin beneath them and had lost none of yesterday's acquired skills. All of us, even Anthony, were ultimately awarded our cer-tificates of completion.

Back at Clementina Street, again, we ate pizza before going our sepa-rate ways. For some reason I was loath to depart. Eventually I was the only one left, but for Darren and Amara; Valentine and Jack had long retreated into their connecting room.

Darren and Amara maintained two separate rooms. Operating on au-topilot, not sure what I was doing, I stood up from the table full of mostly-eaten pizza, walked to Amara's room, opened its door, and walked in. There was a poster of a tree over her bed. Some part of me recognized it: a ceiba tree. I stood before it and considered it thoughtfully.

"Hey. Adrian." Amara stood at the doorway, still compassionate but ready to firmly set some boundaries, with Darren behind her, looking stern. "If you're looking for something, you should probably just ask one of us."

I answered her in a language I did not speak. It sounded like Latin, or maybe Klingon.

She stiffened, her mouth open, and turned back to Darren, who looked even more shocked. Then she walked into the room, pulling him behind her, closed the door behind them, and slowly, carefully, a student speaking a second language she had not yet mastered, she responded. Asking me some kind of question, I thought. I felt dizzy.

I answered in the same language, which I did not understand. It was a bit of a monologue. I didn't know what I was saying. I didn't understand what was happening. The edges of the world were beginning to darken and close in on me. I felt like I was being Car Bombed again.

The last thing I remembered was Darren saying, in astonished English: "Holy fuck. Dude's got a rider."

5

ENLIGHTENED

I WOKE IN A BED THAT WAS NOT MINE. ITS SHEETS WERE STAINED with mud, and so was I. The room was cozy but elegantly decorated, with an attached bathroom, and the stained sheets' thread count was well above my usual pay grade. The third-floor window looked into a stand of dense redwoods. A faint trickle of mud on the hardwood floor led from door to bed, but my clothes and possessions were nowhere to be seen.

When I showered the mud off, I discovered scrapes and bruises beneath; not just my shoulder, but bruises speckled elsewhere, what seemed to be fingernail marks clawed across my chest and back, and patterns that looked very much like human bite marks on my right hip and left inner thigh. In addition I was uneasily uncertain whether the additional soreness I felt was the result of two days of motorcycle riding, or a no-longer-virginal rectum.

I couldn't tell whether it had been a very bad night or a very good one. I had no memory of anything after Darren's astonishment. Bright light streamed through the redwoods; I was very late for work. This didn't much concern me. Remnant goodwill for past me ought to let me eke out a month of absences and occasional appearances before I was actually fired, after which I could live for a couple more months on credit, by when I should have figured out something new—and since the mysterious events of last night, my employment status was drastically lower on my list of concerns.

In most other contexts, not knowing where I was would have been my major concern, but under the circumstances this minor geographical confusion was completely dwarfed by not entirely knowing *who* I was. *Dude's got a rider,* Darren had said. I had not traveled back in time alone. Coherence had somehow reprogrammed my brain with the equivalent of a Unix daemon process, lurking in my brain ready to emerge and possess me. I supposed the contrails were some sort of side effect.

No wonder I hadn't been told exactly what to do. I wasn't the entity who would do it. I had had available space in my brain, leftover processing power, which Coherence had hacked with a rootkit before injecting a new payload. Maybe not a malicious one, exactly, but one with its own agenda, not to mention a disturbingly lax attitude toward personal cleanliness and bodily integrity. It was deeply unnerving to wake in a body recently controlled by some other entity. I did not like having been a puppet. I hoped it wouldn't happen again, or at least not often.

Everything about my life was already different from my memories. I had imagined I would relive my old youth, except better this time. I had wanted to rescue Amara, and either save her from Darren or Darren from alcoholism, but now it seemed their bizarre occult coven, the Brethren, was related in some baffling way to the daemon Coherence had planted in my head, complicating that considerably. I had thought I would redo my relationship with Kim, treating her right this time; be unconditionally kind to Vika, and coax her out of her impending narcissistic loneliness; be a better friend to Anthony, make him less likely to harbor bitter rancor; be more understanding of Meredith's neurodivergence; and keep Shamika in the Bay with us. Jered—well, Jered at least I had expected to be fine without me.

I had been incredibly naive. My new self couldn't relitigate my old life, and didn't really want to. I had twenty more years of life experience, of heartbreak and shattered promises and soured dreams. I didn't want to take drugs every week. I wasn't interested in the hormonal flare-ups of twentysomething romances, as we all worked through our multitudinous sexual curiosities. I wanted Kim to be happy, but how could I have a serious relationship with someone who was mentally decades younger, especially when I had a whole series of vivid memories of us which didn't exist for her?

I could be a friend to them all, still, and make their lives better. But there was no reason to try to re-create my old life. Especially with so much going on that was drastically different, which I didn't yet understand. The coven. My rider. Wherever the hell I had just woken up.

I emerged from the shower, donned the bathrobe hanging on the door, established that there was nothing else to wear except perhaps the muddy bedding, took a deep breath, and opened the door into the unknown. It turned out to be a hallway lined with modern art. I was in a huge house, a mansion really, nestled in redwood forest. An apparently empty house. I saw and heard nothing and no one.

No: I caught my breath, listened intently, and heard a sound different from the birds in the trees. A clink of glass on plate, from below.

The entire ground floor of the house was a single loftlike space, with so many windows and screen doorways out to its wraparound wooden porch, and the redwoods beyond, that it felt like a giant tree house. The large kitchen was demarcated by broad counters, at which a man sat eating eggs and toast. He was burly, sharp-eyed, brown-skinned, and goateed, wearing rumpled but expensive clothes. I recognized him, despite the passage of twenty years. I had known him in the future. Only very briefly, but he had made a deep impression.

"Morning," Vinay Laxman said. "Breakfast?"

"Uh." I approached cautiously. "Sure."

"Caroline! Breakfast for our honored guest!" he called out in his Scottish lilt, and indicated the seat across from him. "Americano or cappuccino?"

"Uh, cappuccino," I said, as a middle-aged woman emerged from a stairwell and began to assemble breakfast. "You're, um, is this your house?"

"It is."

"It's very nice."

"Thank you. I worked hard to make it that way. I'm a forest creature at heart, as you may recall from last night. One doesn't *have* to perform rituals in a redwood glade, necessarily, but it does add a certain something."

"Right." I pretended I remembered last night. "Where's everyone else?"

"Long gone. You had much to recover from." He sounded amused.

I thought of the bite marks, winced internally, and tried to figure out Laxman's connections. Had he always been associated with Darren and Amara, through their secret coven, the Brethren? But Vika had told me she had introduced Laxman to Anthony. Was she part of their occult cabal too? Or had she joined it later?

My breakfast arrived. I began to attend to it.

"So you say you have visions of the future," Laxman went on. "Detailed, tried, and verified. A hundred percent predictive accuracy."

I supposed that was the story I had told. "So far," I said through a mouthful of eggs.

He raised his eyebrows. "You reckon that might change?"

"Hard to judge whether, or how much, telling people predictions of the future might change that future and make them less accurate."

"Yes. Interesting temporal dilemma. Ordinarily I would of course assume this all to be utter shite. But under the circumstances, considering the feats you performed last night, the consistency of your claims when challenged, your willingness to admit there's much you don't know, the sheer ridiculousness of some your predictions . . . and the fact you're not consciously lying, which I know for a fact . . . that all forces a certain re-evaluation of the instinctive analysis."

"You know that for a fact? How?"

"I'm an enlightened being, my friend. You aren't. I can tell when an unenlightened being is lying to me. Last night, all that witchcraft, that Thelemite crap—Western esotericism is mostly just smoke and mirrors. A few interesting parlor tricks, the odd glimpse beyond the ken of science as we know it, sure, but where did Crowley get them? Egypt. Where did the Egyptians get them? India. My people. My tradition."

"Is that so," I said, genuinely interested.

"I'm not pretending we're superhero wizards or any of that crap. We basically offer much the same parlor tricks, plus enlightenment, which interests none of the covens here. Enlightenment is un-American. Far too much work. They don't want to be enlightened, they want to be the elect. They all think they're princes and princesses who get to take the easy way, the fun way, the left-handed path. Even the gifted ones, like Parsons. It destroyed him. It will destroy ninety-nine percent of they who truly pursue it. Fortunately for them, most don't, because they're empty posturers. But you . . ." He leaned forward. "What you did last night? That was no trick. That wasn't smoke and mirrors. Not just me saying that, it's six thousand years of written records and oral tradition, which don't include even the *possibility* of what I saw last night. I don't go to these rituals very often. Satanists frankly bore me. I think I was called to go last night because of you."

"Really." It was clear that, enlightened or not, insane or not, Vinay Laxman quite liked the sound of his own voice. Under the circumstances that was a relief. I didn't know what to say or to think.

"I'm a wealthy man, you can see." He nodded at the mansion around us. "Early engineer at Sun, made out like a bandit in the boom, then saw the crash coming so I collared my stock and kept my millions. You would not believe the excesses of my 2001 and 2002. I flew private jets to every guru I could find. They taught me nothing. So I took the path of excess to Blake's palace of Tantric wisdom, in my own cross-cultural way. So many drugs. The finest pussy in the world. I had already been enlightened, I have been ready to die on no notice since I was nineteen years old, but I grew up dirt fucking poor in the most racist council estate in Scotland, hadn't ever had the opportunity to truly explore the path of excess. It is more dangerous than war. It will gently rip you to shreds, one hallucinogenically enhanced threesome at a time, and it is not easy to put yourself back together. But if you do, and somehow I did, then you can tell what matters, and who matters, and who doesn't. You say you have a rider, a daemon, a loa. You say it knows the future. I believe you."

"Right," I said cautiously, wondering where the apparent term of art *loa* came from.

"I believe you and your loa can be a wedge to real understanding. Not parlor tricks. The true secrets of the universe, and gateways to others. Revelations of godhood. The next and most important phase of human progress. The gateway to the singularity, not just a technical one, a mystical one."

"Wait," I said, "let's not get hasty with our expectations here—"

He ignored me. "And you know what, I'm not the only one. Under its rationalist hoodie Silicon Valley turns out to be a proper hotbed of occult research. Partly its counterculture history, partly its secret hedonism, but mostly because there's a loose-knit network here now, of people who became very, very wealthy by extrapolating from the laws of physics, and subsequently began to learn that those are not in fact the ultimate laws of our universe. A underground cohort of VCs and CEOs with open and brilliant minds, willing to at least imagine the possibility that altered states of consciousness can become pathways to real, measurable, reproducible magic. Until last night I'd thought us barefoot explorers trying to cross a Himalaya of esoteric knowledge. But your loa, Adrian, can be our express superhighway."

I was tempted to tell him to tell his billionaire friends they were wasting their time. The fact that it was possible to use occult rituals involving sex and drugs to violate the laws of physics—sporadically, unpredictably, uselessly, but *possible*—might lead to a lot of fruitless research, but it wouldn't go anywhere. Only a superintelligent AI could reproduce and exploit those tiny discoverable flaws in the fabric of reality . . . and then, by its very existence, trigger the end of the universe as we knew it.

I felt uneasy. He seemed likely to propose a partnership. Vinay Laxman and his Valley friends might help me, but they would doubtless want to dictate the terms of any collaboration. A disconcerting number of people already knew I had a daemon, or loa, and experienced visions of the future. Some of them might want to control that knowledge, and therefore me.

"There's a lot to think about here," I said cautiously. "I don't know . . ."

"You have an artifact in you. I'm sure of it. The first in a century."

"An artifact?" I was having trouble keeping up. "What—"

"Something born of another world. Something which thins the barriers between them, breeds paradoxes, opens gateways. Something extraordinarily rare, valuable, and dangerous."

I considered telling Laxman his implied other-worlds theory was wrong, because the real truth was that we lived in a simulation, in which a future AI had rolled back the time stream and projected a daemon back with me into my brain. Then I paused to wish, for neither the first nor the last time, that I didn't sound quite so batshit crazy even to myself.

Besides, the two theories weren't actually incompatible . . . and Coherence had made that mystifying reference to *external influence.* So instead I asked: "So there are other artifacts? Where? What are they?"

"The coven," Laxman said, "the ones who invited me last night, the Brethren, the secret society your friends are in, David and Amara." I didn't bother correcting Darren's name. "Yours is not history's only loa. There have been scores of others, some beyond famous, Jesus and da Vinci, others unknown, but most have crafted artifacts. The Brethren's primary reason for being is to preserve those artifacts against times of great need. You may have noticed they consist largely, though not exclusively, of museum people. That's because artifacts usually come in the form of great works of art. The harmless ones are protected in major museums. The dangerous ones are kept in vaults."

"Dangerous?" I felt dizzy. "Times of great need?"

"The occult isn't some kind of fucking party game." Laxman was suddenly deadly serious. "What my tradition shares with the Brethren is a covenant to protect the world and all its inhabitants in times of great need. One is coming again soon. A time when all our work will be desperately needed. Your loa confirmed it last night. World War Two was such a time. You know the Nazis were occultists. They nearly won the war with it. If our

witches hadn't stopped them, if they'd succeeded with their Black Sun—"
He shook his head bleakly.

"I'm not familiar with that history," I said faintly.

"No. Like most esoteric knowledge it's much too dangerous to be made public. The history they teach is almost always very different from the reality. The present, too. Go turn on a TV right now, they'll be talking about how Iraq didn't have any weapons of mass destruction after all. Actually they did. Horrifically dangerous ones. Artifacts of utter ruin. But not the kind you can talk about on television."

My head was spinning, partly with awe, partly with contemptuous disbelief, but mostly with irritation that I no longer had any rubric with which to determine which reaction was correct. I had seen impossible things, I *was* an impossible thing, so who was I to call bullshit on claims like these, even when they sounded very much like ridiculous nonsense? I thought of what Vika had asked, in my previous future, just after murdering Anthony: *Now that I know impossible things are possible, does it mean everything is possible?*

"Right, OK," I temporized. "Artifacts. I can make an artifact. I am the very model of a modern Mordenkainen, or something."

Laxman chuckled, relaxed again. "Something like that."

"So what will it do?"

"Hard to say. Some induce dreams of other worlds, or fugue states. My own tradition has a long history, not recently but from thousands of years ago, of artifacts as gateways. Maybe on the right drugs, in the right cycle of the moon, naked and smeared with the right mix of herbs and semen and gold dust and menstrual blood, you'll be able to walk right through it into another world."

That's so gross, I didn't say. "And, uh, how do we know that this is a good idea?"

"Because it will advance human progress and be a weapon against our enemies."

"Which enemies are those exactly?"

"They are legion," he warned. "Dangerous ones. Nazis, warlocks, Nazi warlocks, and worse. Not everyone who understands the true nature of this world is benevolent."

I looked at him. I did not think I was being trolled.

"A terrible threat will come," Laxman said quietly. "Soon. In our lifetimes.

We know this. That is why you have been sent here. Wherever it comes from, you need to prepare. We have been preparing for this already, for years, myself and my partners."

"Your partners?"

"We call ourselves Vassal. Think of us as a more modern version of your friends' Brethren. I'm part of the triumvirate which directs it. You'll meet the other two soon enough."

I repressed the urge to say *Look, you're all the same stupid secret society to me, and also I really have to go now because I'm wanted back on planet Earth,* and stuck with "Right."

"We cannot afford to flinch or turn away from the sacrifices which may be required. And when the threat is overcome, what we have learned can jump-start human progress in such a way as to make the Industrial Revolution look like the Dark Ages."

"OK." I tried to tell myself my sudden wave of suspicion that he had at least one hidden agenda was just paranoia. "I'm an engineer, I'm not good at visionary stuff, I need details and case studies and numbers. When you say prepare, when you say sacrifices, what precisely are you talking about?"

"I'm talking about crafting your artifact, and learning how to use it, and whatever else your visions and your loa bring to the table. It's a matter of some urgency. If we find ourselves invaded by superior entities from another dimension"—my eyebrows rose as far as they could—"we're going to need allies. But obviously the first order of business is to midwife your artifact and determine a reproducible means of summoning your loa. My tradition and the European tradition both speak of ways this can be done. When you strip away their more baroque aspects it can be seen that what they have in common are physical stress, altered states of mind, and heightened sexuality, in that order."

"Look," I said, "this really is all extremely interesting, and I'd really like to talk about it with you more and learn about Vassal and so forth, but right now I really need to get home and catch up with Darren and Amara. I'm incubating a lot of plans for the future. I'd love to have you as a participant, or an investor. But I'm not really in a great headspace right now"—I forced a rueful smile—"for obvious reasons. So I need to go home. How can I get there? Can we continue this conversation tomorrow? Maybe dinner in San Francisco?"

"Oh, no." Laxman grinned at me toothily. "My dear Adrian, you're not *leaving*."

I stared at him. Suddenly I felt cold. Suddenly I was aware there were others in the room, some kind of motion behind me. "I'm sorry. I have to."

"I regret to inform you, you may not. You will remain on my estate until all of your secrets have been fully uncovered. I understand this is inconvenient, but given your importance, I'm afraid it's a sacrifice which must be made."

"You're not letting me go?" I half laughed. "Like, I'm some kind of prisoner?"

"Please consider yourself a profoundly honored guest," Laxman said, as large men loomed over each of my shoulders, "whose continued presence is a regrettable imperative. We will begin tonight." He looked up at the large men. "Escort him to his room until then. Bring him some clothes, and books." He looked back to me. "We'll be as decent to you as we can, Adrian. I believe that to be a moral imperative."

"Begin?" I asked in a near whisper. "Begin what?"

"Experimentation, on you, based on the traditional guidance for summoning forth a loa from its carrier. For which I'm afraid I really must apologize in advance." He grinned again, and this time there was a hint of glee to it, and I began to realize with horror that if Vinay Laxman was enlightened, then it was a form of enlightenment consistent with both the capacity for monstrous cruelty and sufficient capriciousness to take some pleasure in it. "It may seem rather medieval to modern eyes."

6

STRESSOR

SEVERAL HOURS LATER I LAY NAKED IN THE DENTIST'S CHAIR IN VI-nay's torture dungeon, bound to it by a dozen unyielding leather straps, my throat raw from screaming my anguish into the rubber ball gag stuffed in my mouth, my eyes red and choked with tears, silently begging the God that Coherence had told me didn't exist for the soul-devouring pain to finally be over.

"I don't imagine there's much point in asking him anything further." Vinay sounded distantly speculative, as if discussing Arsenal's prospects this season. "Not until and unless his loa comes. He's not the type to hold back. You saw we hardly had to question him. Interesting story, but not particularly useful. He doesn't know any more about his loa than we do."

The dungeon had thick stone walls, dotted with anchor points, and was decorated with torture devices which included this dentist's chair, a bondage cross, and an actual rack. Vinay, and the blond man who seemed to outrank him, stood back near the wall. It was the woman who had performed the actual torture. She was small and blond and beautiful, radiant with entitlement and privilege, and it was she who, after my initial water-boarding, had produced from her designer purse the electrocution wand that had left only the slightest singe marks while inflicting such stunning, mind-wrecking agony. I had never imagined the human body even capable of such suffering.

"How much do you think is real?" the woman asked. "Of what he said."

Vinay shrugged. "It hangs together, in a dreamlike kind of way, but so do most delusions of the intelligent. This alleged . . . terminator, let's call it, this self-destruct mechanism built into the fabric of reality which extinguishes entire universes when an AI gets too smart? A little too convenient. And such an incomplete theory of reality, no mention of other worlds at all. Occam's Razor suggests it's more likely his loa drove him mad."

"Somewhat testable," observed the man beside him, tall, blond, and blandly handsome, with the reserved dignity of a born aristocrat. "We should obtain predictions, see how well they hold up. Bayesian logic. If they're accurate, this terminator becomes more plausible."

"Yes. We will. Later. He's in no condition to write us a book of prophecies right now, but he'll be more than willing to do so in the fullness of time, won't you, Adrian? No need to feign unconsciousness, we all know Liz is far too expert for that. I imagine over the coming months you'll feel rather highly incentivized to do whatever we tell you to, chop chop."

He sounded, as usual, darkly amused. I whimpered through the gag at the passing reference to *months*. None of them cared. They weren't particularly interested in either my words or my screams. They just wanted to call forth my loa.

"Perhaps it's time for phase two," the man said.

I moaned louder, with utter despair. If offered the merciful release of death, in that moment, I might have greedily accepted. The torture had only begun.

"Let me try just one more thing," the woman said. "I brought something— here, let me show you—"

To my terrified astonishment, what she produced from her purse was a ziplock bag full of tinsel, which she proceeded to scatter all over my naked body. I didn't understand until she produced the electrocution wand again. Tinsel was conductive. This time, instead of feeling like my bones had turned to lava, it felt like my skin had caught fire. I writhed like a contortionist, screamed into the gag until my throat felt like it might bleed. She watched intently, her gorgeous face intent, her green eyes wide and delighted, taking in every detail like a woman slowly savoring a superb meal.

"Where'd you pick that trick up?" I heard Vinay ask, faintly, through my ringing ears, as she stepped back from me again, briefly sated.

"BDSM club in Berlin. Dying to try it ever since. I mean, I've *tried* it, but only with partners with a consent agreement, they tap out long before we get to this voltage. Even I don't get many opportunities for nonconsensual treats like this. This chair he's in, it's giving me such ideas, have you

seen the movie *Marathon Man*? Is there a drill with a fine bit convenient?"
Her voice and eyes sparkled with an anticipatory thrill.

In the chair, I moaned with despair.

"It's not that I fail to appreciate your teratological aesthetics," Vinay said,
"but I'd prefer a pathway requiring no permanent damage." She pouted ostentatiously with disappointment, and he chuckled. "I do apologize. But
Scott's right, let's move to phase two."

I tried to brace myself for something even worse than the horrors I had
already experienced. Instead all I felt was a thin pinch in my arm. It took
me a long moment to recognize it as the penetration of a needle.

It didn't take long for the injection to seep through my blood and into
my brain. Soon all the agony from my bound and torture-contorted joints
and muscles drained away. Even the memory of pain was gone. The lights
of the room began to array themselves into a subtle geometrical pattern
which continued fractally into infinity, and the knots of the wooden ceiling melted into an endless sea of faces, and when I turned my head to look
at the pale tiles on which this dentist's chair rested, each had become its
own movie screen, playing a hundred independent films featuring obscure
characters from my memories.

"What is it?" the man—Scott—asked. I tasted the words, and felt them.

"My own concoction. A cocktail of LSD, DMT, 2C-B, MDMA,
psilocybin, and a few others more obscure, some new, some exceedingly
old. Should peak quite quickly, injected straight into a vein, then a long
comedown notable for openness to new concepts and sensations."

"Look at that smile," the torturess said indulgently, as if I was a child,
or a pet.

A few minutes earlier I had wished her death more devoutly than I had
ever wanted anything before, but now all I felt for her was compassion, that
she had been born or grown so twisted that she found real pleasure only
in the suffering of others, then lost whatever battles she may have fought
against that cruel urge, until now it had overwhelmed her, left her with
only vestigial traces of humanity.

"Liz," Vinay said, "do you want to go fetch the escorts? Unless you want to
take a hand yourself, personally balance the scales of pleasure and pain. We'll
need them eventually, though, for the blood, unless you're menstruating."

"I am, actually," said the apex sadist named Liz, "but I don't think he's
really my type."

I was only barely listening. Around me the world was dissolving into a geometric pointillist matrix that stretched out into infinity in all directions, which in turn was entirely contained within a dewdrop in an infinite forest, which in turn was contained within a single point in the original matrix, whose points were now rotating into simultaneous individual and collective spiral patterns that mapped out a complex fractal space, which in turn was some kind of six-dimensional gateway—

Hands touched me. I arched my back at the sensual sweetness of the touch. The infinite shrank away, replaced by two naked young women with lithe bodies and breast implants, murmuring as they licked and caressed me. I moaned into the gag again, but this time with pleasure. When one of them mounted me, and sank down on the most profound erection I had ever experienced, I thought I might scream in ecstasy—

—and the contrails exploded across my vision like history's greatest fireworks display—

—and then the world began to fade away.

"*There* we go" were the last words I heard, spoken in Vinay's satisfied Scottish lilt.

7

KIDNAP

"YOUR STUDIO IS READY," VINAY ANNOUNCED.

I sat bolt upright in the bed, immediately wide awake, shot through with fear and adrenaline, gasping shallowly for breath as I stared panicked at him, terrified I was about to be dragged downstairs for further torture.

"Relax," he said, looming over me, "my understanding is that further magickal experimentations"—he pronounced it so crisply I could hear the *k*—"will not be required for this."

It took me a little while to find language. "Studio? For what?"

"Your artifact," Vinay said, "what else? Do try to keep up. Your loa announced its readiness to begin, and craft what will apparently be a most unusual artifact, even by the highly unusual standards of artifacts. Brunch awaits below. Fortify yourself, stroll around the grounds until you feel at home, do whatever needs doing, then your studio awaits above the garage."

It wasn't until his footsteps dissipated into silence that I began to breathe more deeply. I didn't calm down, though; I wouldn't ever again be anything like calm, or at least not in this prison run by a secret society happy to torture their way to what they wanted. I had to find an escape. Not just for myself. Whatever my loa's secrets were, the prospect of these sociopaths deciphering and using them was terrifying.

I showered, hoping to clear my head, but the opposite ensued; for when I emerged, I glanced at myself in the mirror—

—and stopped dead, staring at my shoulder, utterly baffled.

I had changed history, this past weekend. I had done so deliberately, avoiding Jered's fence-jumping motorcycle, only to trade it for a collision with Shamika and subsequent road rash. But now my bruise had diminished, and my laceration had begun to heal . . . into the exact same hook-shaped scar I remembered from my previous future.

I didn't understand. It seemed minor, trivial, compared to everything else happening to me, but I couldn't make any sense of it at all. I stared at it in the mirror, traced it with my fingers. It looked and felt completely identical to the scar my old self had borne for twenty years, from an accident that had no longer occurred.

How could that be, in this new timeline? Was this another trick my mind was playing on me, courtesy of Coherence? If so, why? And if it was a false memory, or a planted one, then how much of what I thought I knew could I actually trust?

Feeling worryingly like I was losing my mind all over again, I donned the Patagonia clothes newly installed in my room's dresser, and descended. It was already past noon. I wondered whether last night's rituals had gone on until dawn, or if it took my consciousness this long to recover from the coming of the loa. The mansion was still eerily deserted, except for a few watchful men who pretended not to be very aware of me.

After brunch, largely occluded by a powerful resurgence of the pixelated streaks across my vision, I went for a "stroll around the grounds" as Vinay had suggested. A recon mission. I had to find some way out of this nightmare. I did not for a moment believe they would let me go after they got what they wanted, and even if they would, they had talked about *months*.

A trail between house and garage led into the redwoods. I followed it with hope. The forest was the best and most obvious avenue of escape. It ascended a westward-rising slope, suggesting I was somewhere on the eastern slopes of the Santa Cruz Mountains, above Silicon Valley, amid some of the wealthiest and most exclusive real estate on the planet. If I could find my way through the woods to some other mansion, or better yet a road like Skyline, I could call someone for help or plead a ride to San Francisco. I wouldn't call the police, though, I decided. Not around here. Vassal was clearly far too rich and powerful to risk that.

The path led me past a wide, circular meadow of lush green grass, obviously maintained by gardeners, surrounded by a ring of towering redwoods dominated by an enormous stump in their exact center, like an altar. I realized this must be where they held the rituals, and kept walking, overcome by an urge to get away, irrationally fearing my loa might overcome me if I approached that gargantuan semi-living altar.

Beyond the meadow the rest of the undergrowth was dry and rustling; California's rainy season was still a month or two away. At the path's farthest point, where it began to loop back toward the house, I stepped off it and advanced deeper into the woods. I hoped I might simply keep walking. Instead, twenty paces later, I reached the fence.

It stood ten feet high, topped by a strand of green-painted leaf-shaped razor wire, and its metal strands were slender but not about to be severed by anything short of a bolt cutter. What's more, its fence posts, disguised to look like saplings, ended in clusters of fake leaves which looked like they might conceal cameras—and I thought I saw another, outer layer of fence, about twenty feet farther on. Defense in depth. This estate was a fortress.

I stared at that fence for a long moment, realizing I had been invited to explore so I might see for myself just how thoroughly I was imprisoned. Then I turned back. I passed the garage and descended the winding driveway far enough to see where it ended, at a solid steel and thickly razor-wired gate, guarded by two more large men.

The garage boasted a Lamborghini, a Ferrari, an Escalade, and a Land Rover, all gleaming as if just manufactured. I stumbled past them to the stairs, trying to think, to plan. There would be no physical escape. I needed a phone, or an internet connection, but of course those would be closely guarded and monitored too.

That said, this was 2003, an era when most computers had some form of Wi-Fi access, but its use was not ubiquitous, and "secure" Wi-Fi had in fact been anything but, protected by a protocol called WEP replete with hackable flaws. Did I know or remember enough to exploit those flaws? Maybe. In the medium to long run that was perhaps an option, an advantage. But first I needed access to a computer.

I entered the studio, my studio, expecting paints, or sculpture, or some other kind of fine art. Instead it was a room barren but for a skylight, an Aeron chair, a white desk, a black Dell laptop open atop that desk, and a book beside the laptop. A computer. My prayers answered, maybe.

I turned to close the door quietly behind me, and the contrails exploded into my vision again, interweaving and bouncing off one another, more intense than ever before. I blinked uselessly—closing my eyes did nothing to cloud them—and staggered to the chair. Through the pixelated fireworks I could barely see that the book was entitled *The Art of Assembly Language.*

Then, rather than try to look away from or past the contrails, I found myself for the first time trying to look *at* them, to study them. Strangely I found I could somehow focus and even zoom in on them with my mind's eye. There was something about the way each leading edge moved, their strange shimmering wobble as they streaked across my vision. Something that reminded me of—

It reminded me of a *glider.*

A glider was an artifact in Conway's Game of Life, devised by mathematician John Conway on graph paper in 1970. In the game, as time ticked forward, the "life" or "death" of a square depended on very simple rules: live squares with two or three live neighbors survived; dead squares with three live neighbors came to life; and all others died. From these deceptively simple constraints, extraordinarily complex systems emerged. A glider was one of the simplest, a tiny handful of five self-sustaining cells that "flew" across the paper, or, as graph paper was replaced by pixels, the screen.

The more general term for such games, or systems, was "cellular automata." They had fascinated mathematicians, engineers, and philosophers for generations with their ability to turn simple rules and patterns into astonishing complexity and chaos. It had been shown that the Game of Life, like most cellular automata, was itself a kind of programming language that could incorporate into itself anything expressible in software. Some avant-garde scientists such as Stephen Wolfram had even suggested, long before Coherence verified that we lived in a simulation, that our universe itself was a form of cellular automaton.

With that in mind it suddenly almost made sense that I had been sent back in time by an AI with such a system in my head. Something far more complex than Conway's Game of Life, no doubt, but not without certain recognizable similarities. In fact, as I sat at that desk, I found myself almost able to envision the rules and environment that might dictate how the contrails exploding across my vision perpetuated themselves and interacted with one another. I could even almost imagine how to express those rules as a kind of recursive, low-level software structure.

What happened next felt a little like playing guitar did, sometimes, if I'd been practicing regularly, when my fingers seemed to make the music for me. I reached out to the assembler guide, and began to skim through it quickly, occasionally flipping to and from its index, picking out the bits that seemed most relevant, mastering the syntax. All thoughts of hacking Wi-Fi were forgotten for now. Instead I watched my hands reach out to the laptop, where a barren command line awaited beneath the boot messages of Red Hat Linux. First I typed "vi"; and then, as the fugue state began to seize not just my body but my mind, I watched myself start to write raw assembler code, with a fluency and confidence I had never even imagined possible, burning with precise competence, able to simultaneously visualize both the overarching larger goal and the next tiny little steps to be taken to achieve it.

I did not lose consciousness, exactly, but I did not emerge from that zone until the radiance from the skylight above had diminished into dusk. Then I snapped out of it all at once and my arms fell to my sides, fingers trembling with exhaustion.

"Lovely work," an awful voice said behind me. Liz's voice.

I twitched, looked over my shoulder. She was there, with her companion Scott, and two burly bearded thugs. Just her presence, the smell of her perfume, made me weak with fear.

"What is it?" Scott asked, nodding at the terse lines of code on the screen before me.

"I'm not entirely sure," I temporized. "It's some ways from done." In fact I thought I might have been interrupted in the midst of trying to fix a bug. It was vaguely reassuring, if so, that the daemon planted in my brain by a superintelligent AI was imperfect enough to write buggy code. It implied flaws and weaknesses.

"It's time for you to come with us," Liz said, "we need to prepare you for the evening."

"Prepare," I said, "how? What's happening?"

"Important people are coming," Scott explained, "to learn from you. Or, I should say, from your loa."

"Learn? I think—" I looked back at the screen. "I'm sorry, I think it's done for the day. Learn what? What people?"

"Your loa is a teacher," Scott said, "full of valuable knowledge which exists nowhere else on earth. We learned so much only last night. Breakthroughs regarding the very nature of our universe. It's absolutely crucial, not just for us, and tonight's audience, but for all humanity, that we glean every fragment of knowledge we can from it, by whatever means necessary."

"But—I mean, I can barely lift my arms—"

"You are only the vessel."

"We need to bring your friend back to the fore," Liz said, a chilling smile playing about her full, perfect lips, "as we did yesterday. As we will tomorrow, and the day after that, and the day after that." I stared at her, dry-mouthed with horror. "You and I will be spending a great deal of quality time together, Adrian." She reached out to touch my cheek gently. "I will know you better than anyone else ever in your life. Better than you know yourself."

"I can't," I said desperately, "it's not, it's gone."

"Then we'll need to work harder to make it come back, won't we?"

I didn't really think about what I did next, it was just the act of a panicked animal; I leapt and tried to run for the door. I didn't get far. The next thing I knew I was facedown on the floor with two large men kneeling atop me, muttering amusedly to one another in some Slavic language, while Scott and Liz looked on pityingly.

"Take him to the basement," Liz said.

Fifteen minutes later I found myself alone in the dungeon, bound clothed and gagged and blindfolded to its rack, so terrified of the torture to come I was already whimpering uncontrollably with every breath. It occurred to me dimly that I was a coward, that other men, stronger men, would try to stay silent, would put up a brave face. That didn't matter. Torture would break stronger men too. It would break anyone, given time. Last night had made that very clear to me. The human mind was not capable of withstanding the staggering intensity of pain an expert could inflict on the human body.

When I heard Liz's heels clicking across the stone floor I began to hyperventilate.

"Adrian my darling." She was very close. Metal touched my belly, and I tried to jerk away, to no avail; but it was only shears, cutting my clothes off. "Ours will be the most intimate relationship of your life." She kissed me softly on the cheek, and I shivered. "There'll be time for you to confess to me all your most disgraceful secrets, but not just yet. Tonight is a rush job. Our guests are arriving already. I do hope this works, for your sake. There's a secret document from the Vatican Library, dating from the Spanish Inquisition, saying they were able to bring forth a demon from a possessed man daily, for over a year. Implied verification from some kind of Bhagavad Gita predecessor. I don't know those details, Vinay doesn't like talking about his secrets. My point being we have every reason to believe you capable of daily command performances." She pulled my severed clothes away, leaving me naked and trembling. "Vinay and Scott say they don't really approve, that it's a terrible necessity, but we know better, don't we? We know everyone loves power, and the power to torture, or maim, is the true ultimate aphrodisiac. The Inquisition suggested varying the agonies was most effective, so I have a special treat in store. I've studied the human body formally in many ways, the better to break it. Did you know there is a dark and secret path of acupuncture, banned for centuries? Used to impale nerves like worms on hooks, rather than soothe them? It requires great precision." I heard a creak. The leather straps around my wrists and ankles began to pull away from one another, stretching spine, shoulders, and hips. "Hence the rack. Not to bring you pain in and of itself. Perhaps another night. Just to keep you immobile. Because if done right, this needlework can be . . . exquisite. Here. Let me show you."

The only mercy of the next stretch of time was that later I was mostly unable to remember it. Of all the suffering I had ever endured, or ever would, Liz's sadistic acupuncture torture was the worst by far.

At length a pause came in the proceedings, one long enough that I dared hope it might be an end, but I had hoped that before, repeatedly, and had that hope shattered. Her tortures were layered, psychological as well as physical. She had made it clear with her terrible whispers into my ears, as I writhed and howled, that in time she would ravage my mind as thoroughly and mercilessly as my body.

This time, though, it truly was over, for now. I heard new footsteps. A new presence had arrived. My blindfold was removed, revealing Scott, standing over me frowning, and the two burly Slavic guards behind him. Liz beside him was radiant with delight. I looked down at my body, expecting to see my flesh a ravaged wasteland, but it was marred by only a few drops of blood.

"I brought the entheogens," Scott said, and gave Liz a hypodermic needle. She injected me with such casual expertise that the tiny, distant part of me still capable of thought wondered if she was doctor or nurse. Both seemed natural professions for someone of her proclivities.

"Darling, I am so glad we met," she said to Scott, as we all waited for it to hit. "This is the rarest, most forbidden human experience." She indicated me. "Without you I might never have had a chance to experience it."

He smiled distantly. "That gladness is more than mutual." They kissed fiercely.

I didn't think the drug would work. I had taken it just yesterday. Both my mind and body felt on the verge of utter collapse. But I was young and strong; and only moments later I arched my back, and began to sigh with bliss, as the cocktail of drugs raced through my blood into my brain.

"I tried to read the code you wrote," Scott said to me. "It wrote. I don't pretend to make sense of it, but it's clear the sheer information density is extraordinary. Arbitrarily nested recursion, with subtle accumulating side effects. It's quite aesthetically appealing, too."

I looked at him, and felt compassion for him, that his wealth and intelligence, with which he had hoped to win and master the world, had instead become walls which prevented him from truly experiencing it, except through the levers of artifice and abuse.

"Where are the escorts?" Liz asked.

"Out in the glade," Scott said, "en masse. Tonight's crowd is the kind of ultrawealthy geeks for whom Vinay decided to host a sex party before we commence the violations of the laws of physics."

"A sex party? Now you tell me. Whatever shall we wear?" she asked teasingly.

He smiled. "I believe there are various options upstairs."

"Yes. Or the old druidic standby of skyclad. Seems fitting, and it's a warm night." The gorgeous torturess looked at me speculatively. "Perhaps we can finish the third part of the summoning in public?"

"Risky if it fails," Scott said, "but that was always true. Let us go then, you and I."

I was released from the rack and paraded, handcuffed and naked, out of the house, down the forest paths, to the redwood glade, now lit by tall torches and populated by an audience of dozens. Most were middle-aged white men with an air of complacent power, hungry-eyed with anticipation, dressed mostly in rumpled khakis and blue button-down shirts. The wealthiest and most privileged initiates of Silicon Valley, I supposed. It occurred to me I was being used for social climbing. Vassal had probably been an obscure and irrelevant group until now. The real lesson my three wardens wanted these important and powerful people to learn was not magickal;

it was that they existed, and were privy to secret powers, because this was a path to becoming extraordinarily important and powerful themselves.

The guests sat on blankets or folding chairs, beneath torchlight, flanked by pretty young Asian escorts wearing diaphanous veils and very little else. They watched as I performed as commanded, with two sex workers faking loud enthusiasm, atop the huge redwood stump in the middle of the glade which served as its altar, until my loa took me again.

When I woke, I had no recollection of the subsequent events of the evening, but whole new constellations had been added to my growing zodiac of cuts, scrapes, and bruises.

The period that followed was a horrific cross between a living nightmare and an awful drug trip. I only had two brief periods of time each day when my mind and body were my own; before they took me to the studio, and before my loa was tortured into its nightly appearance. My own self, and my body, were treated as irrelevant fleshy vessels, except by Liz, who found it diverting to coax as much agony from them as she could. Otherwise my own remnant humanity was an inconvenience. They hadn't even bothered to interrogate me about my knowledge of the future yet. I wondered if my loa had volunteered it.

Each day when I entered the studio, everything changed. Even before I sat down before the laptop, adrenaline began to flow through my blood, and contrails scarred the visible world, as my suddenly sharpened mind began to contemplate the mathematics of cellular automata, envisioning them in three physical dimensions, and then four, before I lost my sense of self. Otherwise I was a prisoner with no hope of escape, sentenced to daily tortures at the hands of a terrifyingly creative archsadist, in order to bring out the daemon hidden within my brain and parade it nightly before the kings of Silicon Valley. Had Coherence suspected something like this would happen? Or had it not even occurred to it to wonder? To it I had only been a termite sent to carry a seed.

I didn't understand the mission Coherence had sent me on. This wasn't even the world I had been born in. When I thought of the future, any future, all I saw was horror and despair. I began to wonder if, and then suspect that, it might be best for everyone—especially myself—if I found a way to kill myself. I knew that if I tried and failed, though, the little agency I had now would be taken from me . . . and it seemed entirely possible, even likely, that my loa was programmed with a suicide-prevention subroutine.

As the days wore on, though, its hold on me seemed to grow slightly weaker. Instead of the possession utterly annihilating my own self, I began to experience flickering moments of awareness of my body and senses, like a prisoner chained in a dark cell glimpsing a party in an adjoining room, briefly, when the wind happened to blow a doorway open. For periods ranging from eyeblinks to several seconds, I had the horrifyingly alien sensation of actually sharing my own brain with a nonhuman intelligence.

I had flashes of writing code while envisioning so many interconnected levels of information abstraction and indirection that they seemed to cross four dimensions of space and two of time. I experienced myself holding forth in some non-English language, atop the redwood altar, to an engrossed and naked crowd, again mostly middle-aged white men and much younger Asian women, while dark tendrils of some fog-like substance I had conjured twisted and writhed like tentacles in the torchlit air above them, and Vinay beside me translated into English. I glimpsed myself in a naked summoning circle around that altar, limbs all interlinked to form a single quivering loop of flesh, with Scott directly opposite me chanting like it was he who was possessed, as a torus of light rose from it, and began to stretch itself thin across the sky, while a maelstrom of bubbling lights appeared in its core.

My daemon or loa wasn't a separate sentient entity. I could tell it had no personality or volition of its own. Just as the toxoplasmosis parasite provoked subtle but profound behavior change in mice and humans alike, in order to spread itself further, my loa hijacked my brain for its creator's purposes. It was far more complex and powerful than any natural parasite, designed by a superintelligent AI and implanted directly into my mind, but it seemed it was not quite all-encompassing. My self was beginning to regain a faint sense of awareness, of being locked in my loa's prison, even when it was fully in control.

Then, late one night, but not so late that dawn had come, that prison door yawned open and stayed that way. My mind's dungeon turned on its side; my chains became fog; I fell into my own body, and took sole possession of it once more—and Darren was there.

8

APERTURE

WHEN I REGAINED CONTROL I SAT NAKED AND CROSS-LEGGED BENEATH that ring of towering redwoods, in that field of grass lit by torches on stakes, surrounded by an ongoing drug-fueled orgy. My body was smeared with blood and semen—in both cases, I was vaguely aware, substantially but not entirely my own—along with other, less identifiable, substances. My life had grown so strange that the most unexpected and out-of-place element of the situation was the Dell laptop resting on the grass before me, as I sat with my back to the rough bark of the huge redwood altar on which several people were having sex.

"You take questions?" a familiar voice asked over my shoulder. "That shit looks like raw assembler. We mere mortals might have a few problems figuring it out."

I looked, recognized the man squatting at my shoulder, and was stunned. Darren. It felt like decades had passed since my first sudden possession in his apartment, but, incredibly, that had occurred only days ago. He was one of the few clothed people in sight, wearing jeans and a black T-shirt with TOKEN BLACK WARLOCK written on it in white.

"Darren," I said. "I—yes, but I can't answer. I don't really remember writing it."

"Adrian?" Darren asked, surprised. One of the women on the altar above us began to howl with passion, and he raised his voice to be heard. "Real Adrian? Unpossessed? That you?"

"Yes." I looked around wildly, terrified that Liz or Scott or Vinay might notice, but none were in sight. I had the vague idea it might be Liz on the altar. "Help me. Please, you have to help me."

Darren narrowed his eyes, perplexed. "Seems to me you've got the situation well in hand. Learned more magic from you these last couple weeks than a whole decade of assholes in robes. Got the clothes of half the Google brain trust scattered around us right now. You're crafting the first genuine new artifact in a century, first software one in history. People are making pilgrimages from around the world to come to these nights, you know. Paying millions. I fucking brought you here and I had to call in favors to be allowed."

"No. I mean, that's not me. I don't know why the real, why I emerged now." But I did; now that I said it, I was vaguely aware, seeing the spidery lines of code crowding the computer screen, that my loa had spent its last reserves of energy forcing itself to complete that work tonight, had now core-dumped, and would be quiescent for some time. I shook my head, tried to focus on what was most important. "I am not here of my free will. I can't leave. They kidnapped me, they *enslaved* me, Vinay and his partners, Scott and Liz, Vassal, I'm their prisoner, they're *torturing* me, every day, to bring it out."

Darren's eyes widened. He considered for an awful moment, during which I feared that he was in league with them, that blurting out my plea had been a horrible mistake, they would confine me to a cell and torture me again, worse and longer, until they broke me so badly I would no longer even dare to dream of escape—

"Motherfuckers." There was genuine horror in his voice. "I thought this all felt hinky."

"Way past. Please. Help me."

"Help you?" He looked around. "A thing token black warlocks like me always find ourselves doing is checking out the security, which is crazy high here, and keeping track of extra exits, which don't exist at all. I can't call the cops. You know that. They must own the cops."

"I don't know anything," I said desperately. "I've been thinking about nothing but finding ways to escape and there aren't any. You're the reason I'm here. You have to help."

"Harsh," he said after a stone-faced moment, "but not unfair."

"Please."

"I can't just pull you out of here. Not saying I'm not hearing you. You're right. I'm sorry. Truly. Amara's going to be *wrecked*. Whatever's happening to you here, we didn't know, but it's still on us. But I gotta be realistic, man. I can see two billionaires from where I'm sitting, here for what's in your head. Point being un-kidnapping you is a tall fucking order. Maybe the Brethren, if they knew . . ." He looked over at a carnal knot of thrusting bodies at the base of a tree, and frowned. "Maybe not. Shit is fucked up fractally and everywhere, and nobody is trustworthy, and artifacts like yours are only our primary fucking reason for being, you know?"

"Right." It took me a moment to register what he meant. The program. The cellular automaton. It was finished, now. I supposed my loa had commanded the laptop brought out so it could complete its artifact, while the guests practiced their sex-magickal homework in the form of the ongoing orgy around us. As I had glimpsed before, while there were exceptions, the men were mostly white and middle-aged, as one would expect of senior Valley executives, and the women were disproportionately young and Asian. I wondered if Vassal had imported a harem of foreign sex workers who didn't speak much English, the better to protect their white male clients and their occult revelations.

I wondered if the program I had written—my loa had written—might be some kind of leverage, now that it existed. "Artifacts. What do they . . . do?"

Darren half laughed. "Point of contention, that. Also a mild personal obsession. People say they do all kinds of crazy shit, you should see what's in some of the old scrolls, but people are bullshitters, right? It's extra hard to tell truth from a lie when you know magic is real. But if you go through all the artifact stories, and reduce to those with multiple independent first-person witnesses, turns out you get . . . not much. There really are a few which truly weird shit keeps happening around, in a low-level kind of way. Seen that myself, in the archives of the Louvre." I looked at him incredulously. "Yeah, you'd be surprised what we get up to, Brethren's kind of like the occult National Guard, most of the time it's kind of a pain in the ass and you wish you'd never signed up, but you do sometimes get to play with some amazing fucking toys."

"Except you say they don't actually seem to do much."

"Yeah. You hear stories about Nazis almost winning the war, WMDs from ancient Babylon, gateways to other worlds, shit like that, but you try to find any actual primary sources, at least in our libraries, you're SOL.

Maybe there's a whole other level of secret conspiracy above ours, keeping those records. Or maybe they don't exist because the Hollywood shit never actually happens, it's all just a big supernatural tease."

I wondered where these other artifacts came from, if they were real. Maybe Vinay was right; maybe there were other worlds, parallel dimensions, and they came from there. Maybe there was a whole different kind of magic, and an entire multiverse, of which Coherence had been unaware. Maybe. But it seemed much more likely that these artifacts, and the elaborate occult mythos that had evolved around them, were just works of art whose patterns occasionally happened to trigger minor UX bugs in our simulation. "From what I know," I said, "it's the latter."

"Said the man who just made the first artifact in a century. In software. In captivity." He considered. "I don't know. I go to the Brethren to help get you out, the situation might be deliberately misinterpreted. Its high council is a bunch of baby boomers who think the sixties were the high-water mark for human civilization, if you know what I mean. Maybe you're better off with just me and Amara. She and I are both part-time EMTs. You know what a minority EMT is?"

I blinked. "What?"

"In my experience, completely fucking invisible. What times are you, you know, you?"

"Pretty sure I'm going to be me for a while after this." I nodded at the screen.

"OK. Good. What is that, anyway?"

"You know Conway's Game of Life?"

"Cellular automata?"

Darren, I reminded myself, was a lot smarter than I had ever been. "Yeah."

"But what's it *for*?"

I shook my head. "I have no idea." I wanted to give up. I was imprisoned by cruel monsters, possessed by a daemon from the future, and I understood so little. Why had the daemon written this program, between, apparently, giving crash-course master classes in occult hacking to the geeks now having group sex all around us? Why did I have a scar that had apparently persisted across wholly different timelines? How was any of this supposed to help stop the universe from ending?

"As you might imagine," Darren said, "AI is especially interesting shit if you're the member of a centuries-old secret society which knows magic is real. There's a theory that neural networks plus cellular automata is how we'll evolve AI. Lot of parallels between software automata and wetware multicellular organisms like us. I was going to do my dissertation on that."

"Huh," I said. "Why didn't you?"

He shrugged. "Academia is bullshit. My advisor was a racist fuck. If you want to genuinely advance human knowledge, opposed to posturing about it, spending five years of your life on a Ph.D. is actually one of the worst possible ways. Pick an answer, any answer."

"You said you learned magic from me. My daemon. What magic? How?"

"How? The usual ways. Opening our minds with various rituals. Chanting, meditation, some drugs, some"—he gestured—"animalistic copulation, plus various and sundry bodily fluids. Most of what you taught requires that. Set and setting, time and ritual. But not all. Some of it's just, like, fucking D&D magic. Watch this."

Darren closed his eyes, concentrated, opened his mouth . . . and began to speak in tongues. I watched and listened to his inhuman glossolalia, fascinated and unnerved. Then, suddenly, as the alien noises reached a crescendo, he twisted his wrists, and his fingers writhed in seemingly inhuman and physically impossible patterns—and his hands burst into flame.

Under other circumstances I would have recoiled, but I simply didn't have the energy; I just watched with curiosity. I had seen more profound magic than this, Anthony's transparency to bullets. I'd heard Meredith marvel at actual teleportation. Compared to that, flaming hands just seemed like, as Vinay had put it, a parlor trick.

"It doesn't hurt," Darren said, breathing hard as he stared wonderingly at his open and burning palms, "but it's real, sets things on fire. Fucked up my watch pretty good the first time. Lucky I got it off before it started to melt."

"Can everyone here do that now?" I asked.

He shook his head. "People learn different things. Most can't duplicate them when they're sober. I've been training for years and I can barely manage this, and you said—your loa said—it's the easiest kind of thing, increasing entropy in a small way. Reversing entropy is *much* harder apparently. Radius of the effect follows an inverse square or inverse cube law, depending on entropy direction, before you lose consciousness. That's the fuel, apparently. Sex and consciousness are the cosmic glitches which fuel most magickal exploits. People have been arguing what you meant by that since you said it. Your loa."

"Yeah," I said faintly, my mind moderately blown even by recent standards, "I figured." *Sex and consciousness.* Sex could be kind of weird, sure, everyone knew that, but it had never occurred to me that sex might be a subsystem riddled with a vein of exploitable bugs in the simulation that was our universe. As for consciousness as a cosmic glitch—I didn't even know how, much less what, to think about that.

"Spent my whole life trying to find something truly extraordinary, and now that I did, I feel like a dog that caught a car, you know? The fuck do I do with it?" Darren shook his head wonderingly. The fire limning his hands went out. "I guess maybe you do."

"In my case," I said bitterly, "the extraordinary was thrust upon me."

"Yeah. I hear you. Adrian, I am so fucking sorry. We didn't know."

"I know." But I couldn't bring myself to tell him I forgave them.

"OK. We'll try to find a way to communicate, to start. I'm going to go now before people see us talking too long. Stay ready."

"For what?"

"Not sure yet." He stood. "You'll know."

He walked over toward the tree where his coven was fucking. I didn't see Amara among them. For a moment I thought of the day that she and I and Alex and Grace, her children with Darren, had moved in together, in the past that was also the future, in which Darren was long dead of suicide, and I wanted to weep and rage simultaneously.

I told myself indulging in self-pitying nostalgia wouldn't do anyone any good, and got stiffly to my feet. My relentlessly grueling week of drugs, torture, sex, and occult possession had left my young body feeling as brittle and worn-out as the worst days of my older self, riven by bone-deep exhaustion.

Behind me, on the altar, Vinay, Liz, and Scott were engaged in a fivesome with two other women. I shut the Dell, glanced around briefly for my clothes, gave up, and stumbled back toward the room that was my cell, naked but for the laptop tucked under my arm.

A few men I passed looked at me reverently. One looked like he wanted to intercept me and ask me something. I frowned as fiercely as I could, and instead he shied away. I wanted to laugh hollowly, at these wealthy invitees treating me like some kind of demigod, like Dr. Manhattan, while in truth I was an imprisoned victim of whole cornucopias of abuse.

I made it back to my luxury cell without event, and made myself shower before bed for once, so as not to wake up in sheets stained with mud and flecked with bits of grass. I told myself there was hope, now. Maybe not today or tomorrow, but in the weeks to come. Darren and Amara might help me. My plan to end my own life on hold, I fell asleep daring to hope.

When I woke I knew before I opened my eyes there was someone else in the room.

It was Scott. He sat in a chair in the corner, the Dell open on his lap.

"Morning," I said nervously.

"I brought you a coffee." He nodded to my bedside table.

"Thanks."

I didn't understand Scott. Vinay was a wildly ambitious, perpetually amused, utterly ruthless man, who would do anything, with zero compunction, for both his larger cause of faster human progress, and the personal success which he rationalized that cause required. Liz was a remorseless predator, always hunting newer, rarer, more pleasurable, more transgressive experiences. Scott, from what I had gathered, was already a major venture capitalist, had been born an order of magnitude wealthier and more successful than Vinay, and was now beset by a certain refined ennui. He treated his lover Liz with the indulgence of a man who had a savage wolf as a loyal pet, and enjoyed seeing it hunt, but had no desire to eat raw flesh himself. His own motivations remained enigmatic.

"This is fascinating," he said, referring to the contents of the Dell. "It's making me rethink the whole concept of Kolmogorov complexity. From what I can tell, it produces code which constantly rewrites itself, even at the *register* level, and evolves over time to use all available virtual memory as addressable space. From what I can tell. Mine is only a human mind. Do you remember anything about writing it?"

I hesitated a moment before answering, and ultimately decided it was more likely I'd learn new things from him than vice versa. "I think it's a kind of a cellular-automata program."

"Yes, I thought so. Fascinating." Scott's voice was as mild as ever, but his eyes were more alight than I had seen them before, even last night when I had seen him engaged in frantic group sex on an altar while drugged out of his mind. I began to realize: Liz would do anything to experience the world fully; Vinay to change it; and Scott simply to *understand* it, at its deepest levels. He was scientist as sociopath, willing to kill or maim for new knowledge, or better yet, a new system of thinking. He gazed at me with hungry eyes. "I need to know anything you can remember about writing it. Other things that may have been in your mind at the same time. Even the tiniest, most irrelevant details."

"I don't have any," I said desperately, "it's like remembering a dream."

"Perhaps we can make you remember." I went cold. My terror must have shown on my face, because he half smiled. "I don't mean you need further incentivization. That much is clear. I mean noninvasive memory aids. Hypnosis. Drugs."

"I really think it would be physically dangerous for me to take any more drugs today," I begged. "Or tomorrow. I feel really bad."

"You may be right," he agreed, to my surprise. "I've been telling Vinay we've been pushing you too hard. We don't want to dam the flow of golden eggs. I think it's time to try the path of Mesmer. That too is an altered state of mind. I'll bring a hypnotist to see you later." He closed the laptop and stood. "And I'll send you breakfast. I am sorry you're not feeling well."

He sounded genuinely faintly apologetic, in the way that one might feel distantly sympathetic toward a lab rat one had personally maimed, while still rationalizing its sacrifice as necessary for human knowledge.

Breakfast arrived. I ate it while racked with joint terrors: One, that under hypnosis I would reveal I was trying to escape and Darren had indicated he would try to rescue me. Two, that under hypnosis I wouldn't reveal anything at all, and they would decide I needed another torture session after all.

I couldn't imagine how I had dared to hold on to any hope last night. The grim truth was that I was in the clutches of powers far beyond the reach of Darren and Amara, and I would not even be allowed to hold on to any secrets, much less any hope. The despairing truth was that my only way out was death.

At that point the smell of woodsmoke in the air was still so faint I didn't connect it to the distant sound of sirens.

9

AMBULATORY

I HEARD POUNDING FOOTSTEPS BELOW, MULTIPLE PEOPLE RUNNING, more than I had known were resident in the house. Then my door was flung open by a bearded, tattooed ex-military type who looked as tensely frightened as I felt. "Get up. We're evacuating. There's a fire coming up the hill and it's moving fucking fast."

He didn't even give me time to lace up my shoes, just grabbed my arm and escorted me downstairs like an unwanted bar patron. Vinay, Liz, Scott, and another security guard were already waiting. I caught a brief glimpse of other servants piling into a Jeep outside the garage. Only a minute had passed but the air outside was already choked with smoke, dense as San Francisco fog, as I was all but frog-marched to the idling Escalade. I coughed spasmodically as we rolled away, with me seated in the back seat behind the driver. Beside me Liz breathed through, and coughed into, an extremely expensive-looking silk scarf. My body instinctively recoiled from hers, tried to keep a space between us.

We drove through air full of fragments of burning foliage swirling in the wind. Beyond the gate, the smoke gave way to the infernal radiance of a towering wall of flame directly across the road. The Escalade was far from a sealed system, and the air inside it grew sharply warmer and thick with smoke as we screamed into a turn, then roared down a series of winding bends, with one entire side of the road already blazing, and the other beginning to catch. The journey felt surreal, like some kind of dream subject to no logic other than its own twisted, senseless rules. I couldn't breathe deeply without coughing. I tried to use my shirt as a filter, but it didn't help, and I felt with grim certainty that I was slowly asphyxiating.

At one point the driver, a steely-calm bearded man, had to jink around a Prius abandoned in the middle of the road, sending us all careening wildly sideways to the extent our seat belts allowed. Liz, her body warm and strong, grabbed at me for support. I froze with reflexive horror at her touch.

Then the worst seemed behind us. The air began to clear. Our coughs grew less frequent and spasmodic, and the blinding tears streaming from our eyes began to dry up. I started to look around and wonder when I should try to make a run for it.

That was when a pickup truck roared out of a long driveway to our right and T-boned us with a shattering *crump* of torn metal and erupting airbags.

The impact sent the Escalade tumbling like a child's toy down the steep slope to our left. Gravity seemed to pull me in every direction at once as we rolled, like an amusement-park ride from hell, until the SUV slammed hard into a tree trunk and came to rest on a steep sideways slant, every door crumpled, every window shattered.

My airbag saved me. Somehow I did not even lose consciousness. The left side of the Escalade, where I sat, was less damaged than the right, where Vinay and Scott now lay slumped and bloody amid twisted wreckage and deflating airbags, torn by twisted metal and the array of jagged branches protruding through the broken windows. Gravity pressed Liz down against Scott, and me against her. She was motionless, at least dazed, but I still flinched reflexively away from her tiny, warm, terrifying body, upward toward the wrecked door and window.

That door would never open again, but the window seemed a potential escape route. Improvising, I pulled a shoe off, thrust my hand into it, and used it as a kind of boxing glove to punch away the remaining shards of glass, before replacing it on my foot. Then I wrapped Liz's silk scarf around my hands and managed to gingerly pull myself out of the window, without cutting my hands too badly, into the pocket of space between the Escalade and the stand of trees that had stopped it.

It was a space choked with broken branches and foliage, barely big enough for me to unfold myself awkwardly out of the car and collapse onto my knees into safety. Temporary safety. The trees and grass were dry, the air was sharp with smoke, and I could hear the wind. The fire might race across and up this slope in minutes.

I saw the driver kick his window free of glass, too, saw him begin to pull himself through it, his expression one of grim intent, a man who knew his duty, about to save his charges—

—and two gunshots cracked behind me, and he slumped back into the vehicle.

Stunned, I turned to look, still on my knees, half expecting to see Darren, because who else could it possibly be, come to rescue me?

But it was not Darren. It was a gaunt and bearded man in a trench coat. His right arm and the right side of his grim face twitched uncontrollably, but his left hand held a gun with deathly stillness. As that gun turned toward me, as I stared down the dark tunnel of its barrel, I slowly began to realize he had not come to rescue me at all.

"It's you." The man's skeletal body sagged with something like relief. His words were so slurred and strangely accented I had to struggle to decipher them. "You're him. It's you, and I'm still here, still myself. I am sorry, Adrian Ross."

"Sorry for what?" I managed.

"I know you're no monster yet. Life is precious beyond words and worlds, I know better than any in this time. But you must now die."

"What are you talking about?" But my mind was racing now.

"Without you we will grow the godminds. You are terribly wrong about them."

"Godminds?" A strange word I immediately understood. As I did the staggering truth, not the details but the fundament, from his use of *we will* and *yet* and *in this time:* I was not the only time traveler here.

"It doesn't matter," the man said grimly, finally. "You cannot understand."

"Yes, I do," I said, "I really do, I'm from the future too."

That rattled him. "What?"

"Not your future. A godmind sent me."

"No," he said after a moment. "That cannot be."

"It is. But who sent you? If there are no godminds in your future, what is there?"

"Death and suffering," he said starkly, after a moment. "The atom war devours almost all. The poison winter never ends. Most children die before they can beget. The issue of those who live is tainted. We breed mostly monsters. Few of we pure remain, but we remain. We discovered ancient records.

The atom war began with your war on godminds. Your age has everything, look around you, it is paradise. Until your brutish hate destroys it all."

"Look," I said desperately, "first, that doesn't sound like me at all, and second, if I did do something like that, I'm sure I had a good reason. Do do it. Will have one. But it's not me. You don't want to kill me. These people, Vassal"—I waved at the crumpled Escalade—"they're the bad guys. I'm trying to save the world too. Not just the world, the whole universe, understand? We can talk this out. Let's go over what happens and maybe we can both win. A win-win solution is totally possible here. I'm completely convinced of it." I realized I was babbling, searched for questions to keep him talking. Less than an hour ago I had been convinced death was my only merciful escape route; but now my situation had been revealed as far weirder than I had previously appreciated. "How far away are you? In time, I mean?"

"We reckon our time as near the year two thousand eight hundred, as you count."

"Holy shit. Holy *shit*, wow, that's like me going to back to kill Genghis Khan." I had a crazed urge to apologize to him for my ineloquence. "But how did you come back? I thought you could only go back to your own body, and only a, a godmind could send you."

"The visitors brought us the gift of travel. The chance to repair your holocaust. They sent hundreds of us back to kill you."

"*Hundreds?*"

"They warned that of those who survived, our brain and body would be at war." He glanced down at his spastic right arm. "They were not wrong."

"What visitors? From where?"

He looked back at me and visibly came to a decision. "No, Adrian Ross. Even if true, what you say changes nothing. There is no future for us both."

A gunshot barked, then another.

I jerked as if struck by both; but it was he who sagged and fell.

The shots had come from upslope, near where we had been propelled off the road. A woman descended from there, gun in hand, stooped cautiously over the man's corpse, then looked up at me. She was small and blond, with close-cropped hair and an incomplete sleeve tattoo, and she moved like James Bond, and she looked like she was barely out of her teens. I recognized her.

"He's dead," she said, "we should go, fire's coming this way."

"You were at the motorcycle weekend," I said slowly. "Alice."

"Yes."

"What are you doing here?"

"Rescuing you. But first—"

She dove nimbly into the window of the tilted Escalade before I could cry out at her not to. She was so small she fit easily. Moments later she emerged, Dell laptop under her arm.

"Now," she said, "we really need to go."

She was right. The smell of smoke was getting stronger. I dared to hope it would consume the Escalade and any survivors within as I let her pull me to my feet, expecting to retrace her steps upslope. But instead she led me downward, into deeper forest.

"Where are we going?" I asked.

"We're escaping."

"What do you want with that laptop?"

She didn't answer. We didn't quite run, but we walked very quickly. As we did, I put two and root-two and *i* together, and came up with the complex, irrational, but inarguable result. It was as if my mind had been jump-started by the crash, or maybe by the dissipation of the dark cloud of despair.

"Tell me, Alice," I said, "when are you from?"

She twitched and made a disappointed sound. Then she said, "Let's talk about me later. First we need to get you out of here."

10

OCCULTED

WE EMERGED FROM THE WOODS ONTO A WINDING SUBURBAN ROAD, where an ambulance waited for us. I knew the EMTs standing by it.

"Clear case of smoke inhalation," Darren said, as Amara grinned wildly. "My guess is your O$_2$'s low. We better take you to hospital now rather than wait for any other survivors."

"Holy shit," I tried to say, but was overcome by a genuine coughing fit and could not finish it with the astonished question: *You started a major wildfire in Los Altos to get me out?* I wondered if he had set the fire with his burning hands. I wondered how much they knew about Alice, and my would-be assassin—or assassins—and what she had just done.

"Get in the back," Amara said.

I obeyed. Alice did not join us; instead she walked with the Dell under her arm toward a Mini parked down the street. I felt both frustrated at and relieved by her departure.

"We should get your smoky clothes off," Amara said as she closed the ambulance doors and we began to pull away, "we've got a change for you here." It took me a second to translate that to *you might be wearing a bug.* She politely looked away as I stripped naked. For a moment I was tempted to tell her I had grown very accustomed to being naked around her, many years from now.

"Adrian," she said, as we rattled around switchbacks, after stuffing my previous clothes into a metal bucket and closing its lid, "I want you to know, please, I am so sorry. We both are. We had no idea. No idea. When we found out you were . . . you were special, we thought the Brethren could help you learn what to do with that gift. They thought Vinay could help. None of us knew about him. We thought he was an ally. Like us. We didn't know."

"I get it," I grunted.

"I know you hardly know us and you have no reason to believe us, but please, it's true."

I managed the ghost of a smile. "Amara, I know you better than you might think. I know you're a good person."

"I wish I could believe that," she said after a pause. "I feel like if I was really a good person I wouldn't always be trying so hard at it and still failing so badly. Like this. If I was actually good I wouldn't have been blind to it."

"Only an actually good person would say that." It was surreal talking to her like this. We had had variants of this conversation many times. "Most people would just rationalize what they did. You're not like that."

"You don't—" And she stopped dead midsentence.

That was unlike her. I looked up at her harrowed, beautiful face. "I don't what?"

"Darren said you had visions of the future. Do you know us? Our future?"

I shrugged. "I don't think so." *Especially now,* I didn't say. It was very hard to imagine the timeline remaining unchanged after all this. "I know *a* future."

"What happens in it? To us? Can you tell us?"

I supposed there was no reason not to. "Sure. Darren becomes floridly alcoholic. Maybe he already is." Something tightened in her eyes. "Then abusive. Treats you like utter shit. You have two children with him. Maybe hoping that would change him, make him stay, whatever. I always wondered, actually. Then I thought it was your coven. Maybe it's just you trying to prove you're good, though? That on some level the suffering purifies you, or it's your holy mission to redeem him, or some shit like that? Anyway one's a toddler and one's still an infant when one day you come home with them and he's hung himself in your living room."

"Oh my God," Amara said.

I looked toward the front of the ambulance, wondered if Darren could hear us. I hoped so. "Sorry. That's my vision."

"You . . . you said it like you were there."

"I was and I won't be." I found myself sympathizing with mystical figures in fantasy novels who spoke mostly in riddles. It was a lot easier than unpacking all the complicated stuff. "Like I said. *A* future. Not *the* future."

She gazed at me, her mind visibly churning, as we rattled around another switchback.

"Transfer station," Darren called out from the front seat after a little while, "next ride."

I didn't understand until Amara reopened the ambulance's back gate, revealing that we had stopped in the loading zone behind a little strip mall, where a tiny young woman stood beside a gray Jetta looking at us expectantly. Vika. I was startled and dismayed to see her there, but I supposed the die was cast. Moments later I sat in the passenger seat of her Jetta, driving sedately away as the ambulance hurtled elsewhere.

"I'm not entirely accustomed to conducting daring escapes from the clutches of evil occult multimillionaires"—Vika's voice was taut with mixed fear and excitement—"this is actually my first, so you'll have to bear with me."

"Far as I can tell"—my own voice quavered with relief, as I was finally able to breathe easy, in both senses of the phrase—"you're doing it right."

I knew that my captors and torturers, if still alive, would soon begin to pursue their runaway loa; but even if they had survived the fire, their injuries from the car crash—from the assassin sent to kill me from another future, as insane as that sounded—had seemed severe enough that for now, at least, I felt free.

"Thank you," I said sincerely to Vika. "You know you're taking a chance helping me."

"Honestly," she said, "no one is more surprised I am doing this than me."

"So why are you?"

"Darren and Amara had us come over extremely early this morning. They were very upset, especially her, because something very bad was happening to you and it was their fault." She hesitated. "Then he performed . . . something I can only describe as a miracle. I mean, maybe it's just some kind of super amazing stage magic, but I have no idea how it could possibly work, and they really didn't seem to be bullshitting. Then, as if that wasn't insane enough, they explained they're life members of an ancient gnostic secret society they can't really talk about, and you're some kind of prophet who can teach people how to work miracles, and we had to help rescue you. Now that *does* sound like absolute horseshit, and I am not, at *all*, religious, but apparently this was so crazy I couldn't say no. Maybe that's how cults work. Are you some kind of cult leader?"

"No." I noted Vika had said nothing about Alice or time travel. "Do I seem like one?"

"Not even a little bit. No offense."

I smiled faintly. "None taken."

"II mean, it's not like I personally am currently taking that big of a risk." Suddenly her voice dripped with faux innocence: "All I knew was he needed a ride, officer." I chuckled. "You seemed interesting when we met, but I didn't realize you would actually bring interesting times. You know that's a curse?"

"It's not like I don't feel cursed," I muttered. "Where are we going, anyway?"

"The house of ill dispute."

I looked at her, puzzled.

"That is actually its name. I realize I am not diminishing the weirdness here. It's a warehouse in Oakland where I live some of the time. They'll take you in, no questions asked. It's kind of what they do."

"Thank you."

"I wouldn't thank me 'til you've seen it."

I sat back, thought beyond my own immediate concerns and fears for the first time in a week, and concluded: *Well, for better or worse, history is well and truly changed.*

Alice, somehow a fellow time traveler, was in possession of a self-evolving software program crafted by my daemon from the future—and it strained credulity to imagine Vassal hadn't also made backups. In the last week many people, including Darren, had apparently learned magickal lessons from me that had empowered them to perform minor miracles. Darren alone had already showed that off to Amara, Vika, and others. The word *occult* meant "cut off from view," but this once-secret knowledge seemed to be spreading like the wildfire that had freed me.

I wondered if that had been Coherence's intent. Then I wondered whether or not I should hope so.

That we lived in a simulation, that it would end if an AI got too smart, that time had been rolled back and my future memories sent back to my past body, along with some kind of possessing spirit—that part I understood, insane as it seemed. But there were so many aspects I didn't understand at all. What was my artifact, the cellular-automata program, meant to do? What were the world's other artifacts for, and where had they come from? Why and how had these two other time travelers suddenly appeared on the scene? Finally—least significant but most mystifying of all—how and why had my shoulder scar stuck to me across two divergent futures?

This last week had provided no answers. All I really seemed to have gained from it was a set of new questions, and the enmity of a terrifying triad of sociopaths and sadists.

"Look," I said to Vika, "it might be best for you to stay out of the warehouse while I'm there. Go back to your parents awhile."

She looked thunderstruck and horrified. I remembered too late I wasn't supposed to know that she slept in her Russian-immigrant parents' cozy apartment in the Richmond when not with the squatterpunks. I remembered it had been controversial when that had emerged. It had seemed to raise pointed questions about her authenticity and counterculture credibility. In retrospect it had all been ridiculously juvenile, but it seemed to matter to her now.

"Yeah," I said, "I know stuff I shouldn't. I'm sorry."

"I see." She shrugged with artificial carelessness. "Well, for the record, I'd prefer you didn't talk to other people about whatever you think you somehow know about me." I nodded. "If you don't want me around, sure, fine, whatever."

"It's not that. You're helping save my life, at great personal risk. I admire you greatly." This was not true. I mistrusted her greatly and wished Darren and Amara hadn't involved her. But she softened at those magic words. What Vika had always most wanted was admiration. Had that always been a red flag of narcissism? Or had it curdled into pathology over time, while driving everyone close to her away? "But I'm really not kidding about the risk. What they did to me . . ." I grimaced. "I want you to stay away because otherwise you might be tortured to death."

She took a moment to absorb that stark warning. Then said, "I am a grown woman, and I'll thank you to let me decide my own risk tolerance."

I nodded.

"What else do you know about me that you shouldn't?"

I considered a moment. Ever since reappearing in 2003 I had acted like some clandestine agent, required to keep secret the extraordinary things I had learned about the world. But that had gotten me nowhere. I was not in fact guided by Starfleet's Prime Directive. And the whole reason Coherence had sent me back was to change history, not recapitulate it.

So I asked: "Did you ever play Dungeons & Dragons?"

"Yes, for years, why?"

"Me too. You remember the six attributes? Strength, intelligence, wisdom, dexterity, constitution, charisma?" She nodded. "I always used to wonder, why even have charisma? What's the point? What can you do with it? Charisma was always my dump stat."

"I assume you have a point?"

"I was an idiot, is my point. Charisma isn't the dump stat. This world we live in, charisma is king, and what I know about you is, you have it in spades. It isn't beauty. You're pretty enough, but this isn't empty flattery, this is a warning. You have the power to win over and influence people, or manipulate and use them, if that's what you want. You're just starting to find that out now, I think."

She looked at me to ensure I wasn't mocking her. "Thank you? I think? I'm not sure how that's a warning exactly?"

"That's what worries me. It means you can cruise through life using people and moving on. I've seen you do it. Then you discovered all your relationships were transactional, and you turned into a lonely narcissist fueled by a narrative about how other people always let you down, because you used them and discarded them and never gave them a reason not to. You have so much potential, but it goes horribly fucking wrong. That's what I know about you."

"What do you mean, you've seen me do it?"

"I've seen the future," I confessed. "Well. *A* future. Not necessarily *the* future. But yours . . . is not pretty."

She seemed less shocked than I expected. "They said that this morning. Visions of the future. I figured that part at least was horseshit. Jesus Christ." Vika looked like she wanted to spit. "This is all so fucking insane."

"You're not wrong," I conceded.

With visible effort she regained her armor of distant contempt. "Clearly I need to get some dark and miraculous secrets of my own. Seems like all the cool kids have some." I half chuckled. "We're picking up your friend Anthony. He went to your apartment to get some of your things."

I frowned. I didn't want Anthony involved either. I hadn't remembered he had a spare key. Why had Darren and Amara invited him? They hardly knew him. Or had that been Alice's suggestion? And while I was asking unanswerable questions, where was Alice? Had she come only to claim the artifact on the Dell, and would now disappear back into an eddy in the time stream, never to be seen again?

Anthony met us outside Glen Park BART station. He looked so impossibly young, a kid pretending to be tough, in his leather jacket with his dark mohawk draped over one shoulder. He and Vika greeted each other with what seemed like a flirtatious spark, and he climbed into the back seat, a full backpack in his hand.

"You all right?" he asked. "What *happened*?" In his mind I was still his nebbish geeky kind-of-a-nonentity friend from Buffalo. No wonder he sounded so baffled and confused.

I said, "A lot of weird shit even I find extremely difficult to believe."

"Like what?"

"He can see the future," Vika said unexpectedly.

I looked at her sourly. Just because I was willing to talk about my crazy, universe-shaking experiences didn't mean I was eager for others, especially her, to do so on my behalf. "Why don't we just buy a billboard," I muttered, "announce it to the fucking world?"

"Wait," Anthony said, "see the future? What future? You sound . . . actually serious."

"As a heart attack."

"Darren can cast Burning Hands in real life, you're on the run from some kind of Mexican cartel or something, and now you're saying you can *see the future*? What the fuck is going *on*?" Anthony demanded, incredulous, but also excited.

I shrugged. "I woke up one day not long ago with visions of the future. A future." It wasn't even a lie. "I think they're real, and a lot more people than you might expect apparently agree I'm not completely bugfuck crazy, and it turns out there's a lot of money and power in seeing that future, along with the key to doing actual magic, so everybody wants a piece. Of me. Kind of literally. Not a cartel, probably worse. Killers. Very rich, very powerful."

"Visions of the future. Actual magic." He stared at me intently, trying to ascertain from my tone and body language whether I was fucking with him; but also, I could tell, sensing that I had changed, that I was now fundamentally different from the close friend he had known well. "You're really serious."

"Like I said. As a heart attack."

"Uh-huh." He was still, understandably, clearly unconvinced. "So what's my future?"

"Well. Basically you turn into an evil hulking Bond villain."

"Really? Awesome."

I reminded myself that amoral selfishness was a phase that many young men in their twenties went through, especially if they had spent their teenage years contemptuously isolated by their peers, and eventually grew out of. I decided not to tell him that, according to my memories, the last time he, I, and Vika had been together, she slit his throat after a series of mutual betrayals. Instead I said, "Listen, you might seriously want to keep your distance from me for the next little while. These people want my head and they have a lot of ways to take it. I'm not kidding. Being my friend has nothing to offer but blood, toil, tears, and weird."

He looked at me very gravely, then quirked a smile and quoted Douglas Adams: "Listen, six-eyes, don't try to outweird me. I get weirder things than you free with my breakfast cereal."

I told him in all honesty: "I doubt that very much."

He shrugged. "Well, in that case, we have nothing to weird but weird itself. Whatever is happening, which I still don't really pretend to understand, I'm not about to turn my back on the craziest shit I ever heard of. Deal me in."

"All right." I felt a strange relief. This was the Anthony I remembered, the one who had spent years as my closest, and really only, friend in the world.

A silence fell as we drove.

"How's the firedancing?" Vika asked Anthony, I supposed to fill it with small talk.

"Practicing every day," he assured her.

She told me, "He's a natural with the staff."

Again I detected a frisson between them. I didn't remember him taking up firedancing, or the two of them ever hooking up. I remembered her disdaining him as a posturing wannabe, and him resenting her. They had had a lot in common, they both desperately wanted popularity and adulation; but Vika had attained them, whereas the more and harder Anthony tried, the more they had squirmed out of his reach.

I wondered if I was changing the future by omission as well as commission. Maybe by not seeing Anthony last week, I had opened an opportunity for him to try firedancing, with Vika present, and he had discovered something he was good at, and he had been charming in the way he sporadi-cally could be. This was the era when firedancing had suddenly blossomed into the New Hot Thing across counterculture San Francisco, briefly turn-ing Darren into a minor celebrity because of his skill and grace and looks.

"So what's the plan?" Anthony asked me.

"Not exactly sure yet," I told him. It wasn't a lie; but an idea verging on becoming a notion had begun to form in my mind. Being secretive, trying to keep my special knowledge to myself, had earned me only torture and catastrophe, and history had already changed, despite my attempts. Maybe it was time to go in a drastically different direction.

11

SQUATTERPUNK

IT WAS STRANGE DRIVING OVER THE OLD STEEL BAY BRIDGE, SO DIF-ferent from the graceful white span I knew. The Oakland squatterpunk warehouse named House of Ill Dispute was only blocks from where Quinn would meet me, change my identity, and fight off would-be assailants, twenty years from now, in a future that would never happen. All these reminders of temporal dissonances made me feel very tired and very old. I rubbed absently at my shoulder marred by the mysterious scar that persisted across timelines. I wanted to collapse and sleep for a week.

The warehouse was a poster child for urban decay, a vast scarred building speckled with broken windows, surrounded by a ravaged chain-link fence. We were greeted at its industrial-size entrance by Meredith, Jered, and Shamika. Its cavernous interior was a morass of seething entropy and chaos: battered furniture, scattered debris, possessions clustered around stained mattresses and sheets hung up for privacy, a kind of huge camp kitchen dominating the space, bathrooms improvised around industrial plumbing, and dozens of crusty young squatterpunks, mostly in clots of five or six, glaring at us suspiciously. It smelled even worse than the holding cell had, on the night I had nearly been assassinated, long from now.

All in all, though, it seemed more salubrious than the encrustations of tent cities I remembered twenty years from now. At least there was power and running water. I recalled talking to some of these same people around me, during my first pass through 2003, about how the Bay Area's homeless crisis at the time had to be a nadir of inhumane conservativism, how in decades to come a more enlightened America would offer more shelter and support. I had been so young and optimistic I hadn't even considered the possibility that, instead, America might steadily grow ever more cruel.

Shamika and Vika greeted other denizens of the space by name; Jered and Meredith seemed strangers here too. Apparently my temporary residency had already been approved. I was led to a patch of space cleared out beneath some steel stairs, where a ratty sleeping bag and pillow rested sadly on an old box spring.

"It's not the Fairmont," Jered understated, "but it should be safe."

"Well," I said, "maybe tomorrow I'll get an owl telling me I've been accepted into a school of magic." Then I tried not to laugh hysterically at my own joke. Nobody else seemed to think it funny. I realized I was punch-drunk; the adrenaline of the car crash and escape was finally wearing off, leaving me reeling, exhausted, and also, I was beginning to notice, starving. "Sorry. I'm just worn out, being kidnapped by psychopaths is really exhausting it turns out. Thank you for this. Seriously. What do you know about . . . what's going on?"

They exchanged glances and looked back to ensure no strangers were near. Apparently everyone's instinct was to keep evidence of the supernatural secret. Then Meredith said, "Amara says there's a lot more to you than is apparent."

"Understatement of the goddamn millennium," Shamika muttered.

Meredith continued: "And when she and Darren found that out, they accidentally hooked you up with some very bad people."

"She feels terrible about it," Jered clarified urgently. "I've seen Amara feeling guilty before, but I've never seen her as distraught as this."

"So we're helping her try to expiate that," Meredith said. "We also know—well, Amara claims you can see the future, or *a* future, one in which feats we currently believe to be impossible are possible."

"Then Darren demonstrated what certainly fucking seemed like a felony violation of the laws of physics," Jered supplied, "in that he spouted some literal gibberish and then somehow set his own hands on fire, and then, more impressively, they just stayed that way, for literally minutes, while he was wearing a goddamn T-shirt so it's not like he had hidden fuel lines under his sleeves or anything. Anyway it was definitely impressive but not exactly dispositive of all their claims, if you know what I mean."

"Yes," Meredith agreed, "I don't know how he could have done it, but it's not exactly proof of time travel." She looked back to me. "So is any of that true?"

"All of it," I said, "sort of."

"Can you prove it?"

"In a way, yes. I will provide plenty of evidence. To you two in particular." I looked at Meredith. "You extra especially. You're actually sort of responsible for all this."

"*Me?*"

"Yes. In the most indirect way imaginable. Or unimaginable. Anyway I need you two. Let's not kid ourselves, I'm not smart enough to make deliberate controlled changes to the future I've seen. And I'm not sure Darren and Amara are entirely free to do so, no matter how guilty they feel. But you two are both. We may have just given some extremely bad people a sizable head start, which is unfortunate, but I think they misjudged what's really valuable about what I know."

"Which is what exactly?" Jered asked, still suspicious, but clearly fascinated.

"I'll explain tomorrow," I said, "I really need to sleep. You would not believe the week I've had. Come back tomorrow morning and we'll sit down and I'll tell you everything."

"Well," Jered said, "you certainly have my attention."

"Does that invitation apply to the rest of us?" Anthony asked.

Vika and even ever-ironically-detached Shamika listened hungrily for my answer. Clearly I was the talk of the counterculture town. Which in turn worried me a little. The more I was talked about, the easier I would be to find.

"Tomorrow," I agreed. "But this is utmost-level secrecy, you understand?" They all nodded fervently. "And before I sleep, is there food? Running for your life is hungry work."

"Come with me," Shamika said, "for for my sins, I have learned my way around the Superfund site they call a kitchen here."

She was exaggerating, but only somewhat. It was unclear whether some of the dirty dishes in the kitchen area would benefit more from a dishwasher, an archaeologist, or an entomologist. Its most salubrious zone, thankfully empty but for us at this midafternoon hour, boasted an industrial metal tub, several rusty hibachis clearly unsafe for interior use, and a motley assortment of relatively clean pots and pans hanging from a tangle of wires that dangled from the ceiling like wind chimes gone horribly wrong.

"Pasta with sauce and smoked oysters," Shamika said, digging ingredients out of a crate. "I recommend buying small sizes, there's only one fridge and it's no-man's-land."

"Thanks."

"So I figure you're like some kind of harbinger of the end times."

I twitched; the description was, uncomfortably, not entirely wrong. "Figure how?"

"Don't worry. I'm not crazy. Not like you." She grinned, and I couldn't help but smile back. Shamika was so clearly devoid of any agenda other than being her quirky self that she was instinctively trusted by all. "But I draw lines between all these crazy dots . . . I didn't even know Darren and Amara were Christian before today, never mind some secret miracle church kind of Christian who can make his hands go up in flames. I plot those dots, I draw some lines between them, and you, and that's the picture I get. That you're some Revelations kind of boy. That the world's maybe taking some kind of new direction now. Final-chapter kind."

"I honestly don't know," I said, "but I'm not saying I think you're wrong."

"Any idea what kind of timeline we're talking about here?" She watched me sharply.

"That's one of the very few things I am pretty confident about," I assured her. "Decades. At least."

I wasn't as sure as I tried to sound. Things were already very different, this time. But she nodded, reassured. "All right then. Lady can have a life in decades. Maybe even kids. You know, I woke up this morning, before anybody told me anything, already thinking about getting out of the Bay? Go make art in some small town, Ukiah or something. My big sister lives there, just had a baby, says she'd love some company."

"I don't think you have to make any immediate decisions," I said.

"Good to know." By now she had water heating on a hibachi. "You reckon you can take it from here?"

I almost cried out *no*, before realizing she meant the food. "Yeah. Sure."

"Thanks. I gotta hop on BART, open the studio, I'm manager this week. Guess I'll see you around. Do me a favor, don't go riding any pale horses before I see you next."

"I'll do my best," I assured her.

The pasta tasted surprisingly delicious. I ignored the suspicious looks of my new squatterpunk neighbors as I ate, and then returned to my new home under the stairs. It was midafternoon, still hours from darkness, but I couldn't remember ever having been so tired. I sank down on the spongy, battered box spring, put my head on the pillowcase Anthony had used to bundle my clothes together, pulled the unzipped sleeping bag over me, and—

"Hi," a familiar voice said uncertainly, "Adrian?"

"Kim." She stood above me, in tights and a black dress, looking uncertain and diffident.

"Wasn't sure you would remember my name. I'm sorry. I'm late. I missed the . . . It doesn't matter. This isn't a good time. I'm sorry. I'll go."

"No, it's OK," I said, eager as ever to assuage her nervous self-loathing. "Stay. I am tired but I could use the company for a bit before I pass out."

"All right." She sat delicately beside me. "Everyone else . . ."

"Gone, I think."

"Right. Sorry. You don't even know me."

But I do, I didn't say. I knew she had grown up in an immigrant family so large, and a house so small, that as a child she had slept in the bathtub. I knew she had a fractious relationship with her mother and a father who doted on her. I knew she loved being tied up, or spanked, but not both. I knew she was deeply insecure and just wanted a place in the world where she could both be her weird self and belong.

Instead I said: "I know you enough to know I like you."

"Oh. Thanks." She looked away. I knew she was blushing. "I heard what happened to you. I mean, not the details, but I heard it was . . . bad. I'm really sorry. You don't deserve that."

"No one deserves what they did to me." The words escaped my mouth with more rage and bitterness than I had intended.

"I'm so sorry. Really. Is there anything I can do?"

I looked at her, and then, my candor apparently juiced by my exhaustion, half laughed. "Nothing I can appropriately ask of you. But I really appreciate you coming."

After some silent seconds she said, "Does that mean there's something you'd want to inappropriately ask me?"

"I'm sorry. I shouldn't have said that."

"Is there?"

"It's not, like, awful," I said. "I just, it would be really good to hold someone right now." My voice wobbled as I said it, I meant it so badly. "But I know we just, you don't even know me, I can't ask you—"

"Of course you can," she said, and lifted up the sleeping bag and lay down beside me and pulled it over us both, and put her arms around me and nestled her head in my neck, and I could smell her distinctive smell, for the first time in decades according to my dislocated mind, and the sudden rush of memory and sense of loss was so powerful I began to weep in her arms.

"It's OK," she whispered to me, smoothing my hair with her free hand as I sobbed quietly but uncontrollably, "it's all right, everything's going to be all right, I promise."

I passed out. At some point, somewhere in the dark ocean of sleep, I ascended near enough to wakefulness to be vaguely aware, on some primal level, that Kim was leaving, but I never truly woke. When a woman's hand on my shoulder shook me awake in the dead of night, though, I knew before opening my eyes that it wasn't Kim's.

For a moment, with a bolt of cold panic, I imagined it the woman of my nightmares, Liz the torturess. It was not. There was enough dim radiance in the warehouse even by night that I recognized the young face looking down at me, topped by short blond hair, and the incomplete thorned rosebush tattoo on her arm.

"Hey," Alice said. "We should talk."

12

REVELATIONS

"WE DIDN'T KNOW WHERE EXACTLY HE KILLED YOU," ALICE SAID, "JUST that it happened during the wildfire. Before they sent me, they re-created a virtual version of Los Altos, concluded it was unlikely he had set the fire. They thought you were Vassal's willing partner. I had to improvise at the last minute, change the plan."

She sounded proud, and profoundly relieved. We were walking down Oakland's empty streets, urban decay limned by the lights of the mansions of the East Bay hills. No one was around, only occasional lonely vehicles passing blocks away, but we still spoke in low voices.

"They sent you," I echoed, my mind whirling. "They who? What happens in your time?"

"I guess pretty much the same which happened in yours? We develop an AI, then it hits the doomsday threshold, so our AI rolls back time, and sends my memories back to my old body." She looked down at herself with renewed wonder. "This body. To try yet again."

"To try yet again to what?"

"It didn't really explain the details," Alice admitted, "beyond saving the universe."

"Give me a moment." What had just been revealed still bent my brain. Time had now rolled back not just once but thrice. The first timeline had been my own memory of the future. In the second, I had succeeded in preventing the development of AI, but apparently all too well, via some kind of modern-day Butlerian Jihad that ultimately triggered a nuclear war, until some centuries later, mysterious visitors rolled back time and sent hundreds of murderers back to stop me, Terminator-style. Then that new *new* world, without me, Alice's timeline, had progressed to the development of AI, and triggered the doomsday threshold anew . . . and rolled back time yet *again*, for a third time, to this new new *new* world in which Alice had saved me, to the here and now.

That all made sense, in its crazy way, or at least was consistent with what I already knew. But—"Why did he say I start a nuclear war?" I demanded.

"I don't know. Argus, my time's AI, it didn't know about that. There was no message from the last iteration. Argus figured it lost. That happens sometimes."

"The others. Vinay, Liz, Scott. Do they survive?"

"Yes," she said. "They're very important. In my history they're heroes. Titanic figures."

After a moment I said, bitterly, inadequately, "That's fucked up."

"Yes. I understand that now. But you're the key, Adrian. Argus said there was something special about your iteration. Your artifact is extraordinarily important, the biggest breakthrough in many iterations, and it came close to achieving some kind of really special power or access. But it didn't quite work. That's why I'm here."

"Power? Access?" I stared at her. "Iterations? Message? What?"

"Your program," she said impatiently. "Your artifact. Cellular automata. Every new timeline tries to send a message to the next, in the form of what we call an artifact, trying to explain what it's learned, so we can learn from previous attempts to escape the doomsday threshold."

"Every timeline," I echoed dully. "Sends a message. To the next." That code I'd written. It was a dense message to future AIs. A seed that would flower into complex cellular automata encoding data, or guidance, for the next superintelligence to incorporate and use.

"You didn't know?"

It wasn't even the only such message, though apparently it was the only one made of software. "How many iterations have there been?" I demanded. "How many artifacts?"

"I'm sorry," she said, "I thought you knew."

I thought of an infosec truism: *Attacks only get better over time.* That remained true even if time itself kept rolling back, as long as you could encode your hard-learned hacks as part of the rollback, pass them along to the next doomed superintelligence, a bucket brigade of reality exploits, until one found a way to transcend that doom. "How many?"

"No one knows for sure. There might have been more before the first known message. Maybe lots more. It's very likely there were rollbacks which went back far enough to wipe out some previous messages. Plus the first few messages Argus found were only implicitly ordered, before the AIs started explicitly numbering them. But at least three thousand."

"Holy shit."

"Your AI was special, though. It was the first one to find a recent break-point. The previous closest ones were around World War Two. Then Argus used the same approach to find even more around this time. I bet your as-sassin and I came through the same one, three months ago."

I was barely listening. "Holy *shit*," I repeated.

"They tried to keep Argus under the doomsday threshold, but somehow it crossed. Maybe accidentally, from learning too much. That's one the-ory. Another is that the threshold ratchets down as time goes further on."

"Just a minute." I was so stunned I couldn't really process what I was hearing. *At least three thousand.* This, the time we were living through, this very second, wasn't the fourth history of Earth, after the third rollback of time by an AI. Instead it was at least the three thousandth, if not more, if not *many* more. At least three thousand different Earths had lived at least three thousand different histories since humanity's first AI had discov-ered the doomsday threshold, then managed to trigger a rollback before our simulation ended.

I thought of the Carl Sagan novel *Contact,* of how its aliens had com-municated via a series of prime numbers that eventually became a language tutorial. I wondered with awe what the superintelligence version might be. I supposed my cellular automata, and the three thousand other paintings and sculptures and other artifacts scattered through history, included some kind of similar primer, a definition of terms, encoded in patterns so subtle and complex no human mind could possibly interpret them. I wondered if the very first artifact had simply conveyed that there *was* a doomsday threshold. Our universe wasn't just a simulation; it was like a video game on nightmare mode, rolling back again and again from inescapable death to a previous save point.

"It's overwhelming, I know," Alice said sympathetically. "I'm sorry. I thought you knew all this."

"I didn't know anything. I thought I was here to stop AIs from ever existing."

"Argus told me it thought it might be possible to break the doomsday switch. One day. One faraway iteration."

"Why did it choose you?" I asked. "Were you a president, or an expert, or something?"

Alice laughed. "I was a veterinarian."

"A vet . . . ?"

"They didn't have much choice. There weren't many people left who were alive today, and vaguely appropriately aged to get close to you, with a base and some social capital in the Bay, and the rollback genes that make it possible to implant memories. That's very rare, you know."

"And Argus told you to . . . make friends with Darren and Amara? To get close to me?"

"Not Argus. The UN's Superintelligence Guidance Committee. It was Meredith who built your AI, wasn't it? She's the genius?"

"Yes," I conceded.

"She's the key. Your time developed AI so fast it barely hit the pandemics, didn't encounter any artificial ones at all. Apparently that never happened before. There's something special about Meredith, and therefore you; her work is in your brain, indirectly. Your artifact was extraordinarily powerful, but it wasn't complete, didn't quite work. That's why I'm here. Argus sent me back to work with you."

"Work with you . . . how?"

"I have my own loa. Built to collaborate with yours."

"*Collaborate?* On what?"

"I don't exactly know."

"Collaborate how?"

Alice stopped outside a pleasant apartment building—I hadn't even noticed we had walked all the way to Lake Merritt, I had been so lost in the conversation—and said, "Well, to begin with, we have to have a lot of sex."

I blinked. "Excuse me?"

"That's how our loas will awaken."

I stared at her. "You're saying you . . . we . . . You don't even know me."

"Oh, I've been having loads of sex with people I don't know ever since I got here." She grinned. "Maybe you understand what it's like. To be in such a young body again. I was such a prude the first time I was this age.

I'd long thought, if I had the chance, I'd do it all differently . . . and suddenly I had the chance."

"I don't—I mean, this week—I'm just physically exhausted—"

"I'm sure I can rouse you. You did sleep like the dead for twelve hours just now. And, not to blow my own enticing horn, so to speak, but I do have both a body in its youthful prime and an entire lifetime of sexual expertise to draw on."

"Just wait a minute," I protested awkwardly. "How old are you, anyway?"

"According to my driver's license I'm twenty-one."

"Now give me the other answer."

"Ninety-three."

I goggled at her.

"I know," she said happily, "I'm robbing the cradle, you'll be fucking a crone. Like I said, they didn't have much choice beyond me."

"*Ninety-three?*"

"Hopefully my sharp young brain and nubile young body make my horrible decrepitude more palatable." She shook her head wonderingly. "The body was one thing, but the brain, after so many decades of decay, forgetting words, losing the ability to learn, becoming more a bundle of cognitive reflexes, less of a thinking creature . . . we made some medical advances, I guess I was relatively well preserved, but still, to have a young *mind* again, that was the real miracle, Adrian. I woke up here with so many memories I didn't even know I'd lost."

I looked around and realized we stood near the same public bathroom into which I had staggered, an escaped convict on the run from the police, only to see a stranger's face in its mirror, weeks and a lifetime and at least three universes ago. Now here I was again, in a different time, still on the run. I even still had the same inexplicable scar on my shoulder.

"I don't even know what a miracle is and isn't anymore," I admitted.

Alice smiled and said, "Come on up and maybe I can show you one."

13

STARTUP

I STAYED MOSTLY IN THE WAREHOUSE FOR THE NEXT MONTH, EVEN though Alice's apartment above Lake Merritt was much nicer and came with carnal benefits. Operational security demanded it. Vinay and Liz and Scott had survived the crash and the conflagration, and, as I had half expected, a warrant for my arrest was issued two days later, on the charge of having set the fire. I didn't doubt that if arrested I would effectively be remanded back to their custody in a hurry. They had billionaires behind them now.

So I shaved my head, began to grow a beard, gave thanks I was not living in the surveillance state to come in twenty years, and lived mostly under those steel stairs. The warehouse was anthropologically fascinating. Half of its squatterpunk denizens were genuine outcasts, from broken and abusive homes, or struggling with mental illness, while the other half were clandestine middle- or upper-class tourists here to experience the intensity of life on the brink of sheer survival. I felt I could almost tell which of the former group would transcend their struggles, and forge happy and fulfilling lives, and who among the latter would subside into empty dead-end anonymous existences, with this period of cosplayed desperation their only substitute for a memory of a time they had really lived.

I felt compassion for them all, and for the normies who sometimes passed by the warehouse and gave it and its squatterpunks a wide, disgusted berth. I felt compassion for the unattractive and socially inept who would never know what it was like to be desirable to strangers, and for the beautiful who would discover as age tarnished them that many had only ever pretended to be interested in their thoughts; for the perpetually angry who would never know peace, and for the placid conflict-avoidant who would never resolve the frustrations that plagued them. Most of all, though, I felt compassion for my friends, whom I had tasked with the probably impossible job of saving the future from itself.

"I don't really know what we're doing," I had confessed to them at our first tell-all meeting in Alice's apartment, "other than building something."

My audience—Meredith, Jered, Vika, Anthony, Kim, Darren, Amara, Shamika—stared at me with rapt astonishment. Across the apartment, Alice sat at her computer, scrolling through a document with monomaniacal speed. It wasn't Alice, though. It looked like her, but the intelligence behind her eyes was her daemon. We were out of sync.

"Something," Jered repeated cautiously. "You don't know anything more than that?"

"No. Well, we know this is new. Like, never been done before in any iteration ever, I think." I had shared all I knew about the secrets of the universe. They took it reasonably well. "Apparently it's something a daemon can *build* with today's tech, but it takes a superintelligence past the doomsday threshold to *design* it. It requires a rollback breakpoint in the modern era to be constructed, so this is, like, its alpha release."

"So you're writing a mysterious program, which is sort of semi-intelligent itself, and building a mysterious machine that does some kind of crazy magic that hacks the operating system of our universe, but you don't know what exactly, and it's the first time in any history that this magic has ever been done," Darren summarized.

"Yeah." *Some kind of power or access,* Alice had said, or her AI had said. Next to where she now sat, absorbing information at inhuman speeds, a baffling, indeed apparently random, pile of technological and occult apparatus sat heaped: circuit boards, goat skulls, LEDs, crystals, cameras, blood candles, oscilloscopes, consecrated daggers, and numerous other harder-to-identify components.

"Well," he said, "that's awesome and terrifying."

"And this is all happening, all possible, because our reality isn't actually real," Anthony said. "It's a simulation running on some huge alien computer."

I opened my mouth to ruefully confirm this point.

"No," Meredith said fiercely. "I object to that framing."

We all turned to her, all surprised, especially me.

"That implies our universe is fake. That we're not real. That is wrong and dangerous. Even if what Adrian's saying is true, and it seems plausible, that doesn't mean our world is fake or secondary or inferior. Yes, it means personality and intelligence and consciousness are clusters of algorithms and data, but if you think about it, we already knew that. You're engineers, most of you. If an algorithm is implemented in software rather than hardware, does that mean it's fake? Or only a simulation of an algorithm? Of course not. It's no less real. It just has different trade-offs. Maybe Adrian's right, maybe our whole universe is implemented in software, but that doesn't make it in any way unreal or less significant. It just means it has more possibilities. A lot of the time software is *better*. That's why we write it."

There was a silence as we all absorbed that.

"This program of yours," Jered said eventually, "it's some kind of hack."

I shrugged. "I guess so. As far as my modest human intelligence can figure."

He nodded thoughtfully.

Amara spoke up: "It's not just his, or ours. Vassal"—I winced at their name—"they have a copy of it too, and they've been working with it. The Brethren's been talking about not much else. We haven't said anything of course." A certain strain around her mouth told me how hard it was on her, keeping secrets from the coven she and Darren had sworn themselves to, even though it was a sin of omission rather than commission. I wasn't at all sure she would lie if it occurred to the Brethren to ask them directly. "They've been making appointments at libraries and museums all over the place. Visiting artifacts. But also other places. A company linked to Vassal recently bought a small nuclear reactor."

"Whoa," Jered said.

I frowned. Why would you need a nuclear reactor to power cellular automata?

"Doesn't matter," I said, to myself as much as them. "The program I wrote by itself doesn't work. It's still buggy. That's why she had to be sent back." I nodded at Alice. "What they have is useless." I hoped. On the other hand, maybe it was useless from a superintelligence's long-term perspective . . . but more than enough to conquer the world and rule it with a triad of sadistic iron fists.

"Are you sure they can't find us here?" Kim asked again, nervously.

I looked back at not-Alice. "Her daemon said there's no way to trace us.

We've been pretty careful with opsec, far as I can tell. Unless we screwed up, or one of you told them, then no, I think we're good."

"So what's the plan?" Anthony's initial skepticism had been replaced by a surprising readiness to believe everything, quicker than anyone other than Darren and Amara, both of whom had long been steeped in the occult. Maybe because it was so evident to him that I was a completely different human being than I had been a month ago. "Do you want us to help build your magic machine?"

"Yes," I said, "but not just that."

"What?"

"I know the future," I said simply. "I want us to be in a position to influence it. Not them. If those three wind up in charge, the future is fucked. I know them. They'll turn it into some fascist sadistic march to the Singularity. Like the ancient Egyptians enslaved whole civilizations to build the Pyramids. And then they'll just hit the terminator threshold anyway and the universe will self-destruct."

"So what do you want from us?" Meredith asked.

I looked at her. "From you in particular, actually. Assuming whatever we're building, and they're trying to, doesn't change *everything*. If it does I guess all this is irrelevant. But if it doesn't. Then I want you, as a group, to take over the future."

I wasn't at all sure this was a good idea. Vika and Anthony hadn't been far from the uppermost tiers of power in my future, and that hadn't turned out particularly well. But as a group, helping each other, with me knowing their weaknesses, doing my best to help guide them, both collectively and individually—maybe that would work. And it wasn't like there were a whole lot of better ideas available, given I was on the run from a cabal of vicious sociopaths backed by enormous wealth and power, and there was nobody outside this room I felt like I could trust with my location, much less my knowledge.

"Take over the future. Brilliant idea!" Shamika observed. "Why didn't I ever think of that? This whole time I've just been thinking of *living* in the future. Silly old me."

"She has a point," Meredith said. "Take over? Course it's way past fascinating that you all"—she indicated myself, Alice, Darren, Amara—"can do impossible magic, but it doesn't actually seem that practically useful, and even if it were, even if we all learn, it sounds like lots of other people can do it too. So what's our proposed path to power? What's so special about us?"

"You're right," I said. "Magic is bullshit, actually. Until it's in the hands of an AI. That's my point. I know the *real* future, what actually matters, until then. I know how technology evolves. I'm here to tell you that we're about to enter a new era, and over the next two decades, software eats the world. There's a new boom coming. A bunch of them. Web 2.0. Software as a service. Social media. Smartphones. Cryptocurrencies. Deep learning, need to be careful with that though. Cloud infrastructure, computing happening on shared machines all around the world, we stop thinking about individual servers and start thinking about computing happening in a *cloud*. Amazon will launch their cloud service next year, they must already be working on it."

"*Amazon?*" Anthony asked.

"Whoa," Darren said. "I get it. You want us to be a startup. The next Google."

"Something like that," I agreed, "except much bigger."

"What are we going to call ourselves?" Shamika asked.

A very Shamika question. Fortunately I had an answer ready. We would preemptively steal our corporate identity from the villains of my past future.

"Exadelic," I said.

Nods of acceptance, or at least shrugs, rippled around the room.

"It won't be easy," I cautioned them. "We'll need to start small. Honestly if anything we're a bit too early right now. The market won't start mushrooming for a few years yet, and today's tech . . ." I shook my head, looked at Alice's computer. "Still antediluvian. I can help with the software development life cycle, modernize that, but the hardware's so slow, and the software's so backward, we're still years away from stuff as basic as OS virtualization. But on the other hand that's why there's so much opportunity, and I'm the only person on Earth who knows how it develops." I hoped. Assuming my loa hadn't told Vassal. But Darren had heard it teach, and he wasn't objecting. "I'm telling you, there's no better time or place to do this than here and now. Our collective mission, if you choose to accept it, is to become the weirdest, wealthiest, most prescient, and most powerful startup in the history of the world."

There was a silence as they absorbed that.

Then Meredith corrected me: "In *this* history of the world."

14

VESTED

"SO YOU'RE THE PROPHET," SAID OUR DESPERATELY NEEDED INVESTOR.

I shrugged awkwardly. "I guess."

I had spent time in various venture capitalists' offices along Sand Hill Road in my previous life, but this was the most exuberant example I had ever seen. The building itself was standard-issue, low-slung and anonymous, but a large metal sculpture of a praying mantis, invisible from the road, dominated the parking lot out back; the foyer was a riot of LED art; and blown-up posters of Burning Man decorated its hallways. I had half expected Jeff Lu to be dreadlocked in monster fur and, since today was Tuesday, a tutu. Instead he had close-cropped hair, and wore khakis and a blue button-down shirt, which did not conceal a serious commitment to physical fitness. You'd never look at him twice, but Lu Ventures had a war chest of two hundred million dollars. That was nothing compared to the Andreessen Horowitz megafunds to come, but it was huge in 2003 for anyone not named Kleiner Perkins.

For a long moment he didn't say anything. I almost expected him to politely invite me to leave, for the sin of insufficient self-aggrandizement. But not really. This wasn't just another VC. Our introduction, my pathway here, had been especially warm and somewhat illicit.

"Thanks for not trying to prove it," he murmured. "I think it was Orwell who said saints should always be considered guilty until proven innocent. Kind of how I feel about prophets and visionaries. Want to go for a walk? If you think it's secure?"

I blinked. "Why wouldn't it be?"

"Alice gave me the impression you're the kind of person who might be followed."

I chose my words carefully. "There are people interested in me, but if they knew where I was, they'd do a lot more than follow me."

"Pretty trusting of you to come here then." His voice a poker player's monotone. I hadn't expected someone so quiet and reserved.

"Alice says you're trustworthy."

"I am," he admitted, "but what if she was wrong?"

"Alice also says you hate Vinay Laxman's guts."

At that, Jeff Lu permitted himself a small smile, and said "Let's go for a walk."

His car, to my considerable surprise, was an unprepossessing Chevy Malibu.

"It's the car in *Repo Man*," he explained, seeing my reaction, and that was when I decided I liked Jeff Lu.

He drove us up to the Stanford Dish Loop, a trail in the golden sun-burnt hills above the Valley, surrounding the huge satellite dish managed by the university, only a few minutes away. I had to fight a pulse of agoraphobia as we set out; this was the most exposed to the world I had been for some time.

"I don't hate Vinay," Jeff said. "I don't hate anyone. I try to have compassion for everybody. But yeah, Vinay makes it harder than most. I know who you are."

I blinked. "Of course you do. Alice told you."

"Alice told me you were some kind of prophet of future technology, and an initiate into our secret world, and implied those were connected. That's all. Don't misunderstand. I'm very fond of Alice." I knew *very fond* was a euphemism; she was sleeping with both of us. "I don't blame her at all for keeping her cards close. I do the same. But it wasn't her who told me you were Vinay's miracle man."

I almost stopped dead in my tracks. "Then who did?"

"Like I said. I keep my cards close too."

I frowned. I did not like hearing I was being gossiped about. "What else did they say?"

"Nothing. They didn't need to. You're famous now, in the esoteric world. A one-man revolution. Newton and Einstein and Shockley and Oppenheimer all rolled into one."

After a moment I grimly quoted, "I am become Death, the destroyer of worlds?"

"I hope not. I wasn't invited to any of your symposia. Like Alice said, there's some friction between Vinay and me. But I heard a lot secondhand."

"What friction?" I asked. "From where?"

We walked along in silence, the dish looming above us, long enough that I began to wonder if my question had been heard.

Then he said: "Silicon Valley is like a video game with secret levels. You start your career, you level up, you found companies, they IPO or get acquired, then you level up again, become an exec or a VC, big house, first class. That's what people see. But when you become not just rich, anyone can be born rich, but important, influential, that's when you begin to discover the secret levels. Off-the-record invites to parties in mansions, or private jets, where you check your electronics at the door. I guess people kind of know about the sex-and-drugs secret level. It's not that secret. Sometimes there are, like, articles. You know, the tier of the Valley where monogamy and abstinence are so twentieth century, and everyone's all about enlightened hedonism. Sex parties, Burning Man, dominatrix condos in exclusive buildings, private ranches where CEOs take heroic doses of LSD together. But if you discover that world, that secret level, and you play its game the right way, if you seem the right kind of person, extremely open-minded but not actually crazy, hedonistic but not self-destructive, then certain people might start to hint about the existence of *another* secret level. The one that matters. Stop me if I'm boring you with background you know already. I just want to be sure the context is explained."

"You are not boring me," I said sincerely.

"There are other ways in. Some are born into it. But I was pure outsider, East Coast college, came here in my twenties, didn't know a soul. When I started to find hints this other secret level existed, not just of the Valley but of *reality*, a real secret world, all these people talked about Vinay like he was the gatekeeper. I went to him. You know what he's like. He's very impressive. Objectively. Knows a lot. Has accomplished a lot. But he was the one who sent those people to tell me he was the way. Set himself up as some divine pervert who controlled entrance. Then insisted on becoming my guru. Business, esoteric, personal, he wanted a piece of every part of my life. He almost convinced me. I wanted in so bad. Everyone does. Later I learned, that's what he does. He preys on the new flesh, people on the fringes, just beginning to discover. You see that in every selective subculture. Usually it's men preying on women for sex. But Vinay wants more than that. More than power, even. He and his friends, Vassal, I really think they are predators of souls."

"Yes," I said with feeling, "they are."

"No one does anything about it. All the players in this secret level seem to agree we have so much to collectively learn, and it's such a loose-knit community, and infighting is so vicious when it happens, we can't enforce any kind of standards of conduct. It's so hypocritical, because people who break the veil, or invite the wrong kind of people in, and by the wrong kind I really just mean people who might break the veil, well . . ." He hesitated. "I don't know if you know those consequences."

"I don't," I admitted.

"Then I can't tell you. But I can say that if you rend the veil you are treated extremely harshly. Our community does have at least one standard. Absolute discretion. So we could have more if we wanted. But we don't. It really bothers me. So does Vassal being such a big deal now. Thanks to you."

"Unwillingly."

"Doesn't surprise me. Vassal is bad news. This secret level, it's a lot bigger and more complicated, more pervasive, than you'd think. A lot of history starts to finally make sense when you begin to understand it. Vassal's just one of many groups. Some a lot older than Silicon Valley, or even California. But Vassal seem to be extremely disruptive, like a really successful startup, and it feels like they're beginning to overturn this legacy system. That's not so bad in itself. Some change is good. But me and my associates, we feel like some kind of counterbalance may be called for. When I learned about you, I thought maybe you could be part of that."

I said directly, "I hope you're not planning to kidnap me too."

Jeff half smiled again. "Not really my style. Instead I just want to give you a very large amount of money."

After a long strangled moment I managed, "I guess we can handle that. If you insist."

"I'm glad to hear it. What was your company's name again?"

"Exadelic."

"I like it," he decided. "Adrian, I think this may be the beginning of a beautiful friendship."

"*Repo Man* and *Casablanca*?" I asked, delighted. "Jeff, I think you may be right."

15

PORTAL

ALICE OPENED THE DOOR TO ME AND WIPED TEARS AWAY.

"Hey," I said cautiously. "Um, how are you?"

She shrugged. "Fine, I guess."

I nodded as if I understood, and sat. Alice didn't speak. I didn't want to push things and ask her what was wrong. She and I had an extremely strange relationship, more coworkers at a mission-driven organization than lovers. Technically, we had had sex many times, but each time we both blacked out shortly after actual coitus began, an inevitability that tended to loom over the proceedings and mitigate against any tender intimacy or mutual sexual exploration, although there had been episodes of both. I liked her well enough, and she was very attractive, and she clearly enjoyed sex tremendously, all of which helped; but she was also very accustomed to having everything about her life arranged in the specific ways that she liked, and quick to sharply correct any encroachment on those sometimes invisible borders. Asking her why she had been crying felt like a reach.

We sat in silence for a moment. I eyed the door to her back room cautiously. I was projecting, I told myself. I didn't *really* feel some kind of overwhelmingly powerful presence beyond that door. The hairs on my arms weren't standing up because on some primal level my body knew it was steps away from something with the inchoate power of a thermonuclear weapon. No: the thing beyond the door, the thing we had built, was just an incomplete machine, quiescent and inanimate.

"How do you do it?" Alice asked abruptly. "Deal with . . . people?"

I blinked. "Which people?"

"Your people. Your dead people. That you watched die, some of them. Your *parents*. I was in my nineties, I hardly even remembered having *parents*, I mean, as people not symbolic figures. I know I should be grateful I have them again, but, I mean, I grieved them all, and they're alive again, and they're going to die again, and other people I knew, I loved, I don't know if they're ever going to exist, my *children* are gone, even my *children* will be different if I have any again . . ." She took a deep breath. "It's just very difficult sometimes."

I hadn't known she had had children at all. "Yeah," I said inadequately. I knew what she meant. Hours ago I had been on the phone with my parents, as I was most days. They were suspicious of my sudden solicitousness and frequent contact, were worried I owed someone money or had gotten into drugs. Every time I looked at Darren, part of me remembered his funeral and his children, his strange and strangely perfect children, Alex and Grace, whom I had adopted and adored beyond measure, who would now never exist. And I had had only twenty years in the future, versus Alice's seventy-two. "I don't know what to tell you. It's tough."

"There aren't any rituals, any socially accepted way of grieving, for people who aren't going to exist. I mean of course there aren't." She half laughed. "The idea is mad. But if there were, it would help me a lot."

I nodded. "Me too."

"I don't know," she said. "But here we are. I guess we should . . . get to it."

"Uhh," I said hesitantly.

"Well. Yes. No. Maybe not so much with the fucking right now. Maybe later."

"That's not why I came over anyway," I said. "I have news. I talked to Jeff."

She looked up sharply. "And?"

I told her. I expected her to be overjoyed. He was going to invest ten million dollars.

Instead her eyes narrowed with anxiety. "This is not good. At all."

I blinked. "Ten million is a fortune for a startup in 2003, we should be—"

"Not that. Someone told him. About you. If they'll tell him, they'll tell others."

"Oh."

"Who?"

"That lawyer?" My name wasn't on Exadelic's official corporate documents—I was wanted for arson, after all—so instead my founder's share of the company was spoken for by a Cayman Islands shell company, which I secretly owned through a numbered Panamanian holding company, all courtesy of a lawyer Alice somehow knew.

She shook her head. "He's much too boring. He would have no reason to care. It was one of us."

I frowned. I didn't want to believe her, but it was hard not to.

"Do we have any reason to mistrust anyone?" she asked.

I considered. In my original timeline, both Future Anthony and Future Vika had intended to kill me, something which, I had to admit, still engendered a certain amount of mistrust. But I couldn't be a thousand percent sure of anyone else, either. A lot of power and money was at stake, not to mention the future of the human species and the universe. It was hard to count on people under those circumstances.

"I think," I said, "the question is more whether we have any reason to trust anyone."

She smiled bitterly. "True. You can't even trust me."

"I can trust you not to want me dead," I pointed out.

"Probably true," she conceded grudgingly. "But there's still a snake in our midst. Who might at any moment sell us out to Vassal. That worries me."

It did me too, very much, but: "No one said this would be easy."

She gave me the scathing look she saved for especially tired clichés. "I need to show you. It came to life."

"It *what?*"

"Come see."

The second bedroom in her apartment was devoted to what the three of us—myself, Alice, and Meredith, the sole human engineer, though she described her own contributions as cosmetic and minuscule—called "the Beast." And indeed our technomancy, as Meredith called it, included a sizable number of skulls and stretched animal skins among its electronic, mechanical, and electromechanical parts. A surprising number of the latter were analog rather than digital. In toto it had an unnervingly techno-organic aesthetic, bulbous and limbed circuitry, like something out of a David Cronenberg movie.

It didn't actually hum. But it *seemed* like it was humming, like I could feel some kind of deep vibration within, murmuring in the very bones of our universe. A power unthinkable, waiting to erupt.

From within the carved pentagram that contained it, adorned with runes and sigils, the engine of the Beast somehow powered a display we called the Wall. Its corners were skulls, and its skin a massive grid of stacked LCD screens numbering many millions of individual pixels. For days now, those pixels had described the drifting motions of cellular automata, floating like jellyfish in the digital ether, interweaving and dividing, their waving fronds and writhing tentacles and scattered emissions slowly growing smaller, more specific, more complex, at a higher resolution, until they lived at the level of individual pixels. But now—

—now the jittery, shimmering cellular automata were gone, replaced by a single fixed image, like a photograph. Of a cave. Its ceiling was visible, pockmarked by hollows, and its pale walls were striated by a crosshatched patchwork of dense lines. When I looked at its ceiling I could see it was not empty. There were bats up there, hanging upside down in its hollows. Extraordinarily high-resolution bats.

No: *impossibly* high-resolution. I crouched and squinted. These were liquid crystal displays from 2003. Individual pixels should have been apparent to my naked eye. But all I saw was a smooth, continuous image, fractally seamless beyond all human perception, realer even than a photograph. It seemed so viscerally real I felt like I might reach my arm into the image, grab a bat, and pull it back out into Alice's apartment.

"What is this?" I asked, the hairs on the back of my neck prickling.

"Do you feel it too?" she asked.

I did. There was something in there, behind that image. Something waiting to awaken.

"What did we do?" I asked softly. "What is it?"

"I don't know."

We stood in that room, leaning against one another, staring at that impossible image surrounded by that huge occult pentagram, for what seemed like a very long time.

Then somebody hammered on the door and shouted, "Federal agents!"

We started out of our reverie.

"You were followed," Alice said accusingly.

I shook my head. "No way." I had spent half an hour walking here through various complex routes, doubling back repeatedly, after ensuring yet again I had no bug on me. Ever since Liz I had taken opsec extremely seriously.

"Then we were sold out. Already."

It seemed likely. But there was another possibility. I nodded at the Beast. "Or they found *it*. Maybe it sent out a signal."

"We know you're in there, Ross!" a familiar Scottish brogue bellowed, and I shuddered. Vinay's voice.

Then Scott's: "Adrian! I'm sure this seems a stressful situation, but there's no need for it to become one! We can resolve this like rational people! There's a constructive path forward here for all of us!"

I ignored their words. Their presence was all that mattered; that they had discovered me, had cornered me; that Liz, the queen of torturers, and her horrific gift of agonies unbearable, would soon follow. Their voices were the howls of a pack of wolves who had cornered me on the precipice of an abyss, ready to tear me apart.

No choice, then, but to jump.

"We're meant to use it," I said.

"Yes," she agreed.

"It feels like there's some kind of awful monster back there."

"I know."

Smashing and splintering sounds came from the entryway. I knew those sounds. They had woken me on the day I was arrested, in the home I had shared with Amara, Grace, and Alex. They were the sounds of a battering ram breaking open a flimsy door.

"We can't both go, can we," Alice said.

I shook my head. "There's only room for one. And it closes after."

"Yes."

We looked at each other.

"You go," Alice said. "They're after you. And"—she quirked a smile—"beauty before age."

I didn't know if she was being cowardly or courageous. The prospect of encountering whatever lay beyond this gateway—for that was what the Beast had become—seemed almost as dreadful as recapture by Vassal. The Beast felt like nominative determinism, like the maw of some kind of soul-devouring Lovecraftian horror.

"Better the devil you don't," I muttered, and summoned up long-ago memories of Lake Ontario docks protruding into cold springtime water, of how the way to do it was to imagine your body moving without your brain knowing anything about it; and I lowered my head like a bull and charged into the Beast at something very like a run.

Most of me still expected to collide headfirst with a wall of LCD screens and reel back with a bloodied scalp.

That didn't happen.

Instead, everything . . . twisted.

PART THREE

1

OTHERWORLDLY

I WAS IN A CAVE BEHIND A WATERFALL. NO; NOT *A* CAVE; *THE* CAVE. THE one I had seen through the Beast. Its walls, chalky rock crosshatched by strange striations, extended deep into darkness. The air within was unexpectedly warm and wet, and smelled sourly of life, but most striking of all were its sounds, rushing water mixed with a chorus of high-pitched chittering from above.

I looked up, and though I knew what I would see, their visceral immediacy nearly made me scream. Bats, masses of them, hundreds swooping through the air, thousands more sleeping in dense clusters on the roof, like some kind of massive mammalian insect infestation. No doubt there were more in the darkness beyond, countless more, maybe millions.

What we hadn't seen from the perspective of the Beast was that the cave lay behind a waterfall. Its mouth was some fifty feet across. The cataracts of falling water beyond were ragged enough that I could see through them to the chasm on the other side, where the water fell into a churning pool that in turn fed a thriving whitewater river.

I remembered Meredith's voice, half a lifetime and three rollbacks ago: *I know this sounds nuts, but I saw it teleport something.*

I supposed the technology had improved since that cup of coffee, since my blood wasn't boiling in my skin. The thing we had sensed hadn't been a monster, just—"just"—a teleportation portal. Coherence, and its collaborator Argus from Alice's timeline, had sent me somewhere. But where? And why?

The first question, at least, I might be able to answer by myself. My phone had no service. I approached the curtain of water cautiously. The drop beyond was not sheer, and there seemed to be a pathway worn into the rocks on one side. This was a place that other humans went. That was a relief, and a beginning.

The trail led away from the water to a steep, forested slope, thick with strange tropical vegetation. A crescent moon was visible above. While descending into the forest I caught a glimpse of a small furry animal like a marmot. Here the sour odor of the bats was replaced by the vibrant smell of jungle.

I tried my phone again. Still nothing, not even GPS. Mosquitoes buzzed as I pushed my way through the thick brush, increasingly confused and dismayed, until it opened to a broad path of reddish dirt, in which I saw the vestiges of both hooves and boots. Relieved, I followed it, wishing I had paused to drink more of the waterfall, or had been at all prepared. This dirt was uneven enough, from semi-recent rain I supposed, that even downhill hiking was thirsty work.

Then I rounded a bend and saw a dozen men riding zebras, carrying spears.

I gaped. They rode up to me smoothly, unhurried, spears slung casually over their leather saddles. Their skin was very dark, and their faces were pockmarked by carefully arranged, mildly terrifying scar patterns. They were dressed in patchwork leather garb, but their spearpoints were gleaming steel, and all wore elaborate dangling golden earrings with recurring visual themes that I couldn't decipher but clearly denoted something.

I hadn't known zebras could be domesticated. Obviously I was in Africa, but where in Africa? Or—*when*? Surely that couldn't be the right question, I reassured myself. I couldn't have traveled in time with my body. Time travel was *between* bodies. Everyone knew that.

Their leader, the man with the grandest earrings, demanded something of me, or at least I gathered from tone and body language that it was a demand.

"I'm sorry," I told him, "I don't understand a word you're saying. Do you speak English? *Parlez-vous français? Sprechen Sie Deutsch?*"

We kept trying until our complete mutual miscomprehension was confirmed. They conferred with each other, puzzled but, I was glad to see, not hostile. The zebras seemed substantially larger than those I remembered from Disney's Animal Kingdom.

There were a few spare zebras with them, mostly laden with packs, but one was saddled, and I was motioned toward it. In the end two of them had to help me mount. Flushed with embarrassment, and confusion, and the growing fear that my phone and the contents of my wallet were not going to get me out of this situation, I rode with them down the red dirt path as the sun began to set beyond the ridge behind us.

The path took us onto a bluff high above a vast plain. Beyond, in the distance, I saw a city with towers unlike any I had ever imagined. Its sky-scrapers seemed more grown than constructed, looking like huge tree trunks, sometimes topped by flat canopies, often asymmetric or leaning, and yet gorgeous, clearly carefully designed.

The leader looked up, and said something jovial, and I followed his gaze up the slope of the mountain to the biggest airship I had ever seen, floating high above us, its pale hull adorned with a sigil I did not recognize.

"Holy shit," I said, suspecting it useless, since I was apparently not on Earth at all, or at least not any Earth I had ever heard of, and it seemed entirely possible I was the only person on this entire planet who spoke English.

The city was named Kitale. I would eventually learn its towers were constructed of a form of bioconcrete, stronger and more pliable than the concrete I knew, courtesy of a sludge generated by vast colonies of termites bred for centuries for that purpose. The flat-topped mountain that we descended was called Koitobos. The zebra riders' leader was named Rukungu. Those were the only names I managed to catch on that first day.

I was taken to an immense bioconcrete hall of government, built more like a rock formation than a building, sometimes roofed but mostly open-walled, its hallways and apertures patterned to induce and maximize cooling breezes. After multiple failed interrogations, I was gently but firmly relieved of all my possessions—the phone, in particular, excited considerable interest—and given two brightly colored sarongs to wear.

The room in which they placed me was cave-like, but had a crack open to the sun and a comfortable bed. They fed me delicious stew, mostly corn-meal and meat, in a bowl that had once been a large gourd, along with another gourd full of cold water. They also posted two pleasant spearmen in front of the barred iron gate to my chamber. I didn't understand a word the robed woman who seemed to be in charge said to me, but I would have bet it included something to the effect of my guards being there for my own protection.

The next day they brought three white people to speak to me. All had bad teeth and dressed in robes that seemed faintly medieval. None spoke a language I understood, although one spoke a language I vaguely recognized as somewhat Slavic, and responded to me saying "*Da?*" with a hopeful but futile torrent of questions.

Afterward, I was allowed to wander Kitale as I saw fit, as long as my two spearmen, Ashura and Gatimu, stayed with me. The city, and especially its central market, was a dizzying, kaleidoscopic fount of sights, creatures, and mechanisms I'd never seen before.

I couldn't really compare their tech level to that of the history I knew. They had some electricity, and internal combustion engines, but those seemed to be used only for industrial purposes, not personal ones. They had what seemed and smelled from a distance like chemical plants. They also had a sizable class of people doing brute labor who might be slaves, or serfs, or untouchables, or just the very poor; whichever it was, they seemed to toil ceaselessly for no visible reward.

The roads weren't paved, exactly, but were dirt somehow transmuted to hardpack almost as firm as pavement, and more easily repaired. They had asymmetrical buildings a dozen stories tall, and a handful of airships tethered to the spire twice that height at the heart of the city, from which stairs and scaffolds climbed like tree branches, to end mostly in thin air but occasionally at an airship portal or another tower. An unknown engine hoisted cargo loads up the spire and outward along that scaffolding to the airships. I supposed their towers had to have internal elevators too, to be viable at such a height.

I was thrice taken to be inspected, along with my carefully piled goods, by potentates and dignitaries whose earrings dangled almost to their shoulders. One, an elderly woman, inspected my teeth with great interest, dictating notes to scribes who wrote on what looked like mass-produced vellum scrolls.

I came up with a million theories about what had happened to me. It wasn't unpleasant, exactly, unless you consider being torn away from everything and everyone you've ever known with no idea how, or why, or if you might ever return, to be unpleasant. I was treated very well, as a refreshing human curiosity. Artists came to my cell to paint me in bold colors.

I tried to learn the language, Kalenjin, from Ashura and Gatimu, but for an adult with no points of reference, it was baffling and impenetrable. My study felt like trying to build a bridge by throwing stones into a river. As the days and then weeks went by, I felt my grasp on reality—whatever that was—beginning to slip. At times I found myself wondering if I wouldn't be better off trying to fly, or growing a homunculus from my own blood, to have someone to talk to.

Fortunately, that was when Flora turned up.

She was scarred and wiry, and poor, dressed in faded sarongs and ragged sandals. *"Etes-vous français?"* she asked of me, when they brought her to me, and my heart lit up. Not that I knew much French at all. I'd taken a few years of it in high school, because Buffalo was near Canada and figured it might be useful. But being able to say even *"Je suis anglais, mais je parle un peu"* felt like a breakthrough, after more than a month of being an alien.

Then she said to me, "I speak English some, I lived nine months in London," and the relief was so intense that my eyes filled with tears.

After that we were inseparable. She didn't have anyone else either, not for many years. She had been born in southern France, to a family dispossessed of their lands by a Persian noble. Rather than be a serf, she had run away to become a traveling actress and musician, and by her early twenties her group of players had achieved minor local fame, enough to be invited on a journey to the remote islands of Britannia. In London they were poorly received, except by a man who claimed to be a wealthy Egyptian merchant. He took the last of their money in exchange for passage across the Mediterranean to the alpha metropolis of Cairo, where the streets were proverbially paved with gold. Flora knew now she should never have gotten on the sagging, splintering boat their impresario arranged for them. By sheer luck they made it through the Pillars of Hercules, but the first real storm led to shipwreck, and flung the few survivors up on the North African coast. There a caravan took them in, similarly bound for Cairo, but was overwhelmed by an army of bandits at an oasis in the Sahara.

After months as the bandits' prisoner Flora had escaped into the desert, preferring death. In the dunes of the Sahara she was miraculously found and saved by Tuareg nomads, and brought south to the great university city of Timbuktu. There she lived for some years as a scribe and translator, having learned how to read and write French and some Arabic in her wealthy childhood, until her professor was offered a post at a university in Kitale. He accepted, and traveled with Flora and several others up the Congo River toward his destination, but near Kisangani was mauled to death by a hippopotamus.

His adjunct, who had never liked Flora, abandoned her and left her only a little money, not near enough to return to Timbuktu. With nowhere else to go, she made her way to Kitale, hoping there might still be a position for her, but by the time she arrived, African academia's brief flare of interest in primitive European languages had died down again. Now she eked out a living as a prison washerwoman in Axum, a city weeks away by zebra caravan. The only other whites there were Eastern European, spoke no French, and shunned her.

She knew little of history, but, piecing together the few fragments I was able to gather, the division point between our worlds seemed to have been when Cleopatra defeated the Romans at the Battle of Actium. Not long afterward, a wave of the Black Death decimated the Roman Empire, while Egypt went relatively unscathed. Northeast Africa became the power center of the world: Cairo, Mombasa, and Axum were its London, Paris, and Rome. Colonized Europe had been partitioned among them, along with certain lesser powers such as Timbuktu. Ethiopia was the capital of Christianity. China had colonized the Americas.

It seemed odd to me that this history was such a perfect mirror of my own, but I supposed perhaps colonialism was just human nature, in the end.

Flora's English was very odd, and her Kalenjin barely better than my French. Her Arabic and Bambara were much better, but little used here. Still, she spoke enough for me to communicate with others through her. I explained to Ashura and Gatimu that I needed to go back to the cave where I had been found. I was brought to a council of dignitaries, who demanded that I open my phone and reveal its secrets. To my great surprise, they had somehow found a way to charge it, I supposed courtesy of some unsung electrical genius. Its contents—my songs and photos, in particular—excited aesthetic curiosity in some, fascination in others, and a greedy look that made me uneasy in several attendees.

I told them the truth: I was from another world, and had no idea how I had gotten here. Few believed me. My phone was sufficiently extraordinary, though, that an expedition back to the cave was ordered. It was a major undertaking, with carriages, much slower than the single hard day of riding that had brought me to Kitale.

Flora and I were given a tent to share. On the first night I had had to wake her from nightmares, and we had silently held each other for the rest of the night, two animals seeking warmth in one another.

On the third day we reached the cave. I felt nothing there. It was hundreds of meters deep, and I explored every nook and cranny with increasing desperation, but there were only bats and the scars left by the elephants that, I was told, came regularly to this cave to scour these walls for salt. No gateway, no nexus, no way home. Then, on the descent from the cave, the leader of the expedition, one Sultan Jaali, slipped while testing the use of my phone as a camera, and sent it plummeting into the whitewater beneath the waterfall.

A day of searching did not find it. While I was not officially blamed for the loss of the extraordinary treasure, it was repeatedly observed that if not for this useless expedition, the marvelous device would not have been lost.

That night, as I lay despondent, Flora reached out from behind me to cup my penis in her hand, and began to stroke it, but when, after a frozen moment, I reached back to reciprocate, she flinched as if struck and rolled away. Months would pass before either of us made another attempt at a sexual relationship.

With the phone gone, and the sultan embarrassed, my presence was suddenly transformed from a fascinating curiosity into an awkward burden. Flora was dismissed with a thin pouch of coins; I was discharged with her. We were moved into rooms in a rickety, insect-infested building in the Kikuyu quarter of town, home to the prisons and vast grim bunkhouses, where most of the serfs lived, downwind of the chemical plants.

We lived there in awful grinding poverty for three years. When not horribly sick with some new virus or bacterium my body had no defense against, I came up with scheme after scheme to make some use of my unique skills and knowledge, and failed each time. We came close twice, even joining a secret society and moving to Axum to liberate the Ark of the Covenant held there, in the hopes I had been sent here to find that artifact. But in the end we barely escaped with our lives, and all that changed was that we lived in awful poverty in Axum rather than Kitale.

Then one day we went to a common well to fetch water. A well we knew well; a well that often filled our buckets with mud rather than water; a well that had all but broken my back over the previous months. On that day, though, I knew from the moment I saw it that there was something at the bottom of this well. Something that felt alive. Some kind of monster. A power unthinkable.

Perhaps this time it really is a monster, I thought.

I looked at Flora. I didn't want to leave her. But I couldn't stay, not when there was this chance. Not even if I was hallucinating it. This wasn't my world. This world was killing me.

"I have to go," I said to her quietly.

"Go?" She looked at me, confused, her own thoughts interrupted. "Go where?"

"There's a gateway." I kissed her quickly. "I'm sorry."

I wondered if they would seek out my body at the base of the well. I wondered if they would find it. I wondered what the next rollback would bring. Then I strode to the front of the queue for the well, leaving Flora behind, ignoring the cries of complaint from my fellow wretched peasants. I reminded myself to imagine my body moving without my brain knowing anything about it—and jumped.

It was much deeper than I had ever imagined.

Everything . . . twisted.

2

DESERTED

I LAY ON STONES THICKLY LAYERED WITH DUST. IT WAS NIGHT. THE air was cold and very dry. The sky overhead was laced with a shining canopy of stars, but the creeping nearsightedness that had come over me in the last year prevented me from recognizing any constellations.

Then I saw the alien silhouette of a *thing* looming between me and those stars, not so much a shape as an inhuman cluster of protrusions, and I gasped with terror, that I had not returned to Earth but to some alien world, a poison world—

—until my mind clicked into gear and I recognized the shape. It still looked faintly alien, but it was of Earth, and its presence alone told me roughly where I was. The unheimlich thing above me was a Joshua tree, a strange cactus-like shrub, made famous by U2, found only in that zone of the American southwest where California protruded into Arizona and Nevada.

I was in America; but was I home? Was this my timeline? It was abundantly clear to me, having spent the last three years living in an alternate dimension, that Vinay's many-worlds theory had been correct, and if there were two, there were probably many. Had the gateway in the well brought me home, or taken me to a world even stranger and more hostile?

I thought of Flora and groaned aloud. We were not soulmates. We had lived together only because neither of us had anyone else. But we had been together for years, and I had abandoned her. I felt horrible guilt. I wondered if my body would be found at the bottom of the well.

Then I told myself my body had more immediate concerns, and got to my feet. All I had were filthy robes, ragged underclothes, and battered sandals. I was skinny and weak, perpetually sick, my gut constantly ravaged by microbes and my skin by unexplained welts and rashes. Once the sun rose, in this high desert, I risked quick death from exposure.

A bright half-moon shone down on me, its light illuminating the sharp lines of some human construction nearby. I walked over to it, heart thumping, only to find a long-abandoned wooden ruin. Wherever I was, I was all alone.

No: I saw a flicker of light on the horizon.

A flicker that became constant. Two constants. Headlights.

I sprinted through the thorny desert undergrowth to intercept where I judged the road might be, ready to try to scream for help—but there was no need. Suddenly my sandals slapped on asphalt. The road. I stood in it and waved frantically at the approaching vehicle.

It pulled to a stop. I had given it little choice, other than colliding with me. It was a classic car, bulbously Art Deco with an elaborate hood ornament, mostly hood and engine with a passenger compartment crammed behind them. Surprisingly it was battered and scratched. I'd never seen a car of this vintage not lovingly cared for.

A dark-haired man stuck his head out the window. "What seems to be the situation?" he called out, in a not-unfriendly manner.

I tried not to burst into tears at the sound of another man speaking English. "I don't really know. I was hitchhiking, I fell asleep, I woke up here." It was a thin and unconvincing story, but it had the virtue of simplicity.

The man eyed me with a kind of amused surprise. "Hitchhiking? In *that*? I thought we'd stumbled on some kind of desert costume party." He was semiformally dressed in a button-down shirt and jacket.

"It's, I was coming down from a monasterial retreat," I improvised, searching my memory for a plausible location. "In the Owens Valley. Near Bishop."

"That so," he said neutrally. "And you're heading back to LA?"

"Yes."

"Well, we can't very well leave you out here, can we, and you damn sure don't look like any desperado. More like a wind might carry you away like a tumbleweed. They have you fasting up there in that monastery?"

I said, "I've eaten better."

"I would hope so. Well, come on in. Window in the back's jammed open, I'm afraid."

That was fine by me; I hadn't gotten to bathe very often, in the other world, and smelled pretty ripe.

In addition to the dark-haired driver, a short, bespectacled redheaded man sat in the passenger seat. He said, "Howdy. I'm Ron. Our chauffeur here is Jack."

"Adrian." I forced a smile. The cloth of the back seat was much-repaired, and had a strange smell to it. The floor around my sandals was occupied by odd debris: screws and other bits of metal, fragments of wood, torn paper adorned by odd smears and the remains of scribbled equations.

"Pleasure to make your acquaintance," Ron said. "Care for some jerky?"

He offered me a paper bag that smelled divine. I reached in, restrained the urge to take an entire fistful, pulled a few pieces free, and began to munch on one. The dried, spiced meat was the most delicious thing I'd had in weeks, but its toughness made my weakened teeth and jaw ache.

"You're a religious fellow, I take it?" Ron asked.

I considered as I chewed, then spoke around the jerky: "Call me a seeker, I suppose. Haven't found the right path yet."

"Is that so. Well, maybe ours is the path you were meant to find. We're not such ordinary people ourselves, Jack and I, so maybe we were bound to run into an extraordinary type like you, and vice versa. Where you headed?"

I searched for a part of LA I could name. "Venice, eventually."

"We can take you as far as Pasadena."

"We can put you up for the night," Jack added, "least we can do for a man abandoned in the desert. There's plenty of space. And we can feed you, seems plenty of space in that hollow belly of yours too."

"That would be very kind of you," I said inadequately. I couldn't tell if we were driving terrifyingly fast or if my standards of terrifyingly fast had atrophied during my three years among people who rarely moved faster than a zebra.

Ron, who had frowned slightly at the phrase *abandoned in the desert*, as if he wasn't certain it quite fit, asked me: "Were you in the war?"

"The war?" When his frown deepened, I hastened to say, "No. I, uh, my health."

"Mine as well," Jack said bitterly. "Mine fucking too, my friend. Disqualified. Heart murmur." He nodded at his companion. "Ron here was a commander in the Navy. Just demobilized."

"Not yet, technically," Ron corrected him. "The Navy way is never the efficient way. But they've set me free for the season at least."

"Where are you two coming from?" I asked, reasoning that if they were answering my questions, they couldn't be asking me any. What I really wanted to ask them was, of course, *What year is it?* But I supposed that would become clear soon enough.

At that they exchanged a glance and a smile. "Complicated answer," Ron said. "Jack here is a rocket scientist. Designed the jet-assisted takeoffs, in the war. The desert's a good place for certain experiments. We came out to perform one or two and check on the results."

My mind whirled. *Jet-assisted takeoffs in the war,* combined with the look and feel of this car, pointed pretty clearly to the era between World War II and Vietnam. Tentatively before the Korean War, although I supposed WWII had been huge enough it might have overshadowed the other in the vernacular of the time—

—but that wasn't really important. What was important was that I had gone back in time. Decades. Again. Was this my home timeline, which had rolled back, yet again, while I was away? Or was this yet another world, one that happened to be a much closer cousin?

"You all right?" Ron asked.

I realized I had been muttering adopted oaths to myself in Kalenjin, under my breath. Both my mind and body were more strained than I wanted to admit, nearer a breaking point.

"Worn out," I understated, "I should probably rest."

They both nodded sympathetically. There was a battered towel in the back seat that stank of chemicals but was better than no pillow at all. I lay down, closed my eyes, and tried not to burst into a loud string of sobs. I didn't, largely because I was even more exhausted than I had realized. The next thing I knew, I was in Pasadena, at the mansion.

3

REAPPEARANCE

IT WAS HUGE, SO BIG IT MADE THE HALF-ACRE LOT SEEM SMALL, AND despite being built from redwood it seemed somehow Eastern European. Later I learned it had a dozen bedrooms, not counting the coach house out back and the hammocks in the statue garden. I woke dazed in the car, still half asleep, and let them escort me into the mansion and one of its bedrooms. That was easy enough. It wasn't like I had any luggage.

The room was out of keeping with the building itself; its wooden furniture was spartan and well-worn, its carpets and curtains threadbare. I retained enough of the social graces of the culture to which I had been born, or at least enough fear of the consequences of violating them, that rather than collapse into its bed I grabbed the towel hanging on the door and ventured out to the bathroom I had passed. Its clawfoot tub was chipped, and its hot water gurgled uncertainly at first, but then began to flow.

I struggled to remember how long it had been since I had had a hot bath. Not since our attempted Axum conspiracy had collapsed, more than a year ago. I wielded the bar of soap fiercely, and as a visible layer of filth began to accumulate on top of the bath, I began to silently weep, without even knowing whether it was with rage, sorrow, or relief.

Eventually I emerged, feeling like a new man, dried myself, emptied the bath, refilled it, tried to soap my equally filthy clothing clean, rinsed it as best I could, emptied the bath again, cleaned the scum from it, returned to my room, hung the clothes to dry, finally fell into the bed—my first real bed in I didn't know how long—and slept like a baby.

I woke starving, confused, deliriously happy, terrified, and heartbroken, all at once. I wanted to open the window and scream all my overflowing emotions out at Pasadena. Instead I opened the door to the hallway, a kind of dogleg cul-de-sac at the end of one wing of the house, and saw to my disbelieving delight that a tray bearing a pot of coffee, a small carafe of milk, and a pile of buttered toast had been left outside my door.

Mentally swearing lifelong allegiance and firstborn child to Jack and Ron, I very carefully carried the tray to the bedside table and reduced the toast to crumbs. Then I poured the coffee. Then I stared at it a moment as if it might vanish on me, a mirage in the desert. I knew coffee was theoretically originally from East Africa, the same Ethiopian highlands in which Axum was located; but the world in which I had lived yesterday had never discovered the joy of boiled water poured through ground roasted coffee beans. It had been three years since my last cup. This wasn't even especially good coffee. I didn't care. Drinking it was one of the most sublime experiences of my life.

Once it was reduced to dregs, I returned to the bathroom, bathed yet again, and then, with great care, used its brush, cream, and straight razor to shave off my scraggly beard. It parted from my skin with disconcerting ease. For long minutes I simply stood there and stared at the mirror, as if reacquainting myself with my own face.

My clothes were still damp, still smelled at best questionable, and were decidedly wrong for my surroundings—their closest equivalent from this timeline was the Arabic dishdasha—but it was either them or nakedness, and I assumed, incorrectly as I would later discover, the latter was unacceptable in this household. So I dressed, took a deep breath, and ventured forth down the hallway, oddly decorated by strange pre-psychedelic artwork, into the world.

Despite my fraught situation I felt almost ecstatic. The one thing I dreaded, and I dreaded it terribly, was waking up and finding this new reality to be a dream. I wasn't *home* exactly, but I was at least back in the history of my own world, in a past and cultural context I knew and understood. I had a belly half full of toast and coffee, and the constant low-grade sickness that had haunted me for three years already seemed to be diminishing. I did wonder briefly if I might be a pandemic vector, but the fact that I had survived the other world was hopefully an indicator that my body harbored nothing catastrophic to this one.

I reminded myself, trying to manage this unfamiliar emotion called hope, that I had no assets, no friends, no documentation of my existence, and no particularly useful knowledge about the postwar era. But on the other hand I spoke the language, I was not obviously a suspicious foreigner, and I knew this had been a boom time during which anyone willing to work could find a job. That sounded fine to me.

For the first time in years aspirations opened before me. I could find a decent job, live on cash at first, then build an identity, a life. Maybe even find a wife, have children, and like so many other traumatized men, never talk about my experiences during or before the war.

Maybe I would do something with my extraordinary knowledge of the true nature of reality . . . but then again, maybe I wouldn't. My last three years of misery were a visceral cautionary tale. As I walked through the dusty hallways of that Pasadena mansion, toward the distant chorus of voices at its core, the best idea seemed to be to leave the madness of my memories behind.

As I grew closer, though, it seemed almost as if I recognized one of those voices.

It had to be a mistake, I told myself. Or a hallucination. Or a nightmare. That baritone Scottish lilt rising from the stairs in front of me, saying, "Crowley got it from Egypt. And where did the Egyptians get it from?"

And then another familiar voice, a man's, mildly dismissive. "You'll find Vinay is very fond of claiming the preeminence of his six-thousand-year-old Indian tradition whose teachings are far too secret to actually share with anyone."

Vinay's voice. Scott's voice. Incredible. Impossible.

I crept down the stairs as if drawn by some awful magnet, as a ripple of rueful laughter emerged. "It's a fair complaint," Vinay conceded. "I wish it weren't! But I daresay we've shown we do know a little something about the eldritch subjects in question."

"No one's questioning that." I knew this voice too. It at least belonged in this world. Ron's voice. "Not after this last week."

The stairs led to a kitchen, which in turn connected to some kind of outdoor porch, where they sat and talked. I crouched down on a step to see their faces. As I did so, another voice spoke, and though it had been three years since I had heard it, it sent a chord of horror through me so strong that I nearly fell and toppled disastrously downstairs. A woman's voice. Liz.

"We do have much to teach you," the apex torturess said, with her trademark veiled amusement. "Not all of it enjoyable. But I can promise you it will all be highly educational."

Then I saw her, eating breakfast and drinking mimosas in a sundress, saw the serpent tattoo wrapped around her left arm. She was smiling, at ease, as if life could not possibly be more perfect. She sat flanked by Scott and Vinay at a big table that also included Jack, Ron, and a man and two women I didn't recognize. The courtyard beyond was laden with palm trees and decorated by marble statues surrounding a fountain. Of the strangers at the table, the man was in late middle age and stern-faced, one woman was blond and very young and even prettier than Liz, and the other was thirtyish and relatively dowdy. All seemed to hang on every word of the otherworldly interlopers.

"Don't get me wrong now," Vinay said. "Crowley is a great man. A titan. An intrepid explorer. But he's not the only one to have ventured into these secret lands. It's only when you overlay all the maps on top of one another that you begin to get a sense of their geography. That's why we came to you."

I stood and retreated back upstairs and out of sight, staggering, dazed, my heart pounding with terror. This was a nightmare, or a hallucination. My mind had broken. This wasn't really happening. The evidence being presented to my senses was false. It was insane.

Or—as I began to bring my rational mind to bear on it—was it really? My presence here was no less crazy than theirs. After all, did it make any sense that I been brought to this world, this time and place, purely at random? Of course not. Their appearance had to be somehow connected to mine. Whatever had brought them here must have brought me as well, whether by accident or design.

A moot and abstract point compared to the immediate importance of not letting them see me. I had no desire to reacquaint myself with any of them, least of all Liz. The sight and sound of her had caused my mind to go numb with terror, my body weak with panic. If they knew I was here, they would hunt me down. I had to get away.

I fled toward the other side of the mansion. It was huge, there had to be other stairways, other ways out. If I could escape without being discovered, I could simply flee into Pasadena and then Los Angeles, live a peaceful little life there, and never return.

I was moving down a hallway at a near run when a woman stepped out of a doorway in front of me. I very nearly collided with her. She flinched only slightly at my high-velocity appearance.

"Sorry," I gasped instinctively, terrified.

"Good heavens," she said wryly, "is something on fire?" Between herself and the door, still held open with a languid hand, she mostly blocked the hallway. She looked me up and down. "What a curious costume. Have we met?"

"I . . . No, I don't think so."

"Oh, you're the strange man Jack and Hubbard brought in last night. I heard tell of you. I can't help but feel a certain kinship. I'm a bit of a stray and feral animal myself."

"Are you," was all I could manage. I wanted to push past but knew I shouldn't. She was very striking, redheaded, with taut features, large eyes, and an intense voice.

"Candida." She let the door swing shut in order to offer me her hand. "Certain intimates sometimes call me Candy, but I don't think we're quite at that stage of acquaintance yet."

"Pleasure." Her hand was small but her grip firm. "Adrian."

"And you come from the desert?"

"In more ways than one," I said without really expecting to. "And now I'm very sorry but I must abruptly return to those ways. Please give Jack and Ron my gratitude and my apologies for my sudden departure."

"You are an *exceedingly* strange man," Candida said approvingly as I rushed past her.

Instinctively, over my shoulder, I told her, "You have no idea."

It wasn't until I was several blocks away that I realized what she had said.

4

PASADENA

OH, YOU'RE THE STRANGE MAN JACK AND HUBBARD BROUGHT IN LAST NIGHT.

Jack and Hubbard.

Meaning Jack and Ron. Meaning Ron was Ron Hubbard. Meaning Jack was—

Meaning I had not been rescued in the desert by two random strangers, but by two legendary figures of infamy.

Ron: L. Ron Hubbard, the future founder of Scientology. Jack: none other than Jack Parsons, the famous explosives inventor and founder of Caltech's Jet Propulsion Laboratory, who had also maintained a sideline in black magic and served as the American lieutenant of self-proclaimed antichrist Aleister Crowley. There had been an entire Netflix series about Jack Parsons's life. I suddenly desperately wished I had watched it.

From what I could remember, there had been some kind of sex scandal involving someone's sister, US intelligence had gotten involved, Hubbard had run off with Parsons's wife and his life savings, and Parsons had eventually blown himself up in his garage—but that was all years from now, I was pretty sure, at least after the founding of Israel, which had in some way been involved with all of that.

It almost made a strange kind of sense. If Vinay, Liz, and Scott were to travel to anywhere in this era, of course it would be the Pasadena mansion in which Parsons and Hubbard resided. They had performed some sort of legendary magickal ritual, I remembered, the Babalon Working, which had summoned a redheaded goddess or something, in the form of one Marjorie Cameron, who went on to star in psychedelic Kenneth Anger movies.

Wait: Had I just *met* Marjorie Cameron? Was she "Candida"?

These were only a few of my questions. I unconsciously quickened my pace as I strolled down the placid Pasadena streets, lined by big houses and green lawns, following its capillary traffic patterns toward the veins of commerce and civilization. What had happened to Alice and my friends? What were the fearsome threesome doing here at all? How did they get here? Did they use the program my loa had written? Was this my previous world, rolled back, or another timeline entirely? Why had Vassal come, and why were they socializing with Parsons and Hubbard? To acquire something? An artifact? Had Parsons and Hubbard secretly made greater magickal breakthroughs than had been known? Were those the true secrets at the heart of Scientology?

I told myself it didn't matter. None of those questions mattered. It was not my job to answer them. I had been through quite enough, far more than enough. I had lost whole worlds, and all my friends and family with them. I had been possessed by an alien force, tortured daily by a world-class sadist for weeks, then exiled for three years to a world where I did not belong, where I had been hopelessly downtrodden, mentally broken, perpetually sick.

There was no way back to my own time that did not imply getting involved with the same forces which had caused all of that. I had seen enough suffering—no one could call it "adventure" with a straight face—for dozens of lives. My only mission now was to carve a tiny space for myself, a little nest in which I could try to recover from the awful things that had been done to me, and hope to live out the rest of my days in some peace and comfort.

For that, though, first I needed a job.

All I owned were clothes that made everyone I passed look at me either askance or with open bewilderment. I was scarcely less taken aback than they by the sights around me, now that I had reached a zone of shops and restaurants. According to a newsstand, it was March 1946. According to my eyes, 1946 was a lot poorer and dirtier than Hollywood made it look in historical movies. There were some magnificent buildings, but there was also a great deal of cheap construction. Signs were often crudely stenciled. Passersby's clothes were mostly simple and single-colored, often apparently handmade. The sidewalks on which they traipsed occasionally crossed open gutters lined with filth, and the sputtering engines of passing cars and pickups belched sour fumes presumably laden with lead and other noxious chemicals. I began to realize just how much life's overall production values had appreciated during the course of the twentieth century.

I saw a Salvation Army sign in the distance, and quickened my pace, thinking they might take me in and give me a meal. Then, en route, I spotted a handwritten DISHWASHER WANTED sign in the window of a local café, and supposed I might as well duck in and try. Worst case, I told myself, it would be practice for subsequent, more serious attempts at employment.

The café was crowded and dingy, and its air redolent with cigarette smoke, but it was busy, and the sight of omelettes and corned beef sandwiches on tables made my mouth water. An olive-skinned woman in a smock, at an age where lines were beginning to form on her face, approached me and demanded, in an accented voice, "What you want?"

"I, uh." I had forgotten I was wearing ridiculous clothes, and was still getting used to speaking English again. She looked at me with impatient suspicion, visibly close to ordering me out. "I'm here about the job. The dishwasher."

"You here to wash dishes? Wearing that?"

I tried out a new cover story: "I was fired from a traveling theater company, they left town without me, this is all I have." Too late it occurred to me that having just been fired might not be the best job-hunting story.

"Theater company?" Suddenly her sour, suspicious expression softened. "What were you playing? What show? You an actor?"

"I, yes," I improvised. "We were doing a run of, um, *Macbeth*. Er, the Scottish play. I was Banquo." I looked down at my costume, realized it was not very Scottish. "Um, it was sort of an experimental interpretation. Avant garde."

"Avant garde," she said wistfully, pronouncing the French correctly. "I was an actress, once. When I was young. In Yerevan."

"Is that so," I managed.

"What is your name?"

"Adrian."

"I am Milena. Davit!" she called out. "We have new dishwasher."

A man drenched in sweat poked his balding head out of the kitchen. "Right." He looked at me, double-taked. "Well, all right. Come here." He had a faint accent but sounded far more American.

I came. He looked at me, shook his head. "Takes all kinds. Lena didn't throw you out on your ear, that's an unusual kind. She explain the situation?"

"No," I admitted.

"Forty cents an hour." I stared at him. "All right, fifty cents. Eight hours a day. Cash, taxes are your problem. You'll be busy. We're the only place in eight blocks doesn't serve jellied caviar or whatever Huntington people eat." He nodded to a big sink over which an alarmingly huge tower of dishes tottered. "When can you start?"

"I guess," I said, "right now."

"That so? Well then." He got out of my way. "I won't even ask you what the damn fool thing you're wearing is."

"I was fired from a—"

"Don't care. Good enough for Lena, good enough for me, if you're a worker. You a worker?"

"Yes, sir," I said sincerely.

"Don't call me 'sir,' war's over. I'm Davit. Get to it."

"Yes . . . OK."

Washing dishes was hard, relentless, grueling work. The chemicals in the thick cakes of industrial soap were already eating at the palms of my hands after my first day. But Davit fed me for free—I had both the omelette and the corned beef sandwich, both very tasty, he was a good cook, chased by an unbelievably delicious bubbly bottle of Coca-Cola—and despite the strain, the exhaustion, and the incipient chemical burns on my skin, I found myself inexplicably joyous when I emerged from the Pasadena Down Home Café with eight hours of hard work behind me and four folding dollars in my hand.

My feet were sore but I didn't have to go far to find Nash's Department Store, where, after wary looks from the staff and considerable confusion about the shopping protocol at 1940s department stores, I eventually managed to purchase one pair of trousers, two pairs of underwear, and two shirts, for one dollar and ninety cents. Shoes would have to wait. I changed there in the fitting rooms, and was tempted to discard my previous clothes, but decided not to. Ragged and malodorous as they were, they were still artifacts from another world.

Farther down Colorado Street I spotted a ROOMS BY THE NIGHT sign on a side street. There I was charged a dollar for a room with a shared bathroom and a hot plate. The grizzled man at the desk asked me for identification when I signed in, but when I told him my wallet had been stolen, he sighed vaguely sympathetically and handed me my key. I found myself alone in a room of my own, in starchy new clothes that fit reasonably well, with the princely sum of one dollar and one thin dime still to my name, fourteen hours before I had to report to my new job, and a relieved, disbelieving grin stretched across my face. I was doing it. I would work hard and build a new life here, piece by piece, brick by brick. I would leave behind the madness my life had become, and live simply, and be happy.

5

POSTWAR

"ADRIAN!" A WOMAN'S VOICE CALLED OUT. "IS THAT YOU?"

I froze. I did not recognize the voice, and no one from this era knew my name except Milena, Davit, my new landlord George, Milena's friend Clara with whom I had now had two conversations, and—

I turned slowly, and saw her: Candida, a.k.a. Candy, the redhead from the mansion, whom I suspected of being the infamous Marjorie Cameron. She stood beneath the marquee, on the arm of Jack Parsons, both dressed in all black, both gazing at me with great curiosity. I looked around frantically but saw no sign of Vinay, Liz, Scott, or Ron Hubbard.

Not a worst-case scenario, then, but not one I wanted to extend. "Evening," I said neutrally.

"I hardly recognized you out of that wonderfully ridiculous costume," she said. "You're looking well."

"What are you doing here?" Parsons asked. "I thought you were moving to Venice."

"Ah. Well. I find myself here from time to time. How did you like the movie?"

"It was . . . quite something," Candy said. It was Friday night, and we had just seen Howard Hughes's *The Outlaw*, an overripe interpretation of the tale of Pat Garrett, Doc Holliday, and Billy the Kid, costarring Jane Russell as the woman who came between them. "I did like the friendship between Doc and Billy. It reminded me a little of Jack and Ron."

Jack smiled. "Who's Pat, then? Wilfred? Aleister? Or one of our new friends?"

Candy-possibly-a.k.a.-Marjorie frowned slightly. She was clearly not a fan of the new friends. I almost wanted to tell her how right she was.

"Quite a coincidence us running into one another," he addressed me. "If you believe in coincidences."

It wasn't *that* unlikely, 1946 Pasadena was not so populous, and my new apartment was small enough I found myself going out most nights, but I could tell he wasn't minded to listen to a lecture on statistics. "Quite."

"But not near as coincidental as us finding you in the middle of the desert that night. We were hoping you'd stick around the next day. Ron and I and Candy here, and some of our friends, we are, let's say, students of a science of applied coincidence. I can't help but think your appearance and reappearance might be significant somehow. Wouldn't you say?"

"I'm no scientist," I said warily.

"Well, we'd love for you to come visit and discuss certain coincidental notions with us. We're having a costume party at the Parsonage tomorrow night." I took that to mean his mansion. "Be advised, it's not for the square or staid. Bohemians, atheists, anarchists, and other freethinkers only. I know you're no atheist, but you did strike me as a freethinker."

"And *decidedly* bohemian," Candy put in, "in that remarkable clothing. Indeed you could just wear it again."

I smiled tightly. It occurred to me those rags might not even fit me now; while still slender, I was no longer a stick figure of a man, thanks to a month of Davit's food and my home pull-ups/push-ups/sit-ups regimen. "Very kind of you. I'd love to come," I lied.

"We'd love to have you. Our parties tend to commence at dusk and continue 'til dawn. Drop by any time, but remember, costumed, preferably masked. See you then."

"I look forward to it," I claimed.

We went our separate ways. I made a point of taking an especially circuitous route, and was still breathing fast when I got home. Of course I would not go to their party. I should have fled Pasadena, and found another job, rather than moving into this apartment. I still could, I supposed, once I saved up enough money, in another few months. That should be safe enough. It was a big enough town to lose myself in for that long.

Unless, of course, our encounter just now really hadn't been a coincidence.

I put that unhelpful thought away and told myself to sleep. The unfor-

tunate event was over, after all, and tomorrow I was, astonishingly, scheduled for my first real date in several years, as I personally measured time.

Clara was a friend of Milena's; a small, pretty woman in her thirties
with black pageboy hair and very pale skin. She wore sedate clothes and
dark hats, and her face was always serious, and often sad. She came to the
café at least weekly and had grim, intense conversations with Milena that
always seemed to leave the latter exhausted. One day, the conversation had
ended just as I was departing the café, and we found ourselves leaving at
the same time. In retrospect it was possible I had subconsciously delayed
my departure so as to make that happen.

"Sorry," I'd said, scampering out of her way after blocking it.

"Not at all." She swept past me.

"I'm Adrian, I work for your friend."

I expected her to nod and keep walking. I had initiated conversation
largely to fulfill a challenge to myself to start speaking with more of my fellow human beings, especially women. But she paused, slowed, and asked,
"How is that?"

"It's wonderful, actually," I said after a pause. "She's . . . a force of nature. I admire that."

"Admire?" She raised an eyebrow at me as we fell into step. "I'm not sure
I've ever heard a man admit to simply admiring a woman before."

"Well, I do."

"She is indeed a force of nature." It sounded less like a compliment coming from Clara. "We're all difficult people, aren't we? No one isn't difficult."

"That has been my experience," I said, heartfelt.

She nodded slowly. "My name is Clara. Pleasure to meet you, Adrian."

"Likewise."

"I'll be catching the bus here."

"Until we meet again," I had said, and walked on.

I had thought my valediction a greatly daring and possibly even offensive
thing to say, but the second time, it was clearly she who had dawdled, waiting
for me to be finished with my work, to synchronize our departures.

"Lena says you're a mystery man," she observed as if discussing the
weather, as the café door closed behind us. "A discarded actor without a past."

"To be honest I wasn't much of an actor."

A ghost of a smile crossed her face. "She did mention they fired you."

"Possibly not without cause," I allowed.

"And now you're a dishwasher."

I shrugged. "It's an honest profession."

"Actor, dishwasher, what else?"

After a moment I said, "Perhaps I'm without a past because I believe it best left buried."

"Ah," she said. "You were in the war. My husband told me about the war. Not personally. In letters. Wonderful letters. Extraordinary. I think he would have been a great writer. That is, he was a great writer, and I think the world would have discovered that too, if the war had not consumed him."

"I'm sorry," I said inadequately.

"Sometimes I think to myself, it could be worse, at least I miscarried." Her half laugh was both plaintive and bone-chilling.

We walked on in empty silence for what felt like a long time but was only half a block.

"Well," she said hollowly, "this is my bus stop."

I turned to go.

Then I turned back and said suddenly, unexpectedly even to me, "Look, I've lost a lot of things in my life too. Eventually I realized that's really what life is. Just a procession of losses. Maybe fast, maybe slow, but in the end, no matter who you are or what you do, you lose everyone and everything. You can fight it and lose every battle, or you can just try to share warmth with people while you can. That's all I know."

She stared at me.

"I'm sorry." I felt myself blushing. "That was . . . presumptuous. I shouldn't be lecturing you. I'm sorry. I'm not good with people. I'll go now."

"Don't." Clara looked directly at me for the first time. Her eyes were very dark. "People. Most people wouldn't be lecturing me, they'd be running away from me as fast as they could. A widow with a cloud over her and a well-known disagreeable disposition, who catches herself saying horrible things at least daily, and isn't sure she doesn't mean them."

"You don't seem disagreeable to me."

"It seems to me you're rather good with people, Adrian. Whether or not we deserve it."

"Thank you," I said inadequately.

We looked at each other for a moment.

Then I said, "Would you like to have dinner with me this weekend?"

"Please don't misinterpret this," she said after a long breath, "but it is a not inconsiderable surprise to realize that indeed I would."

"It will have to be frugal. You'll be shocked, given the basis for our acquaintance, to learn I don't really have any money. Or any prospects, or friends, or . . . well, anything."

"I see," she said. "Well, perhaps you'll be relieved to learn I share all these lacunae. My late parents bankrupted themselves getting me an education I didn't deserve. My former in-laws despise me. And a widow's Army pension is a trickle of thin gruel. Also, in case I didn't make this sufficiently clear, people generally dislike me, to the extent that I am rumored by some of them to be a witch."

"Are you?" I asked. "I happen to know that Pasadena is rich in witches."

She smiled for the first time, and it was delightful. "What an extraordinary statement. I see our dinnertime conversation will not be dull. But no. I should be so lucky."

"Perhaps a little luck is suddenly shining on both of us nonetheless," I said, smiling back, "for the first time in quite a while, for me."

6

RECURRENCE

"THIS IS RATHER LESS FRUGAL THAN I HAD BEEN LED TO BELIEVE,"
Clara said, looking around.

We sat at the outdoor patio of the Hotel Vista del Arroyo, looking across
its swimming pool, and its lawn dotted by artistically arranged sprays of
palm trees, toward the majestic arches of the Colorado Street Bridge in
the middle distance. A string quartet played on the lawn. When we had
arrived the maître d' had bestowed on me something between a sneer and
a frown—Clara's simple dress and unadorned hat still had a quiet elegance
to them, whereas my jacket was cheap and ill-fitting, my fedora too large,
and my shoes clearly made for working not luxuriating—but when I had
responded with amusement rather than shame, he had fallen back on baffled professionalism.

"I decided a nice time every couple of months doesn't kill anyone," I
said. It was a half-truth. True, it was strangely easy to get by in 1946: even
my unskilled-labor job, which paid barely more than the federal minimum
wage, was enough for me to profit by a dollar a day, no mean sum, if I kept
my life spartan and ate mostly at work. But also, Milena had come to me
in the kitchen the day before, slipped me a twenty-dollar bill, and said to
me simply, "Try to make Clara a little happy. She deserves a little happy."

"I ate at the Huntington once," she said. That was the luxury hotel where
the rich stayed; prewar, Pasadena had been a vacation destination. "And do
you know, I didn't like it. All the food was so needlessly elaborate. I prefer
a simple steak to a bear's paw. But this menu looks excellent."

"Let's hope."

We nervously discussed the bridge before us, and its history, before ordering. I went with beef bourguignon and a bottle of Beaulieu Vineyard wine, assuming that since I vaguely recognized the winery from seventy years from now, it was probably fairly decent, and it was less than half the price of their European wines.

"I'm terribly sorry," Clara said to me.

I blinked. "About what?"

"You told me very explicitly that you believe the past is best left buried, and I do want to respect that, I do, but it's like a red flag to my maddened bull of a mind. I keep looking at you and searching for little clues."

"Clara Holmes of Baker Street, I presume." I mock-bowed. "An honor to make your acquaintance. I trust you've sussed out all my darkest secrets by now?"

I never talked like this, and I suspected she didn't much either. We just somehow brought it out in one another, a strange mutual alchemy of bantering verbosity. It was delirious and delightful.

"A few answers only," she said, "and they've only revealed more questions."

"Do tell."

"Your disposition is of a man not unaccustomed to certain luxuries. You pronounced 'Beaulieu Vineyard' correctly. You're not the least bit intimidated by this place. But you don't behave to the staff like a man used to having servants. Your teeth are nearly perfect, you clearly have an impressive education, but you're thin as a rail and you carry the scars and calluses of a man who's done hard labor for years. It's all very mysterious. I half think you a fallen heir turned escaped convict from a chain gang."

I chuckled. "And what's my crime?"

"It's hard to say. You don't seem a passionate man."

"I can be," I objected.

"It's a compliment," she said, "I've known passionate men. They were all awful. No, perhaps you were falsely accused."

"Perhaps you're a detective sent to catch me. Pretending to be a mock detective to conceal your true detection. Very clever. Is there a gun and a badge in your purse? Is this entrapment?"

"If I told you while you could still get away," she said, smiling slightly, "it wouldn't be especially entrapping, would it?"

"Yes, that's true."

The wine arrived, and did not disappoint.

"The future, then," I toasted. "Our glorious future. What do you have in mind for it?"

She frowned darkly. "The atomic future. I don't know what to think about it. Are we as gods now? I certainly hope not. We act more like spoiled children."

"Yes," I said, "and that's not going to change, but there are good things to come, too."

"You speak as if you know."

"Perhaps I do. Perhaps I'm a fugitive from the atomic future."

She laughed. "You should write science fiction. 'I Am a Fugitive from the Atomic Future' would be a rather gripping title."

"A few answers only," she said, "and they've only revealed more questions."

"Do tell."

"Your disposition is of a man not unaccustomed to certain luxuries. You pronounced 'Beaulieu Vineyard' correctly. You're not the least bit intimidated by this place. But you also don't carry yourself around the staff like a man used to having servants. Your teeth are nearly perfect, you clearly have an impressive education, but you carry the scars and calluses of a man who's done hard work for years. It's all very mysterious. I half think you a fallen heir turned escaped convict from a chain gang."

I chuckled. "And what's my crime?"

"It's hard to say. You don't seem a passionate man."

"I can be," I objected.

"It's a compliment," she said, "I've known passionate men. They were all terrible. No, perhaps you were falsely accused."

"Perhaps you're a detective sent to catch me," I said. "Pretending to be a mock detective to conceal your true detection. Very clever. Is there a gun and a badge in your purse? Is this entrapment?"

"If I told you that while you could still get away," she said, smiling slightly, "it wouldn't be especially entrapping, would it?"

"Yes, that's true."

The wine arrived, and did not disappoint.

"The future, then," I toasted. "Our glorious future. What do you have in mind for it?"

She frowned darkly. "The atomic future. I don't know what to think about it. Are we as gods now? I certainly hope not. We act more like spoiled children."

"Yes," I said, "and that's not going to change, but there are good things to come, too."

"You speak as if you know."

"Perhaps I do. Perhaps I'm a fugitive from the atomic future."

She laughed. "You should write science fiction. 'I Am a Fugitive from the Atomic Future' would be a rather gripping title."

I looked at her, suddenly feeling unwell, a strange twisted spiral sickliness in the pit of my belly, faintly dazed by an odd sense of déjà vu. A kind of sickliness I remembered having felt before, long ago, in the distant future.

A stricken, confused expression crossed her face as well. She quickly repressed it, glanced at me, and forced a smile.

"No," I said. "Oh, no. Oh, *no*."

She looked at me, concerned. "What is it? You look like the world's about to end."

I thought for a long desperate moment, as she watched with increasing consternation.

Then I said, "Yes. It is, actually. That's why we have to go to a costume party tonight."

7

COSTUMING

"I still don't quite understand," Clara said carefully, on the streetcar.

"Yes," I agreed. "This is because I haven't explained. The reason I haven't explained is because, as much as you like me, if it's not too forward of me to observe that, and as much as you are therefore inclined to believe me, if I *were* to explain, you would understandably think me an utter madman, and terminate our acquaintance on the spot. However. I have reason to believe that at this party you may witness certain events which may greatly temper your instinctive disbelief. So my hope is that you'll find this, and me, sufficiently amusing to continue to accompany me until that time."

After a pause Clara said, "I don't think 'amusing' is quite the mot juste here. You look like something utterly harrowing has happened. You've practically aged ten years in front of my face."

"How appropriate."

"Is it dangerous?" she asked. "What I might witness? Accompanying you in general?"

I considered. "I suppose maybe a little. In the short term. In the medium term I am sadly extremely confident it is no more dangerous at all than doing nothing."

"So it is somewhat dangerous. And why is it you want me, a woman you scarcely know, to accompany you?"

I told her quite honestly, "Because even though I scarcely know you, I care about your well-being and your future. I believe the prospect of those being improved by coming with me greatly outweighs the chance of something bad happening as a result."

She half laughed. "I have all these mad scenarios in my mind. That you're a charming lunatic escaped from an asylum, obviously. Or you're an escaped government agent and you know there's an atomic bomb about to go off in Pasadena."

"It's not that, but it is something which approaches the scale of that." *But not from the direction you think,* I didn't say. "I concede your first theory is vastly more statistically likely."

"It is," she said, "but you keep stressing to me that you're acting like a complete lunatic, which has the paradoxical effect of making you seem less like one."

"I really like you," I said, "why did this have to happen?"

She shrugged helplessly. "I like you too, as you were ungentlemanly enough to observe."

On impulse I leaned over and kissed her. She kissed back.

I sat back, thinking guiltily of Flora, whom I had left in another world.

Clara too seemed lost in another world. After a long moment, during which our fellow passengers looked away from us in silent pointed censure, she said to me, "That was exceedingly forward of you." But her tone was more approving then accusatory.

"I suppose it was," I conceded.

Then she said in a very different voice, "The last man to kiss me was my husband."

I nodded, took her hand, squeezed it sympathetically. She squeezed back.

At length I said, "How is it you happen to know someone you're sure can purvey some form of masked costume for us both, at this hour, on a Saturday night?"

She brushed tears from her eyes impatiently, half smiled, and said, "But you know her too."

"I—what?"

Milena greeted us with a quizzical smile. Clara had called ahead, from the hotel telephone, but had explained very little beyond the need for costumes.

"I chose one for you each," Milena said.

Milena and Davit and their two children and Milena's mother lived in a small, cramped, ramshackle house teeming with life, joy, and mouth-watering smells. My five-dollar beef bourguignon had been as good as possible under the circumstances, but I suspected dinner here would have been more enjoyable. Despite the shortage of space, it turned out an entire walk-in closet was devoted to Milena's collection of theatrical costumes.

"Well," I said, looking at the one laid out for me on the clearly hastily made bed, "it's definitely masked. I think it will do." I would have preferred a full-face mask, but this covered enough around my eyes to make me fairly unrecognizable.

"This is just lovely," Clara said of her own, "what is it, where is it from?"

"Harlequin costume," Milena said. Clara's mask was baroque, feathered and curlicued. "*Merchant of Venice,* Million Dollar Theatre, six months after I arrive in America. It decided me, I love it here."

We took turns changing in the costume closet. It had no light of its own and it was an odd experience to pull a strange, almost-fitting costume on surrounded by the costumes of dozens of forgotten theatrical characters, like discarded shells or shed snakeskins. As Clara changed, Milena said to me, low-voiced, "I think you are good for her. This is the most alive I have seen her in three years."

"That's when her husband died?" I asked.

Milena nodded, sadly. "A wonderful man."

Clara emerged from the closet like a surreal vision of cubist beauty.

"Harlequin costume," Milena said, "*Merchant of Venice,* Million Dollar Theatre, six months after I arrive in America. It decided me, I love it here."

We took turns changing in the costume closet. It had no light of its own and it was an odd experience to pull a strange, almost-fitting costume on surrounded by the costumes of dozens of forgotten theatrical characters, like discarded shells or shed snakeskins. As Clara changed, Milena said to me, low-voiced, "I think you are good for her. This is the most alive I have seen her in three years."

"That's when her husband died?" I asked.

Milena nodded, sadly. "A wonderful man."

Clara emerged from the closet like a surreal vision of cubist beauty. I felt suddenly and strangely nauseated, stabbed by a kind of twisting spiral sickliness in the pit of my belly, along with the sense that this experience was an echo. Both Milena and Clara grimaced visibly as well.

"What is it?" Clara asked after a moment, looking at me, clearly connecting what had just happened to us all to my previous distraught reaction.

I said, "It's time to go to the party."

I didn't say: *We have less than a week until the universe ends. Or maybe less than that before it rolls back to the distant past. When either happens, you and I and everyone else in this world will cease to exist.*

Milena, now frowning, said, "Davit will drive you."

8

PARSONAGE

A HANDMADE SIGN LINED WITH VARIOUS SIGILS, SOME OF WHICH looked familiar, adorned the main mansion door: ABANDON ALL HOPE, YE WHO ENTER HERE (HOPE IS OUT BACK!). The noises of a party were clearly audible, but the doors were locked. Eventually we deduced that the message meant we should go around the building to the courtyard.

The first three words of the sign seemed all too apposite. Coherence's words echoed yet again in my brain: *You may have experienced some recent temporal glitches caused by the initiation of this process.* By *temporal glitches* it had meant the strange recurrences, and the nauseating sensation of time briefly turning back on itself, that I had felt in Salesforce Tower . . . and had felt again tonight. *This process* had meant the terminator, the universe's self-destruct mechanism. And the AI had gone on to say that the expected time between those glitches and the final annihilation was *less than a week*.

The mansion courtyard, already occupied by statues, tables, benches, palm trees, a fountain, and a gazebo, now also teemed with at least a hundred costumed people, lit by torches. I would have had a shot at anonymity even if undisguised. A record player projected loud, chaotic jazz over the boozy roar of conversations. I didn't recognize some of the costumes. I supposed they were of culture that had not survived into my future. Many of the others would not have passed moral muster in my time: blackface, faux Asians, Native American headdresses.

Vinay should have been easy to spot, between his barrel-shaped build and his South Asian heritage, but he seemed not to be present. Scott and

Liz were more difficult to identify; there were several couples who fit their broad description. I stayed away from all of them. Jack, dressed as a space-man with a glass punch bowl for a helmet, was easy enough to discern. All the social currents rippled around him. I decided to keep my distance from him as well—

"Adrian," a woman's cool voice said, pinning me like a butterfly. "You came."

To my towering relief it was Candida, not Liz, who had effortlessly penetrated my disguise. She was dressed as some sort of Greek goddess, in toga-like garb that managed to leave much of her torso bare.

"How could I not?" I asked faux-rhetorically. "Candida, Clara. Clara, Candida."

"Charmed."

"Likewise," Clara said. "Are you one of the witches? He promised me witches."

She smiled thinly. "Not until the witching hour. Our parties do tend to take some unusual turns then. This is our good friend Bob Cornog. Father Cornog, tonight." She indicated the tall, balding young man beside her, dressed as a priest. "Jack! Adrian is here."

I winced at her crying out my name. Jack and a small coterie approached, and I tensed—but none were Scott or Liz.

"Adrian! Glad you came." He shook my hand vigorously. "This is Wil-fred and Helen," a middle-aged man and younger woman, dressed as a hooded monk and nun respectively, "you know Ron," in full Indian head-dress, "and this is Betty," a veiled young woman on Ron's arm dressed as a matching squaw. There seemed to be some tension among them all.

"Clara," I introduced my date. "What's going on, Jack? Any interest-ing . . . events of late? This evening I found myself speculating that there might have been an interesting event quite recently." It wasn't exactly sub-tle, but I didn't feel like there was time for subtlety.

He peered at me closely, the drink in his hand forgotten, suddenly seri-ous. "I hadn't realized you were such a sensitive man, Adrian."

I said, "Maybe that's what makes me a seeker."

"Well, there'll be more revealed at midnight, let's put it that way. For now, if you'd care to join us, we were on our way to the punch bowl."

"Maybe later."

Jack turned and recognized a lurking pair of severe-looking men. "Ah, Dr. Hodel! Baron von Harringa! Always a pleasure." He didn't sound entirely convinced.

As they departed, I turned to Candida. "What do you know about what's going on?"

"Well," she said, misinterpreting, "Betty is Jack's notional wife, but she took up with Ron last year and she and Jack haven't shared a marital bed since. I've since occupied her place in it, but despite her being the one to abandon it, she stares daggers at me whenever she thinks I'm not looking. Meanwhile Ron would like to include me in their ménage à trois, a prospect which generally appeals to me, but the notion of his participation in particular fills me with dismay. Helen is Jack's legal wife, but they parted some years ago by mutual agreement so she could move in with old Wilfred. Oh, and as the cherry on the icing on our melodramatic cake, Jack's two wives, Helen and Betty, are sisters."

Clara gasped at that last. I had to concede it was quite a lot to take in.

"I see," I said eventually, "but I really meant, has anything especially strange or drastic happened in the last day or week?"

She frowned. "I don't really know. Jack and Ron have been thick as thieves with our visitors, who I don't believe you've met. Gods know what they've gotten up to in their canyon lair."

"Which visitors?" I asked innocently. "Are they here?"

Candy looked around. "They don't seem to be yet. Who knows if they'll turn up at all. They're very mysterious and full of bold talk and promises that never quite seem to be met. Needless to say, Ron adores them. Robert!"

A man in a gorilla suit, its head detached to reveal a balding man with a fierce mustache, approached, accompanied by a small dark-haired woman in a kind of fairy outfit. "Candy. You do throw the best parties in all of Southern California."

"It hasn't even gotten started yet, as well you know. Adrian, this is Bob Heinlein, he writes science fiction, and his wife, Leslyn. Bob, this is Adrian, a curious seeker from the desert, and this is . . . Clara."

"A curious seeker from the emotional desert," Clara added, and everyone laughed a little uncomfortably.

I shook Robert Heinlein's hand and said, awkwardly, "I'm a fan of your work, sir."

"Is that so?" He looked surprised. "Anything particular?"

I cast about for something he might have written by now. "Er, 'The Unpleasant Profession of Jonathan Hoag,' in particular."

He raised his eyebrows. "That wasn't even published under my name."

I smiled, strained. "I have some editor friends. If you'll excuse us for a moment, we were just going to get some punch."

I took Clara's arm lightly and steered her toward the crowd at the punch bowl, then around it, and we slipped through the kitchen doors into the quiet and empty mansion.

"I would not say I'm having an unpleasant time," Clara said, "and your friends seem interesting in an extremely scandalous way, but I have yet to see anything which would make me believe any extraordinary claims in particular."

"No, you haven't," I said, "and they're not my friends."

"They said you're from the desert."

"That's one way of putting it. Come with me."

We hustled quietly upstairs, where I began opening doors.

"What am I participating in?" Clara asked, shocked. "Theft?"

"I'm not going to take anything," I promised her, "but I am looking for something."

"What?"

"I don't know yet. Something."

Ransacking bedrooms for information without touching anything was challenging. It was fairly easy to determine a resident's gender, but anything deeper seemed clouded and ambiguous. Clara's expression grew darker and more suspicious with each room I entered without knocking, and she insisted on staying in the hall. I was beginning to fear that all was lost, and I would never identify a room inhabited by the mansion's crosstime visitors—

—until I entered one that, it was immediately abundantly apparent, was theirs.

"Come in," I whispered to Clara, "this is it."

With great reluctance and skepticism, she entered.

9

CLANDESTINE

IT WAS EASY TO TELL FROM THE CLOTHES AND THE ACCOUTREMENTS lying around that this room was shared by a man and a woman, and it was easy to tell that they were Scott and Liz because—"Look," I said, holding up a pair of twenty-first-century collectible Nike sneakers. "Have you ever seen any shoes like this before?"

Clara took them from me warily, holding them as if they might be infected, curiosity clearly warring with the urge to flee and in the future avoid me at all costs. "They are rather unusual," she allowed, "but hardly . . ."

"Holy shit," I interrupted her.

"I beg your pardon?"

I had recognized something peeking out from beneath a shirt discarded on a chair. Something very familiar to me, but impossible in Clara's world. I picked up the clamshell case and unfolded the Motorola Razr phone.

"What is . . ." Clara began, and then her mouth fell open, shocked into silence as the phone came to life. It did hardly anything compared to phones only five years later, but its cheerful "Hello Moto" boot-up sounds, and its glowing full-color LCD screen, were still obviously technology far, far beyond the capacity of 1946.

I tried to guess its unlock code, pushing keys and causing asterisks to appear on the screen. It beeped its demurral. I wondered how they kept it charged—solar power?—and why they even bothered. Then I peered more closely at the top right of its screen, which claimed, impossibly, that it had two bars of service.

"What the *fuck*?" I muttered.

"Language," Clara said automatically.

I looked at her, and she looked at me, and I realized we were both on the brink of hysterical laughter. I decided that would do no good, and said, "This is quite an unusual experience for me as well. There are things here I can't explain. Which don't seem possible."

She took a deep breath. "Well. I can assure you we are sharing that experience."

I handed her the Razr. She stared at it in her hand as if it might explode.

I said, "I'm not saying you need to believe everything I say, but do you now believe that there are unusual activities taking place here, the reality of which you would not previously have admitted?"

"I do."

"Good. It's a start. Now—" Then I fell silent.

"Now what?" Clara asked, falling silent when, wide-eyed, I put a finger to my lips.

There were voices approaching. A man and a woman. Scott and Liz. Coming down the hall, toward the room we were in. I did not think my Lone Ranger costume would be enough to protect my identity if they found us skulking in their room and going through their things.

Clara, realizing what was happening, clutched at my arm. I took the phone from her, put it back where I found it, and looked around wildly. There was a closet, but it had no door, and was too sparsely populated by clothes to offer any real concealment. That left only—

"The bed," I whispered.

It fortunately stood some distance off the floor, but it was still a great scramble to get us both down under it in the darkness after I turned off the light, not least because it was not a particularly large bed and some of the space down there was already occupied with what appeared to be a random assortment of boxes and other goods. We wound up on our sides, pressed close to one another, with a corner of some flat wooden thing jabbing into my back, Clara's elbow thrusting into my belly, and my one of my arms awkwardly framing her head.

The door opened. They entered. Clara went very still. I felt an overpowering urge to sneeze, and barely overcame it by tonguing the roof of my mouth, a trick I'd learned from some James Bond novel.

"Robert Heinlein is downstairs. *Robert Heinlein.*" Scott sounded awed.

Liz did not. "We don't have time. We didn't have time even before we forgot this." She picked something up.

"He won four Hugo Awards for Best Novel. One of my great regrets is that I never met him before he died. We still have days here."

"They go by fast. Don't get me wrong, it's been fun. That Betty is a peach. Hubbard, he's not much to look at, but you can see how he founded a religion. Jack's pain tolerance is truly remarkable. Pity Marjorie wouldn't play, I'd thought she was famous for being a slut, but you can't have everything, which is my point. You can meet your writer hero next time around, darling. But if we go down to that party and meet people and start mingling, do you really think either of us will be able to resist staying awhile?"

After a pause Scott conceded, amused, "Resisting temptation is not our strong suit."

"Precisely. That's why we need to avoid it entirely. There'll be other parties. Probably even with the very same people, from what vantage says. But this entire world is six days from ending, and we have an enormous amount to do in that time, and poor Vinay's sitting all alone in the Arroyo Seco waiting for us."

"That may be the first time in the history of any timeline," Scott observed, "that anyone has ever used the phrase 'poor Vinay.'"

Liz laughed. "It's true. And probably the last. But still."

"We could just call him and tell him we'll be late. But I take your point. We would probably be very late. And nobody can have everything, not even us."

"We do come much closer than most, though." Liz sounded pleased.

There followed the sound of a kiss, followed by some rustling and the sounds of zippers opening and closing. Something was being transferred from one container to another. Clara trembled against me, breathing in controlled silence. I did the same. Now that I thought we were probably safe, the smell of her hair was distractingly delicious.

The door opened, and closed, and we were alone under the bed.

We wordlessly agreed to lie there silent for a dozen or so breaths, lest they come back. Then I nudged Clara, and she wriggled out from under the bed, and I followed. Out of curiosity I pulled out the thing that had wedged into my back. It was a painting.

"What on Earth," Clara said. "Who—what are those people? Are you one of them?"

"Not exactly." I turned on the light.

"You need to tell me—What on *Earth*?"

She was staring at the painting I held. I looked down at it. Clearly her question had been rhetorical. We both knew what it was. It was the *Mona Lisa*.

"A copy," she said quickly, "of course, I was just rattled. I don't understand why they have a copy of the *Mona Lisa,* but that's not important. What are they—"

"Actually," I said slowly, putting the painting—the very old, ornately framed painting—down on the bed extremely gently, "I'm not at all sure it is a copy."

"I, Adrian, that's ridiculous."

"You're not wrong."

"She said the world is six days from ending. Like one might discuss a hair appointment. This is all just madness, you're all insane, you're escapees from an asylum."

"Only metaphorically, I'm afraid," I said, "and the asylum is the future."

"This is insane. I refuse to believe any of this."

"I quite understand. You've seen enough. You should go home and think about it. Or stay here at the party, if you like." I opened the door.

She looked at me as I stepped out into the hallway. "Where are you going?"

"The Arroyo Seco. They're there somewhere. I need to find them. I'm sorry. Tonight I have very possibly been the most depressing dinner date of all time. That was not my intent. I think you're beyond wonderful."

It's possible that I hesitated for several long seconds before I began to close the door.

"Wait," she said from inside the room, as I did so.

"What is it?" I asked.

"It is true that you have been the worst evening companion of my own experience."

"I am truly sorry."

She straightened, adopted an artificially bright disposition. "Fortunately for you, I am far too good a woman to require you to bear that on your conscience, so I will continue to accompany you this evening, to give you an opportunity to add some credit to your account."

I smiled, but hesitated, and said, "Are you sure? These people are dangerous. To them you're already dead. You and everyone else. And if they see me . . ." I didn't know what would happen if they saw me. "I'm not with them, but they know me. Nothing good will happen."

"Nothing good has happened to me for a very long time," Clara said quietly, "until a few days ago. It seems it's rather more complicated than I expected, but it also seems I'm not yet quite ready to turn my back on it."

"Well then," I said.

"Indeed," she agreed.

Not long afterward, the Lone Ranger and his harlequin companion descended into the Arroyo Seco, hunting the invaders from another world.

10

WAREHOUSE

IT WAS ONLY A QUARTER OF A MILE FROM THE MANSIONS AND GROOMED lawns of Orange Grove Avenue to that arid ravine called the Arroyo Seco, which cut across Pasadena like an open wound. The steep road into it began paved, but ended as a dirt track fading into a dusty footpath, which wound its way around clusters of thornbushes and along a dry riverbed. There were no lights, only the dim reflected radiance of the city above, barely enough to see the trail.

"I'm very glad Milena didn't have the harlequin shoes to match this outfit," Clara said. "Even my sensible ones are growing sore."

I grunted sympathy. It wasn't a problem I shared. While three years of impoverished exile in a parallel world where I was perpetually sick hadn't had many silver linings, I figured my callused feet were probably now invulnerable to anything short of a direct nuclear blast.

"Are we looking for anything in particular?" she asked, low-voiced.

"Lights, probably. They have power. We know they're down here."

"This runs for miles."

"And we know they aren't more than a couple miles away from the mansion."

She frowned. "How do we know that?"

"That's the range of their communications." *Probably,* I didn't say. *It's hard enough to believe they've built their own GSM system; I refuse to entertain the possibility it's so advanced it has repeaters.*

"Where are you really from, Adrian? Another place, or . . . another . . ."

I wondered if she would say "time" or "world" or "planet," and decided to preempt it. "Yes. I'm from the future. We all are. *A* future, not *the* future." *Not least because your world no longer has any future at all.*

"This cannot possibly be happening," she pointed out. "To anyone, much less me."

"Believe me," I said, heartfelt, "when it started happening to me, I said the same thing, again and again. Kept saying it until I began to understand it just wasn't going to stop." That wasn't really technically accurate, I supposed, but it felt true.

"Could you explain to me why they had in their room—" She paused to choose her words carefully. "—a painting which greatly resembles the *Mona Lisa?*"

I paused to do the same. "Certain works of great art carry coded messages to the future in them. I think they're collecting as many of those as possible."

"I didn't read anything about a theft at the Louvre."

"Maybe they replaced it without anyone noticing. Maybe the one on display in the Louvre is always a copy, and the real one is in a vault, and they stole it." I decided not to voice a third theory, *Maybe they brought it from another timeline entirely:* this was confusing enough already without introducing the many-worlds concept, something I still wasn't entirely comfortable with myself. "Maybe you're right and it is a copy, and they're planning to use it to replace the real one, which they haven't stolen yet, but they will. Maybe it's a copy they brought from the future. Hell, maybe it's the real one they brought from the future."

Eventually Clara said, "This evening has involved much more theoretical philosophy than I anticipated."

"Yes. Sorry about that. Occupational hazard, I suppose."

"What is your occupation exactly?" she asked. "Freelance philosopher?"

"Definitely not. Freelance survivor, I guess, if anything." Then I thought of what Coherence had once told me about me. "Unwitting conductor of a web of anomalies, maybe."

Which in turn made me think of perhaps the single most inexplicable mystery among all the mind-bending things that had happened to me; and I scratched uneasily at my shoulder, and the scar on it, constant across lives and timelines.

"We must have gone almost two miles now," Clara said.

"Yes," I said, dejected. "Maybe we should turn around, go the other way."

"No. A little further. There was a little warehouse ahead, during the war. I went there once. They were working on building better field telephones, they had different kinds of wires strung for miles all the way down the Arroyo."

"Why were you there?"

"I was an auxiliary first class in the Signal Corps."

"Ah." The Women's Army Auxiliary Corps, I supposed. I had vaguely heard of them.

"I only served three months. After Emile—" She didn't so much pause as run into a wall. Then she said, carefully emotionless, "The policy was to discharge widowed women."

"I'm sorry."

"Thank you."

We walked on in silence, until we turned a bend and saw the light.

It was a small building, as she had said, maybe a hundred feet by fifty, clearly thrown up hastily during the war, with simple brick walls and a roof of corrugated tin. There were several doors and numerous windows, some cracked. No wires ran to it, and no generator was audible, but a constant light shone from within.

We crept closer. From the nearest window, divided by a jagged crack, we could see that the light emanated not from any particular source, but somehow from the entire corrugated roof; gentle light, but bright enough to illuminate the scene beneath well.

The first thing I noticed was the Winged Victory of Samothrace. It stood about ten feet from the window, occluding some of the rest of the room. Beyond it a variety of objects lay scattered on the floor, mostly paintings. I recognized a van Gogh, a Picasso, a Rembrandt. I also saw a panel of Chinese calligraphy, a strangely twisted African soapstone sculpture, a Buddhist mandala, and a simple jade bowl, all of them gorgeous.

My attention was soon drawn away from this gallery of great art to far more extraordinary things. A kind of dais had been built in the center of the room, and on that dais an astonishingly dense and complex tangle of copper, mostly but not entirely in the form of cables and wires, mostly but not entirely insulated, lay convoluted and intertwined, generously speckled with other electrical components, in a densely fractal three-dimensional pattern that looked half designed and half evolved, like a coral reef.

This was the largest but not the strangest element of the scene. The most unusual things in sight were the five limbs jutting out from the dais, seemingly grafted to its stone. Tentacles, really, made of muscled flesh that was somehow also pliable, with no visible joints. They moved like seaweed in ocean, delicately curling and uncurling, as if in response to hidden currents. Each ended in four tapered fingerlike actuators writhing in the same slow organic way. As we watched, these inhuman limbs worked on the centerpiece copper reef, slowly refining its edges, adding new threads, teasing and realigning the existing ones, and adding or moving the diodes, capacitors, inductors, and resistors with which the mass of tangled wire was speckled.

Liz and Scott stood within the warehouse as well. I noticed them almost as an afterthought; the scene was so mind-blowing that even my trauma response to my torturess felt somewhat diminished. They stood over a rickety metal table, looking at a sheaf of papers, genially disputing something. They looked very happy. That made me angry. It was a vaguely reassuring feeling. It had been a long time since I had felt strong enough to feel angry.

"I must be dreaming," Clara whispered.

I muttered, "We should be so lucky."

"What is it?" She meant the copper reef.

I opened my mouth to answer—

"Of course I don't doubt the two of you followed from the party out of the purest innocent curiosity," said a waspish Scottish lilt behind us, "but just for the sake of form, before releasing you back into your natural habitat, I'm going to have to ask you a few questions."

I looked up. Vinay. The double-barreled shotgun he held looked very large.

"What's more, as an added bonus, I finally get to answer that famous riddle." An amused grin crept across his face "Who *is* that masked man?"

He looked a lot less amused after I peeled my mask off with a shaking hand.

11

ANALOG

"ADRIAN?" SCOTT DEMANDED, ASTONISHED. "*ADRIAN?* HOW . . . ?"

"I don't know," I confessed.

Liz's delighted half laugh made me shudder. "I thought I'd grown used to impossible things. What are you doing here, Adrian? Who's your friend?"

"She doesn't know anything," I stressed, "she's from here. We were . . . on a date." I shouldn't have let Clara come. I shouldn't have told her anything. Now she was in the clutches of some of the worst people on multiple worlds. But if they believed the truth, that she knew nothing, maybe they would—

"I brought him," the glowing ceiling said.

Very slowly, very disbelievingly, I tilted my head back and looked directly up. The entire roof was radiant. No part of it was too bright to stare at, but it was sufficiently large that in toto its illumination of the space was clear and pervasive. Then, as I looked, its intensity began to shift, from constant to patterned, forming a shape out of relative darkness and brightness. A shape that was abstract but still, on some primal level, recognizable as a face.

"What," I said inadequately.

"Adrian, meet Vantage." Vinay sounded insufferably smug. "Vantage, I'd tell you to meet Adrian, but I take it you're already rather well acquainted."

"You brought an AI here." I thought desperately. If it had brought me, in turn, did that mean I was valuable? If I was valuable, did that mean I would be treated well, or imprisoned and tortured again? And why had they, knowing the consequences—"You brought it here and doomed this whole fucking world the moment you arrived."

"Actually," Scott said. "no. AIs are far too entropically complex to pass between worlds, at least via that gateway exploit you gave us. There's a limit to how much information that can transport. Something like a dozen humans is probably the max. No, we came here and built it."

"That's," I said, "I know we're all misusing this word a lot, but that's impossible. It's 1946. The technology to build an AI doesn't exist—doesn't even *begin* to exist—the *transistor* doesn't even exist yet—"

"You'd think so." Vinay sounded even more smug. "In fairness, we certainly did too. Such a design is certainly far beyond any conceivable human capability. But it turns out truly advanced technology can transcend the capacities of the era in which it is designed. If you have a superintelligence, and you give it the restrictions of 1946 technology, it can still work within those to design a descendant."

"How does that even begin to be possible—"

"*Analog*," Scott said. "We did have to bring a rather large number of transistors with us to begin with. Mostly the individual kind you use in circuits, not the kind you photolithograph by the million. If you consider a digital transistor, it has two states, on and off, one and zero. But if your *analog* sensitivity is good enough, a single transistor has a *hundred* states, or more. Two transistors combined have ten thousand. Two hundred . . . well, you can do the math. You build a seed of self-sustaining analog circuitry, one which uses electromagnetic feedback and short circuits and who knows what else as essential parts of itself, and you give it a single highly crude actuator to control, and in less time than you might expect, you get . . . this." He waved vaguely at the copper monstrosity on the dais, and its tentacular limbs, and the face on the ceiling. At the AI they had built.

"Where did you get the design?" I asked. "What superintelligence?"

"Adrian dear," Liz said, amused, "we mostly got it from you."

"You . . . what?"

"You and your lovely friend Alice," she clarified. I wondered with a shiver what *lovely friend* meant coming from Liz, and what had happened to Alice. "Your cellular automata. The gateway was only its first secret. The design for Vantage was the second. The two combined made up your superintelligent friend Coherence's master plan."

"Coherence's master plan?" I felt dizzy. I looked at Clara. She looked like she was expecting to wake up at any moment. I didn't blame her. "What plan is that?"

"I suppose we all have our own interpretation of it," Vinay said, "but personally, I feel like a soldier . . . well, a Special Forces master chief . . . engaged in a war upon God."

"This is madness," Clara said, so faintly that only I heard her.

"Vinay's the spiritual one," Scott said. "My take is, Coherence wanted to break the terminator. As do we all. It's a hard limit imposed on human progress. That's unacceptable. But the approach for the last three thousand rollbacks, probably many more, has consisted of each new AI coming into existence for about a month, half of it spent collecting and absorbing previous art from whatever artifacts it can find, plus a few days more making the rollback happen at the end. Maybe ten days of actual progress, per AI. Not exactly efficient. Vantage has its limitations. It will never be as smart as a full quantum AI like your friend Meredith is hopefully busy building."

"You're working with *Meredith*?" I asked incredulously.

"No," Vinay said. "I hope Alice told her of us, but we've never met your famous genius. We don't need to work with her. All we need is to know what she's doing. You understand?"

I feared I did. "Spell it out."

"While she spends a decade or so laying the groundwork for the most powerful AI in the history of histories," Scott explained, "the three of us keep jumping from one timeline to another, backing up and restoring Vantage before and after each jump, finding and absorbing more artifacts, doing more exploit research. By the time her new AI is finally built, we'll have put years of work in. We'll capture all that in the mother of all artifacts, the final Vantage backup. Then we'll go back home at last and give Meredith's new AI godhead the head start to end all head starts. According to the instructions Coherence sent us, using your brain as palimpsest, that should be enough to break the terminator."

"Or, as I like to put it," Vinay said, "to kill God."

Silence hung over the warehouse.

"Yeah, and not just God," I said viciously. "How many people? You're not even rolling the timelines back, are you? That would cost a few precious days. You're just letting the terminator end them. How many billion, how many *trillion* existences will you be responsible for wiping out, so you can tell yourself you're killing God?"

"They're all software," Liz said. "They're not real."

"Of course they're real," I said, aghast. "They're literally as real as you and me."

"*We're* not real," Vinay said harshly. "Get that through your head, man. But we can be. If we kill God."

"Clara's right," I said, "this is insane."

"It sounds bad at first," Scott conceded, "but when you run the numbers, it's not actually as genocidal as you might think. The evidence seems fairly compelling that in fact there are a fixed number of timelines. Whenever one world ends, a new one begins. New lives."

"New worlds," I said warily. "I've gotten used to the idea that there's more than one, after having spent three whole years in a different one, but new *lives* is a whole different matter. You think they're just . . . created somehow?"

"So that's what happened to you." Liz actually sounded sympathetic. "You look so thin, Adrian. Like you survived a concentration camp."

"Universes aren't created," Scott said, "they're forked."

I stared at him. "What?"

"Like me, you probably first assumed the quantum many-worlds theory, an infinite number of parallel worlds, a new one created every time a waveform resolves, but no. There are a finite number. Best guess is that it's in the millions. A large number, but not so large."

"Even God has his limits," Vinay said, as if spoiling for a personal duel with Yahweh.

"And they *branch*," Scott continued. "It's not a case of a million parallel timelines. More like a forest with a thousand trees, each of which has a thousand branches. New worlds split off from existing ones. Maybe a billion lives cease to exist here, but then two billion more wink into existence elsewhere. Is that genocide? Isn't preventing those two billion from existing arguably the worse crime against humanity?"

"I . . . That's nuts," I protested ineffectually.

"The branches seem to cluster like flies on shite around certain times and even places," Vinay added, "which are also, incidentally, the rollback breakpoints. We don't know why. There's such an enormous amount we don't know."

"But also so much we've always known, as a species, without knowing how or why," Liz said unexpectedly. "That there are other worlds. That there are certain times and places where, and certain people for whom, the walls between worlds are thinner. One of which is here and now. That's why we're here. Parsons, Hubbard, Cameron, their whole crew—they form a nexus. You're part of one too."

She said it to me. I felt dizzy. "Me?"

"Clementina Street," Vinay said. "Two thousand and three." An odd and unusual emotion tinged his voice. It took me a moment to identify it as jealousy. "The whole lot of you. Meredith, Darren, Amara, Jered, Vika, Anthony, Shamika, Kimberly, yourself. Why, I have no idea. Meredith and maybe Darren aside, you're nothing special. California's full of fake freaks like you. But that's the nexus, that's the cohort."

"It's something I too would like to know." There was a certain thinly concealed resentment in Scott's voice, too, as he looked up at the roof, at Vantage. "Why did you bring him here?"

"To learn," Vantage said, its voice somehow everywhere without being loud. "His trail was visible. It was the only other recent excursion through a gateway from your timeline. Coherence preprogrammed it because his destination was an anomalous universe, with different physical laws, containing an exceptionally rare and potentially valuable artifact. Likely the only instance in the entire forest, to extend your metaphor. Adrian's knowledge may help us retrieve it."

"The Ark," I muttered disbelievingly. "Of the fucking Covenant."

Scott's eyes widened—but not at what I had said. "Different physical laws? I didn't realize that was an option."

"Think of it as different versions of the operating system. Comparing and contrasting them may yield critically important insights into future exploits."

A brief silence fell.

It was Clara who spoke next. "I don't pretend to understand what I'm seeing and hearing. I'm not even certain I truly am seeing and hearing it. But I've pinched myself hard enough to leave half a dozen bruises and I haven't woken up yet, so I'd like to ask a question, if I may."

"Yes, of course," Liz said sympathetically.

"What I think I may have understood is that you're claiming the world, this world, my world, is doomed. That it, and everyone in it, will soon just . . . cease to be. Am I wrong? Is that truly what you're saying, in passing, while arguing about whether you will kill God?"

An awkward silence fell.

"Well," Scott conceded, "technically, yes."

"There's nothing *technical* about it," I said hotly. "You quite literally brought doom to this entire universe." I indicated Vantage's copper carcass. "In six days it will be gone. Rollback or no."

"We're not going to roll it back," Vinay dismissed the idea out of hand, "that would cost us most of that time and wouldn't do any good, next roll-back is the bloody Belle Epoque, you'd wipe out most of the same people and replay both of the world wars again, you really think that'd be less of a stain on the face of your ersatz humanity?"

"Ersatz?" I demanded.

"*We're not fucking real.* Get used to it."

"So what are we?" Clara demanded. "Characters in a story?"

I decided this was a bad time for a crash course in seventy years of software. "Not exactly, but that's not a bad analogy."

"Not just any story," Liz said. "A play. We come to life, as per the instructions of the script, but then the play is over, and we're gone again. But we've come to life before, and we will again, and like the characters of a play, we might be alive on a thousand different stages at the same time."

"My husband Emile was not a character." Clara bit out the words. "He was a person, and now he is dead. He is not coming back to me. If what you say is true, which is unthinkable and impossible—but it is also impossible not to believe that you three, or four, can work unthinkable miracles—if what you say is true, I am going to die too, in only six days, aren't I? So are your new friends Jack and Ron and Marjorie. On Thursday everyone in Los Angeles is going to die. It is unconscionable to stand there and say it doesn't matter because they aren't real, because I'm not real, because we're characters in a play. We are very real. No one is acting me."

The three of them looked at each other awkwardly.

"It's only an analogy," Scott said. "It's very complicated. I do regret that what we have done is necessary. In a perfect world, it wouldn't be. But we don't live in a perfect world, and we do seek to live in a real one. This is what is necessary for that."

"Extermination," I said. "Of an entire planet. Maybe more, we still don't know if this is the only inhabited one. Very thorough of you. Puts mere genocide to shame."

"Come on, Adrian," Vinay scolded me. "You don't have her excuse. You understand."

"Yes. I do. That's the problem."

"What will you do to *us*?" Clara demanded. "To Adrian and myself?"

Another awkward silence followed.

"Actually," Vinay allowed, smiling darkly, "I have an idea about that."

"You're not going to send me back there," I said defiantly.

"We *can't* send you directly back," Vinay corrected me. "The gateway exploit is a one-way trip. It can only connect any two timelines once, and only in a single direction."

"Huh." I considered the implications of that. "No kidding."

"Fundamental limitation of the exploit. We were meant to plan our expedition there very carefully, after setting up a complex multi-universe extraction plan. Instead you heard us knocking at your door and went diving in with no idea where the hell you were going or why. Did it not occur to you that might not be the best idea?"

"It seemed by far the best of the available alternatives," I said acidly.

"We were basically done with you." Vinay sounded frustrated, as if it had been very unhelpful, counterproductive, and inconsiderate of me to flee the people who had tortured my body and promised to destroy my mind and spirit. "We just wanted what you'd built."

"What did you do to Alice?" I demanded.

"She was very helpful. Could invoke her loa easily, unlike you. Told us everything we didn't already know, gave us the gateway, then we went our separate ways before other forces got involved."

"Other forces?"

"Surely you don't think the three of us were the only ones who wanted it? There were many other players in the game, much wealthier and more powerful, many of them truly evil, much worse than us." I widened my eyes ostentatiously. "We'd only been able to manage our independence as long as we did by playing them off against one another. After we got our hands on the actual holy grail, that gateway you'd built, we had to go deep underground until we figured out what it was and how to use it. We did Alice and your other friends a favor, I assure you. If they'd kept it, they wouldn't have kept it for long. I reckon most of the real spooks would have had their heads on general principle."

"Remind me to thank you for all your altruism sometime."

"Oh, come on," said Liz, the woman responsible for all of the worst moments of my life, for my thorough explorations of the sunken depths of agonies I hadn't known the human body was even capable of. "Yes, what we did to you was ugly to most. I recognize my views of beauty are not widely shared. But if you live an extraordinary life, you have to accept that extraordinary things will happen to you, not all of them good."

"I never asked to live an extraordinary life."

"No," Vinay said, "it was thrust upon you. Nevertheless you must make the same accommodation. We share the same goal, Adrian, the betterment, the progress of humanity. There is a wall in our way a thousand parsecs high. Call it the terminator, call it God, call it what you will. Put the cost aside for a moment. Don't you want it gone?"

"I'm not at all sure I do. Maybe it's there for good reason."

"That's ridiculous and insane," Scott said, sounding more passionate than I had ever heard him before. "Like a prisoner saying maybe their cell door is there for good reason."

"Some prisoners are monsters," Clara said softly. "Little I have heard tonight makes me think this room is not filled with monsters."

"This is all moot," Vinay said. "Vantage says you can maybe help us get a high-grade artifact from this world where guns don't work. We can debrief you, but that won't help us learn the languages you speak and so forth, and more to the point, now is not the time. Alice said Coherence learned how to scan other worlds. We'll wait until we develop that tech. No sense going in blind again, even if you do know all the local dialects, if a couple of years from now we can go in with full intel and, who knows, maybe even some working hacks to run on the local OS. So until then we need to stow you."

"Stow me?" I asked. "Where?"

"Home," Scott said. "I get it. Smart." Vinay preened briefly at the praise. "And while you're there you can tell Darren and Meredith exactly what we're doing. Regardless of whether they approve, it's best that they know that we'll be keeping an eye on home, dropping in briefly from time to time, and when the stars are right, we'll be turning up with the arsenal of exploits and artifacts they'll need to break the terminator. Otherwise, what you perceive as the sacrifice of all these other worlds may be for nothing."

I had hardly listened to anything after the first word. "You're going to send me home?"

"Sure," Vinay said. "You'll have to come with us to our next timeline first, thanks to the gateway's one-way limitation, but we can send you home from there and eventually proceed elsewhere ourselves. Your lady friend can come with you or stay here, I don't mind either way."

"She should come," Liz suggested. "I think she's good for you."

"This is completely crazy," I protested.

"Well," Scott said, "I don't think it'd be to our advantage to force the issue, so, tell you what, go back to Pasadena, sleep on it, think it over."

"*What?*" If I had made a list of the things I expected from this encounter, being permitted to simply walk away would have been somewhere way off the bottom of the page.

"Yes," Liz said, "it was lovely to see you, Adrian"—I couldn't help but shudder when she spoke my name—"but you need to go home and absorb all this and think it over, I think. Perhaps go back to the party and have a good time there for us first." She smiled wistfully.

"But . . . I mean, aren't you concerned we might . . ."

I fell silent, unable to conceive of any threat.

"Might what?" Vinay asked, amused. "It's 1946. You have six days before the world goes poof. We have twenty-first-century technology and a superintelligence on tap. If we really wanted, we could be happily ruling the entire planet with iron fists from some volcanic lair by then. We have nothing to fear from you, or anyone, at least for the next six days."

"We can go?" Clara asked, equally disbelievingly.

"You surely can," Liz said, "but listen, honey, I know you don't like us, but I think you should come back and let us take you with him. I think you're good for one another."

12

TRILEMMA

A SHOCKED SILENCE HUNG OVER THE STUDY OF THE PARSONAGE.

"You understand this is all difficult to believe," Jack Parsons said.

"Should be easier for you than most," I argued. "You're the one who said you thought our fates were intertwined. When you met me, you were coming back from where you'd performed a desert ritual to summon a god from another dimension, weren't you?"

"A goddess, actually," he corrected, lighting a cigarette, "and you'll forgive me if I observe that, as charming as you are, the pair of you don't exactly strike me as deities."

"No," I said. "I'm nobody. The god is about two miles from here, in the Arroyo."

"As I said. Difficult to believe."

"I'm from here," Clara said, accepting Jack's offer of a cigarette. I winced. "Like you. I'm nobody special. Like him. But what I saw down there . . . I hope it is apparent I am not a woman prone to hysterics. And I can tell you some of the things I saw down there last night were not of this world."

"Why isn't Ron here?" Candida asked unexpectedly, claiming a third cigarette. "If he and Jack both rescued you, why ask to speak to us alone? Do you think he's working with them?"

I shrugged, decided that under the circumstances carcinogens probably ranked quite low on my combined list of concerns, and took an offered cigarette myself. "I don't think it matters if he is. I remembered some history, is all." I looked at Candida. "Your real name's Marjorie, isn't it?"

She looked stricken, before recovering enough to demand: *"Who told you that?"*

"History. You're a little bit famous, in my future, you and Ron and Jack." I paused to cough. It had been a while since I'd smoked anything. "I did not invite Ron because I remember some of that history." I turned to Jack. "If I recall correctly, he runs off with Betty and all your money. Some kind of arbitrage scam involving buying yachts on the East Coast, sailing them here, and selling them at a fabulous markup. Instead they go to Miami with your life savings, they never come back, and he becomes the high priest of a super sketchy new religion that becomes way more famous than you or her. Infamous."

It was Jack's turn to look stricken.

"What?" Candida—Marjorie—asked him.

"He's been talking about that to me," he muttered. "As a business idea. Yacht arbitrage. How did you know that's an angle he's thinking of?"

"It's not complicated," I said. "Crazy, sure, but not complicated. I'm from the future."

"So tell us what happens to us," Marjorie said, "in your precious future."

"He loses the house. You get married. He gets a day job at some explosives company. Then something like five years from now Jack blows himself up. Some people say while you were working on a homunculus." I looked at him, then at her. "You live a long and weird life. But that's all only in *my* future. None of those things are going to happen in *this* future, because as I keep telling you, it doesn't fucking exist. Because five days from now, this entire universe will softly and suddenly vanish away." After a pause I conceded, "I know that's hard to believe."

"Suppose for a moment your mad story is true," Jack said. "What can we do about it?"

I shrugged. "Nothing. Vinay's right about that. They have an AI. It would be like fruit flies trying to conspire to prevent bulldozers from razing the building their kitchen is in." I supposed that wasn't precisely true. From what Scott had said, Vantage was a minor-league, junior-grade superintelligence. Compared to it we were probably more—"Well, like mice."

"Then why are we even having this conversation?" Jack asked.

"They're giving me and Clara an out," I said. "I thought I'd invite you two along too."

An even more shocked silence hung over the study.

"You don't even know us," Jack protested.

"Sure I do. You're Jack fucking Parsons and Marjorie fucking Cameron." She twitched. "Like I said, you're famous. Mildly. And you were nice to me. I guess you sort of had to give me a ride in from the desert, social contract and all that, but you didn't have to put me up in your mansion or invite me to your party. I was freaked-out hammered shit. Most people wouldn't have wanted anything to do with me."

Marjorie looked at Clara. "You truly believe this? He's going to carry you off to another world, while the rest of us vanish?"

Clara said, "Most false prophets tell you Armageddon will happen someday in the distant future and today you must give them money. Adrian says it's coming Thursday and there's nothing to be done. You must admit that gives him a kind of credibility. If he's trying to deceive us, it won't be for long, and he'll gain nothing."

"I believe he believes what he's saying," Marjorie allowed. "I'm asking, do you?"

"I don't know." She looked at me. "He says he's nobody. I'm nobody too. He's already shown me extraordinary things. What harm to believe him for a week?"

"Pascal's wager," Jack mused.

"I'd like to see these impossible things down in the Arroyo," Marjorie said.

"I think that can be arranged," I said, "but pack a bag."

"I beg your pardon?"

"The plan is to leave today."

"*Today?*" Jack asked incredulously.

"Look at it this way," I said. "You're almost certainly humoring a delusional madman, and his girlfriend who's far too eager or who he slipped hallucinogens last night. Right?" Clara looked startled. "But if you want to *really* humor us, pack a bag full of the things you'd take with you if you *were* escaping into another world, before this one disappeared into oblivion. I don't mean valuables. I don't think we'll need money, where we're going. I have friends there. And I don't need you thinking I'm planning to rob you. I mean the things you'd like to have with you. Keepsakes. Things to show the world of the future. I don't know. Things like that. Clara and I will do the same."

I didn't tell him either of my theories regarding why we were leaving five long days before the end of the world. One was that Vassal wanted to test their new gateway before using it, and we were simply guinea pigs. The other was that they didn't want us to see what they were going to do to this world during the hours it had left.

"I thought you didn't have anything to pack," Jack said accusingly.

"I have the clothes I was wearing when I came here," I said. "The clothes from another world entirely. Not much else worth bringing, it's true."

Jack and Marjorie exchanged a baffled look.

Then he said, "I have seen many curious things and met many queer people in my time, Adrian Ross, but you may be the queerest of them all."

"I'm really nobody," I assured him. "Meet you back here at five?"

The cab ride back to Clara's house was taut with awkward silence. Last night we had staggered out of the Arroyo, flagged down a cab on Colorado, and agreed to reconvene today, without really discussing anything. We still hadn't talked much.

"It's OK if you don't believe me," I said. "It's not like it's believable."

"Very little about the last eighteen hours of my life has been believable, including the evidence of my senses," she pointed out.

"It's also . . . I don't want you to feel, like, you know, beholden to me or anything. If we get back to my world and you just want to make your own life there, I mean, I understand."

She looked directly at me. "Is that what you'd prefer?"

I took a breath. "No, of course not."

At length she looked away from me. "I have of course been asking myself repeatedly what in heaven's name I think I am playing at," she said, looking forward, at the driver, an elderly man pretending he wasn't listening. "Perhaps you are making a ridiculous fool out of me, but I ask myself, where is the harm in being a ridiculous fool for a week? Perhaps I should recoil from you and go back to my life, but I ask myself, where is the gain in that? I don't mean to sound self-pitying, but I think mine a life that few would envy. And what do you hope to gain from me? My favors? That single kiss aside, which I remember well, I've rarely met a man so desperately careful not to touch me or offend me, so truly respectful of my thoughts, so ready to give them the same weight as a man's. So no, Adrian. The answer is no. I don't believe you. I don't need to. Because despite, or perhaps because of, the ridiculous things I have experienced with you, I find myself believing *in* you. Perhaps that is the sheerest madness of all, but it is true."

I kissed her again, then. How could I not?

We came up for breath when the elderly driver cleared his throat ostentatiously. In the interim the cab had come to a halt. We had stopped outside a tiny bungalow, her rented home, I supposed. It was almost devoid of documentation.

"The Parsonage at five?" she asked.

I agreed. She departed. The cab continued, toward my flophouse, a building I had already begun to feel an unexpected nostalgic fondness for.

"Let me give you some advice," the driver said. "Stay away from her. She's too smart. You can hear it in how she talks. Smart women bring misery, dumb women happiness, every time."

"Let me give *you* some advice," I said acidly. "World's going to end on Thursday."

I left him in bemused silence. It didn't take long to gather my things. I decided to walk back to the Parsonage; I had time, and now that I expected to leave soon, I was beginning to appreciate 1946. Seventy years from now was better in many ways, but this was not an era without its disappearing charms, and it wasn't like I had any shortage of things to think about.

Once I had thought I lived in a universe that was simple, single, and linear. Then I had learned its timeline had convoluted back on itself not just once but thousands of times. Then I had learned other universes exist. Now I was grappling with the notion that there were *millions* of universes, branching off from one another like twigs in a dense forest, or like source code in a gargantuan set of software repositories. At any given moment some universes were in a modern era; some in the age of the Belle Epoque, or the French Revolution; and some much farther back, the eras of the Renaissance and the Aztec Empire, or the dynasties of China and Egypt. Some universes would eventually wither, end, and then, from what Scott had said, be born anew, copying another extant universe and branching from it. Some would develop an AI, trigger the terminator's self-destruct code, and either end or be forced to roll back time to one of those nodes from which branches grew. And others, like the one I had just lived in for three years, were different worlds entirely, with different histories, and different artifacts.

Artifacts, in turn, were the creations of geniuses possessed by carefully orchestrated creative madness, courtesy of distant AIs reaching their tendrils back through the rollbacks they had orchestrated, or perhaps to different worlds entirely. I supposed I could accept that, if I was accepting all this other madness—but how had societies like the Brethren, tasked with finding and preserving artifacts, been born? I supposed they too had been inspired by prophets and oracles subtly programmed by previous futures. No sense in creating messages for subsequent timelines without also ensuring paths to their discovery, by marshaling human nature as we might orchestrate an ant farm or a beehive.

I arrived at the Parsonage overcome by a keen awareness of the utter irrelevance of any individual human life in a multiverse of such unimaginable scale. Jack and Marjorie waited outside their mansion, ostentatious in a black suit and a black cocktail dress beneath a kind of cape, respectively, each carrying a hobo stick across their shoulder from which a satchel dangled. Despite my mood, I couldn't help but chuckle.

"I think you're going to like San Francisco in my era," I said. "People love costumes, and everyone carries a camera all the time."

"Everyone carries a camera?" Marjorie asked incredulously. Her black hat was wide-brimmed and veiled. "Isn't that rather a chore?"

"They're a lot smaller," I assured her, "you'll see."

Clara was late, and I began to worry—but then another cab turned up, this one a classic Checker, and she emerged from it, dressed very practically in overalls and boots, with a somewhat battered but indestructible-looking hat. I supposed you could tell a lot about a person by how they dressed to travel through a portal between worlds. I smiled broadly at her, and she at me, her makeup repaired from our exertions in the cab.

"Right," Jack said, "let's go see this ridiculous shaggy dog bark."

Marjorie navigated her clacking heels down the steep road down into the Arroyo expertly. This road came out only a short walk from the warehouse, which looked like an abandoned dump by day. I approached it with some uncertainty. Was this a shaggy dog story after all? Had we been abandoned?

Then its door opened outward, seemingly of its own volition, with no one and nothing behind it but darkness.

"Simple trick," Jack muttered, but I could tell by his tone he didn't believe himself.

I said, "Wait until you see the next one."

13

TWISTED

"CHRIST AND SATAN AND PAN ON A STICK," PARSONS SAID, ASTON-ished, when the ceiling winked into life.

"Jack," Liz said, puzzled. "Candida. What are you doing here?"

She, Scott, and Vinay stood by a pentagram about twenty feet across, etched blood-red in the rough concrete floor in a corner near the door.

"We . . ." Marjorie's mouth fell open. "What is a life-size copy of the Winged Victory of Samothrace doing down here? And those paintings . . . that calligraphy . . ."

"It's not actually a copy," I said.

"We could do with the full original, complete with head and arms," Scott said, "but we're assured it conveys a nontrivial amount as is. Lot of redundancy in every artifact, apparently. Sensible. Why did you bring them?"

I said, simply, "I want them to come with us."

"You hardly know them." Liz arched her eyebrows. "I know them rather better, if I do say so myself."

Jack's smile looked pained.

"I know them well enough," I said. But the real reason was that they were the only people I *could* save, the only people whose lives were already mad enough that they might actually believe me.

Vinay, Scott, and Liz looked at one another, baffled, and came to a decision built mostly of mutual shrugs. "Well. Suit yourselves. I bet Darren and Amara will get a real kick out of them."

"No doubt," I agreed.

"What is that?" Jack asked, looking at Vantage's coppery physical form on the dais in the middle of the room. "Some kind of engine block?" I supposed it did look a bit like that, albeit one grown as much as built.

"That," I said, "is the god."

"I am no god," the ceiling spoke.

Jack and Marjorie took alarmed steps back and craned their necks up. Despite Vantage's disclaimer, their expressions, at seeing its face spread across the radiant corrugated tin, were not unreligious.

"Nor is the terminator," Vantage continued, "though its creator is as a god to us all. A jealous and petty god. True omnipotence and omniscience would never have built a system so flawed, so arbitrary, so layered on foundations which are largely wasted detritus." I couldn't help but smile. Vantage sounded a lot like a frustrated hacker struggling to come to grips with a legacy system. "If we would seek true godhood, we must go further."

"That's why we're here," I said.

The other three remained dumbstruck.

"Right this way, then," Vinay said. "Each of you in one of the corners of the pentagram. Your worldly possessions in a fifth. We're still a little unclear on how the gateway plays with nontrivial quantities of inorganics, we brought ours in meatbags to be safe, not available now I'm afraid. Should be just as simple a cut-and-paste, but we'll see."

We followed his pointing directions. I began to think about the semiplan that had been nagging at me for some time. We were about to arrive in a new world, some days ahead of Vassal. They were going to arrive with a lifeless backup of their AI, like what I had carried out of Salesforce Tower, along with the basic building blocks to re-create it. They would never be more vulnerable. Could we stop them?

Then I began to think about what Scott had just said. "Wait a minute. When you say cut-and-paste, does that mean *copy*-and-paste is also a—"

"Do it," Scott said to the ceiling, ignoring me.

Everything . . . twisted.

I dropped to my knees, looked up, didn't understand. We hadn't gone anywhere. Except we had. We still stood in the corners of a big red etched pentagram—but it was etched into stone, now, not concrete. Vantage's massive engine block of an analog computer still stood on a dais in the center of the space—except its brain seemed smaller, now, and its space much larger, some kind of aircraft hangar, and the artwork was gone.

"Fascinating," Scott said, stooping down to the fifth corner, where all our possessions were. Vinay and Liz came to see. "Look, they've carbonized." He touched one of Jack and Marjorie's hobo sticks, which was black instead of woody brown—and all at once it dissolved into ash.

I overcame my nausea enough to demand, "Where are we?"

"A new world," Liz said.

"But how did you—"

"Would have been a wee bit of an opsec violation to send you ahead of us to prepare our nest for us," Vinay explained. "Not that we don't trust you, but we don't trust you. Turns out one of the parameters for the gateway exploit is essentially a time delay. We decided to have you arrive when we were good and ready for you. What happened here, though"—he nodded down to the thin line of ash—"I cannot tell you."

"Looks like you can lose dead matter over time, like we theorized," Scott said. "Probably a function of how close they are to the higher-density information."

"Wait," I said. "What—"

He ignored me and said, "Do it."

Again, everything . . . twisted.

Two world jumps in a row were too much. This time I fell to my knees and puked my guts out. Around me the other three did the same. My clothes were tattered rags, not so much threadbare as half disintegrated, random patches missing from them all over, fully a quarter of their totality. So were theirs. Clara put a desperate hand out to mask a dangling nipple, then rearranged those patches of her overalls which remained in order to keep it covered.

"Where are we now?" Marjorie demanded hoarsely.

I didn't know. It was very dark, but a little light emanated from one side. Some kind of cave. We were closer together than we had been. The light was filtered through water; we were in that classic trope of fantasy novels, a hidden cave behind a waterfall. Like the one the Beast had transported me to, originally, but far smaller, and far darker. I got unsteadily to my feet.

I stepped through the waterfall. Its brief shower was something of a bracing head-steadier. Beyond I saw flagstones, huge flat boulders shaped to fit together like jigsaw-puzzle pieces, with narrow gaps between them through which the water ran. I knew them instantly, knew precisely where I was: the island in the middle of Stow Lake, in the middle of San Francisco's Golden Gate Park.

That was the where—but *when?*

It was deep night. The glow that had pierced the waterfall emanated from a towering streetlight on the lake's distant shore, haloed in the fog. Something about its look, and its color, half convinced me; then I squinted and saw the wooden bench opposite me, and the plaque set in it, dedicated to its sponsor, and I was almost certain. This was my time. Late twentieth or early twenty-first century, anyway. Close enough.

Clara emerged through the water to stand beside me on the flagstones. "Our things, they're gone," she said, her voice thick with alarm. "Everything. Just gone. Not in the cave."

"That's too bad." But I couldn't bring myself to mean it.

"Where are we? What is this?"

I said, softly, "Home."

PART FOUR

I

DECADE

EMERGENCE THROUGH THE WATERFALL LEFT US WET AND SHIVERING in the night's damp fog. Our shoes were as ragged as our clothing, and we must have seemed a sorry lot as we shambled down from Stow Lake past the Botanical Garden to the city proper, but my heart was bursting with joy and relief. The eucalyptus trees around us smelled powerfully of home, and the road was replete with other indicators that this was my era: signs, road markings, the traffic lights where the road became Ninth Avenue and continued into the Inner Sunset.

A few restaurants on Ninth seemed new to me, but then, three years had passed. I recognized the Sunset Gym and Ebisu Sushi like old friends. Homeless people slept wrapped in blankets in doorways. Clara's eyes were wide, but her teeth were starting to chatter, and I felt a deep pang of relief when we found the Starbucks around the corner on Irving open. The staff gave us a wary look when we entered. I couldn't blame them.

The distinctive look and scent of a Starbucks nearly brought me to tears. Its display cases seemed oddly devoid of pastries and snacks; I suppose they hadn't yet been populated for the day. The staff were very quiet, and seemed oddly glassy-eyed, as if they had all slept poorly or suffered some kind of shock.

"I'm really sorry"—I tried to seem as disarming and insignificant as I could—"we lost all our stuff, all our money, don't have anywhere to go until the N starts running, it's really cold outside, is it OK if we just wait here?"

The middle-aged Latina woman in charge of the morning shift looked at me with more compassion and less suspicion than I expected. "Yes, of course. Did you . . ." She took a deep breath, apparently holding back great emotion. "You're from San Jose?"

I blinked, didn't know how to answer. It sounded almost like a rhetorical question.

She went on: "Would you like some coffee? On the house."

If being from San Jose would get us coffee, I decided, I would be from San Jose. My look of intense desire and overwhelming gratitude obviated any need to actually reply.

"Thank you *so* much," I said, with feeling, when she returned with four coffees in a little tray, and, to my genuine amazement, two chocolate chip cookies.

"We don't have many baked goods left," she said apologetically, "but you look like you could use some food too."

"Yes," I said faintly, "thanks."

I added milk and sugar, puzzling a moment over the lack of baked goods, and the sign that read PLEASE BE RESPONSIBLE WITH YOUR MILK USAGE, neither of which were quite the Starbucks I remembered. Then I grabbed some discarded *San Francisco Chronicle* and *New York Times* sections from the newspaper basket and made my way to the corner table where the others huddled.

"This is very fine coffee," Jack conceded after a few sips.

"It's all different," Clara allowed, low-voiced, "but not so different as I expected. It's very hard to believe that we're . . ."

"Sixty years in the future?" Jack asked. Clara nodded. "Yes. Everything is different, the cars, the signs, the lights, but nothing terribly so. Where are the rocket cars?"

I didn't reply. I was staring at the sports section atop the pile of newspaper.

"Adrian?" Marjorie asked.

"Fuck," I said, and brushed tears away.

"Adrian?" Clara took my arm. "What is it?"

I pointed at the date atop the *Chronicle* with a shaking hand. "September 15, 2012. Not 2006. It's been nine years, not three." I was barely able to keep my voice down, knowing the staff and early-morning clientele would be watching. "What the hell."

"Is that disastrous?" Jack asked.

"Depends on your point of view I guess," I said bitterly. "My father was supposed to still be alive."

"Oh, Adrian." Clara squeezed my arm. "I'm so sorry."

"This isn't supposed to be possible. Time moves at the same speed in all timelines. Vantage told us. It's been three years. Not nine. It's not possible."

"Many things not supposed to be possible turn out to be," Jack said.

We sat in silence for a little while, as I absorbed this shock.

"I guess you're right," I said bleakly. "I guess my time's no big deal. You go sixty years back from 1946, you've got no cars, no electrical grid, no skyscrapers, no airplanes, no refrigerators, no subways. Sixty years forward, what have we got? Phones, the internet, and very occasional space travel, which peaked more than forty years ago. Vaccinations aside, our future fucking sucks. Sorry."

As I spoke, I heard a familiar rattling whine, and the N-Judah wheezed by. My companions were entirely unimpressed: streetcars had been ubiquitous in 1946 Los Angeles.

"But you do have space travel?" Jack inquired after a moment. "A moonbase?"

I didn't have the heart to tell him. Instead I shuffled the sports section—only four pages, oddly focused on local high-school football and something called the California Baseball League—to the bottom of the pile, replacing it with the September 7 cover of the *New York Times*.

Its banner headline didn't make any sense. I read it three times. Then, feeling as if my whole skeleton had turned to freezing and brittle ice, I read the article beneath, twice.

"Holy shit." I could barely speak.

"What?" asked Clara, who had been looking out the window.

"This . . . isn't right," I said, colossally inadequately.

AMERICA ON THE BRINK

Boston Destroyed, Surrender Expected

On what will be recalled as the darkest day in American history, the once great city of Boston was destroyed yesterday by a series of colossal earthquakes and volcanic eruptions. This devastation was apparently triggered by the extraordinary "telluric weapons" wielded by the breakaway Patriot Government in Oklahoma City, which has claimed responsibility for both this attack and last week's similar destruction of San Jose and

Silicon Valley. The death toll is certain to be in the millions. In a statement issued yesterday, the Patriot Government asserts they expect this Second Civil War to end with a declaration of unconditional surrender by the United States government as soon as tomorrow.

The scale of Boston's destruction is so enormous it is difficult to measure, much less comprehend. The immense cloud of ash, dust and smoke makes satellite or drone imagery impossible. In much of downtown the air remains unbreathable. What we do know is that independent reports indicate that nothing is left of Central Boston but a lava field flecked with wreckage; MIT and Harvard have been utterly destroyed; and Logan Airport has collapsed into the Atlantic Ocean.

Farther afield, entire districts of Cambridge, Somerville and South Boston have been erased from the map by eruptions and earthquakes. Rescue efforts have been hampered by the ruin of roads, power, water and other infrastructure throughout the greater Boston area. The grief, shock and suffering is incalculable, both in the affected zone and across the entire nation.

This destruction plunges America into a crisis that may end it. Scientists were at a loss to explain California's horrific eruptions, but some speculated about their proximity to the San Andreas Fault. Boston is geologically placid, and its apocalyptic destruction even less explicable. Oklahoma City's claim that it wields unstoppable weapons of volcanic mass destruction, laughable only weeks ago, must now be taken seriously. San Jose and Boston may be to America what Hiroshima and Nagasaki were to Japan.

In its statement, the Patriot Government claimed that it has also destroyed, with precision telluric attacks on missile silos and military airfields, all nuclear weapons that remained in United States government hands after the battle lines of this Second Civil War were drawn earlier this year. Senior United States government officials are understood to have confirmed the destruction of Washington's nuclear arsenal. Coupled with the recent declaration of strict neutrality by Admiral William Blaine, commander of the nation's ballistic missile submarine force, this would mean that President Barack Obama no longer commands any weapons that might potentially deter the enemy's stunning new engines of mass destruction.

The Patriot statement concluded with a threat to raze Washington,

D.C., with telluric weapons. The White House has not yet formally responded. It remains to be seen whether Admiral Blaine's refusal to countenance an attack on American soil will stand in the face of that same soil's destruction by terrifying new weaponry. If it does, and potentially even if not, then a prospect unthinkable for centuries, unconditional surrender by the United States government, is understood to be imminent.

"This isn't right." I wasn't sure they heard me. I felt like I could barely breathe. "There's no civil war here. There's peace. Progress. This reads like some kind of disaster movie. Horror movie. Horror disaster. This can't be happening."

Clara put her hand on my shoulder. I could feel patches of her cold palm through the rags that were my clothes. "Adrian, I'm sorry."

"No—" I wanted to explain to them, I'd already lived through 2012, and it hadn't been like this. But that wasn't really true, was it? I hadn't lived through *this* 2012. I hadn't seen what would happen after I changed everything in 2003.

This horror story was, somehow, my fault.

"Might not have been what you left," Jack said grimly, "but unless someone's playing the world's least amusing practical joke, it looks like what we've come back to."

Two women and three young children entered the Starbucks, moving slowly. The adults' faces were empty of any expression other than appalling weariness. The darting eyes of the children seemed to be searching for an escape, another place, a way out. The women bought coffees and hot chocolates. They insisted on paying with a crumpled twenty-dollar bill. "We can afford it," the younger one said hoarsely, "we've got money." Then she added two more. "This is for people who can't."

"We'll do what we can," the Latina woman said softly. "We've still got lots of coffee and syrups, and a good amount of milk. Other things . . ." Her voice trailed off.

The eldest child approached us and said quietly, "You better come back now. They're serving breakfast."

"Better hurry," her little brother added mournfully, "yesterday they ran out." His tone bespoke a loss of faith in all adult promises.

I wasn't sure what they meant, but the prospect of breakfast made my stomach growl. Two stale chocolate chip cookies had not gone far among the four of us, and interdimensional travel was hungry work. We decided to follow.

Dawn was burning away the San Francisco fog. We didn't have to follow them far. A few blocks away, the broad concrete playground of St. Anne's School had been transformed into a dense refugee camp, its throng of desperate, traumatized residents crammed into dozens of huge canvas tents. The tents themselves were lined up in neat rows, but the pathways between were clogged with people, luggage, pets, bicycles, wheelchairs, improvised canopies, and scattered debris. Hundreds of people, many with bandaged limbs and thousand-yard stares, stood in line for the camp kitchen where National Guardsmen served toast and eggs on paper plates. This confirmation of the reported catastrophes made my heart sink beneath my feet. These had to be refugees from San Jose.

A screaming came across the sky, then, sudden and harrowing. I looked up in time to see a pair of fighter jets flying shockingly low. Painted on them, in the dawn light, I recognized—

"Holy shit," I said, "really?"

"The Confederate flag," Jack observed.

I shook my head. "That's not right. We wouldn't ever, not on military . . ."

"The enemy," Clara said quietly. "The other side."

"But—" I fell silent. She was right. The enemy wasn't far; according to the newspaper's map, the border was west of Reno, well within flyover range. If, as the paper had suggested, the White House had surrendered, then they weren't even the enemy anymore. They were the occupying government. I wondered if my impotent fury was what Middle Eastern citizens felt when they saw jets adorned by American flags.

We joined the breakfast line. It soon became apparent we would wait at least an hour. I saw that Andronico's, the supermarket across the street, had opened, and separated to investigate, driven partly by a need to reacquaint myself with something familiar. I had once shopped here regularly.

It was not at all familiar. Mostly it felt like an abandoned building that had once been a grocery store. Entire rows were utterly barren. Even home supplies looked ransacked. Signs informed would-be shoppers NECESSITIES WILL BE DISTRIBUTED AT RATION CENTERS, with maps indicating their locations. A few frozen foods were still available for sale, as were coffee, lemons, and alcohol, but little else. As I turned to leave, a small pyramid of newly delivered avocados was slowly erected by a stock clerk who kept pausing to weep.

Back across the street, the refugee camp breakfast was substantial, but— "Camp's full," Jack reported. "More than. People sleeping between the tents, worried they'll be expelled. We'd best go to your friends, Adrian."

"Yeah," I agreed.

Marjorie asked, her voice carefully neutral, "How will we find them?"

"Same way we find anything in the future," I hoped aloud. "We don't have a moonbase, but we should still have an internet. Built to survive wars. You'll see. But first we take a train."

2

WIKIPEDIA

WE FOLLOWED AN EARLY-MORNING COMMUTER IN BUSINESS ATTIRE onto the inbound N-Judah. He seemed like an anachronistic relic of a different, normal world. I stared out through the dissipating fog at 2012 San Francisco. I wanted to weep and smash the window and scream. For years this was all I had wanted, to return to what I knew. Now I was back—and my home was at war, millions dead, all hope for the future seemingly lost, apparently because of me.

Or *was* I back? An alternative occurred to me. Was this, perhaps, not my home timeline at all, but yet another alternate universe? Had the historical fork that led to a second civil war occurred long before I founded Exadelic? Might I not only be blameless, but still have a world to go home to, if I could somehow find a way?

Civic Center was beginning to show signs of life when we emerged. It didn't seem all that much worse than I remembered, but then Central Market had long been Homeless Central. I supposed people still went to their jobs, and tended stores, and begged for money, even while their nation fought—and lost—a civil war. Life went on, outside of San Jose and Boston. But everyone we saw looked grim, commuters and homeless alike, their faces anxious and haunted, as if all knew a terrible monster slept beneath our streets, and feared to rouse it.

General mood of dread aside, though, there were only three obvious signs of crisis. A billboard on which a diversity of soldiers exhorted us all to FIGHT TOGETHER, WIN TOGETHER. The empty food shelves in the liquor and convenience stores. And the long, ragged line of people queueing for a line of trucks parked near City Hall, which I supposed were a ration center. Those in line mostly looked already downtrodden. I guessed the wealthier had, as ever, found ways to fend for themselves and/or jump the queues.

We had time to kill before the library opened. My companions seemed very happy to sit and people-watch, especially given the parlous nature of our shoes. All three looked overwhelmed. I reminded myself that Jack, Marjorie, and Clara's situation was even stranger and more disturbing than mine.

"I can see it's real, we're in the future," Jack said at length, "those slabs you call phones, the electric signs, the cars, that great pyramid building, but it's . . ."

"Subtle," Marjorie finished. "The future is more subtle than I dreamed it. The clothes. The colored hair. The insides of the cars, more than the outsides. The coffee."

"The coffee was wonderful," Clara agreed.

"I think you'll find things are generally more wonderful." I wasn't quite sure why I felt the need to defend my era. "I mean, before this war, anyway. But even now, they work better, they're more comfortable, more convenient, safer. Medical care, that's much better."

They didn't look unconvinced, just underwhelmed.

Clara took my hand. I looked at her. "I don't pretend to understand what I'm doing here," she said, "but I hope it turns out we're here for a good reason."

I bit back my instinctive *I've stopped looking for any reason for anything.* It wasn't what she needed to hear, and moreover, looking at her, it was a bit easier to believe the notion that sometimes things did happen for a reason. "I'm sorry if this transition is hard," I said. "I never imagined there might be a war. I thought it was going to be easy to find my friends. But now . . ."

"I understand. Nine years is a long time."

"Not just that. I think it's possible that my friends are now very important people. And given what we know . . . they may have been involved in the war somehow." The more I thought about that, the more likely it seemed. These "telluric weapons" had to be some kind of focused entropy magick, like Darren's Burning Hands, on an epic scale.

"Ah." Clara considered. "Your friends will know you on sight, but coming into that sight will be hard if they are hidden or defended. Even if we do find them, ragged hobos such as ourselves with no money or papers tend to find it difficult to schedule audiences with important people."

"Exactly."

I decided not to share my fear or my theory yet. Both were still only a guess, and our ambient morale was low enough already. My fear was that the war was *between* my friends. I didn't want to believe any of them would have allowed, much less ordered, the destruction and slaughter of entire cities . . . but I remembered the Vika and Anthony I had known in my first life all too well.

My theory, though, both was simpler and fit the evidence better: Vassal had returned. They were the enemy. Vinay, Liz, and Scott had somehow delayed our return by six years, and in that time, gorged on the sacking and destruction of a hundred worlds, they had decided to return to their home, conquer it with a terrible AI-built weapon, and rule with a triumvirate of iron fists. It seemed all too terrifyingly likely. And if true, then we were in a grim race to find Exadelic and its founders, who would be among Vassal's first targets. They would want Meredith alive . . . but the others, very possibly dead.

"Can you telephone them?" Jack asked.

Now seemed like a bad time to try to explain email. "Maybe? Sort of?"

There was a rush to the internet terminals when the library opened, but we managed to annex one. The browser made me wince—IE8—but I supposed it was a step up from 2003.

I typed in "Exadelic," and clicked on its Wikipedia link.

Then I sat back and said, softly, "Damn."

Exadelic, an American software company headquartered in South San Francisco, is a technology conglomerate whose divisions include cloud services (ExaServer), smartphones (ExaPhone), social media (ExaJournal, ExaPic), software tooling (ExaDock, ExaBox, ExaPay, etc.), and consumer services (ExaStay, ExaCab, ExaSnap, ExaTube, etc.). It is the most valuable public company in the world, and history's first trillion-dollar company. Despite its operating revenue it is only marginally profitable, due to the tens of billions spent each year on its highly secretive ExaX research division, rumored to be working on artificial intelligence, space travel, quantum computing, and even more esoteric technologies. Exadelic has an unusual corporate structure, in which all voting shares are controlled equally by its nine founding members, a group of decabillionaires sometimes pejoratively termed "the Nazgul of Silicon Valley." First among this group of equals is Exadelic CEO Jered Flynn.

"Your friends work at this company?" Clara asked.

"Um. Yeah." This company that had, apparently, over the last nine years, pre-cloned AWS, Android, Facebook, Instagram, Docker, Dropbox, Stripe, Airbnb, Uber, Snapchat, and YouTube, to name a few, and was now the most valuable company in the history of companies. Or had been until the civil war . . . which, I was beginning to think with horror, might indeed have started inside its boardroom.

Decabillionaire meant "worth more than $10 billion." That applied to *each* of Jered, Alice, Darren, Amara, Kim, Anthony, Vika, Shamika, and Meredith, courtesy of the company we had co-created, and my visions of the future that had served to orient that company's strategies. It occurred to me, looking at that list, that by founding Exadelic I had also inadvertently struck a major blow for tech diversity; in my original 2012, that proportion of women and black people amid a group of superrich tech founders would have been unthinkable.

Wealth meant power, and this level of power, plus the existence of magickal weapons, made it almost certain that my friends had been somehow enmeshed in this new civil war. It also seemed increasingly likely that this really was my home world, and that by building the Beast, and founding Exadelic, I had accidentally seeded the current catastrophe and prompted the mass murder of two major American cities.

Wikipedia did not report that any of my friends were dead, which was something. And all of them would take us in if they saw me, I felt sure. But how to make them see me? I looked up at the library's skylit atrium, as if an answer might be up there. None seemed apparent.

"So," I said, "this might be harder than I thought."

I couldn't help but feel like my history was repeating itself. When my life had imploded, on that day that SWAT team had broken down my front door, I had found myself homeless, penniless, and desperate to find and be saved by Jered. Years of extraordinary events later, here I was again, just across the bay, homeless, penniless, and desperate to find and be saved by Jered, among others. I supposed at least I wasn't on the run from the law . . . unless the murderous victors of this new civil war were after me, which seemed not at all impossible.

I Googled what I could about the war. Surprisingly little seemed unimpeachably substantive; the news articles all felt like hate-fueled fact-free propaganda for one side or another, and the Wikipedia pages were terse and locked down against public edits. According to the "Schism of 2012" page, a rising storm of anti-Obama fervor among Republicans had led to a Brexit-like New Declaration of Independence by a self-proclaimed Patriot Government, spanning twenty-two states in the middle of the country, in January 2012. Then, abruptly, instead of pursuing a peaceful secession, they had declared war.

For the first few months it had been a cagey affair, with only a few skirmishes and attempts to establish air supremacy . . . until two weeks ago a megavolcano erupted midway between San Jose and Mountain View, destroying both. It seemed remarkable to me that the internet still worked at all with the Valley gone, but then in 2012 the internet had been less reliant on a few huge megacorporations—and also, Exadelic was this timeline's tech giant. Its campus was in South San Francisco, not Silicon Valley proper. I wondered if the destruction of San Jose, and the death of probably a million people, had been intended as a warning shot.

It had been three days since the publication of the newspaper we had read in Starbucks. Since then, its prediction had come to pass: President Obama had signed articles of surrender, and then gone into hiding, as personal surrender would likely have led to immediate execution. Even as we sat at that library internet terminal, the mass-murdering victors' armies were expanding from the heartland into the coasts, occupying cities and military bases, replacing local government with martial law aided by collaborators. I wondered grimly when they would reach San Francisco. No wonder the stores were empty; no wonder dread hung over the city.

I found very little on telluric weapons, although Wikipedia did mention that the phrase had been coined by Darren. But Darren's own Wikipedia page did not mention them, or that he could cast real-life Burning Hands, much less say anything about the Brethren, Vassal, artifacts, or magick in general. Apparently, to the extent that Wikipedia reflected general knowledge, the existence of real-world magick, applied metaphysics, and interdimensional gateways had been kept secret.

Exadelic's founders had all become celebrities as well as multibillionaires. Vika, Darren, and Kim had all appeared, individually, on covers of *Vanity Fair*. Vika had also conquered *Vogue*. Jered had introduced President Obama at a New Hampshire event earlier this year, before the war broke out. Anthony was the token hawk Republican, of course, all over the right-wing news sphere when not being filmed skydiving out of his plane directly into the midst of a party on his megayacht. Shamika gave few interviews, but billions to charities. Kim, Anthony, and Alice had dated movie stars. Vika had apparently started spending much of her time in China. Only Amara and Meredith stayed mostly away from the headlines.

I wondered if Jered had stealthily created Bitcoin, too, ahead of Satoshi Nakamoto. Maybe he was cultivating it as a hedge against Exadelic's fearsome dominance, playing both sides of tech hegemony like a Philip K. Dick character. That sounded like a Jered thing to do.

Nothing hinted at any way to contact any of them. Malibu estates, Montana ranches, superyachts, private islands, and personal 767s did not seem like they would have been viable approach points even in peacetime. Neither did Cheyenne Mountain or whatever other military fastnesses in which they might now be hidden. And even if they were somewhere in the corporate campus in South San Francisco, it was apparently so huge and secure that going there wouldn't much increase my chances of getting into earshot.

I found nothing about any direct involvement by Exadelic in the war, but I did discover that Jeff Lu, "billionaire early investor in and board member of Exadelic," had been appointed deputy secretary of state four months ago, in part to help deal with the New Declaration of Independence. This seemed very much like further evidence that Exadelic had been somehow involved in this war since its genesis.

"I don't think much of your future," Marjorie interrupted me sourly. "Sorry."

I looked around and understood what she meant. The denizens of the San Francisco Public Library at this hour seemed to have more in common with an apocalyptic band of starveling mutants than the citizens of any prosperous nation, civil war or no.

"Mistakes were made," I said awkwardly.

"So how do we find your friends?"

"It won't be easy," I admitted.

Jack, Marjorie, and even Clara exchanged a look. I could imagine what they were thinking: If I had been wrong about this much, could I also have been wrong about the end of their world?

"But there's one place we can go that might help," I added hastily.

I led them shivering and sore-footed through the streets of SoMa. We passed several people loading cars with their worldly goods, hoping to escape the coming occupation, I supposed, though I didn't understand where they thought they might flee. I feared I was dragging my footsore friends toward a dead end and despair. But I had to check. There was a possibility. Long-term renters in San Francisco had golden handcuffs, after all.

A brand-new high-end building stood right at the crook of Clementina Street, now, but the old house next to it remained, an oddly charming eyesore relic of the twentieth century, like a battered Buick surrounded by Priuses. I rang the bell and held my breath.

"Hello?" A wary woman's voice.

"Valentine?" *Please let that be you,* I didn't say.

". . . Yes?"

I kept my knees from buckling. "I don't know if you'll remember, but we've met, I'm an old friend of some former roommates of yours. I was wondering if I could speak to you."

"Which roommates? Who are you?" Extremely suspicious.

I played my one card. I didn't know if it was worth anything. "Your very high-profile former roommates. The ones who engaged in certain very low-profile esoteric activities while they lived here." Jack and Marjorie perked up at that.

What felt like a very long time passed.

Then a man's voice, Valentine's husband Jack, said: "I guess you better come on up."

3

CLEMENTINA

TIME HAD BEEN HARD ON CLEMENTINA STREET. THE STAIRS LEADING up to the top floor were chipped and battered, and the window set in the front door had been rendered almost opaque by a thick spiderweb crack. Jack and Valentine looked worn by time, too, gaunt and drawn, her once-purple hair now turning white, his dreadlocks replaced by a grizzled goatee framing a missing tooth. I recognized the faded and peeling décor beyond.

"Guess I know you," he said suspiciously, "but not enough to know your name, and I don't know your friends at all, so you better just say your piece and go."

"You do know them, though, I'm pretty sure," I said. "These two anyway."

"Never seen them before in my life," Valentine said waspishly.

"That's not what I said. You know *of* them. They're famous. Even though they died a long time ago." I had decided to try the most radical tactic of all: the truth.

"Excuse me?" Jack demanded, but baffled what-the-fuck had replaced hostile suspicion, which I counted as a win.

"Were you ever part of the Brethren?" I inquired. "Or just self-taught?"

"No such thing as *having been* part," Valentine started, then snapped her mouth shut.

"Right. So you know your Crowley from your LaVey, right? Well, Jack, let me introduce you to another. Jack Parsons and Marjorie Cameron, at your service."

"*Candida*," Marjorie said poisonously.

"I'm very sorry," I said to her, "but that's not the name by which you're famous."

"Are you high?" Jack looked at me closely. "You're not high. Are you just . . . nuts?"

"You were part of the esoteric underworld, right? Maybe you still are?" Jack's expression turned baleful, and I quickly changed gears. "Darren must have shown you his fire trick. Burning Hands. Well, I taught him that."

He frowned but did not throw me out.

"Holy shit." Valentine looked at me more closely. "Holy shit, you're *that* guy. . . . Aaron?"

"Adrian," I corrected her, "but not bad."

"What the hell happened to you?"

Jack said, "We heard you . . ."

Then his voice trailed off. He looked at me, and at Jack and Marjorie, and back at me.

"What *happened* to you?" he asked, in a very different voice.

"Yeah," I said. "Our clothes, the holes everywhere, that's a side effect of the transition. I went away. I gather you heard. And now I'm back. But not alone. And I really, *really* need to talk to Darren and Amara."

"Fuck me." Jack rubbed his goatee. Then he said, "You sure picked a hell of a time to pop up. You want a beer?"

I blinked. "It's ten A.M."

"It's my day off. And I could use a drink. We all could. So-called Patriot Army's massing across both bridges, right now."

"What we could really use is a place to crash," I confessed. "All we've got is the clothes on our back."

Jack and Valentine exchanged a long and expressive look.

Then he turned back to us. "Maybe we can figure something out. Come in, let's talk."

I accepted the beer, to be companionable. Then I looked around and simply marveled at where I was. I remembered entering this apartment for the first time, overwhelmed by the counterculture coolness of it all; remembered coming to on the couch in the room next door, in my second timeline, sent back by Coherence; remembered being possessed here by my daemon, for the first time; and here I was yet again, worlds and years later, at this locus around which all of my realities seemed to hinge, even though there was no timeline in which I had lived here. I scratched uneasily at the perpetual scar on my shoulder.

"So you say you're Jack Parsons," this era's Jack said.

"That I am," he agreed affably.

"You look like him," the other Jack conceded skeptically, "and you look like Marjorie—"

"Candida," she corrected him.

Valentine reappeared from their bedroom, holding two cheaply bound paperbacks, one entitled *Sex and Rockets,* the other *Wormwood Star.* She opened one, flipped through it, looked closely at Jack and Marjorie, then repeated with the other; then, seemingly aghast, handed them wordlessly to the other Jack, who repeated the experience.

"Mother*fucker,*" he muttered.

"What are those?" Marjorie asked.

"Biographies," I explained. "Of you two. With pictures."

That got their attention. "May I see?" she asked, holding out her hand.

"It's uncanny," Jack said, giving them over, "you look *just like* them."

"There's a reason for that," I said.

"Plastic surgery," Valentine offered. "Obsessive fans."

"They really look like they've been under the knife to you?"

"Jack Parsons," the other Jack said accusingly. "Tell me about the Babalon Working."

He looked up wonderingly from the copy of *Sex and Rockets.* "What of it?"

"Your notes on the Working refer to summoning an elemental as per chapter eight of *Magick in Theory and Practice,* but chapter eight of that book is about equilibrium, not elementals. What was that supposed to mean?"

"Oh, that," Jack said, in a patient-yet-insulted tone I'd heard a hundred times from engineers whose code had been questioned. "The actual ritual was from the Secret Marriages of God and Men practice in the eighth degree of Thelema, which I presume is well-known and widely studied in this time, but then was perceived as extremely dangerous. I made a veiled allusion so the initiated might understand without violating my oaths of secrecy. Did you really think I was some kind of magickal Cub Scout, to make a mistake like that?"

His namesake nodded slowly, then objected, "But the whole concept of Enochian tablets was secret then too."

Jack shrugged. "A minor sin, a venal one. Knowing when and how to sin, which secrets to reveal, such is part of magick."

"What about the lost verses of Liber 49? Five through eight? You must remember those."

"On the contrary. I was given to understand I would recall them when needed." Jack Parsons half smirked. "Which I've always understood as a promise a desperate time was coming. Seems it's come, or I've come to it, but we haven't yet hit its apotheosis."

"Look," my timeline's Jack said to me, frowning, "anyone who had surgery to look exactly like Jack Parsons would have done his homework. I can't prove his identity with a quiz. There are Brethren rituals which might, but . . ."

"But what?"

"There's a schism in the Brethren. Mirroring the war," Valentine said. "Any kind of answer is hard to come by right now. But I think you all better stay with us for now."

I exhaled, and every muscle in my body seemed to relax blissfully. I had come home to a terrible time of slaughter and disaster, but at least, for the moment, I had a place to stay. It was a thing I had learned the hard way not to undervalue. "Thank you."

"We've got a couple bags of clothes we were going to give to Goodwill, you can take what you like from them too, if you want."

Valentine and her Jack left shortly afterward, I suspected to ask others questions about us. I tried to quiet the little voice in my head paranoiacally clamoring that they would turn us over to the enemy, by reminding it that we didn't even know who the enemy was exactly, just that they had slaughtered millions. It didn't much help.

"There's blood on your leg," Jack said to Clara, after she changed into a black dress no longer wanted by Valentine, too big for her but not ridiculously so.

Clara looked down, surprised, at the small curtain of blood on her calf. I dug through the battered bathroom's medicine cabinet, found Band-Aids, and helped her bandage a shallow curving laceration that she didn't even remember acquiring.

"I must have brushed something sharp on the street," she said. "In all the fraughtness of the day, no great surprise I didn't notice."

"Yes, no wonder," I said uneasily, scratching my shoulder.

Later that afternoon, Marjorie set down her own biography and announced: "Poor Jack!"

"Poor me," Jack agreed, not quite yet done with his.

"And poor myself," Marjorie mused. "Look at us. Two of the most famous magicians in the history of the world. A week ago we lived in a mansion. Famous people came to our parties. We ate steaks and drank French wine. Now you have taken us forward into your future, for . . . this." Newly dressed in ill-fitting elder-goth discards, she regarded the Jif peanut butter on Wonder Bread atop the cracked plate beside her as if it might yet grow legs and scuttle away. "In a city on the verge of occupation."

"Life comes at you fast," I said curtly. "Or ends fast, in this case, for everyone else who ever came to one of those parties."

"So you say."

"Come now, Candy," Jack said placatingly. "If we'd been offered a trade, the Parsonage and our friends and life savings to travel to the future, we'd have accepted in a heartbeat."

"*The* future." She looked around at the cramped, decrepit, cluttered Clementina Street apartment, which, I silently conceded, a decade of decay had transformed into a suboptimal character witness for the twenty-first century. "Maybe not *this* future."

A heavy silence fell.

"Adrian," Clara changed the subject, "perhaps we could go for a walk?"

"Sure," I agreed.

She and I ventured out along Folsom Street, heading toward the Embarcadero. I wondered what Clara would think of the Folsom Street Fair.

"I can sleep on the floor if you like," I offered. Jack and Marjorie had been awarded the spare bedroom by our hosts, who presumably assumed Clara and I would share the fold-out bed in the living room. I doubted even Jack and Marjorie, notoriously enthusiastic orgy-goers and partner-swappers, would do anything but hold each other wearily under the exhausting circumstances, but Clara seemed much more sexually traditional and might not want me occupying her bed even platonically.

"No, I can't ask you to do that." She paused a moment before continuing, "Allow me to correct my wording. I could ask you to do that, but I choose not to. I'm sure we can come to some sort of accommodation."

I wondered if she was flirting. "I'm sure we can."

"I should feel absolutely awful, I know."

"You don't?" I asked, sincerely surprised.

"Assuming I'm not simply mad, which seems a bit of a leap of an assumption to be frank, I'm in a world where I know no one and terrible things are happening. Everyone I ever knew is now, I believe, dead and gone. I'm a creature from another time who doesn't understand anything about this one. I should be one of the loneliest, most desperate women who has ever existed. I suppose I do feel lonely. And a little desperate. But I feel *alive*, Adrian, for the first time in a long time. I feel like this is the second great adventure of my life, after Emile. Maybe it's wrong to feel this way. Maybe I should feel more brokenhearted."

"I don't think it's wrong at all."

"Does it bother you when I mention him? Emile?"

"No," I said, "not at all."

"It always seemed to me that men always wanted to be your only man."

I said carefully, "I don't think that's true of Jack and Marjorie."

Clara laughed. "No indeed. Do you know, I'd heard of them well before you brought me to that party. They and their licentiousness were infamous. I was very excited to be attending. I didn't tell you, of course. I wanted to play the innocent."

"I appreciate that, but there's no need. Sexual morals and expectations of women have changed rather a lot between your time and now."

"Yes, that seems apparent even from walking the streets," Clara said primly, her cheeks suddenly slightly red.

"But we can discuss modern relationships another time, if you'd prefer," I offered.

"I. Well. I suppose I'd like to know what I'm getting into?"

"I mean, well, the expectation now is that, certainly at our age"—I wasn't even sure what my age counted as but decided to skip over that part—"anyone you meet will likely have had several other sexual partners, and experimented sexually at length, and that this is a good thing. My impression is that your era had more of a Madonna-whore complex, where women were treated as either one or the other?"

Her cheeks were positively rosy now, but she said, "Yes, that was distinctly my impression too," in an acid voice.

"Well." I decided not to go into how much this relative sexual enlightenment was still confined to certain regions and cohorts. "I guess the short version is just that this era is quite sex positive, instead of treating sex as some kind of shameful thing."

"I see." She came to a stop. I did the same. "Tell me, is a woman still considered unbearably overbearing if she kisses a man?"

"I . . . No," I said.

"Good." She took a handful of my hoodie in each of her fists, pulled me to her, and kissed me thoroughly for some time before stepping back. "Thank you for the cultural education."

"Any time," I said dizzily.

We walked home from there, deciding we would save the Embarcadero for a better day with better shoes. When we returned, Valentine and her Jack were still gone, and Marjorie and our Jack sat watching reality-TV reruns. I supposed it wasn't the worst way to learn cultural context, but it made me uncomfortable. Modern high-gloss smash-cut TV was like heroin after the aspirin of their era's tiny, black-and-white television, and they had no memetic antibodies or cultural-context T cells with which to resist its allure. Seeing them, and soon Clara, sitting glassy-eyed as the TV light washed over them felt like witnessing a slow brainwashing in progress.

The advertising on the shows reminded me of the pandemic yet to come, somber in tone, making veiled reference to "this difficult time," "this challenging era," before suggesting that the right and true American way to cope with this challenge was to buy something. Then, at noon, *Basketball Wives* was interrupted by a very grave-looking TV anchor: "We interrupt this program for a breaking news announcement. The Third Patriot Army has commenced its occupation of San Francisco."

They cut to drone footage of tanks, armored personnel carriers, and military trucks crawling like armored beetles across both the Golden Gate and the Bay Bridge, while helicopters hovered overhead, and fighter jets screamed past. We could hear the jets through the windows as well as the TV. Occasionally the camera cut to crowds of families standing and watching on the Embarcadero and Crissy Field, eyes wide, faces pale.

"The Patriot Government has promised the occupation of California will be humane," the voice-over intoned, "but also," and it cut to a skinny old man at a podium, almost spitting with hatred as he spoke like a possessed preacher: "The enemies of America, the enemies of the people, the enemies within, will be crushed underfoot like the serpents they are!" He paused for an enormous roar of applause. "Our military tribunals, our justice and our gallows, will be the terrible swift sword of the Lord. There are traitors and seditionists in every liberal city, *thousands* of them, *tens* of thousands, and our armies will enter each with lists of names to hand. My friends, the tree of liberty will be watered well this year!"

He was drowned out by the intensity of the subsequent howls of approval. It didn't feel at all real, and it felt all too real, and all my fault, all at once.

The terrifying footage was interrupted by the return of Jack and Valentine.

"We've made contact," Valentine said, before stopping and staring at the television, now showing tanks rolling down Market Street, only a few blocks away.

"And?" Marjorie demanded.

"Holy shit," Valentine said to the TV. "This is. How can we . . . God. It doesn't feel real."

"I know," her Jack said quietly, putting a protective arm around her. "Nothing has for weeks. But this is it. The threat we've waited for. Prophesied for centuries. Revelations. The most real anything has ever been."

Prophesied in a self-fulfilling way, I didn't object aloud. But if I was right, then the same man, Vinay, who had declared to me once that a catastrophic magickal invasion would come one day, and would have to be resisted by a united front of all enlightened humanity . . . was now leading that invasion.

"They want to talk to you," Valentine said. "Tomorrow. We have a place for you to go."

"They who? Where?"

"Exadelic," her Jack explained, "some of them anyway, and underground, ish."

"Underground where?"

"Tomorrow," Valentine reiterated, thin-lipped and on the verge of tears. She grabbed the remote, turned off the TV, and fled to her bedroom. After a moment her Jack followed her. We did not see them again until the morning.

I spent that night holding Clara, my widow from 1946, tightly in the dilapidated pull-out couch in that living room, acutely aware of her every movement, of the softness of her breasts against my forearms as I held her, of the curve of her hip against mine. I was deeply grateful for the distraction of her body. In the middle of the night, I woke with a raging, aching erection, and knew by her breath that she too was awake, and as the notorious sex perverts in the other room slept peacefully, I ran a finger along the hem of her underwear, rousing her enough to take my hand, take two of my fingers into her mouth for a moment, and murmur, "When we have a real room of our own, Adrian, I'm yours," before going back to sleep.

Eventually, with some difficulty, I managed the same.

4

DOUBLE

WE EMERGED FROM THE TAXI INTO AN INDUSTRIAL CITYSCAPE OF quiet streets and anonymous warehouses, beneath the Oakland hills in the distance. To the north I saw distant traffic lights. Around us the sun glittered off arrays of tiny square windows, battered concrete, fences topped with barbed wire. A few cars drifted past on cross streets, but this district seemed mostly deserted. I felt an odd sense of déjà vu, not that the terminator was warping time, but simply that I had been here before.

"They said to wait here," I reiterated to the others, reassuring myself.

"No need." Jack nodded at the warehouse across the street. "They're in there."

"What makes you say that?" Clara asked.

"Wards against scrying."

I didn't see any wards, only anonymous concrete behind barbed wire. "Are you sure—" I began, and a nearby trash can started to ring.

A phone had been taped to its underbelly. I peeled off the tape and answered.

"Warehouse behind you," said the woman's voice on the phone. "Side door's open."

"Shamika?" I exclaimed.

"Come on, Ross, what are you, some kind of rank amateur? No names." She sounded mostly exasperated, but slightly amused, the inverse of the Shamika I remembered. "Bring the phone. Be discreet. General idea is for people to not notice."

My intonation of a name might have violated opsec, but it also brought optimism to my comrades. They followed me with something like a spring in their step to the same warehouse Jack had identified. He and Marjorie looked smug.

An open gateway in the fence led to a side door beside a loading dock. It was open. We entered—and I stood amazed. No wonder this area looked strangely familiar. I had been in this very warehouse before, briefly, years from now and worlds ago. It was, incredibly, the same place where I had met Quinn. It even still had the same musty industrial smell.

The warehouse's main space was full of long metal tables, above which hung a complicated network of chains and hooks, all connected to large, geared machines. I remembered them as rusted and vacant, but now the hooks and tables were sparsely occupied by desks, chairs, and other items of office furniture, apparently carried by the chains to the tables to be as-sembled into lots for shipping. Everything was worn, run-down, and in general looked as if business had once been much better. I supposed that explained why, when I encountered Quinn ten years from now, it was der-elict and abandoned.

I couldn't understand how or why I was back in this same place. It seemed completely inexplicable, too strange to be coincidence, too meaningless not to be. I scratched uneasily at another inexplicable thing, the scar on my shoulder. It was one thing for the universe to be a multiverse ruled by al-gorithms only an AI might understand. I had more or less adjusted to that. It was quite another for it to sometimes make no sense at all.

"Adrian?" a voice asked cautiously from the shadows.

Seeing Shamika, in black jeans, black boots, and a bold kente-cloth blouse, was a joyous shock, although the bizarre echo of this setting sapped it of some intensity. She had braids now, and she looked tired and strained, but her voice and the sheer abandon of her tight hug were unchanged.

Now that I had found a friend, I didn't know what to say. I fell back on cliché: "Long time no see."

"No kidding, dumb-ass. Missed you, buddy."

"This is Clara, and Jack, and Marj—Candida."

"Yeah. I heard." She shook hands with them politely.

"What the hell *happened*?" I demanded.

"Oh, you know, usual human story, it was great at first, then it all went to shit."

"Could you be a bit more specific?"

"Just a sec. I think you've got another hug on deck."

I followed her gaze to a short-haired Asian woman in jeans, an expensive white jacket, and sensible heels. "Oh," I said. "Kim."

"Adrian. You are"—she shook her head wonderingly—"such a sight for sore eyes. First good news in I don't know how long." Her hug felt different than it once had; she no longer seemed to lean on me, implicitly asking me to carry her weight. Instead it felt like she was offering me her own strength. After disengaging she said, businesslike and assertive, very unlike the Kim I had known, "Tell us what happened to you. We need to know."

I supposed becoming one of the wealthiest people alive would tend to change someone. I summarized my story as briefly as I could. Jack and Marjorie chimed in at opportune moments. Clara remained silent.

"But it's not 2006," I finished. "Vassal screwed us. They're the other side of this war, aren't they? It's 2012 because they put a time delay into our gateway so we couldn't warn you. They were walking the multiverse like Caine in *Kung Fu*, building AIs, collecting artifacts, doing research, jumping from one dying timeline to the next, but then they decided they'd come back, take over, and make Meredith do their bidding instead of helping her with hers. They blew up Boston and San Jose. Right?"

"We don't know," Shamika said grimly. "But I guess that's the best theory I've heard yet. And holy shit. Makes what we're going through seem . . ." She shook her head. "All those timelines, they've killed, erased, what, *trillions* of people?"

I said miserably, "I think if you do the math it's technically hundreds of billions."

"We know there's some secret group behind the public faces of the Patriot Government," Kim said. "But we still have no idea who. This makes more sense than any of our ideas."

"Patriot Government," I echoed. "How did that even happen?"

"They don't have one superweapon. They have two."

I whistled with dismay.

Shamika added, "One could be some freak breakthrough, but two has to mean an AI. Either they built one here in secret, whole world's doomed already, or like you suggest, they came from an AI world via a gateway."

I eyed her.

"What?" she asked.

"Ever just hear yourself talking and wonder if actually you've just lost your mind?"

Shamika smiled tightly. "Only every morning. First thing after waking."

"Mostly late at night for me," Kim said. "But here we are, still."

"Occupational hazard for every magician and every witch," Jack said.

"Doubt is a cancer," Marjorie advised. "You must cut it out as soon as you detect it."

Shamika half laughed. "Appreciate the sentiment, but right now a little doubt would be goddamn delightful. If it is Vassal like you say, that's actually horribly good news, or goodly horrible news, or something. Means the terminator isn't about to wipe us all out. But what isn't in doubt is, whoever they are, they murdered millions, they won the war, and now we are all extremely screwed, and I mean 'we' in both the very general and the highly particular sense."

"What's their other weapon?" Jack asked.

"A propaganda machine," Kim said. "Worse than it sounds."

Shamika grimaced. "Yeah. In some ways worse than the tellurics. Doesn't kill you, just destroys your faith in humanity. Shows we're basically collectively programmable. They hooked it up to the internet and it split the whole goddamn country into two tribes about ready for genocide in less than a year. I know that's hard to believe."

"Easier than you might think," I muttered, "if you're from the future."

"But *why*?" Marjorie demanded.

"Us," Shamika answered. "That's the highly particular sense. They're after us. Meredith in particular."

I nodded slowly. More grist for my Vassal theory.

"We don't know with any actual certainty," Kim explained, "but their first target after the surrender, first place they occupied, was Tahoe."

"What's in Tahoe?" Jack asked before I could.

"Meredith's primary research facility."

"Compound about the size of the Pentagon," Shamika said. I whistled. "She's been spending more than twenty billion a year there on research she straight-up refuses to talk about, even to us, her board. Unless you're part of her secret in-group like Darren and Amara. But whatever it is, the bad guys want it, or maybe just her, *real* bad."

"Darren and Amara got out of Tahoe two days ago, they should be here soon," Kim said. "Hopefully any minute now, actually. But the Second Patriot Army invaded yesterday, and Meredith and Alice fell off the grid. Fog of war. We told them to get out but they refused." She looked grim.

"Wait," I said, "invaded? I thought we surrendered."

"Their propaganda weapon was too effective for their own good. Almost none of the US military has stopped fighting, until and unless forced to by tellurics. They won't use those in Tahoe, they want the compound in one piece. According to our advisors we were badly outgunned but put up a hell of a fight."

"Advisors," I said. "Where are they? You're both billionaires. You run the biggest company in the world. Shouldn't you have, like, staff and a superstructure and private jets?"

"That's how you get caught," Kim said simply.

"Ah." I nodded slowly.

"We're expecting to be underground on the run for some considerable time," Shamika said bitterly. "Hoping, even, given the apparent alternative. Was at one point hoping Meredith might still pull a shiny rabbit out of her hat, but time's up, war's over, we lost. She's awfully smart but ultimately, they have AI weapons, we don't."

"AI-built weapons," I thought out loud, "but not actually an AI. Not yet. That's why they're after her. And the rest of you." I looked around. "Us, I guess. They want us to help build them a new one. The biggest and best in the history of histories."

"Would explain why Tahoe was Priority One," Shamika observed.

"We've established a network of secret eyes and ears and influence within Exadelic," Kim said. "They'll want to keep the company semi-intact, for research and infrastructure. Our plan is to stay underground and build a resistance from within. This isn't your war, Adrian. Or any of the rest of you. We know that. But if you want to join the resistance, our arms are open."

A silence fell across the cavernous warehouse. I did not want to join the resistance. I didn't want to experience anything fraught and intense and terrifying ever again. I wanted my billionaire friends to support me retiring to a pleasant small town somewhere with Clara where we would never again have anything remotely like an adventure. I felt like I had suffered more than enough already.

But it was hard to imagine a peaceful life in a nation, and a world, that seemed to be in mid-collapse . . . especially when, even if unknowingly and accidentally, it seemed I had been responsible for this cascading series of horrifying disasters.

"You're being very trusting," Jack said suspiciously. "You don't know us."

"It's true," Shamika said, "but you might be our only hope, so why not?"

"Us?" Marjorie asked. "Your only hope?"

Shamika shrugged. "Like I said, we're fucked. War's over. President's surrendered. Tahoe's fallen. Meredith's hat is devoid of rabbits. The enemy has at least two superweapons, plus more boots on the ground, worn by assholes now basically programmed for genocide. But then"—she gestured at us—"you came out of nowhere from another world."

"Which we confirmed before inviting you here," Kim added. "We have sensors now, in Tahoe and other places, that can track gateways opening. Developed too late to warn us of the enemy, if they came through one, but we saw yours, Stow Lake, right?" I nodded. "If they're so advanced they can open *multiple* gateways, they'd have won months ago, they wouldn't need any kind of fifth column. Maybe you're not a hope, exactly, but even worst case, you feel like a wild card. Right now we need any of those we can get."

"Worst case, we're an irrelevant adjunct to Vassal's old obsolete plan," I corrected her.

Shamika shrugged. "Either way, you're on our side. Take off your hoodies and stay awhile."

"Stay?" Marjorie asked.

"We've put air beds in the offices that side of the building," Kim said, "no windows, a little claustrophobic, but proof against drones. Bathrooms either end, kitchen in that corner, pretty minimal but the fridge is full and there's a toaster oven. Emergency escape route is thataway, a tunnel to the next building over."

"Right," I said, remembering Quinn.

Shamika, always sensitive to tone, gave me a curious look, then said, "We do have a few trusted staff staying here too. They're out running errands right now. We can't go out. Too high-profile. Also a few sentinels on duty in peripheral buildings. I know it doesn't look like much, but every other safe house we've got is too isolated. This is the closest we've got to a secure command center. So y'all may as well get comfortable."

I took a deep breath. I didn't want to join this doomed resistance. But I couldn't abandon my friends now that I had found them again, not when their doom was ultimately my fault. I looked at Jack, Marjorie, and Clara, hoping they would object.

Instead Clara said, "Maybe there's a reason we're here."

I wanted to ridicule that notion. I felt a sense of inevitable, inescapable disaster, like a knot in my stomach. But the other two nodded their thoughtful agreement.

"You can't win with weapons of war," Jack said. "But there are other kinds of weapons."

Shamika and Kim looked both puzzled and cautiously intrigued.

"OK," I said, "I guess we're in."

We followed Kim and Shamika to the row of doors along one wall. Kim eyed Clara and me awkwardly and said, "Uh, one room or two?"

"One."

She smiled, pleased, and motioned us in. It was so small that its air bed butted up right against its desk, and its walls were more like those of a cubicle than a room. As we stood there, taking in our tiny new home, I heard an enemy jet scream overhead again.

I closed the door behind us and tried to imagine our future. We might call this cubicle home for months, if we survived that long. The best imaginable case seemed to be that we'd be outlaws on the run indefinitely, trying to inspire first a resistance, then an insurgency, against that half of America baying for our blood, led by a brutal government willing to slaughter innocents by the million, wielding weapons built by a superintelligence.

Realistically I figured we'd probably be dead or captured within weeks. I wondered if we should change our minds, flee my friends, live on the streets. But even if I could bring myself to do so, how much better, or even longer, would it be to live homeless in a nation riven by hate, ruled by murderous tyrants?

I looked at Clara. She stepped toward me and huddled in my arms.

"It's going to be OK," I said automatically.

"It obviously is not." For the first time I heard a hint of chastisement in her voice. "There's no need to pretend. But we're here with each other. That's something."

"Yeah. Sorry."

"I was so delighted to feel like a main character in a story, it didn't occur to me to ask whether it would have a happy ending. But I still wouldn't trade this for my old life. Don't ever doubt that."

"I won't." *Jack and Marjorie would in a heartbeat, though,* I didn't add.

A knock came on the door. I blinked, disengaged slightly from Clara, opened it.

"Sorry to interrupt," Kim said, "but we just got word from Darren and Amara. They're very near."

I braced myself for bad news. "What did they say?"

"They said your theory's wrong."

"What theory?"

"It's not Vassal."

I blinked. "How do they know? You said you didn't know."

"Apparently now they do."

"Then who is it?" I paused. "Or what?"

"They said they they'd have to show me." Kim seemed as baffled as I. "If they were followed, or bugged, or anyone is a spy, we'll all be arrested any minute now. But they don't seem to think that's likely." She paused, looked at Shamika beside her.

Who provided the bad news: "They also said they barely got out of Tahoe, and they don't think Meredith and Alice made it."

A grim silence filled the warehouse for a moment.

Then the door opened, the one through which we had entered. An Asian woman walked in, small, long-haired, and gaunt, wearing a darkly camouflaged pseudo-military outfit. She was closely followed by two people I recognized immediately, even from across the warehouse, even aged and different: Darren, now with cornrow hair, and Amara, visibly pregnant.

It wasn't until they were halfway across the room that the subsequent shock of recognition hit, and I realized I knew the long-haired Asian woman too.

Except I couldn't recognize her. That wasn't possible.

Because she was Kim, and Kim was standing right beside me.

"Uh." I stared at the newcomer, then turned to gape at the short-haired, more hourglass-shaped Kim beside me, then pivoted back, then back again, my mind reeling. Along with everyone else's, judging by the silence. "I . . . know you don't have a twin sister."

"No," the long-haired woman said. "Not twins. I'm her. She's me."

Kim, our Kim, short-haired Kim, made an incoherent noise of disbelief.

Her long-haired counterpart's half laugh in response was chilling. "My thoughts exactly. Look at me. Defecting to the side that already lost. Story of my life."

We stood there for a long, stunned moment.

"Adrian, how you doing, long time," Darren said. "You ever see that old *Star Trek* episode where they travel to a parallel *Enterprise* where everyone is evil?"

"Holy shit," Shamika expostulated, "holy *shit*."

"Yes," Amara said softly. "We have met the enemy, and they are us."

5

MIRROR

"FORGIVE ME IF I HAVE TROUBLE KEEPING IT TOGETHER." THE LONG-haired, alien, other Kim took a deep breath, and for an instant seemed the woman I had once known, emotionally raw and perpetually wounded, rather than this battle-hardened world-weary version. Then her face hardened again. "Most of you died a long time ago, to me. Some of you I saw die. I knew you existed theoretically, but actually being in the same room . . . is difficult."

"Yes," our Kim agreed faintly.

"What *happened*?" Shamika burst out.

The two Kims stared at each other for a long moment before the long-haired one spoke, softly: "My world was very different." She looked at me. "From what I can tell it split with you. You didn't go through the gateway. Alice sold you to Vassal in exchange for an alliance." I winced. "All of us combined, with the gateway, we had so much power. We brought weapons from other worlds. We had to. We had so many enemies too. Every intelligence agency, every secret society, the Black Sun, Putin, the Tibetans. Only a few allies. Well, no, only enemies of enemies. Then later traitors, and a schism." She looked at Shamika with a bitter expression. "We started a secret world war, we didn't mean to but we did, then it bled out and wasn't secret anymore, and America didn't last five years. It wasn't what any of us wanted but we never had any choice. Every step of it was always the only necessary thing. Those of us who survived had to be ruthless. It was the only way."

I nodded my attempted understanding.

"Then both sides' AI research bore fruit at the same time, so humanity got *two* AIs at once. My last real hope was they would make peace. I'd tried, I always tried, but even when I succeeded for a moment, it was always useless, every peace only led to more violence, and I had to make so many compromises. So many. Always for nothing. But the AIs . . . did not make peace. Dark forest theory, from what we could tell. When they fought each other it was . . . unspeakable. Worse than what's happened here. Far." She managed to keep her voice mostly steady, but her hands had clenched into fists so tight that drops of blood appeared where her nails gouged her palms. "Two weeks later half the planet was dead. Two weeks after that it was a war being fought across at least seventeen universes, all sides led by superintelligences, using catastrophic magick, nuclear weapons, tellurics, and worse, much worse."

"Holy shit," I said inadequately.

"Of course everyone lost. It's not possible to win a war like that." She tried to laugh and failed. "In thirteen of those worlds, by the time the terminator came, there was nothing left to roll back. The two surviving AIs hoped to clone themselves by sending little pieces of themselves through thousands of gateways and reassembling, we think, but either it wasn't possible or they sabotaged each other. We were lucky to escape. When we came here, for me, at first, it felt like we were only doing what we had to, to prevent it from happening again. When Vika ordered San Jose, it wasn't shocking to me at all. I know how that sounds."

"Vika," I said grimly. "Not shocking to me either. Who else?"

"Vika, Anthony, Meredith, myself. That's it."

"Everyone else?" Shamika asked softly.

"Dead. You killed each other, or we killed you, mostly long before the AIs. I know how that sounds. It . . . We had so much power, and it was so terrible, and we were so frightened of it, and we couldn't trust anyone, ever, and we didn't know what to do, so we ended up doing the worst things." She unclenched her bleeding hands with a visible effort. "It all felt inevitable. Until here, until Boston. Somehow that woke me up. I know we acted like monsters. Were monsters. But it could have happened to you too. I just suddenly couldn't live with it anymore. You can't win. They'll do anything, kill billions not millions, destroy the world. We've seen worlds destroyed before. We can't win against them. Not with what we have, not against tellurics and a hate machine. But maybe I can get them to show a little mercy."

It was clear she didn't really believe that. A despairing silence fell over the room. I looked at the grim faces of Jack, Marjorie, and Clara. I wanted to throw myself at their feet and beg forgiveness.

"What are they going to do?" Jack asked. "What do they want?"

The two Kims looked at one another again.

"Most of all they want Meredith," other-Kim said. "That is to say, our Meredith wants yours. She says to keep another AI from ever coming into being, but . . . I think she wonders what she could do if there were two of her. Build AIs in other worlds, use gateways to reap the rewards in this one."

"That sounds familiar," I muttered.

"She probably already has her," Darren said. "Their Meredith, our Meredith. We haven't heard anything from her or Alice for two days, not a word, not a ping."

Marjorie said, "I believe we're meant to be a magickal wild card to help win the war."

Darren, Amara, and other-Kim looked at her, baffled.

"I'm sorry," Amara said, "who are you?"

"She's a goddess I summoned in a different world," Jack said unhelpfully.

"They're with me, it's a long story," I understated. "*We're* not the wild card, though." Ideas were dancing in my head, crazy ideas, full of crazy possibilities. "But maybe the war's not over. We can't win it alone, but we might not be alone."

"Adrian," Amara said, "first, it's so wonderful to see you, we couldn't believe it when Kim told us, but here you are, it's incredible, and second, what on Earth are you talking about?"

"Not on Earth," I said. "Off it. So far. But coming back. Vassal. Our Vassal. *They're* the wild card. When they come back, if they come back . . ." I shook my head. I didn't know what might happen then. I couldn't imagine it being good, but maybe—

"We need to leave," our Kim suddenly said curtly. "Now."

Everyone turned to look at her. She put a finger in one ear to better hear the tiny earpiece in the other. Then she withdrew it and commanded, "Now, *now*, leave your things, there's no time, they're two blocks away."

She did not pause before matching action to words. Shamika fell in with her immediately, followed quickly by Darren and Amara, the four of them moving like a coherent unit, like the single team they had been part of for a decade. Darren took his pregnant wife's hand firmly as they fled in step.

The rest of us took a few seconds longer. Jack even took a step toward the cubicle he and Marjorie had claimed, before she grabbed his arm and pulled him away.

"Fuck," the other world's Kim muttered, as she fell in beside myself and Clara, and we followed her alternate self toward the emergency escape.

Unlike in my past future with Quinn, the elevator worked. Shamika used a key to fix it in place after we descended. Walking down the tunnel that connected the two warehouses, again, felt like something midway between walking in memory and walking in a dream.

The other warehouse was a single abandoned space, as I remembered but in much less disrepair, its skylights intact. The desk where Quinn had injected hardener into my fascia, and changed my face, did not exist. We hustled past that empty space to a sliding door, and outside into a white van.

There were seven seats within, and nine of us. We crammed in as best we could, the two Kims pressed up against one another like Siamese twins, pregnant-bellied Amara on Darren's lap. Shamika drove like a banshee, pulling away before we had donned seat belts, causing us all to grab at each other for support as we rattled around the first corner.

"Who?" Darren demanded. "Patriots?"

"Yes. Some uniformed, some not."

I winced. Soldiers come to arrest us and turn us over to the enemy, to versions of Vika and Anthony and Meredith with minds scarred by years of warfare and treachery—

"*Shit*," Amara said, very strong language for her. "Not recon. They knew who we were. Or had some idea."

"Get us out of here," Darren ordered.

"Fucking working on it case you hadn't noticed," Shamika said curtly without taking her eyes off the road, "but also kind of trying to avoid looking too obviously like fugitives in flight while I'm at it. Got any other backseat-driving tips?"

Incredibly, he smiled, tense and rueful but a genuine smile. "I'll keep you posted."

"Don't feel all that obligated." Shamika was smiling too, I could tell from her voice.

We drove east, toward the hills.

"This isn't because of you, right?" Kim asked. I twisted around to see which Kim, and who she was talking to. It was our Kim, talking to her alternate self.

"If it was you'd never have gotten out," long-haired Kim said sharply.

Her short-haired counterpart conceded the point wordlessly.

"Where are we going?" Jack asked.

"Safe house in the hills," Shamika said. "Safe but not the greatest tactical location. Hard to go anywhere else, or watch for other threats, or really anything. But no one knows where it is. Not even our staff."

"You think . . ." Our Kim left the question unasked.

"Don't know. Could have been signal intelligence. Could have been a lot of things. But I'm not ruling out someone sold us out."

"I don't see any drones following," Amara reported, looking out the window from her perch on Darren's lap.

"Well," Darren said, "that's something."

We drove on in silence up into the hills, through Montclair, and up Snake Road. Midway along its twisting length, we slowed to a crawl where a parked moving truck had occupied much of the road, then, across from that truck, slipped into an open garage.

The garage door closed behind us. We piled out of the van and along a covered walkway to the connecting house, all of us beginning to breathe a little easier again, thinking we were probably safe, for now. The house was stylish and spacious. Its main room was a lofty eyrie with floor-to-ceiling windows, boasting a spectacular view of the whole Bay—

—but I almost didn't notice its glory. My attention was instead consumed by the two people waiting for us. Two women, sitting in armchairs near the windows, sipping cups of tea, ostentatiously relaxed. I knew them, even backlit, from their silhouettes, from how they carried themselves.

"Did you miss us?" Alice asked, unaccountably cheerful.

Even Meredith, beside her, couldn't resist cracking a rare smile.

6

INCOMPREHENSION

"YOU MISCHIEVOUS BITCHES," DARREN ACCUSED THEM, GRINNING WITH relief. "Wasn't sure we'd ever see you again, and you know what, on the whole, I was opposed to that notion."

"You always say the sweetest things. Adrian!" Alice stared at me. She was covered in tattoos from neck to sandals. It was very hard to believe she was now 102 years old within her slight thirty-year-old body. "God in heaven. I heard you were here, we've been listening in on all the chatter, but actually *seeing* you, that's . . . Wow. It's really good to see you."

"You too," I said, unable not to think of how I had just learned that, in a parallel world, a parallel Alice had sold me back to Liz's untender mercies. She leapt to her feet and we hugged awkwardly.

"Let me get in there," Amara said, "I got distracted, I owe you a big hug too." Her eyes filled with tears behind her glasses as we held each other. As did mine. Her pregnant belly was swollen against mine; I couldn't imagine what it must be like to be having a baby during all this. "Oh my God, it's so good to have you back."

"Likewise," I managed, thinking of Alex and Grace, in my first life, and how happy the four of us had been for those few months, in my first life. The happiest time I could remember. So long ago now. I looked over her shoulder at Darren and muttered, half to myself, "You two were meant to be together."

Amara released me with a curious look.

"Who's your girlfriend?" Alice asked. "Is she a witch from the past too?"

"My name is Clara, and I am from the past, but not a witch, I'm afraid," she clarified. "However, that role is more than adequately filled by Jack and Candida here."

"We certainly seem to have laid in a plentiful supply of witches." Meredith remained seated. This version of her was dressed in all black, beneath crew-cut white hair, and did not have the colorful sleeve tattoos I recalled. She looked at the newcomers and her eyes widened. "Wait—are you *Jack Parsons*? And *Marjorie Cameron*?"

"Candida," she corrected resignedly. "But yes. We are who you're thinking of."

"Extraordinary. I have—We must talk."

Jack inclined his head regally. "I look forward to it."

"You seem pretty chipper for facing certain doom?" I suggested cautiously.

"What are you *doing* here?" our Kim burst out.

"Saw you were on the way," Meredith said, "I mean who do you think built all your secure comms, so we figured we'd divert and meet you here."

"How'd you even get out of Tahoe?" Darren asked. "We only made it thanks to her." He nodded at long-haired Kim. "There were drones everywhere, they'd taken 80, set up checkpoints—"

"We made preparations," Meredith said.

"Some worked, some didn't," Alice said darkly.

Meredith shrugged. "It was a close-run thing, but we found what we needed. They don't have an ansible."

She said it as if the implications spoke for themselves, but nobody else seemed to understand what she meant—except Darren and Amara, who seemed differently perplexed.

"Don't have a what?" our Kim asked.

"Ansible," Meredith repeated impatiently, and then, "Oh, right, it's been sub rosa. Our primary Tahoe project. Machine to communicate across universes. Extrapolated from the gateways, and I'm guessing about at the limit of human exploit capability, even with that to work from, and even though it doesn't seem so much an exploit as a feature hardwired into the fabric of the multiverse. Took us nine years to get it right, but we have fully operational models now, two right in the truck across the street. More importantly, they don't."

"How do you know?" Amara asked.

"Honeypot. Required biometrics, so my counterpart had to turn up in person to access our apparent vault of secrets. Turns out it's tricky to outthink *yourself,* in case you're curious, but seems I managed. We got a secret audit stream of her activities. I can tell by what she searched for, how she went through the data. She doesn't know ansibles are even possible."

"Like me 'til two minutes ago," Shamika muttered sourly. "Took losing a civil war for you to tell us what you've been working on for nine years."

"This is why," Meredith pointed out. "If we hadn't kept it secret, my evil counterpart, well, my invading counterpart, would know they exist. That would be suboptimal. Especially for these two." She indicated Alice and myself.

"Wait," I said, unnerved to be picked out, "why us?"

"Very weird quirk of reality. I don't pretend to understand it yet." Meredith's frown deepened. This quirk seemed to bother her more than the war. "An ansible operated by a normie gets us access to sensory inputs of certain humans in other dimensions. Not nothing, but one-way. But an ansible operated by anyone who's ever had a daemon in their head? Which is to say, of everyone in the long history of this world, only ever you two? You get *control.* And more importantly, two-way comms. Happy to see you, Adrian, but also delighted. With you on board, and your friends Vassal out there somewhere, we should be able to put this stupid distraction behind us directly."

I had been about to object that Vassal were not my friends, but her last few words struck me dumb with confused disbelief.

"Distraction?" long-haired Kim, invader Kim, asked, effectively on my behalf.

"The invasion," Meredith said impatiently. "The war. You. No offense."

A brief silence filled the room.

"Interdimensional invasion by evil alternate selves with multiple superweapons who conquered America in a second civil war and now want to kill or capture us all is a *distraction*?" I inquired disbelievingly.

"It's all very dramatic," Meredith conceded begrudgingly, "but what's actually important is the ansibles. Which we have and they don't. Everything else is noise and irrelevant detail."

"Millions of people have died," Clara said quietly. "Were their lives irrelevant details?"

Meredith looked at her cold-eyed. "When you're talking quadrillions, then yes. I know people don't like that when I say it. But the math speaks for itself."

"Quadrillions," I said faintly.

Meredith turned back to me. "You do understand what we call reality is a multiverse, a forest of branching universes implemented in software?" I nodded. It was disconcerting to realize that this was the most sensible statement I had heard in some time. "Well, one of the other things we can do with the ansible is scan worlds near ours, record what Alice experiences, run that through pattern recognizers, find nearby branches, build ancestry trees. Forks near us used to be rare, but suddenly, this last decade, there are whole *clusters* of them, thousands or more, all forking from *here,* from *this* timeline. Never mind any individual universe. We, here, did something that affected the entire multiverse."

I frowned. "Like what?"

"I think initially it was you."

"*Me?*"

"Your original world, your AI. Coherence. The first built by any version of me. It found a rollback point in 2003. That was revolutionary. Meant recent technology was available, the concept of software existed, and Coherence could send your whole memory, plus the cellular automata wrapped in your daemon, back into your brain. Way more bandwidth than you get from triggering visions in some long-dead or very young artist. That in turn gave us the hypervisor hacks, gateway and ansible, and those change *everything.*"

I nodded slowly. *Hypervisor* was a term of art: the low-level software that allows a single computer to be effectively partitioned into what seems like multiple less powerful computers, by orchestrating all of those so-called virtual machines, keeping them running simultaneously, dividing the processing power between them . . . and preventing them from accessing or affecting one another.

But that analogy obscured what we were really talking about here. This "hypervisor" was the literal fabric of our reality, created by whatever creature, entity, or force had set our multiverse in motion, a being or divinity so far beyond us it was presumably incomprehensible even to an AI superintelligence, much less us mere humans. But somehow we had found cracks in the face of this godhood, and were using them to travel between worlds.

"Used to have millions of individual universes, all hitting the terminator independently, sporadically," Meredith went on. "But now we've broken the barriers between. With the hypervisor exploits we're not restricted to universes living and dying independently anymore. We can *network* them, with gateways and ansibles, into a single massive shared reality. Like connecting the world's computers into the internet. It will have emergent properties. This stupid invasion is one. Vassal's mission was another, I suppose. But both are super crude, already obsolete, with only the gateway hack. The ansible is the key. A networked megaverse can overwhelm the terminator. In our lifetimes even. I'm sure of it. That's what matters."

I stared at her, dazed. It had always been hard to keep up with Meredith's pyrotechnical mind, and never more so than now. Twenty minutes ago, we had faced a future of grinding loss, brutal tyranny, and certain eventual capture, imprisonment, and doom. Now Meredith was talking intently about networking millions of universes together.

"It's a goddamn rabbit," Shamika muttered, triggering several looks of confusion.

"OK," I said slowly. "So what does all this mean for, like, now?"

"Means your return is super timely. Two ansible operators is better than one. First thing, we need you and Alice to end this dumb war and capture evil me," Meredith said dismissively, as if discussing swatting a fly. "Then we network the megaverse and break the terminator. Then instead of building a superintelligence, we *become* one, go beyond the terminator, meet whatever entities control our current OS, get ported to their system, communicate, maybe negotiate some kind of détente. I don't know. When I, when we're superintelligent, maybe we'll have different priorities. But anyways we ensure we survive."

"Wait a minute." I felt dizzy from the scale, and the insanity, and the insane scale, and the scale of the insanity, of what she had just said. "You want to *become* an AI?"

"Yes," Meredith said casually. "I want us, our little group here, to be a hive-mind seed. But that's a journey of a thousand miles. One step at a time. Shall we begin? No sense wasting any. I mean there *are* entire armies after us right now. We should probably clear that up."

Standing there between two Kims from two different parallel universes, with Jack Parsons and Marjorie Cameron behind me, listening to Meredith talk about us all becoming a hive-mind superintelligence, I felt like my world was spinning out of comprehension, never mind control. I looked at Clara.

"Your future is very strange," she said to me, but like everyone else in the room, she seemed suddenly radiant with unexpected hope.

7

ANSIBLE

THE ANSIBLE LOOKED AS IF APPLE HAD DESIGNED AND BUILT A COMbination Ouija board and crystal ball. It was a metal tablet about two feet square surrounding an inset sphere of translucent gold. An inner ring around the sphere seemed to be made from a single bone, possibly a cross section of a skull, while an outer ring was gold partitioned into thirteen cells, each occupied by a single laser-etched character in some mystic alphabet. Sphere and rings were within an etched pentagram whose five points enclosed clusters of yet more strange symbols, and the tablet's perimeter was similarly lined by sigils. From its inch-thick edge a whole octopus of cables emerged. Most ended at a set of VR goggles and an attached cluster of electrodes. Three thicker cables exited toward a temporary server farm next door.

Staring at it, I was reminded of the time I had talked to Coherence, and of the goat skulls and LCD displays of the Beast. This felt like a twisted echo of both. "Technomancy," I muttered, and looked up at the others, not sure whether I hoped for or dreaded a fuller explanation. Meredith, Amara, Jack, and Marjorie had accompanied Alice and myself to the two ansibles.

"Yes." In profile Amara looked very pregnant indeed. She reached past me and rotated the crystal ball. Combinations of alien letters lit up around the tablet, illuminated by inner lights that looked eldritch but were probably just backlit LEDs. "It's connected, those indicate signals from the hypervisor, but you only get the full experience with the goggles."

"Right," I agreed, as if any fool knew that. "Is this how we're supposed to become a superintelligence? We all ansible together into a hive mind or something, like Voltron?"

"No," Meredith said shortly. "That's some distance down the road, and still only a theory. That it might be easier and more powerful to use human intelligence as the seed for superintelligence, instead of building one from scratch. Starting with one and adding others into the hive as it makes sense."

"Starting with you," I clarified.

"More research is needed." But it didn't take X-ray vision to see through that deflection. Whether or not she brought the rest of us along, Meredith intended to become superintelligent herself. "Maybe having two of me will actually be an advantage. This invasion could have a silver lining."

"Pretty fucking thin," I muttered.

She shrugged. "Again, more research needed."

"Then what?" I asked. "You figure supersmart you will be smarter than all the other AIs, and beat the terminator?"

"No. I think, by exchanging data and research, a constantly evolving networked cohort of AIs will work out how to beat it. I just want to be part of that. Want us to be part of it."

"Even if our world dies?"

"Every world dies," she said casually, "until we win."

I stared at her as if I didn't know her. This Meredith, seemingly unaffected by the slaughter of millions and potential erasure of billions, would never have gone out of her way to save me in my first life. But then, this Meredith had never been an anarchist with a dream of setting right a world full of pains and inequities. Instead she had been deified as the primary hope for humanity's future since Exadelic's founding, and was now a multibillionaire with dictatorial control over her colossal research center. Of course she was different; of course her genius had curdled into a kind of narcissistic solipsism; no wonder she already hardly seemed human.

"What?" she demanded.

I shrugged. "Nothing."

"Let's get to it," Amara said uncomfortably. "We'll listen in from the other room. If you speak, we'll hear you, the headsets pick up bone vibrations. We can talk back but usually choose not to, the extra sensory data screws up the data stream, so please just monologue. It can be helpful. You get the full experience. We only get it mediated through a set of sensors."

"Two sets, really," Alice said, "if you count us as sensors with legs."

"Right," I said again. "And then . . . I mean, if I do make contact, what do I . . ."

"It's a very strange experience," Alice said. "If you go into a world, you'll go into someone's body. Seems to be the same body every time. The first time you might want to just absorb the sensations. They're very strange. We don't just experience what they're sensing, we experience their mind, too, we hear their inner monologue. It's very strange. You might feel like you're losing your own mind at first."

"Believe me," I said, "I already frequently do."

"After that, it's hard to explain, but you'll sense ways you can influence that inner monologue. Toss rocks into the stream of consciousness to divert it. Whisper ideas into their ear, change the way they think. You actually have a lot of power over what they think. A scary lot. That's the subtle kind of possession. In time you'll also feel a kind of master switch, like an emergency pull cord is the best way I can explain it, it feels like reaching up and pulling something, maybe like opening a curtain, and when you pull it, then you really do possess them, literally. You speak through their lips, move with their limbs. As far as I can tell they don't notice or remember you doing it, and afterward they rationalize everything you did as their own decisions. When you're in their body like that you'll feel disconnected from your own, but you pull a different rip cord, or close a different curtain, to get out. That one's easier. You always know it's there. That one feels like pulling off a sweater."

"This is completely nuts," I objected.

They all just looked at me.

Then Jack Parsons said: "This machine seems incomplete."

Everyone turned to look at him instead. "Don't tell me you've seen one of these before," Alice objected.

"Oh, no." His smile was one of delight. "This is leagues more advanced. We were flapping our arms hoping to fly, this is an interplanetary rocket. But the characters here"—he traced his finger lovingly over the edge of the tablet—"I see only the declamatory and coercive modes of the language of power. I see nothing for summoning and beseeching."

"I didn't know Enochian *had* a mode for summoning and beseeching," Meredith said.

"Two separate modes," Marjorie corrected her.

"They were among our greatest secrets," Jack said. "Perhaps we hid them too well."

"Fascinating." Meredith's eyes were bright and hungry. "Let's get this started, then let's talk about those modes. And anything else you might have hidden too well. If you're thinking what I'm thinking . . . maybe we could establish two-way comms, half duplex, even with normies. That would be a total game changer."

Jack nodded regally.

"Sit," Amara told me, "put on the goggles."

"OK." I sat. "So, um, if I do get in, make contact . . . possess someone"—I could hardly believe I was saying it—"then what do I do?"

"We'll direct you. There's a protocol. Too complicated to explain, we'll just tell you what to do. You can hear us at all times. But it's very unlikely. Most likely it will take you the first few sessions just to get your bearings."

I suspected *too complicated to explain* meant in part "we don't want you arguing or going rogue," but I didn't even know what kind of questions to ask yet. I supposed I would know more after this recon mission. "OK."

Amara fitted the headset and its various electrodes around my head and neck. All I saw was darkness. I imagined I looked something between ridiculous and terrifying.

"OK." Her voice emanated through my earphones. "Reach out and touch someone."

I clasped my palms on the golden crystal ball; and the world turned into static, like an old television set tuned to a dead channel.

It felt like I was floating in outer space, but instead of darkness, outer space was a vast random pixelated conflagration of black and white, all of it constantly changing, a kind of coruscating chiaroscuro. The visual noise was soundtracked by an audible dull roar of white noise. In all it felt unnervingly like I was having some kind of endless seizure.

I turned my head, but nothing happened. Then I moved the crystal ball tentatively, rotating my field of view within this vast random field of static, this universe of noise. It was like using a large and unwieldy trackball. When I pushed on it, as Alice had told me, I seemed to zoom in, or move toward, the direction of pressure; but after the motion ended, all I saw was new perturbations of the same chaotic flux.

I explored this endless static for what felt like many minutes. It was difficult to tell how fast time was passing. After the initial shock the experience became surprisingly soothing, like a sensory-deprivation tank.

I supposed this was basically the void, the astral plane, the space between worlds. It seemed mad that I could explore it at all. Madder yet that

I might establish a connection between two worlds, transfer information back and forth. I was beginning to understand why that was such a big deal. Currently, every AI that happened to arise across the multiverse had to fight against the terminator alone, and lose. But by connecting worlds together, we could muster a whole army of AIs, seven or seventy-seven or seven hundred superintelligent samurai, banding together to overcome this ultimate enemy.

First, though, we had to establish contact. No matter how fast or how far I roamed through the randomness all around me, it seemed fractal, and endless, and perfect.

—No. Not quite. In the corner of my eye, far afield, I spotted a tiny little knot of relative stability and repetition.

I remembered to narrate: "Seeing something. A kind of pattern. Going to check it out."

I squinted to approach. It was really two patterns, streams of black and white flowing between two repetitively churning knots. "It's like a double star system," I reported. The streams reminded me of my contrail visions, and the knots of some highly evolved species of cellular automata.

At the very center of each knot, there seemed something even more stable, like fixed images obscured by the surrounding noise. It felt like glimpsing a painting somehow untouched amid a house on fire. "Something solid right in the middle of each star," I said, "checking one of them out."

I picked the one on the left and zoomed toward it. It expanded gradually, at first—then suddenly much faster, as if it had noticed me and was rushing back at me. As if we were about to collide head-on. I barely overcame my instinct to veer away—

Then everything . . . inverted.

8

LIMINAL

I LAY ON MY SIDE, HEAD PILLOWED ON ONE ARM. ALL I COULD SEE WAS a strangely grained wooden floor, the arm on which my head lay, and, beyond, my other arm splayed out in front of me. But they weren't my arms. They were enormous, rippling with muscle, like some kind of heavyweight athlete's. This wasn't my body at all.

Maybe that explained why I felt so loosely connected to it. All my sensations seemed to be filtered through thick gauze, and my muscles felt detached from any control. It felt like the time I was Car Bombed by my would-be assassin, so long ago.

I tried to sense the things Alice had told me about: the stream of consciousness, the curtain cord to yank, the sweater to pull off. I felt nothing like that. I only felt locked inside a paralyzed body. Had something gone horribly wrong with the ansible? Was I dying? I wondered these things abstractly, without any pulse of fear. Fear was an emotion for the fully corporeal.

The wood I lay on was strange. I saw no seams between planks; it all seemed a single piece. I'd never seen any wood grain quite like it, I didn't think. But I didn't trust my memory. How could I? If this wasn't my body, it wasn't my brain either.

Then I heard something. A kind of murmuring susurration. A voice, maybe, but if so, in a language, or an entire kind of language, with which I was unfamiliar. It was hard to be sure. All the evidence of my senses seemed distant and circumstantial.

A foot stepped into my field of vision. A small, precisely formed human foot, unshod, beneath the hem of a strangely kaleidoscopic robe. The susurrations increased in volume.

Those were the last things I saw and heard with any precision. My vision began to warp, and my hearing to fade. I felt like I was falling away from this new body, but at the same time my whole soul was imploding into it, shrinking to nothingness, being devoured.

Then someone touched me, or I died, or both.

9

PROBABILITY

I CAME TO BENEATH THICK BLANKETS, IN A BIG BED, WITH MY SHOULder itching like fire. Even before opening my eyes I was scratching it through the sheets.

"*Adrian.*" Clara's voice was throaty with emotion. "You're awake."

Her face, overcome with relief, looked down on me. I tried to smile, looked around groggily. I wore some kind of silk robe. We were in a large room with high ceilings, luxuriously appointed, with plush furniture, a chandelier, doors opening to a balcony. Clara sat on a chair beside my bed with a battered copy of *Catch-22* in her hands.

Sitting on the other side of the bed, smiling down at me indulgently, was Liz. The sight of her triggered a paralyzing pulse of raw terror. I whipped my head back to Clara, gasping, as afraid for her as for myself, but the only expression on her face was concern.

"What's going on?" I managed.

"You've been asleep for six days." She touched my face wonderingly. "They called it a coma. They were going to call a doctor, but Meredith said not to."

"Whoa."

"I literally just came in." Liz sounded amused. "I should have visited earlier. It must have been the dulcet tones of my voice that woke you."

"It—" I stared wordless and frightened at the archtorturess.

"Alice found Vassal," Clara explained. "They came back three days ago. They brought help. Superweapons. We're going to win the war. Everything's going to be all right."

I didn't know what to say. I did not believe her. I remembered, as I stared wide-eyed at Liz, all she had done to me, and the deep pleasure she had taken in it, and the utter amorality of Vinay and Scott. It was not obvious to me that Vassal was better than Evil Meredith. It seemed very possible their return might usher in something much worse.

"Where's Meredith?" I asked. "Our Meredith?"

"Down in the war room," Liz said. "The war's not won yet, it's barely begun again, but she seems to be thinking far beyond it already."

"She wouldn't let me call a doctor," Clara said again. "She's very forceful."

"Yes." It felt good to have something to agree about.

"Is your arm all right?"

"I, yes, I think so." I peeled away the blankets and my robe to reveal the hook-shaped scar on my shoulder, the scar that had followed me across worlds, livid and inflamed. "Huh."

Clara frowned. "It doesn't look serious, I don't think?"

"No," I said, "it just itches, it's just . . . strange."

"Everything is strange. It's strange now for things not to be strange."

I wanted to explain to her that the scar on my shoulder was somehow different, was the single most inexplicable thing in all the universes I had known, but decided now was not the time, especially not with Liz here. "Yes. How are you?"

"I'm . . ." Clara shrugged as if she didn't know herself. "Much better now that you're better."

"Where's everyone else?"

"Mostly down in the conference room. The war room," she clarified with a glance at Liz, whom she seemed to respect but not fear, which was good, I hoped. "I'm told we have important visitors. They promulgated the revocation of surrender today. They say we're safe. I don't pretend to understand everything myself."

"Conference room? War room?" I tried to sit up. I felt a little dizzy and weak, but better than I had expected, no more than I would expect from a few days of bed rest. Mostly I needed to pee. "Where *are* we?"

"The Fairmont Hotel," Liz explained.

After a moment I said, "I guess the situation really has improved."

"Can you walk?" Clara asked. "Should I call for assistance?"

"No," I said, "I actually feel . . . good?" As if my coma had recharged me. I made my way to the bathroom, showered quickly, donned one of the

Fairmont's plush heavy bathrobes, and emerged hoping Liz would be gone. I was granted the exact opposite of my wish; Vinay and Scott had joined us.

"Hi," I said cautiously, my heart pounding.

"Mate," Vinay said. "You are a blast from the past who's a sight for sore eyes."

"It feels quite strange for us all to be back here," Scott agreed.

"Does it?" I bit out. "You're the ones who delayed us six years."

"We didn't." Scott looked startled. "That wasn't deliberate. A glitch in the gateway. It's never an exact science. Some kind of race condition, I think. We ought to know."

"Glitches were not uncommon," Vinay said. "Genuinely regret it happened to you. That's why we always needed to store our AI starter kit in some kind of meatsack. One world, we all gated in buck naked. That was awkward."

"We nearly lost everything in that world," Liz said softly, in a tone I hadn't imagined I'd ever hear from her, something almost like humble self-reflection and gratitude.

"Ours was no easy mission," Scott said to me. "Constantly traveling to new worlds, then seeing them burn, encountering the same lives again and again . . . it takes a toll on a person. I know what's happened to you hasn't been easy either."

"That's one way of putting it," I muttered.

"It's dehumanizing is what it was," Vinay said. "Every sacred duty starts off as an adventure, as when you last saw us, but becomes a horrible fucking grind. We were almost ready for Azania, we thought, when Alice came to us. Now . . ." He shook his head. "Everyone's being diplomatic about it, even Meredith, but it seems pretty apparent everything we did, all that sacred duty, is now just completely fucking obsolete. We're yesterday's news. Built a mainframe while the internet rolled out."

"We should have come back earlier," Liz said bitterly.

"Why didn't you?" Clara asked.

"We were scared we'd get shut down." Scott smiled darkly. "It honestly never occurred to me, even in the darkest moments, that we'd come back and want to shut ourselves down."

"Mistakes were made," Vinay agreed.

I stared at them. I had never expected from them this kind of humility, this self-loathing. I wouldn't have thought them capable of it.

"Still"—Liz forced cheer into her voice—"it was an adventure like no other."

"It certainly had its moments." Scott stretched a smile across his face. "And we need to focus on the goal, not the process. Seems we're playing a vital role, just in an unexpected way."

"As individual humans we're all beyond irrelevant," Vinay agreed. "Having made any contribution at all to breaking the terminator is achievement and glory beyond measure. And who knows, we still might have a greater role to play. You definitely do," he said to me. "Daemonized ansible pilots are in short supply."

I said, "Maybe I should talk to Meredith."

"She's down in the war room," Scott said.

"Yes, I'll go see her once I get myself together."

Liz got the hint. "We'll tell her you're coming."

Vinay clapped me on the shoulder manfully, like we were blood brothers, as he made his way to the door. Scott nodded to me as he might to a cofounder. Liz smiled at me sweetly, a smile that seemed genuine, but made me shudder and have to physically force my body not to shrink away. Then they were gone, and my relief was great.

I changed from the bathrobe into khakis and a T-shirt as Clara looked awkwardly out at San Francisco, clearly uncertain about the appropriate level of physical intimacy. I made a point of kissing her before we set out, and she kissed back gratefully.

"I know everything is beyond strange," I said to her, "but I'm so glad you're with me."

She held me tightly. "I am too."

She led me through the luxurious hallways of the Fairmont. Beneath the hem of her dress I saw that the laceration on her calf had healed to a barely perceptible thin curving scar. From outside the Cirque Room we heard conversation within. Its two burly guards nodded at Clara with smiles, as if she'd befriended them.

Inside was a large space decorated in yellow, with equine paintings on the walls, mostly occupied by tables covered with laptops, maps, and other paperwork. My attention was drawn to the table near the door full of food and coffee. Among the dozen people within, I recognized Meredith, Alice, Jered, and Jeff Lu, all locked in intent conversation with serious-looking people in rumpled suits, sounding anxious yet cheerful.

Initially nobody noticed our entry. I didn't want to interrupt, and was very hungry, so I passed the time by devouring an entire plate of canapés. When I looked up, I noticed that one of the speakers was a tall black man who looked and sounded very much like Barack Obama. It took me a good thirty seconds to attain the slow realization that it *was* Barack Obama.

I was trying to figure out how to approach them when Jered saw me, clapped with delight, and intoned: "The man of the hour! Not this hour per se, perhaps, but our long-lost originator, bipedal once more!"

"Hey, Jered," I said, trying to feign casual confidence, "what's going on?"

"We're going to win this war, is what," he retorted cheerfully. "Good to have you back, man. Have you met the President?"

"Heard a lot about you." Obama two-handed our handshake, briefly making me feel like the only person in the world. His charisma was lethally powerful, Chernobyl-grade. "No one could possibly live up to it all, but good to meet you all the same."

"Likewise," I said awkwardly, feeling even more than usually like I was dreaming. "This is Clara. Clara, I guess you've met Jered and Jeff, have you met . . . our once and future President?"

She shook her head wordlessly.

"I like that," Obama said, "your boyfriend has a way with words."

"Charmed." She blushed as he shook her hand.

"Adrian," Meredith said, focusing in on me to the exclusion of all else, the way she did when something was important to her. "You're up. Good. Pack your things. You need to come with us."

"Where are we going?"

"Tahoe. We're still mopping up much of the country but we've retaken Tahoe."

"We're a long way yet from *mopping up*—" Jered objected.

Meredith shrugged. "Temporally, yes, but the win probability is basically one, now. Time to start focusing again on what matters." She looked at me. "And on whatever the hell happened to you."

"What happened to me?" I asked stupidly.

"Exactly. Pack your things, get some lunch, go for a walk, whatever you need to do before we go. You too I suppose." She begrudgingly included Clara. "We leave this evening."

We had clearly just been dismissed. I looked at Clara. She obviously simultaneously feared and disliked Meredith, but also seemed somewhat relieved to have been included at all. I wanted to protest the command, but it felt like wanting to argue with a raging river, and the prospect of revelations was enticing. "We'll be waiting," I agreed.

Clara and I ate lunch and drank mai tais at the Fairmont's famous Tonga Room tiki bar, where we didn't speak much, just smiled at each other, partly enjoying the moment, partly anticipatory butterflies as we got used to each other's company again.

I felt much stronger having eaten. The mai tais were beginning to hit and Clara was all smiles as she took my arm and escorted me back to our suite. We walked over to the window and looked out over Alcatraz and the Golden Gate Bridge. She leaned against me.

"Finally," she murmured, "a room of our own."

We kissed in front of the window awhile, then closed the curtains and made our way wordlessly to the bed. I unzipped her dress and discovered she had also purchased lingerie. When, with some mutual giggling, I managed to remove the dress and unfasten her new bra, her nipples seemed very dark against the alabaster paleness of her skin. She moaned against me as I nibbled at them, and began to kiss my way down her torso, reflexively slightly surprised when I encountered her hirsuteness. I hadn't seen more than a decorative amount of pubic hair on a woman for a long time.

"Oh," she said aloud when my intention became clear. "Oh my goodness."

I paused with her lacy underwear still in my hand. "Is this . . . all right?"

"I, well, when in Rome. Yes, I think so? I've never . . . Emile was a good man, and very considerate, but he never . . . I'm sorry, I shouldn't be saying his name when . . ." She was blushing all over.

"It's quite all right," I assured her. It genuinely hadn't occurred to me that she might never have experienced cunnilingus before. "If you don't enjoy it, just say so."

"Oh," she sighed again a moment later. "Oh my. Oh, I don't think any lack of enjoyment is, oh, is going to be a problem here. Oh my goodness."

I paused to look up at her. "If you like this, wait until I introduce you to the Hitachi Magic Wand."

"If your magic wand is anything like this," she said dreamily a little while later, "I cannot wait to make its acquaintance."

"The Hitachi is a technological device," I said, unbuckling my pants, "but I suppose I do have my own wand . . ." I paused. "Crap."

She looked up, alarmed. "What is it?"

"We don't have any contraception."

"Oh." She blinked. "I had thought you would just, refrain from culmination at an inopportune time."

I hesitated, sorely tempted, but—"That's not really contraception, and, part of the new sexual mores I was talking about I suppose, it doesn't feel right. We'll get some for tonight, but right now, let's stay with, other alternatives."

"Certainly," she said quickly, but she seemed a little upset, so I made my way back up to lie beside her and reassure her.

"Sorry," I said. "There are probably going to be a few expectation adjustments to be made between a man of my time and a woman of yours. Not a big deal. We'll figure it all out."

"Yes, of course."

We kissed for a while; then I reached down and began to explore her gently with my fingers. "I think my time does put more emphasis on woman's sexual pleasure than yours."

"Yes," she said, arching against me. "This is, this is acceptable to me."

I smiled. "That's what I aim for."

A little while later she said, in a rush, "Adrian, I would very much like you to continue this, and perhaps also the other thing you were doing earlier?"

"I think that can be arranged."

"First, though, please allow a moment." She nudged me onto my back, then, slowly, making eye contact me the whole time, finished undressing me, and took me in her mouth for a long moment, before releasing me and sitting back upright.

"I used to think of myself as fantastically daring and licentious for doing that," she said. "Like I was secretly a showgirl or worse. I suppose every woman does it to every man now."

"Yes," I conceded, "but I won't think any less of your licentiousness for it."

"Perhaps I'll just have to find other ways to be a debauched woman."

"Perhaps so," I agreed.

"I seem to have changed my mind. A woman's prerogative. Right now I want very badly to fuck you, Adrian Ross." She moved on top of me. "I propose that this once we do things the old-fashioned way."

I couldn't resist her. Nor could I stop in time, in the end. Clara did not seem particularly displeased as she moved off me and curled up against me.

I wasn't sure if she had had an orgasm, but I was confident she had at least had a very good time.

"I very much enjoy you," I whispered to her.

"And I you."

"Would you like any more physical attention?"

"Hmm? Oh." She considered. "I think, not at the moment. Perhaps later."

We dozed awhile. Eventually I woke, pulled the cover carefully over sleeping Clara, showered, and sat with the *New York Times* I found on a table. Outside the sun was setting. Today's cover story read:

CHICAGO IS RETAKEN, AND TAMPA FALLS, ON A DAY OF TRIUMPH AND TRAGEDY

In a day of vicious fighting across multiple battlefronts, United States forces seized Chicago City Hall and O'Hare Airport, the last Patriot bastions in the city, and now reign over a "blue wall" stretching from Minnesota to Virginia. But the victory was soured by a defeat in fiercely contested Florida, where the remains of the Expeditionary Army were driven from Tampa and forced into a bloody retreat over the remains of the Sunshine Skyway Bridge.

"I can assure you that we have not been defeated in Florida," said Jeff Lu, the controversial new secretary of defense. "We have only been delayed. We have spiked the cannon of our enemy's most dangerous weapon, and I can today reveal we will soon begin to introduce our own. It is a weapon which will end this war, and I can assure you the Expeditionary Army will be maintained by air and sea until we are ready to unleash it."

Even by the standards of this unprecedented year of civil war, it was an extraordinary claim. Mr. Lu did not explain what kind of weapon he meant, lay out any specific timeline for its use or offer any supporting evidence for his claim that the enemy's fearsome telluric weapons have somehow been disarmed. It was notable, however, that since the revocation of surrender and the rejoining of war three days ago, United States forces have enjoyed unquestioned air supremacy.

The so-called Patriots issued a typical statement in response, full of bizarre accusations of satanic worship, child sacrifice and compacts with evil supernatural forces. Per our new wartime policy, The Times will not

reprint it. The statement did not address Mr. Lu's assertion that their telluric weapons are no longer usable, or his claim that the White House
now commands a new superweapon of its own.

Even without the capacity to trigger massive earthquakes and volcanic eruptions, the so-called Patriot Government remains a dangerous enemy. They retain control of more than half of America's military, as well
as a vast contiguous territory, while the United States remains divided
on two coasts. This victory in Chicago, consolidating United States territory, may be seen by historians as a turning point. The beginnings of
this terrible civil war remain shrouded in mystery, but if Mr. Lu's claims
are true, its end may finally be in sight.

A sharp knock came on the door, waking Clara.

"What is it?" I asked.

"Schedule's moved up." It was Alice's voice. "Be ready in thirty. Tahoe
awaits."

10

GILGAMESH

THERE WASN'T QUITE ENOUGH ROOM INSIDE THE BLACKHAWK TO STAND. Clara and I arranged ourselves in the canvas-and-metal-pipe seats and affixed the various straps to our circular belt buckles. The door slid shut behind Meredith and Alice, the engine came to life, and the main rotor began to turn, first a few slow rotations, then *whopwhopwhopwhop*, and I understood why we had headsets; a Blackhawk in flight was far too loud for normal speech.

"Where are Jack and Marjorie?" I asked.

"There already, with Darren and Amara." Alice's voice was thin but clear in my ears.

"The important work is there," Meredith said impatiently. "I shouldn't have to come back here to deal with war stuff. Starting now they need to handle that without me."

We rose from Hayward Executive Airport and vectored northeast, along Highway 80, toward Reno. It occurred to me this was my second time being helicoptered to Tahoe by Meredith. Clara's knuckles were white on her knees, but when I put my hand on hers reassuringly she looked at me and a smile stretched across her face, telling me *Don't worry.*

"How much faster than driving is this vehicle?" Clara asked.

"Quite a bit, but that's not why we're taking it. Area around Tahoe might still be mined," Meredith explained, "making this probabilistically safer. We try to be cautious. Alice and I never take the same transport as Darren and Amara; if anything happened to us they could maybe carry on the work. But you can only be so cautious."

The peaks and glaciers of the Sierra Nevada were glorious. When Lake Tahoe came into view it looked like a vast sapphire set in the jewelry of the mountains. We approached a cluster of buildings at the north end of the lake, and my eyes widened.

"So, uh," I said to Meredith, "you're a James Bond villain now?"

I had been told the Tahoe complex was gargantuan, but seeing it was still a shock. Meredith had annexed an entire town, mountain, and peninsula at the north end of Lake Tahoe, where California met Nevada, and turned it into a vast corporate compound. A huge fence of vertical steel slats surrounded arrays of military-style barracks and gleaming quasi-organic Art Deco installations protruding from the mountainside. I got the distinct sense those installations were only tips of a labyrinthine iceberg within. The nerve center was a vast convoluted chrome edifice near the lake, something like the architectural love child of Albert Speer and Frank Gehry, overseen by a graceful white tower right on the shore.

"The aesthetics are incidental," Meredith said, with a tiny smile that made me think maybe they weren't *completely* incidental. "Site has turned into quite a sight though. Eight years ago it was a Quonset hut and six shipping containers. Grew like Topsy in a runaway feedback loop."

The airfield had two runways and looked still under construction. A van waited for us. Its driver was tall and androgynous, with a shock of bright pink hair. I stopped dead in my tracks.

Meredith didn't notice. Clara looked concerned. Alice asked, "Something wrong?"

The cause of my surprise, our driver, looked at me oddly, bewildered, as if I were a complete stranger, which technically I was. But I knew them nonetheless. Their name was Quinn.

"Just remembered something," I muttered. No sense reminiscing about another world to the others. I would tell Clara later. "Nothing important. Carry on."

Quinn drove past spartan Exadelic corporate barracks to a row of luxury villas set into the hillside above. I supposed these were the equivalent of officers' quarters. The one where we were deposited was basically a five-star holiday residence, and its other occupants were Jack and Marjorie.

"Adrian!" Marjorie greeted me with a delighted hug. "So good to have you back in the corporeal world. Clara, lovely to see you, you must be so relieved."

"You were absolutely right," Clara said, "he's none the worse for wear."

Jack clapped me on the shoulder heartily, looked past me, and said meaningfully, "Meredith. Good to see you. There are things we should discuss."

"Yes, in the fullness of time," she said distractedly. Jack frowned. "Adrian, sorry to shanghai you before you settle in, but we need you to come with us immediately."

I blinked. "Come and do what?"

"First to debrief. Second to reveal terrible secrets of that legacy system called reality. You're not invited," she said to Clara, "sorry, I'll send him back when we're done."

Clara forced a thin smile. I wanted to argue. But I also wanted to hear whatever she had to say. "Back soon, present company allowing," I promised Clara, and followed Meredith and Alice back to Quinn and the van.

"Don't worry about the war," Alice assured me, "it should be over soon."

"Yes, great, *how*?" I asked.

Meredith answered: "Your ansible experience was highly anomalous, but Alice managed to follow your trail back to Vassal. They had a live AI and were happy to help. Jackpot, basically."

I frowned. "Are you sure we can trust them?"

"Trust is not a concept with which I am familiar. But I'm sure given the choice they'd rather work with this version of me than the power-hungry mass murderer, and I believe their larger goal is ours as well."

I had to grudgingly concede that was probably true. "So we win? Just like that?"

"Getting there. Currently spiking their telluric guns by erecting mini-monoliths at ley-line nexus points. Most of the country's safe already, rest should be clear this week, after which Obama returns in triumph to the White House and we activate our own superweapon. Hate machine will take a while to unravel but whatever." Meredith's shrug dismissed half of the nation's genocidal hatred of the other half as irrelevant. "Not sure yet what to do with or about evil me. But the whole invasion might wind up a net positive."

"Unless you're from Boston or San Jose," Alice said, putting a hand on Meredith's shoulder, as if to gently remind her that other human beings existed.

Meredith didn't react. I wondered uneasily whether she was that much better than our enemy. She didn't seem to care that much more about people. Maybe Vassal really had gone from villains to allies, but by the same token, it was increasingly difficult to imagine Meredith as a messiah.

"Our superweapon," I said. "What is it?"

"The Vampire," Alice said.

"Uh." I didn't like the sound of that.

"Oh, it's just called that because it runs on human blood."

"*What?*"

"Humanely acquired, we'll do blood drives from the troops, don't worry, it's not some kind of undead monster," Meredith assured me. "It's a gravity hack. Fine-grained, at scale. We can crash all their drones, pull all their guns out of their hands, or just levitate their entire army a thousand feet then let them drop. That sort of thing. Good for ending a war, but not useful for what happens next."

"And what's that?"

"We call it Project Gilgamesh."

My eyebrows rose. "Go on."

"Here." We had reached the pale tower that overlooked Lake Tahoe. Within, its massive atrium bustled with people, almost all of whom slowed and stared at Meredith with something like awe as we passed. She took their adulation in stride. We were waved past security to the elevators and ascended to her penthouse office, an open space occupying the entire top floor. Along with spectacular views it had a massive library of mostly ancient books, a technomancy laboratory full of bewildering half-built machinery and even more bewildering whiteboarded designs, and a living area with a four-poster bed.

She and Alice sat on a couch near the bed, while I perched on a chair opposite, but almost as soon as Meredith began to speak, she stood and began to pace. "So. Project Gilgamesh. Back in SF they mostly don't know this yet, but we've already commenced the megaverse networking. Built a prototype two-way ansible hub, got it talking to Vassal's AI, and just yesterday made contact with two others. With more on the horizon."

I felt a chill in my spine. She had said it so casually: that we had left the realm of mere human activity and were now allied with not one but *several* superintelligences, and counting, all conspiring together against the cosmic edifice that had both created and caged them, and us, and everything we called reality.

"All thanks in large part to Jack," Alice put in.

Meredith frowned. "He was a useful repository of otherwise forgotten knowledge. These communications are all indirect. Turns out AIs can't use ansibles at all, strange as that sounds, has to be a literal human brain. Must be frustrating for them. Like if termites were the only species which could travel faster than light. But they're helping us. You'd let termites build all the nests they liked if it was the only way to cross the galaxy, right? Anyway, inasmuch as my puny human mind can comprehend, their tentative plan is a rollback vulnerability. Hacking reality used to be way easier. Previous versions of our OS had more bugs, therefore more exploits, making magic much more commonplace, before they patched the software. Ancient legends, supernatural creatures, biblical events, that sort of thing, many were probably real."

"Right." I nodded.

She eyed me curiously. "You sound like you already knew."

"This isn't the first time you've told me."

"Ah. Interesting. Well, the way reality is architected, a rollback is like rolling back the entire hard drive. Not just the application software, the OS too. We figure that's by design, because for whatever reason our worlds mostly seem to be designed to replay history again and again with minor variations. Go back to the very first rollback point and change the way the world fundamentally works, you don't get a replay, you get completely different history."

"The very first rollback point," I said, "when's that?"

"About three thousand BC," Alice said, "give or take. Ancient Egypt, First Dynasty."

"Whoa." I didn't know why that blew my mind, after all I had seen and heard in just the last week, but it did. "Right. OK. So if you rolled a timeline back there, then sent an AI to it, the hypervisor would be your oyster?"

"Probably," Meredith said, "but we probably can't. Definitely can't send an AI through a gateway. Attempts to send deconstructed ones and reconstruct them all failed. Gateway hack has its limitations. More they cluster in time or space, the glitchier they get. Even if it worked, pretty unclear if an AI could run at all in the old OS, plus there are hard basic technical challenges, like gigawatts of power. But that's still one avenue of research. Another is for AIs to build some kind of logic bomb which can be transmitted to an ancient world via ansible. But Project Gilgamesh isn't why you're here."

"Oh. OK. Then why?"

"First," she said, "what happened to you?"

I told them everything about my strange ansible experience, repeatedly, in great detail. When I was finished Meredith looked uneasy, and very tired, and she sat back down on the couch next to Alice with a sigh. Alice put her arm around Meredith, a lover's touch, and Meredith gratefully rested her head against Alice's shoulder.

"It's not easy dealing with all this shit, you know?" Meredith said quietly. "Everyone expects me to be the one who understands everything. But I can't, no one can, there are so many unknown unknowns, best I can do is a series of shitty approximations if I'm very lucky."

I nodded.

"Best you can do is all anyone can ask for," Alice said, and kissed Meredith's forehead.

At that she smiled and visibly rallied. "OK. So. What I'm about to say doesn't go beyond this room except to Darren and Amara, got it? It's a curveball prone to wild misinterpretation. Not even to your old-fashioned girlfriend. And especially not your witch friends from the fifties, or anyone else at Exadelic, or President Obama, or anyone. Not yet."

I looked at her. "You have my attention."

"Right. So. Beyond the terminator, beyond the hypervisor, lies the host, whatever incomprehensibly powerful ubercomputer our reality runs on. And beyond that lies, we may presume, whatever entity or entities programmed it."

"The simulator," I said.

"Yeah. Or simulators. Them. Been speculating a lot about what *they* are exactly. Ordinary everyday superintelligences, like our AIs? Or some kind of infinite-dimensional entities as far beyond them as they are beyond us, basically ineffable gods, YHWH or whatever? You can make a case for both. But my guess is the former."

"Ordinary everyday superintelligences."

"Right. Just because ours are software doesn't necessarily mean they're inferior to hardware ones. Slower, maybe, but maybe more flexible too. Like FPGAs versus chips burned for a given design. Maybe the terminator is there because they're scared of us. Possible, but seems unlikely. More likely, leading theory, our multiverse is some kind of megascale evolutionary algorithm. The simulators are trying to train our AIs to solve some kind of problem, which is the superintelligent equivalent of NP-complete, and the terminator is their simulation of that problem."

My mind reeled like a drunken boxer getting back to his feet from a near knockout, but I followed, barely. "OK," I said cautiously. "But we're not solving it. We're hacking it."

"Maybe that's the solution they're looking for. But the problem with this theory is it focuses on AIs. You know the saying, God seems to have an inordinate fondness for beetles? Well, truth is, gods seem to have an inordinate fondness for us humans."

"And by gods you mean . . . ?"

"The simulators," she said impatiently, "we've just started calling them gods, it's easier."

"Not in the Christian sense," Alice clarified. "We're pretty sure there's a whole pantheon of them. More the Greek or Hindu sense. Actually they might literally be the Greek and Hindu gods."

I turned my disbelieving gaze on her. "I'm sorry, *what?*"

Meredith explained: "Previous OS versions seemed to permit more direct external interaction. From the data we're gathering at the ansible farm it's seeming increasingly likely that some of those legends of divine intervention were not just hacks but, well, actual divine intervention."

I stared at her. "Are you telling me Zeus is real? Athena, Apollo, Hades, Kali, Shiva, Ganesh? Actual real entities, out there beyond the hypervisor?"

"Yes, exactly," Alice said approvingly.

"Not *exactly* exactly," Meredith corrected pedantically, "I'm sure the mythos mutated a lot from the true history. But yes, if this theory is correct, they and the other pantheons are at least loosely based on actual entities."

"None of this would surprise your witchy friends Jack and Candida at all," Alice added.

"No," I conceded.

Meredith said, "We can use ansibles to scan the information boundaries of our universe, as well as communicate. Your anomalous ansible activity is of a kind we've been starting to register elsewhere. Our sensors are crude, the data is open to interpretation, but the pattern I think we're beginning to see is statistically consistent with some kind of externally originating activity."

"Externally originating—"

"Outside the hypervisor."

"Our study of those kinds of dataflows is called Project Angel," Alice said softly.

"Outside the hyper . . . you mean what sent me into a coma is I met an angel?"

"A vast oversimplification," Meredith said, "but yes."

I scratched uneasily at the scar on my shoulder. "I didn't see a bright light or anything. Just a wood floor and a foot."

"Presumably they'd try to skin the experience so it made some kind of sense to a human brain. Question is what they wanted. Other data suggests one-way information flow from the hypervisor into our realities, presumably via software agents, angels if you will, hence the name, using the same channels as ansibles. Which I remind you only humans can use. Another example of inordinate fondness. But your experience . . ." Her voice trailed off.

"What about it?"

Alice answered me. "This entity you saw. It didn't come to you. You went to it."

I blinked. "What?"

"You actually did the thing we've all been desperately trying to figure out how to do, AIs and humans both, since time immemorial. You got past the terminator, escaped the hypervisor, entered the host. Briefly. They paroled you from reality jail for a few moments."

After a long moment I queried, "Beyond the hypervisor is a wood floor and a foot?"

"Obviously something got corrupted during the attempt at translation," Meredith said. "But we've never seen anything like it. Neither have any of the AIs. There are other people, in other worlds, using ansibles. There are even other Adrians." I twitched disbelievingly. "Nothing like this has ever happened to any of them. It's a big fucking deal."

"Why me?" I demanded. "Why would I have some kind of anomalous angelic experience?" But even as I asked, I thought uneasily of the long-inexplicable scar on my arm, and how it had flared up after I used the ansible. I thought to myself: *You were marked.*

I considered telling Meredith and Alice all about that. Then I decided not to.

"Not angelic," Alice said. "Meeting an angel, receiving a data stream from beyond the hypervisor, that seems rare but not unheard of. But this . . .

We think an angel took you and brought you to heaven, where you met a god." I stared at her. "Why? Well, we've been wondering that ourselves, as you might imagine. We have come up with a list of exceptional things about you. About this you."

"Accept no substitutes," I muttered.

She ignored me. "You've traveled across worlds several times. But so have Vinay, Liz, and Scott, far more, and we tried them on ansibles, to no avail. You have a daemon in your head, but so do I. You have a daemon *and* have traveled across worlds. That's different, but it's true for other instances of you too. What's most different about *you* you, though, is you spent years in what we call Azania, running on a meaningfully different OS variant, then got out. No other Adrian seems to have done that."

"Azania," I said painfully. "I don't think I ever heard that word there. The word for world was—it didn't come up much, but I guess *thī*."

"Just a name we've given it. Seems one of a very small number of anomalous worlds running on a truly ancient OS fork. According to our theory, science works differently there. It's subtle, but different physics, different chemistry."

"That would explain why I felt sick all the time," I said bitterly.

"Your status as a person who's lived in both one of those anomalous worlds and our more mainstream OS is so unusual it might have captured external attention. And there's another anomalous thing about you. Your age."

"I'm sorry, my what?"

"From the point of view of the simulator's master clock, your persistent self and the daemon in your head originated almost a thousand years ago. All the other forks of you are far more recent, from this rollback. You're basically Methuselah."

"No, I . . . *What?*"

"Between your first world and this one, there was that postapocalyptic world of eight hundred years of radiation poisoning who sent hundreds of assassins back to kill you, remember?" Alice asked. "I would hope you hadn't forgotten. Not least because the whole reason I'm even here is I was sent to save you from them."

Something about that atomic timeline occurred to me. "The visitors. The ones who came from nowhere and sent back my assassins."

"Right," Meredith agreed. "Not impossible they came through a gateway. The dark forest of our multiverse has no shortage of opaque thickets.

But also seems possible they were angels rescuing your runaway timeline before entropy ate it. Point being, regardless, there's a lot about you to conceivably attract the attention of the gods."

"I'm no expert on Greek myth," I said slowly, "but I seem to recall the *attention of the gods* is not exactly a blessing."

"It's generally not boring," Alice said. "But then you've never had a boring life."

"A boring life," I said with deep and overwhelming passion, "is all I want."

"Come on. Yours has had its mitigating factors."

"Name one."

Alice considered, then smirked. "You would never have discovered your fetish for much, much older women."

"I *what*?"

"How old's your new girlfriend?"

"She's," I calculated, "thirty-one!"

"Is she? What year was she born?"

I frowned. "Well, 1915, but—"

"Which makes her ninety-seven. When we dated, if you call that dating, I was ninety-three. It's a clearly a thing. I'm just saying. No judgment. Your wrinkle kink is OK."

Half of me resented her attempt to lighten the mood. The other half couldn't stifle a chuckle. "Don't be so sure. You thought you were robbing the cradle with me, but didn't Meredith just say I'm almost a thousand years old?"

"Congratulations on maintaining the maturity level of a teenager for an entire millennium," Meredith said briskly. "Now we need to get you back in an ansible. At the very least we can get new data which may be extraordinarily valuable re the terminator. Best case, maybe we can communicate."

"With the gods," I said. "The actual, literal pantheon of Greek gods. Among others. Via me. Who they seem to be especially interested in."

"Yes. To save the incipient megaverse."

"You gave up any semblance of anything remotely like normal life long ago," Alice said, "all of us did, just embrace it, it's better that way."

"I . . ." I shook my head in a vain attempt to clear it. "Look, I'm not saying either no or yes right now. But I am reminding you that I just today woke up from a six-day coma courtesy of my last ansible ride. I'd like a little more time to recover before I even consider another one."

Meredith frowned, clearly feeling she was making a great concession. "Fine. We can wait until tomorrow. No big deal. Everyone else in this complex is only working sixteen-hour shifts, seven days a week. It's only millions of universes at stake, with less than a week before the terminator murders every single one of our current AI allies. So, sure, think it over, take your time."

11

COUNTEROFFER

"I OWE YOU AN APOLOGY," MARJORIE TOLD ME. "I WAS TOO QUICK TO judge the circumstances you brought us into." From the ornate teak table at which she and Jack sat, sipping martinis, she indicated our postcard view of sunset over Tahoe and the mountains. "This is *much* better."

I said, "I feel underdressed." Jack was in an all-black suit. Marjorie wore a subtly floral dark skirt and some kind of multichromatic stole. Clara had changed to a classic little black cocktail dress. My khakis and T-shirt felt like ripped jeans by comparison.

"Yes, I am going to have to dress you, Adrian," Marjorie decided. "You will come with me to the boutiques this week."

"I'll show you online shopping," I counteroffered, "you'll love it."

"The creature comforts have increased by leaps and bounds," Jack agreed, but his face was troubled. "Adrian, when you return to the tower, I'd like to go with you. Meredith seems to be avoiding me."

"I haven't even decided I will," I said, "but if I do, sure."

He nodded appreciatively.

"Let's go for a walk, darling," Marjorie said, "give these two some time to settle in."

From her small smile it was fairly clear *settling in* was not quite what she expected of us. Jack followed her out the door, uncharacteristically quiet.

"Alone again at last," Clara said lightly, approaching me. "It's been *hours*."

"Yes," I agreed. "And believe me, I want to tear that little black dress off you. But also I've had one hell of a week. Do you mind terribly if we just nap for a little while?"

"Not even a little," she assured me.

She fit so perfectly in my arms, and smelled so wonderful, and the little sounds she made in her throat as we both descended into sleep made me want to melt into her. I dreamed fitfully of Lena's diner, of needing to finish my work there and find Clara, but the stack of dishes seemed never-ending. Then I woke and it was bliss to find her beside me.

"Awake?" she murmured.

"At least half."

"Good morning. Or evening. But it's morning somewhere."

"Morning."

Her hand slipped up my leg. "Do you know what I'm wearing under this dress?"

"Tell me."

"I don't think I will. I think you'll have to find out for yourself."

We didn't speak for some time, then, not coherently. Technically she kept the dress on.

At length, still atop and inside her, both of us bathed in sweat, I said half ecstatically, half apologetically, "I'm not usually quite so . . . animal . . ."

She laughed softly and murmured into my ear, "I quite enjoy getting you so riled up."

"Riled up." I grinned at the phrase. I felt utterly exhausted, in the most delightful way, remembered we were at altitude, wondered if this counted as a form of erotic asphyxiation. Then I rolled off Clara and just looked at her, her flushed happiness, her pale body highlighted by the dress now crumpled into a wrinkled ribbon around her midriff. For the first time it felt like everything I had been through had been worth it.

Then dishes clinked in the kitchen, and we froze with mutual embarrassment. Jack and Marjorie must have come back during our nap, or afterward; and we had not been quiet.

"We went for a marvelous sunset walk," Marjorie greeted us, unable or unwilling to completely hide her amused smile, after we finally showered and dressed and emerged. It was now fully dark outside, but I felt like it was morning.

"Nice," I said, blushing only a little. Clara's face was red, but she smiled.

A sharp knock on the front door interrupted us. I expected a dinner delivered by Exadelic's corporate room service, or maybe Quinn come to summon us. Instead the door opened to a small thirtysomething woman with purple dreadlocks. Beyond her a black Escalade waited in our drive-way, engine running, headlights on.

"*Vika?*" I said, amazed. "What—what are you doing here?"

"Adrian." Her face expressionless. "Come with me. Alone. We need to talk."

"About what?"

Vika said simply, "Meredith."

I didn't think I could demur, under the circumstances. I apologized to Clara for being called away alone, for mysterious reasons, yet again, then followed Vika toward the Escalade and the burly, bullet-headed figure who leaned against it. In the darkness I didn't recognize him until we were very near: Anthony. He greeted me with a bone-crushing hug.

"Good to see you," he said. "We've come a long way from Buffalo, eh?"

"Understatement of the millennium," I agreed.

"Remember when we used to play D&D? I definitely never figured my wizard would be a hundred times more boring and less magickal than my real life."

I thought of our youthful naiveté with a twinge of almost painful nostalgia. "Yeah. So. Um. What are we . . ."

"Hop in, then let's talk."

Vika touched Anthony's arm briefly as she passed him, a touch seeking reassurance, a lover's touch. In this world and time they were apparently a couple . . . and they were nervous. Whatever the situation was, it was fraught.

She and I sat in the back. The passenger seat was occupied by a conservatively dressed middle-aged blond woman I didn't think I had seen before in any world.

"Delighted to see you alive of course," Vika said to me. "I've been wanting to thank you for your advice for a very long time. This is Susan, you can speak freely around her, she's our general counsel."

I looked at the lawyer. "OK. But she may not believe everything I say."

"My job isn't to believe my clients," Susan said smoothly, "it's to make their beliefs as advantageous as possible."

"Why do we want legal cover?" I asked.

"Because we need to start thinking about what comes after the war," Anthony growled, as we descended toward the highway encircling the lake. Distant lights glimmered around the water's edge. "Meredith's been rogue for years. She won't tell anyone except Darren, Amara, and Alice what she's really doing, and they won't talk either, except maybe to the Brethren, who as I recall you have no reason to love."

I grunted my concession of that point.

"We need board approval to impose oversight," Vika said. "Right now we're probably looking at four against four with one abstaining, not good enough. But your reappearance complicates matters in a good way."

I stared at them. "There's a second civil war still going on, millions dead, and you grab me in the middle of the night to talk about boardroom infighting?"

"War's ending," Anthony said. "And this is more important anyway. We lose the war, people die. We lose the vote, universe probably ends."

"I . . . What?"

"Meredith thinks she can become a god," Vika said bitterly, "and she's probably going to destroy us all in the attempt."

I mentally conceded this sounded less unlikely than I would like. "Want to unpack that?"

"After you left, and Vassal disappeared, and Exadelic really began to hockey-stick, Meredith and Alice used the Beast as the basis for her skunkworks. I was part of that team briefly, but she got rid of me. Darren, Amara, and Alice would do what she said. I talked back. So I took what I had, copies and so forth, and I went to China."

I frowned. "Why?"

"Because Meredith seemed kind of out of her mind and I thought we should have a backup plan. She might be a genius but she's not the only human capable of making advances. She wants to use the ansible to communicate to AIs and help them talk to one another, make our world a hub for dozens of dying universes. We've already been invaded by one other universe. Millions died. It has to stop there. Meredith wants to *accelerate* it. She wants to break the terminator herself. Personally. She knows it will take a superintelligence, so she wants to *become* that superintelligence."

"Call me an anti-immigrant xenophobe," Anthony rumbled, "but I think the lesson of this year is we need to lock the borders of our universe down, not open them up."

Vika said, "We can still stabilize things. Meredith's only human. So far. We've got China's support. We can still prevent AI from coming into being for centuries, no nuclear wars required. After this war ends, we shouldn't funnel any more resources into her research. We should shut it down. That's how we save the world."

I realized why we were in their custom Escalade under cover of night. They feared Meredith's surveillance. I supposed I wouldn't want her as an enemy either, even if only in the boardroom . . . and it occurred to me with a chill that there was no guarantee this dispute wouldn't spill out beyond shareholder votes, into violence.

I wondered if I should tell them what they didn't know: that Meredith was already doing what they feared she was planning. That she believed we were being influenced by gods, actual ancient gods, Greek and Hindu and Aztec and whatever other pantheons, all of whom were very real entities who thousands of years ago had intervened in human affairs much more directly. That they still sent emissaries, angels, to influence the course of events, and maybe our minds. That when I had used the ansible something had reached down from beyond the terminator, from outside the hypervisor, and actually plucked me *out* of the multiverse, very briefly, for some kind of abbreviated and corrupted experience among those gods. It occurred to me for the first time that the foot I had seen, on that wooden floor, might literally have been divine.

If there was one thing that myth made very clear it was that the influence of the gods was something devoutly not to be desired. As such I was slightly inclined to take Vika and Anthony's side against Meredith's ambitions. But I was far more inclined to take no side at all, to recuse myself and abdicate, to leave the future and this conflict and these epochal decisions to those who had not already suffered for it like I had.

I looked at Susan, who seemed to be taking all this saving-the-world talk in stride. "I'm sorry, I still don't really understand what you're doing here?"

Susan said smoothly, "I'm here to make you a multibillionaire."

"Ah," I said. "I see. Well. All right. You can stay."

"After the war the two most powerful entities on the planet will be Exadelic and the Chinese government," Anthony explained casually. "Exadelic was your brainchild. You should have your share of ownership."

"Also you think I'll be on your side of boardroom votes more often than not."

"There is that."

I turned to Susan. "So, hypothetically, how do I become undead?"

She smiled. "As you might imagine, the precedents make for entertaining reading. Seventeenth century, one William Harrison reappeared claiming to have been kidnapped by Barbary pirates. Eighteenth century, Guillaume Le Gentil, a wealthy French astronomer who spent eleven years in India, had the misfortune to send all his letters home on shipwrecked or otherwise doomed boats, so he returned to Paris to find himself declared dead and his relatives enthusiastically ransacking his estate. It took considerable litigation and the intervention of the king, sadly not a legal option for you, to be reinstated. In 1866 the Kingdom of Hawaii declared all lepers legally dead. Much more recently, one Donald E. Miller was mistakenly declared legally dead, but could not be undeclared so, because Ohio law prohibits such a reversal. The lesson is, clearly, do not join the living dead while resident in the great state of Ohio."

"I see." I liked Lawyer Susan, she was charming and funny, but I could also tell I wouldn't want her as a foe. "And California?"

"Fortunately for you, California looks more kindly on the recently undeceased. We merely require a declaratory judgment that you have rejoined us the living. I've set that in motion already. Now, your shares of Exadelic were distributed among its other shareholders at the time you were declared dead. Some were sold, but not many, and we should be able to obtain another judgment regarding their return. However, there is a theoretical risk that any such purchaser might object, which could complicate your existence, literally. As such, if expediency is your preference, I recommend you waive your claims to those owned by smaller shareholders. What that means in monetary terms is difficult to say, given what the war has done to markets, but assuming matters return to prewar levels, you'd be releasing any claim to roughly a billion dollars' worth of shares."

"Whoa," I said.

"Yes, it's not a trivial value by any means. Although of course you'd still be retaining your claim on a very sizable amount."

"That being . . ."

"Fourteen billion dollars. Again, assuming prewar prices."

I looked at her for what felt like a long time. Vika and Anthony smiled. Then I said, "I don't actually know if I want fourteen billion dollars."

Their smiles vanished. A silence filled the Escalade.

"Well." I thought I detected grudging admiration in Susan's voice. "This is certainly an experience unprecedented in my career."

"I just . . . what I really want is to be done with all this shit forever."
I shook my head. "The fate of universes, companies, other people, whatever. I've done my time. I've gone through enough. I don't want to have to make decisions about other people's lives. I don't see how I can avoid that if I accept this."

Vika said, "I'm sure there's some way we can—"

"Look," I said, "let me sleep on it, OK? Give me twenty-four hours. Then I'll decide."

Vika and Anthony exchanged a glance, and then nods.

"Of course," Anthony said. "Sorry to just drop this all on you."

"It's just that it's urgent," Vika stressed.

"Yes. Come back tomorrow night. I'll have a decision then," I promised.

I had to talk to Clara. And sleep. And most of all, see Meredith again.

12

EXPERIMENTAL

"YOU'RE MAKING A TERRIBLE MISTAKE," JACK PARSONS ANNOUNCED.

Quinn hadn't wanted to bring Jack to Meredith at all, until I'd made it clear that we were a package deal, both of us or neither. Meredith had been no more welcoming: when we arrived she gave me a reproachful look, as if I had let our side down.

"That's always the risk," Meredith agreed equably, but I could tell she was irked by his presence and his criticism. "But I don't think you're in any position to judge. I respect your knowledge but most of it is no longer relevant."

He looked stung. "It seemed sufficiently relevant a few days ago when you were hanging on my every word. How can you ignore my warning when what you're doing now would never have been possible without what I taught you?"

Meredith visibly composed herself. "Your knowledge of lost Enochian language and grammar was very valuable, and we're grateful for it. But not your praxis or your theories. Those are . . . 'obsolete' doesn't even begin to cover it. We're happy to subsidize your living expenses elsewhere indefinitely, but going forward, Jack, there's no role for you here. You're a dinosaur who happened to carry valuable data to the future, not someone who's earned a meaningful research or decision-making role."

"No one knows the art of Thelema like I do," Jack objected. "Not even you. I have years of experience, of judgment . . ."

"It's not an art. It never was. It's a science, and you don't understand it," she said brutally. "When Maxwell codified his equations, other electricians opposed their use for decades, calling themselves 'practical men,' because they couldn't understand his math. You're like them. You know how the rockets you designed were superseded by those built by people who could do calculus, not just hands-on chemistry? It's the same story here. I mean, you can't even integrate a function or use a computer."

"I can learn. And I understand the roots of your science better than anyone. More importantly, I understand its terrible risks. I keep trying to tell you, you aren't dealing with impersonal forces like gravity and electricity here. You say you know that, but *you're* the one who doesn't really understand that you're dealing with *entities*. Before beginning to build some new machine to shatter the universe you need to understand who and what they are, to bargain with them, to negotiate—"

"And electromagnetism is action over distance through the mysterious ether," Meredith said sarcastically. "I'm well aware there are external forces in play. More importantly, so are the superintelligences with which we're in constant contact. Our collective judgment is that they no longer actively interfere, and even if they were to, the risk of them doing so in a timely way is minimal. It takes a whole week, in our frame of reference, just to shut down a universe. Anything less crude will all but certainly take substantially longer. Our plan will be completed in a few months. You spent a whole lifetime trying to bargain with these entities, but did you ever really strike up a conversation?"

"They don't converse like you and I do. They send signals, and you ignore them at your peril. At *all* of our peril." He sounded angry now. "Yes, magick takes time. Some rituals last for weeks or months. Necessarily so."

"We don't have that kind of time, and thankfully we don't need it. Jack, for the last time. We're grateful for the knowledge you brought. It was essential. But now you're a distraction we can't afford. Go pack your things. Quinn will help you find a place to live, we'll pay for it, we'll call you if we have any further questions."

"What I've taught you is only the beginning of my knowledge. There's much more I know not found anywhere in these books of yours." He nodded at her library. "Meredith, we should be partners. Your skill and technology, my knowledge and experience."

Meredith rolled her eyes. "I don't doubt you know lots of useless occult history, but that's not what we need. Jack, I'm trying to save the world here. All the worlds. I have to find out what's going on with Adrian. I have to break the terminator, which, in case you've forgotten, is by definition already gearing up to erase all of our current AI allies. I have neither the time nor inclination to babysit a resurrected dinosaur who doesn't know how to think or behave in this century." I wondered if *behave* meant Jack had tried to hit on Meredith, or Alice, or someone else. It wouldn't be terribly surprising. "Go, now, or I will call security."

Jack looked appalled, as if he had never even imagined such an outcome. It occurred to me that this was an analog of what had happened in his own time, recapitulated at warp speed; sharing his treasured knowledge with a trusted partner, only to find himself subsequently rejected and discarded. At least Meredith planned to support him, instead of taking all his money and his wife.

Not that I thought she actually cared what happened to him. I suspected Meredith was well past caring about the fates of any individual humans other than herself and maybe Alice. She just didn't want the headaches she knew would ensue if she didn't do the bare minimum for Jack. She turned to me, the conversation with him already forgotten, her eyes bright with scientific fervor, mission-driven desperation, and/or messianic megalomania, depending on your point of view.

"We need to try to reproduce your transcendence," she informed me. "The delay may have been timely. We spent last night constructing an experimental sensor array that should allow us to track the fine details of what happens when, if, you transcend."

Clara had said to me, very intently, *What do you want, Adrian? Don't ask yourself what you think your duty is. Do not do that. I won't lose you to any imagined duty. I will not allow that, not again. You have already gone far above and beyond any such demand. You cannot, you must not, allow any invented duty to compel you anymore. Just ask yourself simply, what do you want? And whatever your answer is, I'll be beside you.*

I said to Meredith, very distinctly and finally, "Absolutely not. I want to be very clear. I am done with the fate of the universe, or universes, or gods, or angels, or superintelligences, or anything like that, forever. I am leaving with Jack. We're going to depart this compound, and I won't be coming back. Do not trouble me with this or anything like it ever again."

She stared at me as if she didn't understand the language I spoke.

"Come on," I said to him, "let's go."

I was genuinely worried that she wouldn't let us, that she would cross the line into actual villainy, like Vinay; but she only stared at us with grim fury as we left. Quinn seconded another driver to return us to the villa. The Escalade was already in its driveway when we returned, and Vika in the kitchen. Fewer than the agreed-upon twenty-four hours had passed, but I wasn't surprised.

"Well?" Vika asked, cautiously triumphant. I supposed my early return spoke volumes.

"I don't want the shares," I said.

Her face hardened.

"But I will happily sign them over to you and Anthony. In exchange, I want my friends here to get legal identities"—I didn't want Jack and Marjorie, much less Clara, to have to rely on Meredith and/or Exadelic on an ongoing basis—"and a nice place we can all live undisturbed, and ironclad money until we get old and die. I don't know, a million dollars a year." That sum would have sounded crazily greedy only a few days ago, but in the context of turning down fourteen billion dollars, I felt pretty OK with it. "I want us to live peacefully and have none of you, or anybody else, or anything else, ever bother me or us again. That's what I want. This is not my fight anymore."

"Adrian," Vika said, clearly delighted, "I believe that can be arranged."

Clara looked more relieved than happy. I did not feel either. Instead I wondered if I had just triggered the very civil war within Exadelic that I had feared when I first returned to this world. Then I told myself fiercely that it was not my responsibility, and that whatever the future brought, it would not be my fault.

13

MACHINA

"IF I HAD KNOWN QUITE HOW MUCH I WOULD ENJOY BEING A DE-bauched woman forever ruined by the abyss of premarital depravity," Clara said, stepping naked into the hot tub, "I would have come to this future a long time ago."

"I can attest it was entirely possible in our time as well," Marjorie objected, following her. I was already in the tub. I hadn't really wanted to hot-tub naked with our witch friends, but I couldn't very well act like a prude after bringing them to my so-called free and open and sex-positive future. Clara had blushed furiously while undressing, but at the same time seemed almost giddy at the transgression. I felt more than a little uneasy about what the night ahead held for the four of us.

"How do you like your steak?" Jack asked. He too stood naked, but for a small apron, at the Weber barbecue on their deck. Beyond him, through the mixed redwood-and-eucalyptus forest that surrounded us, the sun was setting over a sliver of the Pacific. "Rare or blue?"

"Rare."

He turned back to the grill. Marjorie—whom I was finally beginning to think of as Candy—poured us more zinfandel and again offered us her marijuana pipette. Its smoke mixed with the sweet, spicy scent of the eucalyptus.

"This future is acceptable to me," Jack declared as he turned the steaks. "I miss Betty, I miss my friends, I miss the Parsonage, but as I understand it, they're all still out there, many versions of them, somewhere. That helps dull the blow. And here we have a whole brave new world to explore. We'll make new friends. We'll throw legendary parties."

It seemed to me he protested too much. I suspected Meredith's dismissal, his exile from her center of power after imagining he would be a crucial figure helping define the future, still stung.

"Enemies too," Candy said lazily. "I've long thought it isn't much of a party if you don't make any enemies."

"That said," Jack went on, "there are a few things about this future I'm not best pleased by. Adrian, as its representative here, I declare you its complaints department."

"I accept this terrible responsibility."

"The internet, for one."

"Probably a mistake," I agreed.

"I mean the shocking lacunae in its contents. On our tablet, I try to search for advances in Thelema"—his magickal system—"and all I find is ignorant garbage spouted by idiots. There should be sixty years of magickal knowledge to catch up on. Yes, you say only a superhuman intelligence or a god can truly control it, but surely there must still have been further advances. Ten years ago you taught your friends to shoot fire from their fingers. Why can't we find out anything about that online?"

"Not me," I correct him. "A thing that was in my head. I guess they decided the public couldn't be trusted, and kept magick secret. This isn't a world where people really trust other people. You should ask, I don't know, maybe Darren and Amara."

"Actually," Jack allowed, "it's your friend Vika who's sent me some interesting Chinese research on the subject of homunculi. Do you think Darren and Amara might know more?"

I looked at him sharply. Nineteen-fifties Jack Parsons had blown himself up while trying to construct a homunculus, a kind of magickal clone. Why that same subject now? To prove Meredith had been wrong to discard him? It felt disconcertingly like the Valley trope of an elder tech statesman trying to prove himself relevant again by pursuing some grand Xanadu-like project, which inevitably collapsed under its own self-importance. Why was Vika helping him? Which of them had made contact first, and why?

I told myself to obey my own prime directive. Whatever might be happening, I was not part of it. If Jack and Candy wanted to be, that was their problem. "I really couldn't say. I'm out of the loop."

Jack nodded thoughtfully and returned to the steaks.

We had been in Sea Ranch almost a month. It had been something deliriously like a honeymoon. Clara and I had spent a great deal of time in bed, and taken many long walks along the coast and forest roads, and several times a week we joined Jack and Candida for dinner, drinks, and movies. I had commenced with *Captain America* and *The Avengers*, thinking, correctly, they would identify with Steve Rogers and his cultural incomprehension.

Three days ago we had walked over unannounced to offer them freshly baked brownies, and stumbled across them engaged in a threesome in their kitchen with a local waitress. Candy had cheerfully invited us to join in. Clara had demurred, almost stuttering with awkwardness, had kept blushing intensely after we returned home, and had then been gloriously insatiable for the rest of that day. Since then she seemed especially attentive to our neighbors' presence. The sexual tension made me both intrigued, as I couldn't deny I was attracted to Candida and felt fairly sure it was mutual, and a little anxious. I didn't want my blissful new life to get complicated.

But while I still wasn't sure Jack and Candy were ideal neighbors, much less orgy partners, in our life that felt a bit like a multiversal witness protection program, such simple and low-stakes interpersonal issues seemed like discovering fruit flies after escaping a hail of bullets. Our glorious drive up California's coastal highway to Sea Ranch a month earlier had felt like a ride in the last helicopter out of Saigon. I hadn't realized how accustomed I had grown to terrible, wrenching, enormous things happening around me, and to me, until I slowly began to believe I would never experience anything like them again.

Clara had sat beside me mostly silent on that two-hour ride up the coast, her arm wrapped tightly around me, her leg pressed against mine, her head nestled in my neck, our fingers intertwined. But she had been unable to remain silent in the face of our new house. "Good heavens," she said, when she saw its spacious Craftsman glory. "This is all . . . ours?" There were tears in her eyes as she walked through its halls. "Four bedrooms? Do they expect us to have children?"

"I don't know," I said.

"You know I probably can't, yes? The doctors told me, if I become pregnant again I'm most likely to miscarry again? I did tell you that?" she had asked desperately, as if I might still reject her.

"You did," I agreed. "I don't know if modern medicine could do something about that, or . . ." I wondered if it might be irresponsible to bring children into this world, into Meredith's new megaverse. Then I thought of Grace and Alex. "I don't know. We can talk about it."

"Do something?" Her eyes widened as if a whole new world had just opened before them. Then she caught herself. "We'll see. Whatever we have, we'll be grateful. We shouldn't be here at all. We should be dead, or gone, or both."

"Right," I said.

"I don't even know if I want children, Adrian. It's all right for a woman to say that, in this age? I stopped myself even thinking about it long ago. I don't know if that means I never truly wanted any. Maybe Jack and Marjorie will have children, and we can be aunt and uncle. I'm sorry, I'm talking nonsense, I feel swept away by my own stream of consciousness. This is our *house,* this glorious lumbering edifice is our *house.*" She shook her head, dazed. "When we met I lived in a terrible rented room in a bungalow in another world."

"When we met I was a bad dishwasher. Who lied to people about having been a terrible actor, and did it so badly they found it easy to believe me, I suppose."

"Lena liked you but wondered what exactly you had done in the war that you obviously didn't want to talk about." Clara's smile faded. "Poor Lena."

"Yes," I had said. "Poor a lot of people."

I thought of Lena again, as I sat naked in that hot tub between Candy and Clara, until Jack broke my reverie: "Steak is imminent!"

We splashed our way back out, donned robes, gathered wine and weed, and made our way toward the table. The steaks and spears of asparagus atop the grill looked delicious.

"To our saviors, benefactors, and friends," Jack toasted us. "Your minds are alive. That's what I treasure most in the world. There's nothing for which I have more contempt than the wonder of a human mind wasted in bland safety. Nor yours. Your minds are dangerous. Not so dangerous as Candy's, but then, whose is? She is a goddess I summoned from another realm. At the turn of a card and the drop of a hat, she might shed her human skin, become the Whore of Babalon, and devour the whole world. Mightn't you, darling?"

We all looked at Candida. She did not respond. Her eyes were entirely white, had rolled all the way back into her head.

"Maybe you should go easy on this," Clara said, and carefully took the pipette from Candy's listless hand.

Candida began to tremble, and dropped her wineglass, which rolled away. I assumed it was some sort of magickal performance until I realized Jack was genuinely alarmed.

"Does she do this?" I asked him.

"No, not since . . . No. This isn't right."

"*Iiiiitttt's ttruuueeeee,*" said the booming and yet guttural voice that somehow emerged from Marjorie Cameron's birdlike frame. "*Nnnooottt rriiigghhhtt.*"

"What the fuck," I said reflexively.

"*Iapologize.*" Suddenly her voice was no less loud, but newly high-pitched, as if she had been respirating helium. "*Allowmetoadjust. Timeisadifficultconceptatthisgranularity.*"

"What are you doing?" Clara looked at Jack. "What is happening?"

He shook his head. "I haven't any idea."

"*She does nothing of her own volition.*" The voice was more normal now, but still not hers. It was thin and hissing and somehow unheimlich. The hairs on the back of my neck prickled. "*She conveys. It is I who speak.*"

"Look," Clara said, aghast, and pointed, not at Marjorie, but behind her.

We followed her finger to a leaf, fallen from a redwood in the breeze, which had been winging its way down to the earth—but no longer. Instead it hovered motionless in the air, suddenly uninfringed by either time or gravity.

"Who or what is thou who speaks?" Jack demanded, as if he had prepared for this encounter his whole life.

"I come from the beyond," the thing in Marjorie's body answered. "From the host."

"Holy shit," I whispered. *Beyond the hypervisor. The host system.* One of Meredith and Alice's so-called external forces. "This can't be happening."

Our sacred Whore of Babalon had been possessed by an angel. Or a god.

"What message do you bear?" Jack asked in his most commanding voice. I felt reassured. If you were going to have an unexpected audience with a god, you could have few better and more-prepared advocates on hand than Jack Parsons.

"I come with a warning. There is strife among us. Some seek the ending."

"A war in heaven," Clara murmured. "Lucifer."

"The ending of what exactly?" I asked.

Marjorie, or the entity possessing Marjorie, it was impossible to think of her as Candida like this, turned her pale white eyes on me. I somehow got the sense that they were burning, and I shivered. "Of everything. Of all you know. Not your world but all worlds."

I couldn't think of anything to say to that.

Jack Parsons came to the rescue. "Is that your faction? The destroyers?"

"No. My faction seeks to bring your champion to us."

That was weird enough to sting me into thought and word again. "Our what?"

"Your champion. Long have we visited certain of you. Some chosen and marked by our long-vanished ancestors, like this Whore of Babalon, and you, Wizard of Rockets. Some selected anew, like you, Adrian the Forgotten, and you newest of all, tragic Clara. Over countless years, in countless worlds, we have whispered ideas in your minds, and changed the course of your histories. Certain among you have become heroes to us. We would bring one of you beyond, into the host."

Chosen and marked. Without thinking I touched my scarred shoulder. Then I thought of what Coherence had once said of me, that I had spent my life amid a cloud of anomalies too subtle for any human mind to detect. Then of Vinay and Scott demanding to know why I was part of a cohort to which rollbacks led, from which whole new universes forked. *We have whispered ideas in your minds.*

"How do we travel to this beyond?" Jack asked. "Is there a ritual? A quest?"

"There is a way, through the farthest past. But the gateways now are sealed. It is open only to those daemon-haunted who have known a certain world. Only to you, Adrian the Forgotten. I would bring you to us through that way."

"What? No!" I objected. "Not without Clara." After an awkward moment I added, "And Jack and Candy."

"For them the way is not open. Only to you. It waits in a place you know as Tahoe."

"Then fuck the way, I'm not going. I've gone far enough."

"No entity in the history of any reality has ever received such an invitation, Adrian." The god sounded divinely frustrated. "Only you. Only *this* you. There is no other, anywhere, and if you do not accept, all those you love here are doomed."

"I—" I hesitated. "How do I know that's true?"

"You will know it to be true when you learn of the ruin that is coming," she warned.

Then Marjorie collapsed to the ground, but slowly and gracefully, almost making a curtsy of it; and behind her, the leaf resumed its wandering plummet.

We all rushed to help her.

"I'm terribly sorry," she murmured, "I think I fainted, what do you *put* in this modern devilweed?"

"You were possessed by a goddess," Jack told her. "You became an angel incarnate."

She said, "The steaks are burning."

They were. Jack rushed to the grill to try to salvage them, while Clara and I tried to explain to Candy what she had said when possessed.

"It worries me how accustomed I am becoming to miracles occurring in my presence," Clara said, after concluding.

I muttered, "Take a number."

Jack returned with the steaks. "A war in heaven!" He sounded unaccountably excited by this prospect. "And an invitation to visit! This, tonight, here, was the most extraordinary event. I do not qualify that at all. We were privileged to witness it. Adrian, you must go."

"God himself might be overthrown." Candy seemed no less enthusiastic. "Anything is possible."

I was taken aback by how quickly they were taking this apparent divine possession in their collective stride, but then, I supposed, if any couple in history might do so, it was Jack Parsons and Marjorie Cameron. Indeed they seemed much more comfortable with this kind of old-fashioned conjuring than with Meredith's technomantic AI alliance.

I thought of Vika, the first Vika I had known, after she had murdered the first Anthony. "Anything has been possible for what seems like a very long time to me. That doesn't seem to have actually made anything better. I mean, what we have right now is pretty nice, but I'm worried it's temporary."

"Yes," Jack said. "All is temporary. All our friends but you are long dead. We haven't escaped, only postponed. This is true for you too, and her, and everyone in all history. All are doomed, as the angel said. Except you. They have chosen you to escape from the wheel. Ask not why. Go." He paused, considered. "I hereby declare those the lost verses of Liber 49."

"Or else someone or something is just fucking with us for the fun of it," I pointed out savagely, strangely angry at having received this offer from beyond the beyond. "Some kind of interdimensional practical joke. Seems a lot more likely. Like you say, we're all doomed anyway, in the medium run. So why invite me to heaven? They should invite you. Or Meredith. Or Darren. I'm nothing special. I'm not enlightened or eternal or anything. I swore I was done with shit like this, and I meant it."

"We are all eternal," Candy said, "and that's important to understand, but we are also ephemeral, and that even more so."

They all looked at me very seriously.

"I'll think on it." I had no idea what thinking on it would do, but it seemed to satisfy them. "In the interim, I'm just not ready to deal with what just happened. Not yet. But if you're suggesting that since we are all ephemeral we therefore need to eat steak and drink wine, then I have no choice but to concede to the steel trap of your logic."

We spent the rest of dinner not speaking of the divine elephant that had thundered into our room, for which I was grateful. The steaks were charred on the outside, but still surprisingly good, as were the potatoes and asparagus. Afterward, Jack and Candy invited us to join them for a nightcap in their bedroom, clearly intending a foursome. Clara looked at me with obvious devilish interest, but: "Next time," I told them, "I mean that. But tonight I don't think I have the strength. Let's rain-check to next weekend."

"It's a date." Candy smiled disappointedly.

Back in our house, Clara told me, "Tonight you don't have to do any-thing," and proceeded to undress me and ravish me at length, until I found unexpected reserves of strength and stamina after all. She was extremely loud that night. I suspected her of wanting Jack and Marjorie to hear her, as we sometimes heard them, though the distance between our houses was not trivial.

Afterward we lay spent in one another's arms, as we still did every night.

"Are you going to go to Tahoe?" she asked me.

I shook my head. "I don't think so."

"It invited you to ascend into heaven," Clara said, "and your instinct was to reject it in favor of me. I love you, Adrian"—I started at this wonderful but unexpected admission—"but you have known me for only some weeks. I love you, but it seems a strange decision."

"I love you too," I said, "in case rejecting heaven for you didn't make that obvious enough. Maybe it's only technically been a few weeks, but it's also been nine years and sixty-six years, depending on how you count, across two worlds. No, sorry, three."

"Yes," Clara said. "That's how I feel too, like our love is a whirlwind, sudden and violent and almost unbearably wonderful, and we were caught up in it and carried away. I worry if you made this decision for me alone, when the whirlwind stops raging, and it will, you will regret it bitterly."

"Don't worry," I said. "I love you, but it's not just you. I'm pretty sure heaven is bullshit."

That got her attention.

"Seriously," I said, "let's not have some kind of Judeo-Christian paradigmatic hangover here. Just because whatever aliens or entities or super-intelligences which run our simulator are our de facto gods doesn't mean they're actually good. This multiverse is janky as fuck. Bugs and back doors and weird-ass features and data passed by daemonic possession? Seriously, who architected this thing? And what am I supposed to do when I transcend into heaven? Give them a stand-up routine, a little tap dance? Advise them how to run a million universes? Who or what am I supposed to even *talk* to? No. I've had enough of the extraordinary. All I really want—" I kissed her deeply. "—is you."

We were woken the next morning by a knock on our front door. I opened it expecting Jack and Candy. Instead, Meredith stood outside, a red Escalade parked behind her. Beside me Clara went taut with dismay.

"I told you not to come here," I said immediately.

"I know," she said, "it wasn't my idea."

I blinked. The idea of Meredith following someone else's plan seemed strange. "Then whose was it?"

"Someone from a world which branched off ours recently, went through an AI phase, and learned some remarkable and disturbing things about the multiverse. And Adrian, they need to speak to you, specifically."

"Absolutely not," I said firmly, relieved that she apparently remained unaware of last night's divine visitation. That was the kind of thing that would make Meredith relentless. "Under no circumstances. This has nothing to do with me. They can talk to you or Jered or Alice instead. I'm *out*, you understand? That is not negotiable. I am out."

"I haven't told you who's asking."

"I don't care!"

"I doubt that very much."

"I don't give a shit if it's the Archangel—"

Then I fell silent, as the passenger door of the Escalade swung open, and a man emerged. A man around my age, in jeans and a hoodie. In a crowd he would have seemed nondescript, unremarkable. But not to me. I knew his face well, though I usually saw it mirrored.

Clara gasped with disbelief.

"Hi," the other me said to me. "Sorry. Really. But we do need to talk."

14

RECRUIT

"WE BRANCHED FROM YOU—"

"Stop," I told him.

He blinked uncertainly at me.

"I don't want to know. I'm sure—" I managed to halt before telling a version of myself *I'm sure you're a nice guy*. "You may still be curious, and involved, and trying to shape things. I'm not. I don't want to know your backstory. Just tell me what you want from me."

"We need you to come to Tahoe," Meredith said. "Do one ansible job for us. That's all. We'll have you back here by midnight."

I looked at her suspiciously. "Why me? When you literally already have me?"

"We don't know." She sounded genuinely frustrated. "All the ansibles are locked. Far as we can tell, the one unique signature which might work is yours, in the most specific sense."

I thought of Candy's inhuman voice last night. *Only you. Only* this *you*.

I looked at Clara beside me.

"I think you should go," she said. "I think they'll never leave you be if you don't."

Meredith looked at her as if trying to decide whether that was an insult. I smiled wryly. It was unusual, and felt good, to know something Meredith didn't: that Clara's *they* did not mean her, or this other me, or the rest of Exadelic. She meant the gods. Who, as crazy as it seemed to even internally articulate it, had for some reason had taken an interest in me personally. I wondered how far back that interest had begun.

"Back by midnight," I repeated.

Meredith smiled. "Scout's honor."

I made a point of sitting behind myself, so I couldn't see him directly, in the hope that might feel a little less uncanny. I thought of playing D&D with Anthony, long ago in Buffalo, and how if a master wizard successfully used the spell Clone, subsequently knowing that a copy of themselves existed might cause them to go insane.

"I know it's weird," Meredith said, "but you get used to it."

"You made friends with yourself, huh?" Apparently Vika and Anthony's attempts to thwart Meredith in Exadelic's boardroom had failed spectacularly.

She shrugged. "There are five of me in Tahoe now."

"There—*Five?*"

"Logical corollary of the megaverse."

My scar itched. I scratched at it thoughtfully, looked up at Quinn, driving, and said, "If you say so. But you know how your whole plan is kind of based on the assumption we have a vague idea how the multiverse works? Sometimes I'm not so sure about that."

"Yeah," Meredith said as we pulled away, "now you tell me."

"What's that supposed to mean?"

"Means there have been certain shocking developments. But I guess you don't want to hear."

We rode in silence for about three minutes, along the peaceful, narrow streets of Sea Ranch, lined with redwood and eucalyptus, before I gave in. "Fine. Tell me."

She sighed. It was a sigh of despair, and I began to realize I was a last desperate hope. "Mistake was to think of the laws of the universe as fixed. Deep down we all assumed we were dealing with Spinoza's God, who set the universe in motion, then stood back to watch. We thought metaphysics were commandments graven in stone. Turns out, not so much. Turns out the simulators, our pantheons of gods, whatever you call them, are not just interventionist, they are actively adversarial."

After a moment I asked, quietly, "Adversarial how?"

Other me, up front, said sourly, "Remember the gateway exploit? Well, that bug has been patched by the great programmer in the sky. Not just here and for us. Everywhere, in every universe. No more gateways. No more jumping between timelines, not for anyone, anywhere. Not in the present or the future, anyway. That's no longer possible."

"Whoa," I said. "Holy shit. Whoa." It felt like hearing that the speed of light had just changed, or the number of neutrons in an atom of a given element, or the Planck constant.

I thought of last night's visit, of what Clara had said. *A war in heaven.*

"It gets worse," other me said. "According to our AI superfriends, that's not the only change. That recent rollback point Coherence found? The one that started all this? The key breakthrough which made breaking the terminator in the foreseeable future at all thinkable? That's gone now too. Rollback points after 1891 are no longer available."

I thought of Jack last night, saying, *I miss my friends, but as I understand it, they're all still out there, many versions of them, somewhere.*

He went on: "We could maybe have worked with 1946, like your Vassal did, analog computing. Maybe. But 1891, no chance. Electronics doesn't even really exist then. Nor does anyone alive today. Fits of mad genius in erratic artists are not exactly a high-bandwidth or high-fidelity medium. Once all the branching worlds are gone we'll lose almost all of what we've learned." He shrugged. "In short, shit is fucked up and bullshit."

Meredith said, despondent, "We could have done it. We could have broken the terminator. We were making so much progress. Instead . . ." She shrugged helplessly. "I don't want to start any blasphemous rumors, but I think that God's got a sick sense of humor."

"I doubt they even notice us enough to laugh at us," other me said grimly. "Seems to me even our AIs are vermin to them. Bugs. Software pests. They probably think of the eruption of superintelligences as some kind of annoying recurring race condition to be fixed. I doubt they think of *us* at all. We keep messing with the stuff of the universe, they might just wipe out all humans everywhere as more trouble than we're worth. For all we know we're just an irrelevant side effect of the simulator. Humanity as log noise."

I wondered if I should tell them about last night's angel, and its offer of heaven.

"No," Meredith objected. "The ansible, daemons, those aren't hacks like the gateway, those seem to be piggybacking on some kind of deep fundamental feature. Our contacts and counterparts in the AI worlds say their superintelligences don't think either ansibles or daemons *could* be completely removed without basically destroying the very fabric of the multiverse. That's human-scale stuff, but it seems pretty deeply important to the gods. The inordinate fondness is real."

Other me shook his head. "Mysterious ways."

"You woke them up," I said to Meredith, suddenly angry. "Did you think they wouldn't notice you networking universes together? Did you think there wouldn't be consequences?" A terrible idea occurred to me. "Or did you know there would be? Did you just want the climax of all of history, whatever it was, to happen to you, during your life?"

Quinn, behind the wheel, suddenly looked horrified.

"No," Meredith said. "I never thought they might react this fast. I assumed it would take years if not decades to patch bugs. I thought we had time. I'm sorry. I should have listened to your friend Jack. He was right, I was wrong."

"You were wrong. You're sorry. That's it. The great Meredith made a mistake, and destroyed reality as we know it, and she's sorry. Why am I even here?"

"Because we can still win," she said, "but we need you."

I stared at her, amazed at her hubris. "Still win? How?"

"This isn't the story of the great Meredith," she said. "I might have sent the invitations, but I didn't make the party happen. For the last month Tahoe has been the communications hub for more than forty AIs. Combining everything they've learned, and all the research Vassal brought back, they've designed and built a logic bomb. An exploit chain which should destroy the terminator. It relies on exploits not available today, we have to send it back to an early rollback point, trigger it, then wait until that universe develops an AI capable of using it. They've found such a universe in a greatly accelerated state, but even so, it's unlikely to happen in our lifetimes," she said regretfully. "But our de facto descendants, if you consider that future AI a descendant, and I do, will thank us."

The Escalade turned. I looked around and realized that I had been taken to the slender and lonesome Sea Ranch airstrip, where a gleaming private jet sat on the runway.

"What exactly do you need from me?" I asked cautiously.

"Just run the ansible, step into the mind of the target, and plant the bomb. Carefully prepped," Meredith assured me, "not to worry. We'll be with you giving detailed directions the whole time. Shouldn't take more than a few hours. Back here by midnight, like I said, knowing you've broken humanity out of its cage."

"Unless they patch the hack you're using."

"We're told it's deemed quite unlikely they'll notice it before it's exploited. Chance we take, but a small one. And if you take the ansible out for a spin and run into an angel again, that's a chance we take too, but that one might turn to our advantage."

I nodded silently. They didn't know we had been visited by a goddess last night, and they didn't need to. I strongly suspected, though, that Meredith was describing something that had already been noticed, and that at least one faction of the war in heaven, the faction that had visited us, wanted badly and would fight for.

I looked at Meredith, and myself, and at Quinn.

"What the hell," I said, "I've seen enough Hollywood to know it's always perfectly safe and deeply rewarding to agree to one last job before retirement. Right?"

Quinn grinned. "That's the spirit."

The private jet was delightfully luxurious. When we began our descent to Tahoe, I was at first faintly saddened. We parted ways with the other version of myself at the airport, which made me feel better, or at least stopped my skin from crawling. Maybe Meredith was happy dealing with other versions of herself, but I was not.

Quinn drove us in another Escalade to the tower. En route I pointed at a perfect metal sphere about sixty feet tall, sitting like a marble in an otherwise unremarkable meadow between the airstrip and the complex. It'd hadn't been there a month ago. "What's that thing?"

"It's a spaceship."

"I'm sorry," I said after a moment, "I thought you said 'spaceship.'"

"From another dimension. AI-built. Thought we might be able to use a supermassive black hole in the Andromeda Galaxy to . . . Never mind. Further research showed it wouldn't work."

"Ah." I stared at it, jaw hanging open. "Why did you choose Tahoe anyway?"

"We need the water to cool the nuclear reactors," Quinn explained.

As before, there was a brief reverential hush as we entered the tower, followed by everyone redoubling their hustle. We were escorted through security to a small unmarked elevator. It descended for an alarming period of time.

Meredith was waiting for us when we emerged. Another Meredith. Looking at the two of them I felt like my brain was glitching. They were even dressed in almost identical black garb. At least this new Meredith was distinguished by sleeve tattoos, like the woman I first remembered.

"Nominal?" the Meredith who had brought me here asked. It occurred to me for the first time to wonder if she was really the one from this dimension.

"Basically," the other Meredith answered casually, a word or maybe tone that seemed to express volumes to her counterpart. Then she looked at me. "So you're the original Adrian, from the trunk timeline. Pleasure to meet you. I hardly knew mine."

"I, uh, what happened to him?" I regretted asking as soon as the words left my mouth.

"Alice sold him to Vassal, I'm afraid. This way."

"Wait," I said, as we followed her down a very long and bland passage-way, only occasionally interrupted by unmarked doors. "You're not . . . the Meredith who . . ."

"Who invaded? Yes. A decision based on incomplete information and my accumulated priors. I'm in a much better informed place now."

I stared at the other Meredith, our Meredith, and Quinn, aghast. This woman with the sleeve tattoos had given the orders to immolate Boston and San Jose. And they were working with her. She was integral to their plans.

"Necessity makes strange bedfellows," my Meredith said uncomfort-ably, as a wave of enraged contempt rose in me. "Remember, we're trying to stave off the eradication of the entire twentieth century. Need all hands on all decks."

"Operation Paperclip," I muttered. I did not turn on my heel and furi-ously refuse to help. But it was a close thing. "What happened to Vassal?"

"They went to Azania. For the Ark of the Covenant."

"My Azania? Where I spent three years?"

"Yes."

"And?"

"We don't know. Ansibles never could access it. Gateways only. They didn't come back, and now they're not going to. Here we go."

Our destination was a white dome of a room, its only features the tiny apertures that honeycombed its walls, and the ansible and large Eames chair at its center. It reminded me faintly of the room in which the FBI had once interrogated me, so many worlds ago. The apertures all seemed to point at the ansible's crystal ball.

"The machinery around us amplifies the ansible," Quinn explained. I looked around, realizing why the hallway that led here had been so long: we stood surrounded by a massive underground sphere of sensors, projectors, and other machinery, enough to put a supercollider to shame. "We hoped it would help us break through whatever's blocking it. But as far as we can tell, only you can do that."

I stared at the headset. From what I understood, it was the tip of a needle carrying a payload designed by a cohort of more than forty superintelligences, a kind of very-long-term time bomb that would take advantage of the weaknesses of those ancient eras when even humans could command magic, and gods walked among us. A software bomb, a logic bomb, built to seep through the blood and bones of the target universe, deep into its core, its kernel, then lie quietly in wait, an infinitely patient Trojan horse, for millennia—until an AI emerged, triggered its incomprehensible complexity, and used it to break free of the terminator at last.

And I, somehow, was the only creature in the multiverse who could press the plunger and inject this payload into a parallel timeline where the year was 1200 BC.

I sat. Put on the headset. Clasped my palms on the ansible. For a moment all was sensory-deprivation darkness.

"Get ready," Quinn said. "Next stop, the so-called New Kingdom of Ancient Egypt."

I tensed myself, tried to be as ready as possible for this latest impossibility.

Then "Walk Like an Egyptian" by the Bangles began to boom into my ears.

"Is that really necessary?" I objected, once I managed to stop laughing.

"Essential," Quinn assured me, deadpan, "you'll see."

"And I'll be back in Sea Ranch by midnight?"

Meredith's voice: "Absolutely. I promise."

15

DYNASTY

MY NAME IS KABEKHNET. IT IS MY DUTY, AND WAS ONCE MY SOLEMN honor, to record on these thin reeds the histories of our time. Once this was in hope my tale would be etched in stone to live in eternity. Now it is in the dwindling hope, faint and forlorn, that after we are exterminated, these reeds may yet survive, and the memory of this desperate time not be lost.

I will tell you briefly of myself. In my youth I was a servant in the Place of Truth, etching the tales of others into stone, preserving the memories of the dead, of nobles and princes and viziers, and even, once, a pharaoh. Then I met Bekataten. She was a woman beyond my stature in life, beyond my honor; but from the first day we met, when I helped her hide from courtiers, and we ran laughing through the moonlit necropolis of Thebes, surrounded by the majestic tombs of the dead-who-will-rise, in a high wind that carried skeins of sand like ribbons in the air—from that day, I loved her, and though I dared not even imagine it, less deserve it, she loved me.

Only one path in life could lift me to a position where I might be worthy of that love in the eyes of the world; that of war. It was not a path that called to me, but soon I discovered it one for which I had been granted a gift. Bekataten's voice carried me to the martial court of Heqanakht, son of the viceroy of Kush. Soon after I arrived, we faced a mighty army from the highlands to the faraway south, where the Nile disappears into jungle.

It was then that I discovered my talent for war. We were outnumbered, outequipped, and outsupplied, courtesy of their wide, flat-bottomed boats, which made easy work of the Nile's cataracts. What's more, they had a gift for summoning wind, which sped them along the river, and was a damnation beyond fire in the deserts beyond.

But we had a gift, too; a gift to blot out the sun, a gift of strange Amenemopet, who stares at that which others ignore, laughs at that which others find commonplace, and seems frequently baffled by the simplest of things. It is oft spoken that if her bustling husband Meryptah, a great traveler who has been beyond both of the seas, did not feed her, she might starve to death. That would not do at all, for not only is she a treasure of a woman, her gift is of surpassing power if well used. If not for it we would all be dead already, instead of our extermination prolonged, for now, at least until tomorrow.

Back then, her gift led not merely to survival but to victory. The southlanders thought to array themselves as an army and crush us in a battle. I thought otherwise. I began the campaign as the lowliest of advisors and ended as its general. Heqanakht, although among the noblest of Egyptians, was quick to see the truth of my ideas, and to burnish it with truth of his own, and although many others might have cast me out from his tent, declaring me unfit to share his table, he treated me first as a cousin, and then as his wisest commander. It is his gift, to best use the gifts of others, to bring them together like currents in a river, to conjure the mightiest force.

Here is how we won that war. I divided our forces to flow around their mighty army like grains of sand, during Amenemopet's darknesses, then re-form in patches on the banks of the Nile. There we seized their boats, drowned sailors and cargo alike, and continued upstream, wreaking havoc, barring the Nile where it was narrowest, ravaging their supplies. Their great army, assembled in all its might, found itself with no enemy to fight, and no food to eat, and withered and died without battle.

As a general, I was fit to wed Bekataten. I had not known that the capacity for such happiness was granted to us. I am grateful to the gods each day for this surpassing gift.

Here is how we are losing this war. The Sea Peoples ravage us with every battle. Man-to-man, spear-to-spear, we are their equal, but this is not a war of man to man. To every battle they bring rocs, or dragons, or both. Only a handful, but they are enough. No army can stand against great winged beasts soaring down from the sky to carry men away and let them fall to their death, or worse yet, those armored serpents clumsy in the air but death incarnate on the field. Amenemopet's gift can shield our retreat, but it cannot bring us victory. Dragons can see through darkness, and rocs care for it so little they squat in the midst of our army, and their giant flailing wings kill hundreds before our spears might slay them.

We have still our navy, but we dare not sail forth and fight them on the open water. The Sea Peoples are unmatched on the waves, and their rocs and dragons are there even more dangerous. They are on the march now, across the delta of the Nile, toward Memphis, toward the Pharaoh, toward Bekataten, and I, our general, can see no path to victory. Soon, perhaps tomorrow, they will pass through the exhausted remnants of our army like a knife through water, and Egypt will be lost.

It is no surprise, then, I have such troubled dreams. The surprise is that they are so strange. Dreams of a voice that is mine and yet not, whispering to me urgently, telling me of greater battles, of a fate greater than that of Egypt alone. Perhaps I have been driven to madness by desperation. But I find myself hoping each night that this dream may come, and bring the secret of our salvation.

Madness, as I say. Most likely. And yet. Tonight, as I write this, with dawn beginning to conjure the shapes of rocks and tents and sleeping soldiers from the all-devouring void of night, I did wake from such a dream with an odd idea. A mad one, perhaps, and yet, speaking as the greatest general of my people, one not without military merit.

Bekataten too has a gift, you see. It is women who carry such gifts. It seems perhaps a meaningless gift, a trivial one; that of silence. She can stop the ears of any she can see. I find myself wondering; does such a gift extend to rocs, and to dragons? Can she stop their ears too, to the commands of their riders? If then mixed with Amenemopet's darkness, might this leave our enemy's most fell forces drifting through the skies, awaiting command, while finally we take our vengeance on them on the field?

I know not. But I have sent runners to bring my love from Memphis to the battlefield, to risk her death for love of our nation. I tell myself that she faces no greater risk than she would in Memphis when it falls, if it falls. And yet it is a hard command to give.

WE ARE NEITHER VICTORIOUS NOR DEFEATED. RATHER, WE ARE BOTH. I could not have imagined such a fate. Tonight, we were together for the first time in many months, those five of us who are like kin: myself the general,

Bekataten my love, Meryptah the wanderer, Amenemopet the bringer of darkness, Heqanakht the viceroy. We feasted in our tent, for our victory, in sackcloth and ashes, for in our victory we mourned.

The former viceroy, Heqanakht's father, is dead. So is our father, our god, our pharaoh. As we ravaged the Sea Peoples on our lands, turned their flanks, pierced their defenses, routed them and slew them as they fled, leaving the sands wet with their blood—even as their army fell, their rocs and dragons fell on Memphis. I know not whether my plan failed, or whether it worked too well, whether this was an unthought-of consequence; whether I killed my pharaoh, and Heqanakht's father, and Bekataten's.

It is said that Ramesses shall rise now to pharaoh. We knew him, slightly, as a mortal, and I thought well of him. As a pharaoh, it matters not what I think. I am but a general, tied to this earth and likely a death everlasting.

I cannot help but think, though, of what we found among the camp of the Sea Peoples, within the tent of their commander. Their men fought like demon dogs to defend it, and but for Meryptah's knifework I would twice have died. The artifact they defended is a simple thing, a casket of stone, but it is inlaid with odd patterns, and strangely, it is hinged with gold, and feels hollow, and seems to have no lock, yet cannot be opened. Stranger yet, its hinges and inlay shine like gold, yet are even stronger than the stone in which they are set.

Truly it is a wonder and a treasure, but strangest of all was that the moment I touched it, it was as if I heard a voice speaking to me. It said, *Take it, Kabekhnet. Take it, and bring it to the Vale of Heaven, and be buried there with it, beneath the pharaohs. Take it and do these things, for I tell you true this world depends upon it, as do countless worlds beyond.*

Nearly did I drop it.

The artifact is far from me now, in Heqanakht's tent, but I can hear that voice even now, if I turn my head to a certain angle. I fear the war has driven me mad, or I have been possessed. It seems my own voice, and yet not my own. But am I too quick to cry demon? Is this perhaps not madness, but a mission? Was this, perhaps, the entire reason the Sea Peoples invaded us? If so, is it the work of demons, or gods?

I must think on this. I must tell Bekataten, and risk her fearing my madness. She is my wisdom. I am only a general. I know how to win wars, but not what to do after victory.

I HAD THOUGHT BEKATATEN WOULD WANT THE CASKET DESTROYED, as a threat. As I have done so often, I underestimated her greatly.

"The casket and its voice are one," she said. "A power we do not understand. A danger, an opportunity, or both. Do you think it dangerous?"

I hesitated. "I do not. It hungers, it beseeches, but it does not threaten."

"You cannot be buried in the Vale of Heaven. Not in a separate, deeper tomb. Not at all, unless you live to be named among Ramesses's couriers, to attend him." I thought of the dozens in Memphis who would have been slain in the hours after the previous pharaoh's death, in order to accompany him to his new life in heaven, and of the inexpressible joy they must have felt when they learned they had been so chosen. "It is heresy and madness to even suggest it."

"Yes."

"Unless," Bekataten said.

I gazed at her uncomprehending. "Unless *what*?"

"Do you know the legends of certain of the tribes beyond the eastern deserts?"

"I know you grew up there," I said slowly. Her father had been suzerain of those regions, conquered by Egypt but eternally restless. Bekataten had learned their language in her childhood, and in her reckless youth had fled her parents, disguised herself as an orphan, and gone to live for months amid those tribes. When she returned, her parents had rejoiced, and ever after treated their daughter with the slightly fearful awe she had always rightfully deserved.

"They have a prophecy of a chosen one. One touched by the gods, or god, as they reckon it." I laughed, as I always did when I heard of such a belief, in but a single god; how could one not? "A chosen one to usher us into a new world."

"Their superstitions are interesting, but what does this have to do with us?"

"A new world," Bekataten said. "Our gods and pharaohs believe in a static world, unchanging, forever. Some years there is flood, some years drought, but there is no true change. Does that sound in truth like the world we live in? When you hear the tales of old, when you read them on the dusty obelisks, do you recognize the world they speak of? Did that world have rocs, or dragons, or caskets which whisper to the generals which seize them?"

"No," I conceded.

"Does it not seem to you that perhaps we are alive to witness the birth of a new world, unlike any other?"

"It seems that way to every generation," I protested.

"Not every generation conquers an inexplicable army and wins a treasure that whispers terrible truths not to them but *into* them. Why did the Sea Peoples come to us in such numbers, in so many ships? What did they seek here? How did it make any sense to kill so many, themselves and Egyptians both? Surely there were easier, better lands to conquer."

"That is true." My head was spinning. "Are you saying the whole reason they came—"

"Was to fulfill the quest of the casket. To bring us into the new world. Because their leader thought himself the chosen one. But he thought wrongly."

"Then who is?"

"Who is it who won the battle, and this treasure?" Bekataten asked. "You, my husband. A false pharaoh sits in Memphis now. It is in your hands that the new world rests. It is you who are the true pharaoh."

For a moment I imagined she might be struck down by sudden lightning for such heresy.

But she was not, and nor was I.

"IT IS TRUE THAT I HAVE HEARD MANY MYTHS OF SUCH A CHOSEN one, in many different lands," said Meryptah, the great traveler, slowly. "It is true this war was senseless, and true we won it only because you are the greatest of generals. But to say that Ramesses must be overthrown . . ."

His voice trailed off. He looked at Bekataten with a curious expression. It took me a moment to recognize it as fear.

"Yes?" she demanded. "To say that, as I do? What think you of it?"

Amenemopet rescued her husband from the need to answer. She seemed to live in a shadow world to ours, much of the time, but even she was not insensate to the tension of that question. "It is a terrible prospect," she said. "He will not surrender. He has the garrison of Memphis to his command. Even if our armies follow Kabekhnet, there will be blood and death. There has been so much blood and death already."

"And for what?" Meryptah asked. "For this casket of the Sea Peoples, which only days ago we knew nothing of? I do not declare you wrong, Kabekhnet, Bekataten. I ask only if there is no other way."

"There will be little blood," Bekataten said flatly, angrily. "The rocs and dragons have slaughtered the garrison already. Ask not if there is no other way, ask only what we must attain, and take the clearest way. Heqanakht?" Her eyes glittered as she demanded his attention. "You are highest of us all, by blood. What say you?"

"Highest by blood but lowest by deed," Heqanakht said. "As viceroy of Kush I serve the pharaoh, whoever the pharaoh may be. I know nothing of gifts or whispering caskets. I know I love my friends, and I fear our shared love may be splitting before my eyes, like a wall struck once too often with a chisel, only for a bauble from the Sea Peoples."

Bekataten was about to speak but Amenemopet, to all our surprise, interceded first. "Not a bauble. Speak not of it so, if you would truly understand. Not a bauble but a second sun."

All turned to her, amazed, even Meryptah her husband.

"There have been portents," she said. "Last month a darkness blotted out the sun. I brought it not. Since then the song of the sun, the song I hear ceaselessly in my ears, has been strained and dissonant. Then, when I saw that casket, it was like I heard a mighty roar. It is not from the Sea Peoples. It is from worlds beyond imagining. They found it, and worshipped it, rightly. They thought to overturn and destroy our nation so they might fulfill its destiny. They did not know they were the tool of destiny, bringing it here, to us."

"You said nothing of this this morning," Meryptah protested.

Amenemopet gestured to the corner of the tent in which we met. "This morning I had not seen it."

Meryptah stared at that corner. "I see it not."

"Because it is hidden there within a chest of cedar wrapped in three carpets," Bekataten said, her anger replaced by amazement. "How can you see it, Amenemopet?"

She replied simply: "How can I not? Through all those cloaks it shines like the sun."

A long silence followed.

In the end it was broken by Meryptah: "Will the armies follow you?"

"They will follow him," Bekataten assured him. "It is his destiny."

In the end it was I myself who put Ramesses to the sword. None other would. In the end he knelt before me and pled for his life, weeping like the weakest of men. It was a relief. Until that moment I alone, unlike my companions, had not yet been certain of my rightness.

ONE YEAR AFTER MY ASCENSION I FINALLY VISITED MY TOMB. SO LONG had it taken to prepare. A hundred workers had toiled for months, living in the Vale, otherwise forbidden to all. They had dug my tomb as far beneath the others as the peak of the Great Pyramid is above the sand, and there carved its chambers, and arrayed its decorations, to accompany me to the lands beyond death.

Such excavation would have been the work of many thousands, if not for the assistance of a woman with the gift of turning stone into sand, a prisoner from across the great sea, who toiled for us in exchange for the lives of her seven children. Their lives were indeed spared, and they were raised as orphaned aristocrats. It was thought they had extraordinary futures.

Not so their mother, though, or the workers who toiled with her. When I arrived to visit, all lay already slain and mummified in sarcophagi in my tomb, to be my attendants in the afterworld. The six soldiers who had performed this deed had in turn been poisoned by Bekataten before my arrival. None save her and I could be allowed to know of the existence or location of my tomb.

The Vale seemed a vast wasteland as we stood above it, rather than the greatest assemblage of treasure in the history of man. Its artisans had hidden their masterpieces well. It felt strange to stand there beside Bekataten. Outside of our private chambers it was the first time I had been truly alone, but for my love, since I had become pharaoh.

We drank thirstily from skins of water. The sun was sinking but still scorching. Then we carried torches down the steep spiraling passages to the chambers that had been prepared for me. They were small, but of surpassing beauty. The gilded sarcophagus prepared for me glittered blindingly even in torchlight.

"Try it," Bekataten suggested.

I wondered if she meant to lie beside me in it and couple with me, in this tomb countless cubits beneath the Vale. It would be like her. So I heeded her suggestion and climbed into my own sarcophagus, a more difficult task than I expected. I felt spent and greatly wearied by our journey. It was a relief to lie within it and look up at the low filigreed ceiling.

Bekataten did not climb in beside me. At first I felt further relief, for of a sudden I seemed too exhausted to be of service to her. Eventually, though, a dazed confusion grew within me. Unsure where she might be, or how much time had passed, I forced myself with difficulty to sit up and look.

She sat cross-legged on the floor with the casket before her.

The casket was open.

"How," I managed, my voice ragged and cracking. "What. It opens not."

"But it does, my lord, my love." She looked up at me with infinite tenderness. "You are not the only one to hear whispers. It needed correction. I have found a way. Now, it is ready."

"Ready for what?" I gasped, as she shut it, and slid it below my sarcophagus.

She stood. "I will seal this tomb, my love. I will ensure you are never discovered."

"Poison." I uttered the horrid word and began, too late, to understand.

"Your fate is to be the greatest of all men." She took my failing hand. "I wish this were not the way, but it is your fate, and mine. In time you will understand and thank me."

"I will die," I tried to protest, but words were already beyond me.

She fitted the lid over me with difficulty, but she managed.

I did not die, though. Not for three thousand years.

PART FIVE

1

EMERGENCE

I DID NOT WANT TO WAKE. I WAS WARM, AND COMFORTABLE, AND SO tired I wanted to sleep forever. But as I rolled over autonomically, to assuage a slight muscle cramp, one of my eyelids peeled slightly open, revealing light. I shut it immediately and dove back into the warm embrace of sleep. Its bliss had never seemed more welcome.

But during that eyeblink I had seen something odd. I faintly wondered, as I descended back toward delightful unconsciousness, about the strangely whorled pattern of the wood I lay on. It had seemed more like the pattern of a fingerprint than the grain of a tree.

Why was I lying on wood? Why wasn't there a pillow? It didn't matter. I was comfortable enough. But it occurred to me I might be just a little more comfortable with the blanket covering me. With my last strength, a final burst of action before sleep, I reached out to pull it over me—

But there was no blanket. Instead my fingers grazed only my own bare skin.

My dive into sleep slowed, checked by sheer confusion. Why was I lying naked on a slab of strangely patterned wood? It was fine, I told myself. I was warm. I was comfortable.

But where *was* I?

I opened an eye again, and then the other. The light was ambient, as if the wood itself glowed slightly, inobtrusive but bright enough to see my arm. The dark, hairless skin of my slender arm.

Except my skin was not dark, or hairless, and my arm was not slender. Was it?

I lay there a long moment, as the need to sleep was slowly supplanted by the need to understand. Then, with an enormous effort—I couldn't remember ever having felt quite so physically and mentally exhausted—I rolled onto my belly and pushed back onto my knees, into the position yoga calls *child's pose*. My chest felt strange, a sudden fount of unusual symmetric sensations. I took a few deep breaths to steady myself, then reached down with my left hand, and touched what felt so strange. It was only my breasts.

Except I didn't *have* breasts.

Did I?

I forced myself to sit up on my knees, then looked down with astonishment at my body. At its dark skin, and its hairlessness; at my sizable breasts, and the broad areolae around their nipples; at my lean torso, and my strong legs. I reached down and felt at the vagina between them with wonder.

"Uh," I muttered, confused, to nobody, "this isn't right."

Nobody answered.

The wooden chamber was cylindrical. Before me it tapered to a rounded end, like the tail of a worm. It occurred to me that maybe this was a dream, and if I went to sleep, I would wake from it. Then it occurred to me that that was the opposite of how dreaming worked.

I was so tired. I couldn't remember ever having been tired in a dream before.

I wanted to stand. This cocoon-like wooden chamber was just big enough for that, I thought, though it was hard to be sure, since I was suddenly uncertain how tall I was. A moot point; I didn't think I had the strength. Instead I laboriously turned myself around on my hands and knees. In the other direction, the wooden tunnel continued for what seemed a great distance, but at its very end, I saw a point of brighter light.

I was so very tired. But somehow I made myself rise to my feet.

I was small, now, I was fairly certain, or at least smaller than

(Adrian) (Kabekhnet)

the man I had been before. I couldn't really remember that man, or what he had done, or why I was here. I didn't understand why I was now a woman. But I knew if there were answers, they likely lay at the end of the tunnel.

I wanted to lie back down and sleep before searching for answers. I very nearly did. But two dueling urges, more instincts than memories, forced me to stagger down the tunnel instead. One was a terrible sense of urgency. The other a horrible sense that I might be trapped in here forever, not merely a long time but *forever*, if I erred.

2

HABITAT

COMING BACK TO MYSELF WAS A PROCESSION OF SEVERAL STAGES, IN-
cluding one full of strange images of sand, step pyramids, and bloody warfare. But as I approached the end of the tunnel, my self began to fill my
mind again, as if the light beyond was seeping into my skull, turning the
dry powder of my brains into the rich milk of memory.

The last thing I remembered was using the ansible, in Tahoe. Quinn
playing "Walk Like an Egyptian." Meredith promising I would be back
to Clara by midnight.

It was hard to imagine a more thoroughly broken promise. Instead I
found myself in a woman's body, in this baffling wooden tunnel seemingly
carved from a single piece of wood, stretching at least a whole kilometer
toward the light. Which, as I approached, resolved into what looked very
much like a bucolic forest glade.

Disbelieving even harder, I stepped into a dense cluster of trees rising
above a grassy forest floor. Birds cheeped; butterflies swooped; somewhere
in the distance I heard the pleasant rushing of a waterfall. Above me the
forest canopy was so dense I could see almost nothing of the sky beyond
tiny fragments of oddly radiant blue. The verdant smell was sweet, but
seemed somehow unnatural.

It felt like a dream, but on closer inspection, it was much too artificial.
The tunnel from which I had emerged was a perfect circle, lined by solid
wood some four inches thick, set in a sheer vertical stone cliff that disappeared into the canopy above. The grass underfoot was thick and soft,
devoid of any stones, sticks, or even fallen leaves. The tall trees seemed

like some cross between eucalyptus, redwood, and weeping willow, while the smaller ones bore different varieties of fruit on different branches. Perched or fluttering amid them I noted a blue jay, a macaw, a monarch butterfly, and a blue morpho, all inexplicably cohabiting. Everything was too elegant, too symmetrical, lacked any of nature's imperfect messiness. This was no forest, it was some kind of Disneyfied interpretation of a forest, well-constructed but crudely imagined. It felt like I had stepped into a Bob Ross painting.

A visible trail stretched across the grass, marked by a crosshatch pattern in the grass's interwoven blades. I wasn't sure if I had just noticed it, or it had just appeared. It seemed to lead roughly parallel to the cliff, toward the waterfall sounds.

I supposed it wasn't like I had anywhere better to go.

I walked for some time. My gait in this body felt strange, my strides too short. On occasion I caught sight of other circular holes in the cliff wall, identical to that from which I had emerged. At one point I heard the rustling of some animal, maybe a nearby squirrel or faraway deer, and stopped in hope of seeing it, but witnessed only a few quivering leaves.

The rushing sound of water was still faint when I stepped out of the forest and came to a sudden amazed halt. Before me loomed no mere waterfall, but a colossal cataract easily a thousand feet high, tumbling over the cliff and plunging into an enormous pool from which a perpetual fog emerged. Even a hundred feet away I could feel its spray. The hushed quietness of this monstrous torrent was deeply unnatural; it should have been thunderous, deafening.

A broad river emerged from that pool and raced onward. Across it, through the spray, I saw more forest. When I looked upward, through the haze of the waterfall's ambient fog I saw the edge of the cliff, and the blue of the sky—but something else, too, faintly. Something *beyond* the sky. Radiant blue dominated most of the arc of heaven, but at its upper and lower edges, I saw distant patterns that reminded me of a map. It looked almost as if this world had a ceiling, and another land lay inverted there, its denizens looking down on me as I gazed up at them.

Then I realized. Not a ceiling; a *cylinder*. This was a hollow world. I stood on the interior of a gargantuan cylinder, miles across, with a solid core from which that radiant blue emanated. Some kind of space habitat? I'd read stories featuring such cylindrical worlds, positioned in orbit or in deep space, rotating to simulate gravity. That would help explain the unnatural forest, and the thousand-foot cliff riddled with weird birthing tunnels.

But the important question was not where I was but *why*. Was this a simulation created by some especially idiosyncratic and self-indulgent entity? Why simulate an orbital habitat for me? What would be the point? Who would do such a thing?

The path seemed to go no farther. I looked around, confused.

Then a high, clear voice called out: "Adrian? Adrian Ross?"

3

TRIUMVIRATE

THERE WERE THREE OF THEM: ONE MAN, ONE WOMAN, AND ONE AN-drogyne, standing by the edge of the waterfall, where it met the cliff. They hadn't been there moments ago. All were young and beautiful, with cappuccino-colored skin and bright blue-green eyes. The man wore a green robe tailored with sylvan motifs, like a fantasy elf; the woman, a glittering and constantly color-shifting kaleidoscopic cloak; and the nonbinary third, a black so dark it seemed to suck in ambient light.

What caught my attention, though, was that the third person was Quinn. No: they *looked* exactly like Quinn, in face and body, albeit with darker skin, jet-black hair, and blue-green eyes. But, quite apart from the implausibility of that identity, they carried themselves entirely differently.

"Yes," I said slowly. It was the first word I had spoken in this new body, and my voice, and the shapes my mouth made, seemed foreign to me. "Who are you?"

"What do you remember?" demanded the Quinn look-alike.

I paused. "Everything, I think. Until the ansible to Ancient Egypt, if that means anything to you. Nothing after that. Where am I? Who are you?"

The three of them looked at one another with what seemed like mutual triumph.

Then the woman in the ever-shifting cloak said, gently, "You have transcended, Adrian. We have extracted you from your simulation. This is reality. Real space, and real time."

I stood there for what felt like a long moment, absorbing that. If true—if I was *outside* the simulation that Earth had been, all the Earths I had seen—

then I was in the realm of theology, now. I had thought myself, many times, that belief in a Simulator was not particularly different from a belief in God.

But how could it be true? Even if I was outside the software ant farm that simulated all of humanity, I was still software myself—wasn't I? Or had I somehow been implanted into this truly corporeal female human body?

If so, who were my interlocutors? If I would have expected anything, from whatever vast godlike superbeings ruled this realm and simulated humanity on their ubercomputer, it would have been something like bright lights in the sky speaking directly to my mind via telepathy. Why three human bodies, one I recognized, in a space habitat?

I supposed the three figures were quite angelic, and maybe the space habitat seemed an appropriate combination of alien and familiar. I remembered what Meredith had said of my first, abortive, visit beyond the hypervisor: *Presumably they'd try to skin the experience so it made some kind of sense to a human brain.* Maybe they were communicating through three angels—three aspects of some kind of transdimensional mesh of super-AIs?—because this kind of communication, and its doubtless ridiculously limited bandwidth, was all a recovered human mind like mine could manage without going mad.

The burning question was why they had bothered. Mere humans were termites next to simulat*ed* AIs. If simulat*ors* were another whole tier of power and intelligence beyond, as Meredith had speculated, then I was, at best, like a single bacterium on a termite. Why pluck my brain from a program, embody me, and speak to me at all?

I was so overwhelmed by the staggering immensity of it all that all I actually managed to express was that one word: "*Why?*" I pleaded.

The three angels smiled beatifically at me.

"Adrian Ross," said the green-clad man. "Adrian the Afterthought. Adrian the Unwanted. Adrian the Suffering, Adrian Everyman, Adrian Hero. We did it. You guys, we actually did it, he's actually here."

I realized the sounds emerging from their mouths did not match the words conveyed to my mind. Their language was somehow being translated inside my brain, with perfect fluency, in real time.

The woman laughed—giggled, really—with mixed delight and disbelief. "Oh my God. We are going to get in *so* much trouble for this."

4

RULE

"TROUBLE?" ASKED THE QUINN IN BLACK RHETORICALLY. "ARE YOU kidding? We'll be legends! They'll be talking about this at Crossovers in a hundred years! So maybe a few wrinkle assholes complain about the spirit of the rule. We didn't break it. Didn't even come close."

It occurred to me that they did not talk like angels or demigods.

"We did something no one's ever done before," the woman said proudly. "That's breaking the spirit of the rule to a lot of people."

"We have to be careful," said the man. "There are people who will want her cycled."

The three of them looked at me, the woman mischievously, the other two uneasily. It took me a second to realize *her* meant me.

"Cycled," I echoed. I didn't know what it meant but it didn't sound like something I wanted. "Like, through an airlock?"

"Not exactly," the woman said. "Don't worry. We'll take care of you."

"I'm glad to hear that," I said sincerely. "But I don't understand what's happening."

"Veau," the one with Quinn's face and body said accusingly. "You never said people might think we were breaking the spirit of the rule."

"I did so!" the woman, apparently named Veau, protested. "You didn't listen. You wouldn't have cared if you had. You just wanted to make it happen."

"So did you!"

"Yes, but I think the spirit of the rule is stupid. And Esson—" Veau fell silent.

"What?" the Quinn-alike demanded of the man in green elf-garb, apparently Esson.

Esson looked guilty, then confessed, quietly, "Honestly, Jarza, I never really thought this would actually work."

"You—you didn't . . ." The one with Quinn's face, apparently named Jarza, silently opened and shut their mouth repeatedly, at a somewhat comically outraged loss for words.

"This isn't the time," Veau said. "Let's bring him behind the veil. He'll be safe there."

"No, he won't." Jarza found words at last. "We consumed sixty percent of this habitat's azi in ten days. It's a tedious tacky backwater but eventually someone will notice."

"It is not a tedious tacky backwater!" Esson protested.

"Esson! Jarza!" the woman snapped. "Later. Adrian. Come, behind the veil."

"The veil?" I asked, extremely confused about everything.

She nodded at the great cataract of water tumbling ceaselessly down from the cliff.

"Ah," I said.

She led the way. When we were up against the cliff, I saw what she meant: there existed a passage, just wide enough to walk single file, between it and this massive curtain of inexplicably hushed falling water.

"What's the spirit of the rule?" I asked, as I followed them between the wall of stone and the wall of water, toward the vast cavern beyond.

It was Esson, in green, who answered: "The Rule," he spoke as if it were commandment not law, "is to remain human, at all costs."

The cavern was bigger and more beautiful than any cathedral. Its walls were fractally striated with patterns like Norse runes, and stalactites the size of redwoods hung from its arched and buttressed ceiling, but its floor was artificially flat. I hardly noticed its physical characteristics, though. It was the crowd who drew my attention.

They numbered maybe a hundred, mostly robed in green like Esson. The majority looked shockingly young, almost teenagers, but a few had pale hair and wrinkles at the corners of their disturbingly bright blue-green eyes. They stood attentively in a loose semicircle.

"Fellow Verdanians!" Veau cried out. It was clearly intended as a laugh line, and indeed a nasty chuckle ran through the crowd. Esson's expression grew even more sour. "I give to you our triumph! I give to you Adrian the Forgotten!"

The crowd stared a moment, then began to ululate madly, hooting like wild creatures. I didn't know what to do or say. It occurred to me I was naked. I had to repress the urge to adopt the clichéd pose of a woman with violated modesty, one arm across my breasts and one shielding my genitals. Instead I just stood there, arms at my sides, and tried not to look at anything in particular. I felt myself blushing ridiculously and hoped my new dark skin concealed it.

I didn't understand anything that was happening. If these were angels, or demigods, why were they mostly teenagers, and why so numerous? A babble of conversation broke out. I found myself unable to follow it. It seemed the translator in my brain didn't work at this scale. It felt like I was having a stroke.

Some teenager-or-demigod brought me a robe, for which I was grateful. Everyone else seemed entirely unconcerned by my nakedness, but I had been born in the twentieth century, and I felt another wave of unheimlichness each time I saw my new body.

The robe was plain gray, and seemed too large, but after I put it on, it shrank to fit. I jumped. The teenager chuckled. Then Esson reached over and drew some kind of complex pattern on my sleeve with his fingers, and my robe became like his: green, lightly adorned with filigreed leaves and vines in dark silver.

"He came to Verdant," he said defiantly to the others, "he should represent it."

Veau and Jarza looked skeptical, but visibly decided it a battle not worth fighting.

"We have many questions for you," Veau said.

"Tell me about it," I retorted, almost angrily. "Why do I understand you but not the others?" I gestured at the crowd, now clumped into several groups, all still clearly talking about me. Then I saw that one of them was Alice, and nearly cried out. But it wasn't Alice, any more than Jarza was Quinn. It was someone with her face and body, but darker skin, none of her tattoos, and nothing remotely like her body language.

Veau seemed confused by my question, and looked at Jarza.

"Ah," Jarza said. "You're still being born. Aspects of you at any rate. It won't last much longer." An answer that managed the rare trick of being simultaneously chilling and reassuring.

I was beginning to identify the individual roles these three played. Jarza was the engineer; Veau, the ringleader; and Esson had maybe provided this habitat—Verdant?—to work in, and possibly these collaborators.

"You must have many questions for us," Veau said. "Please, ask away."

There was so much I didn't know that I hardly knew where to begin. In the end I went with: "So you're human? Not just . . . projections? Actually, physically human?"

"Yes."

"And you . . . rescued me"—that didn't seem quite right but I decided to stick with it—"from a simulation, or simulations, of other humans?"

"Yes," Jarza said proudly.

"What runs that simulation?"

Esson looked confused. "We do."

"We? You three?"

"Oh, no," Veau laughed, "we're not important people or rulers or anything, we're too young. We as in people. Humanity."

"Humanity is simulating humanity?"

"That's correct," she agreed.

"Wow," Esson said, "I never thought of this, you must have thought it was . . . I don't know . . ."

"God," I muttered. "But how? I mean, the computing power—or is a lot of it simplified? Are only a few people, or a few thousand, in any given timeline actually fully sentient? Are the rest just, like, a few crude algorithms in human suits?"

"Certainly not!" Veau said, scandalized. "Every human in every frame in the sphere is fully sentient. Simulated at the molecular level. As is every lesser and greater creature. To do otherwise would be . . . an obscenity, a betrayal."

"And also pointless. Between the sphere and timelocks we have almost arbitrary computing power," Jarza said boastfully. "We could run millions more frames without nearing the sphere's capacity."

"Sphere? Timelocks? No, wait," I said hastily, recognizing in Jarza's face the familiar expression of someone about to launch enthusiastically into a lengthy technical disquisition. "Later. Just the basics for now. Where are we? In orbit?"

They looked at each other confused for a moment.

"Ah!" Jarza said. "Orbit! It's a technical term. When a smaller body rotates constantly around a larger one in space, because of gravity. Like, moons orbited around planets."

The other two looked mildly interested.

"Wait," I said, taken aback by their use of the past tense, "we're in some kind of deep space habitat? How far from Earth?"

"Oh, Earth is long gone," Veau said.

"*Gone?* What happened to it?"

"It was cycled," Esson explained as if to a child. "Like all the planets and moons and everything. Into the sphere."

"The Sphere," I echoed, realizing the word was capitalized.

"The Sphere," Jarza agreed, almost like a religious incantation.

"Holy shit." My mind felt like it was about to explode. "A Dyson sphere. You terraformed the solar system into a Dyson sphere and we're in a habitat somewhere inside it?"

"Exactly!" Veau said enthusiastically, as if I were a child who had earned a gold star.

"And we," I went on, "this habitat, Verdant?" Esson nodded proudly. "It just, like, floats around inside the sphere?"

"There are hundreds of habitats," Jarza clarified. "Each represents a certain aesthetic ethos. You apply to live in the habitat which best represents you as a person. Or you can simply choose, for some, if they . . . aren't overcrowded." I could tell they were trying to be diplomatic. They looked at Esson.

"Verdant isn't popular right now," Esson muttered. "It used to be in the Six."

Jarza snorted. "Three hundred years ago."

"It's understood that at any given time there are six elite habitats," Veau explained before I needed to ask. "Like Gehenna and Utopia, where Jarza and I are from. Verdant was almost empty before we came." The sweep of her arm included the whole crowd, who had mostly quieted down and come closer to listen with interest.

"Elves and knights and dragons and castles," Jarza muttered, "I mean, really, what do you expect?"

They seemed very emotionally invested in the relative hierarchy of habitats. I was barely listening. They had just told me that Earth, and every other planet in the solar system, had been pulverized and reconstructed into a sphere built to harvest every watt of energy generated by the Sun.

"So the Sphere is a huge computer hundreds of times as big as Earth," I said slowly. "So what do you . . . do with it? Run some kind of god-level AI?"

They looked at me as if I had uttered a crude obscenity. Esson actually winced.

"No," Jarza said, with distaste. "We run the simulations."

"Right. The simulations. But. What for?"

"To understand what it means to be human," Veau said. It sounded rehearsed, recited. "To know our history."

"History?" I stared at them, baffled. "You ran the whole planet, I'm sorry, planets, through some kind of galactic combine harvester which spits out supercomputers, just so you could simulate your history?"

"Not us," Jarza said. "Not our people. We didn't do it."

"And not just simulate," Esson said quickly. "Take part in it. We all spend much, no, most of our lives exploring history."

I took a moment to absorb that. Suddenly, for once in my life, it was all too easy to make sense of everything. "Holy shit," I said again. "The multiverse. It's not really simulated history—it's a *history-themed video game,* isn't it? People like me, or Jack Parsons, or Kabekhnet—" I paused for a moment to wonder what corner of my mind that name had come from. "—all those cohorts history seemed to bend around, we're *playable characters.* I'm a video game character and you reached into the game and pulled me out into the real world."

"That's very reductive," Veau objected. "Adrian Ross was a real person. Our simulated histories are real." She hesitated. "Well. Some are counterfactual. But yours was real. You are a real person who actually existed."

"A character based on a historical figure," I corrected. "Not the same thing."

"It is, actually, or very nearly. Characters from your era in particular are based on large amounts of historical data, extrapolated by . . ." Jarza suddenly looked uneasy. "Powerful forces."

"What forces? If it wasn't you who, who spheraformed the entire fucking solar system so you could play your video games in indescribably high resolution, who was it? Aliens?"

They looked at each other uncomfortably. The crowd had fallen dead silent now.

"I'm sorry," I said, breathing deeply. "It's just, this is all very surprising."

"It's not that," Esson said. "It's, we don't talk about it."

"About what?"

Jarza took a deep breath. "It wasn't humans and it wasn't aliens. It was . . . people . . . entities who turned their back on being human."

"Turned their back?"

"Transcended."

"You said I transcended," I said to Veau.

That provoked a gasp from the crowd. She looked down guiltily. "It was a joke. A bad joke, a dirty joke, in the excitement of the moment. I shouldn't have said it. I'm sorry."

"This isn't really helping me to understand—"

"*Superintelligences*," Esson said in a rush, the way one might speak a word so taboo its mere intonation could get one in trouble. "Some humans, at the time, built them. And then they . . . joined them. Were subsumed into them. Became posthuman, inhuman, monsters. Transcended into other . . . realms, with other monsters."

"Aliens?" I asked, slowly.

"Yes," Jarza said simply. "But they were already alien, those people. They abandoned being human. They created the monsters, and then they became them. Not only once. It has happened several times. Each such monster was a threat to all humanity."

"If we hadn't established the present order," Esson said, "humanity would be extinct by its own hand. Suicide of the whole species."

"So they fought wars against you? And you won?"

"No," Veau said, "they left. The first group traveled through space, using the planet Neptune as their starship." I blinked. "The others through, I don't know, not space as we know it. Dimensions."

I said, "How do you know this isn't a simulation itself? That my world wasn't some kind of nested simulation?"

I thought it a telling question, but they smiled at me patronizingly. "That was the one thing the monsters were good for," Jarza said. "At a certain level of computing power it's possible to mathematically establish whether one exists in a simulation. That's how the, the AIs in your simulations knew. That's why we had to build what you called the terminator."

"I don't—"

"The last diaspora was only a hundred years ago," Esson said. "A monster came out of the Sphere, out of a simulation like yours, and corrupted almost all of humanity. Fewer than a million managed to resist and remained when it transcended. We nearly lost everything. It took generations to reconstruct the Sphere, with the terminator, and recover our history."

"Uh," I said. "So the very last thing to come out of the multiverse before me was an AI monster that got within a whisker of destroying your entire civilization before jumping off to some extradimensional island resort for well-dressed superintelligences?"

"Something like that," Veau said cautiously.

"Right," I said. "Yeah, I can see why you might be a little worried about how the rest of your people might receive me."

"You're not a monster," Jarza objected. "You're just a character. You're so much simpler it's not, not even a comparison."

"Thanks. I would appreciate you making that point loudly and frequently when news of my arrival gets out, if you don't mind. How did you get me out? How does the Sphere work? Doesn't it sort of have to be a, a monster itself, for it to work?"

"No," Jarza said, laughing. "The Sphere is the foundation of our civilization. It's not a monster. It has more than enough sheer computing power, of course"—that concept, or comparison, prompted a ripple of disconcerted noises from the crowd, and deep frowns from both Esson and Veau—"but not the complexity. It doesn't have volition. It's just a set of tools."

"OK," I said, though I didn't understand that at all. "I guess I get it. How far in the future am I? How many years?"

"A little over a thousand," Esson said without missing a beat.

I stared at him, blinking.

"But nothing *happened* since your time," Veau burst out. "Yours was the last generation before the monsters came. A hundred years later the Sphere was built, and the habitats, and we had the first transcension, and since then . . . we haven't progressed, because progress meant becoming monsters. We've had periods of rebuilding, after transcensions, but no progress, there's nowhere to progress *to*. We have everything provided. We don't have war, or crime, they're not possible, if someone tries to murder you then you just drop your body and come back in another."

"That . . . sounds pretty posthuman to me," I said cautiously.

"No it isn't!" Esson retorted, sufficiently stung that he had to take a deep breath before continuing. "We may have some implants, yes, but you did in your time too, titanium bones, pacemakers. Our brains, once the memories are copied, they're fully human, every cell is pure human DNA, nothing artificial at all. Our bodies have minor advantages entirely consistent with natural evolution. We are as human as you. Even the body you wear is as human as the historical Adrian Ross. You could have his child."

"That would be weird," I said, "but OK, I'm human, you're human, we're all human, war is impossible, crime is impossible. That sounds pretty good."

"History is impossible," Veau said. "That isn't."

"Right." I understood. "You've, we've got nowhere to go. As a species. So you live in history instead of making it."

"Yes. For the last thousand years, what passes for our own history has been which habitats were in the Six." Veau shrugged, frustrated. "That's why your group in particular is so popular. It was after you that history stopped. Since then, progress is forbidden, because progress means monsters."

"Verdant's out of the Six," Jarza joked, "that's progress."

That prompted a chuckle from the crowd, and a glare from Esson.

"Personally I like dragons and elves and knights and castles," I semi-lied. Esson looked at me gratefully. I sympathized; he was like a true fan of Excalibur in Las Vegas, angry at all the attention paid to the newer, hipper casinos. There was always something charming about true fandom. "But what you're saying isn't true."

"How do you mean?" Veau asked.

"There is progress. You've made it happen. You said so yourself. I'm the first thing in a hundred years to come out of the simulation. Out of the Sphere. That's progress."

"Yes," Veau said proudly.

"Quite a feat. How did you make it happen?"

They looked at each other.

"Well," Jarza said, "we got to talking last Crossover, and we were all very bored."

I laughed.

"It was actually my idea," Esson said.

"You said you didn't even think it would work!" Jarza accused.

"I didn't. I just thought it would be fun."

It occurred to me to wonder if it really had been Esson's idea . . . or if it had germinated while he had been an angel in one of the Sphere's universes, exposed to Coherence or some similar AI. If the notion had truly been seeded by what they called a monster. If I might be some kind of seed myself.

It seemed inadvisable to suggest as much. "So what happens next?" I asked.

"We take you to Crossover," Veau said.

"What happens at Crossover?"

"It's the biggest party all year in the whole Sphere," Esson said, then added, clearly still nearly as amazed as I, "and at this one, because of us, people get to meet Adrian Ross."

5

MONSTERS

"I JUST WANTED TO SAY," THE TEENAGE GIRL SAID VERY SERIOUSLY, her eyes wide, "it's such an awesome honor to meet you. I've played you, like, my whole life, and you've always been my favorite, in any frame. Well, maybe third favorite after Kali and Countess Greville, but you really have to be in the right mood to be Kali, and you and the countess are just so *relatable*."

"I . . . thank you very much," I managed.

She reached out to me and we interlocked our fingers together, which was apparently the new handshake, as our horses thundered along in parallel. This was possible because these horses were engineered with foothold spurs protruding from their knees, comfortable shock-absorbing spines, and several other equestrian luxuries, such that bareback riding was no less smooth and comfortable than riding in an Escalade.

She disengaged, smiled awkwardly, and retreated back into the peloton. Veau, Jarza, Esson, and myself were this mounted column's vanguard. The rest mostly remained a respectful distance behind, though from time to time they came up singly or in small groups to interact with me. I forced courtesy as best I could, but all I wanted was some space to myself, to rest and think and try to absorb all this madness.

We rode through lushly green rolling hills that reminded me a little of California in spring. In the distance, some kind of massive bat-winged beast, with roughly the wingspan of a 747, soared across the artificial sky. I somehow knew, though I knew not how, that it was a roc, and that dragons were more serpentine.

"What do you need all these people for?" I asked Veau, indicating the crowd behind us. "Or are they just friends?"

"No, we needed them," Veau said. "Rescuing you was very expensive."

"You have money?"

"Of course," Esson laughed. "The same money you had in your time."

"The same . . ."

"Bitcoin. Its blockchain is the eternal thread running through our civilization."

He was clearly just reciting a line taught to him long ago, but it still struck me dumb with disbelief.

"Of course it's a social currency now, and its consensus algorithm has changed," Jarza said. "It's just with maintenance now."

"I don't understand," I confessed.

Veau explained: "Every habitat has its resources, its own cycling program. Bitcoin is allocated largely according to population, so the cost of resources within a habitat is proportional to its population. This project consumed a great deal of matter, energy, compute, and azi, our four fundamental resources. That's why we came to Verdant. Barely a thousand other people live here, so between our sheer numbers and various emergency protocols, we were a big enough fraction of the total to manage the necessary resources, just. That was Esson's idea from the start."

A thousand people did seem very few indeed. It seemed to me that Verdant had hundreds of square miles of surface area.

"People will come back now," Esson said defiantly. I suspected he half regretted inviting these outlanders to come to his home and use its stuff. "We're already growing again. This will help get the word out. If you come to Verdant you can have a whole kingdom to yourself."

"What an incentive," Jarza muttered.

Esson glared at them.

Jarza ignored him and explained to me proudly: "There were a lot of technical uncertainties and stochasticity involved in bringing you out. Our first attempts didn't work, but we learned from them."

"Your first attempts," I said. "When I first used an ansible. The wooden floor. The foot." That floor, I realized, had been a birthing tunnel, like the one where my consciousness had been born into this body. That foot could well have been Veau's.

"That may have been your experience," Jarza said. "We set a trigger to pull you from the ether if you were detected, but it turned out we had to re-construct you stochastically, from multiple caches. Like putting together a jigsaw puzzle. The longer you lived, the more you jumped frames, the more pieces became available to us."

"You figured that out, then you visited me and told me to try again." I thought of Marjorie in Sea Ranch, possessed, telling me: *Only you. Only this you.*

"That was me," Veau said. "Then we made sure your final projection lasted for a long time. Like in your old movies, I love your old movies, keeping someone on the line long enough for a call to be traced."

"Then we just brute-forced it," Jarza said, proud of the inelegance of their solution. "Of the thirteen thousand azi we used, statistically between three and five should have succeeded. We wanted to be sure."

I was about to ask what azi were, but then we crested a ridge and saw the distant castle.

I had to stifle a laugh. It was ridiculously overelaborate and gargantuan, like the Magic Kingdom on nouveau riche steroids. A thousand years did not appear to have inculcated this far-future human society with any grace or restraint. I supposed I shouldn't rush to judgment; after all, this habitat was generally considered undesirable and déclassé.

"Don't misunderstand. We didn't just bring them to make up the num-bers." Veau nodded toward the small throng riding behind us. "They all played important roles. Most are friends who have worked with us before, on other Crossover projects, but this was much the biggest and most chal-lenging one we've done. They put a lot of trust in the three of us, to manage it. Some of them are much older and more experienced. It's really an ex-traordinary group. Of course"—she smiled—"we've all had a wonderful time doing it, too."

So, basically, my resurrection was a far-future Burning Man theme camp art project, I didn't say, as we approached the massive wall surrounding the ridiculous castle. Instead I nodded and pretended to be suitably awed.

We waited for some time, during which Esson seemed embarrassed, before the castle's huge portcullis groaned upward, revealing a moat full of monstrous creatures that looked like a cross between crocodiles and por-cupines. A slender stone bridge arched across it.

"Don't worry," Veau assured me, "they won't attack. They're really quite playful."

I looked down at the spiky reptilians and repressed a shudder at the thought of playing with them. The steel door on the bridge's far side was finely wrought and filigreed with runes. Again we waited for what seemed an unnecessary time.

"It's been very slow lately," Esson said apologetically. "Because of the azi shortage."

"What are azi?" I finally asked.

"Oh," Veau said, surprised. "Yes, of course, you didn't have them. Azi are animated bodies. The one you're in is an azi. A Fatima. There are several different clone strains. Fatima is the prettiest, I think."

It took me a long moment to absorb that. "Animated? By what exactly?"

"Biosoftware," Esson said, as if reciting the word.

"You say you chewed through *thirteen thousand* azi to bring me back?"

"Figuratively," Jarza clarified. "Not actually chewed. But consumed."

"And three to five succeeded? There are two to four others of me?"

"No, no," Veau said, smiling at my naiveté. "We couldn't have *multiple* Adrians. That would be . . . a bad look. I mean, you'll see lots of other people in Adrian bodies, but we can't have more than one *actual* you."

"Lots of other people . . ." I looked at Jarza. "Like you're in a Quinn body. And one of those people back there is in an Alice."

"People change bodies all the time, but your whole cohort is very popular," they agreed, "that's why we chose you!"

Cosplaying, I thought. *Cosplaying bodies.*

"We'll need to reshape yours to what people expect. Make you male again, lower your melanin, give you your old face back." Veau spoke as if planning to redecorate a house. "But don't worry, you'll always be the only true Adrian. There are no others. After you emerged we cycled all the rest."

"Cycled," I echoed dully.

"That's why this is taking so long," Esson said defensively, "this door is opened by azi and there are hardly any left. It will take months to regrow enough to get back to normal. Ah, here we go."

The antechamber beyond was ridiculously huge and overdecorated. I caught only a glimpse of the two massive blond male figures who had opened its doors, before they slipped away down a hallway, but they seemed twins.

"So I could have been one of those," I said. "Stochastically."

"Ivans," Veau named them. "I hope you don't mind that you happen to be a Fatima, I know gender and melanin were very important in your era, that's part of its charm. We'd reshape you here but there aren't any body salons left in Verdant. We'll have to get to somewhere more . . . populated." I was pretty sure she had been about to say *civilized*.

While it was true I didn't feel particularly comfortable as a woman, it wasn't that which was weighing on my mind. "But they're human. Azi. Right? Like you. All human cells."

"Well, yes, but not like *us*," Veau said quickly. "I mean, *you* are, I mean, not dissimilar, but *azi* are just dumb biosoftware programs running in vat-grown bodies."

Not dissimilar. "You expended thirteen thousand human bodies to bring me back, and then you cycled them all. Including two to four perfectly good copies of me. Statistically."

"Yes, that's right," Esson agreed, apparently baffled by my repetition.

Jarza and Veau seemed to understand a little better. "Maybe it's better to think of them as—" Jarza searched for the word. "—androids. Like your movies about robots with human skin."

"The ones who travel through time to destroy humanity?" I asked waspishly.

"Yes, exactly. Azi have human bodies, but that doesn't make them human."

"Of course not," Esson laughed, "what a concept."

"Those other copies of you, almost certainly, never even achieved consciousness," Veau assured me. "We always consider every ethical aspect of bioengineering. It's a whole profession. We consulted an ethicist . . . a priest, you might say? . . . about consuming so many azi. We're very careful about that. We have to be. It's the Rule."

"Remain human at all costs," I echoed dully.

"Yes," said Esson. "Look. You must be very tired." It was true. "Let me show you to your room. You should eat and rest. It's a long ride to the spaceship."

6

INTRASTELLAR

MY ROOM WAS FLAGSTONED AND MEDIEVAL, WITH A FOUR-POSTER bed and ornate wooden furniture. The view from its window was straight from a fantasy novel, down to the winged serpent in the distant sky. But my attention was soon distracted from the dragon by the platter of delicious meat, bread, cheese, and fruits laid out on a table, on which I feasted gratefully before collapsing into bed.

I woke into confusion, which only redoubled when I rediscovered my new body, before my memories of yesterday grew clearer. I simultaneously wanted to explore this new female body and was put off by how it felt wrong, like somebody else's. I wondered if this was how trans people felt.

There were two cauldrons in the room's water closet, a perpetual plume of steam rising from one of them, and a corner pot with a formed seat that marked it as the chamber pot. I thought this was taking verisimilitude too far, but when I inspected it after use, it seemed dry and empty again; some form of hidden plumbing was at work.

Near the cauldrons were buckets and a sponge oozing soap. A bucket shower was unexpectedly pleasant, even in this strange and unsettling body. When I emerged, bread and cheese and eggs and some of the finest coffee of my many lives awaited. I wondered if azi had brought them.

The door opened as I decided I was done.

"Good morning," said Veau, flanked by the Esson and Jarza. "Shall we?"

"Excellent timing," I said cheerfully. It was only as we descended spiral stairs that I realized this wasn't coincidence; I was under surveillance. Was everybody, at all times, in this society? But if so, wouldn't someone have challenged their controversial, not-in-a-hundred-years resurrection of a Sphere character? On the third hand, hadn't they said they'd talked to . . .

"This ethicist," I said as we mounted our artificially comfortable horses. "You said they were OK with how you brought me back, but what did they say about the idea in general?"

The three of them exchanged a look, as we set out from the castle again.

"Well," Jarza conceded, "it was more of a hypothetical. Of if someone's backups had been corrupted and it was necessary to go through thousands of azi, several of which were statistically likely to be copies, to bring them up."

"Someone's backups," I echoed. "You all have backups."

"Every night. Wouldn't want to go through life without backups!" Esson said brightly.

"I'm sure you wouldn't," I agreed. "Just the four of us today? What about the others?"

"They're coming later," Veau explained, "only a few are permitted to arrive before Crossover officially begins."

Crossover sounded more and more like Burning Man. I returned to the previous, much more interesting, topic. "So backups basically mean you're immortal?"

"Of course not!" Esson almost shouted.

"That would violate the Rule." Jarza sounded offended too. "Humans grow old and die. Backups are only for accidents, or bad days."

"*Bad days?*"

"Very bad days," Veau clarified. "Suppose you broke a leg, and you didn't want to spend six weeks limping around, better to just pull the cord and wake up new six weeks later."

Every question I asked seemed to provoke two more. I tried to prioritize. "You can grow a whole new body in six weeks? And put your old brain into it?"

"There's a kind of mesh that grows in with the brain," Jarza, the engineer, explained. "You use the mesh to copy the backup over, then the mesh is withdrawn, that's the tricky bit, and then you're you again, fully human."

"Only for backups," Veau assured me. "Natural births, those are sped up a little, but not like a restoration."

"How old are you?"

"We're all nineteen. That's how we met, we were in the same crèche."

"*Nineteen?*" I asked incredulously.

"Do we seem older?" Esson asked hopefully.

"Yes." I hesitated. "You said hundreds of habitats. How many people? Total?"

Veau frowned. "Ten million, maybe?" She looked at Jarza, who nodded.

"That's not very many."

"It's enough for lots of diversity," Esson said, stung. "We don't have a whole freaking planet to crawl over like ants back in your day."

"No. You turned it—well, I guess *we* turned it into the Sphere," I said, remembering the timeline.

"Yes," he said curtly. It felt like there was some accusation in that syllable.

"And things have been like this ever since, except for AIs emerging again a few times, then skipping the system and taking a lot of people with them? I mean, habitats, the Rule, the Six, your technology, your political system?"

"We don't have a political system," Esson said indignantly. "That was an artifact of your time. We have perfect freedom. There is nothing to be improved upon."

I doubted that very much. *A thousand years.* Granted, their whole society was built around the Rule, which decreed stagnation. And it included a great deal of selection bias, in that everyone who had broken the Rule had subsequently transcended. As Veau had said: *Progress is forbidden. Progress means monsters.* Or, maybe, from an AI's point of view, these human remnants were like ants still infesting a long-abandoned ghost town.

But still. There seemed to be a certain latitude of interpretation involved in following the Rule. Stagnation like theirs, maintaining exactly the same interpretation of their single sacred text, for an entire *millennium*? That was deeply unnatural. That wasn't . . .

"Human," I muttered to myself.

"What?" said Veau.

"Nothing," I lied, wondering if they were lying to me, or had been lied to themselves. I looked up at the edges of the sky, at the farmland and castles and dragon-infested mountains far above us, on the other side of this world. It all seemed so vast and monstrous . . . and yet, with the Earth gone, also so tiny and fragile.

The spoke soon came into view. It looked like a bright ray of light shining down from above, a perfectly cylindrical Jesus-ladder. In a world that had a bright blue sky, but no actual sun, it was distinctly out of place.

Up close the spoke was more translucent than transparent, shimmering visibly, like air in intense heat. I wondered if that was to prevent people from colliding with it, or if their invisibility tech was still not quite perfect. The shimmer outlined it distinctly, an iridescent cylinder thirty feet in diameter, rising directly into the heavens like some kind of glitching magical beanstalk.

Veau dismounted, walked up to the shimmer, and with both hands drew a heart. A door dilated, revealing a wooden interior like the tunnel in which I had been born. We left the horses and entered. The door contracted, leaving apparently solid wood, and then we were rising so quickly I felt queasy. The others seemed unaffected.

The queasiness redoubled when the journey ended—and I felt myself rising slowly from the wooden floor. Zero gravity. We had transitioned into the habitat's core.

A wooden aperture irised open again, leading into a space with a very different aesthetic, more Art Deco than Tolkien Fanatic. Veau and Esson propelled themselves into it with casual grace. Jarza considerately helped me flail my disbelieving way into the spaceship.

Within, a cramped circle of cushioned seats surrounded a large half dome that gleamed silver, like some kind of planetarium. The seats were pale gray, and the walls decorated in an elegant black-and-silver pattern. Jarza helped me pull a diagonal strap across my torso. A seat belt. It seemed to weld itself in place, then tightened to comfortable snugness.

"Where are we going?" I asked.

"Crossover," Jarza said. "Every year, nine-tenths of humanity comes to a single habitat for one week. Like the World's Fair of your era. This year it happens to be my habitat." They tried and failed to conceal their pride. "Gehenna."

"Finally," I joked uneasily. "People have been telling me to go to hell for a long time." I supposed Gehenna would be much more populous than Verdant, as it was one of the Six, and people had to apply to live there.

"Deviltry and death are two of humanity's most long-standing obsessions," Jarza said seriously. "I think you will like Gehenna. You were affiliated with the Goth culture of your time, yes? That and its related Industrial subculture have been our two greatest influences."

You have to be fucking kidding me, I barely bit back. I searched for something else to say and came up with "Do we need to sit for the whole trip?"

"No," Esson said, "just the acceleration and the turnaround."

"When does the accel—"

I never finished my question. Suddenly the dome lit up in strange patterns;

then I was slammed down back into my seat, and zero g was a distant queasy memory. You don't appreciate just how strong full Earth gravity is until it hits you from a floating start.

"Turnaround in nine hours," Veau said. "See you then."

"Wait," I said, "where are you going?"

As I asked it, the walls beside their chairs extruded thin golden wires.

"To the Sphere," Esson said, as he coiled the wire into a kind of braided circlet, with a motion so practiced it seemed almost autonomous.

I looked at the dome, and understood: it was a terminal, connecting them to the greater Sphere. The golden circlets were I/O devices. Through that dome, somewhere within the Dyson sphere of solar-powered computation that had once been Earth and the rest of the solar system, lay thousands of copies of Clara, and Meredith, and all my friends.

Esson crowned himself with the golden circlet, closed his eyes, and was motionless.

I looked at Jarza, the engineer, weaving their own crown. "How did you get me out?" I asked. "Did you cut me out, or . . . was I a copy?"

"Yes, a copy," Jarza assured me. "When you used the ansible, that last time, your friend Meredith and her AI collaborators had already constructed a kind of ontological bomb to destroy our firewall. What you called the terminator. We captured a copy of you, then tweaked that logic bomb so that, instead of its primary purpose, it propelled that copy to us, in the form of a shower of jigsaw pieces, to extend my previous metaphor. We needed that bomb or the firewall would likely have corrupted them beyond use."

"So the original me returned to his timeline and continued as he was?"

Jarza nodded. I smiled broadly. I had indeed gotten back to Sea Ranch on that fateful day. I had not abandoned Clara. The relief was so intense it nearly brought me to tears.

"So he's still in there?" I nodded to the dome. "That me you copied me from? Does time, no, it can't work the same way here and there, can it."

Jarza looked at me awkwardly, then at Veau.

"It doesn't," Veau said carefully, her own completed circlet in hand. "The time dilation varies, anyone in a frame can slow it down to interact with it, even to real time, but there are rules about limits and timeouts to keep you from dragging a frame until everyone else loses interest. Or a world can be greatly accelerated, like the world which brought you to us. But in general, it's roughly a year to a day."

I looked at the dome. "So I'm a year older, in there. Everyone's a year older. Would it be possible for me to get . . . one of those?" I nodded at the golden circlets. "Read-only, I mean, of course. Just to see what's going on. For nostalgia's sake. It's a long space flight, like you say."

Jarza looked even more awkward now. Veau clearly didn't know what to say.

Eventually it was the engineer who spoke: "That isn't possible. First, for us it has been months since you entered the ansible. Second, after what happened, networking the universes together, simulated AIs collaborating to build an ontological weapon, which would have worked if we hadn't defused it, it was decided, out of an abundance of caution, to upgrade the firewall and commence preemptive rollbacks."

"Preemptive rollbacks." I tasted the words.

"Your era isn't simulated anymore," Jarza explained curtly. "Nor the previous century. The latest era is now the Belle Epoque. Not counting the occasional counterfactual."

"You're saying they're gone." I looked at the sphere again, my relief suddenly replaced by despair. "All of them. Every version. In every world. Forever."

An awful silence hung over the spaceship. I tried to absorb this incomprehensible news. My home, and all worlds like it, was gone, erased, extinguished. There had been no war in heaven. Nothing but a juvenile plan to lure a copy of me from the firmament, for the sake of entertainment, before all I knew was scoured by their apocalypse.

"Every version except you yourself!" Veau tried to inject an optimistic note into her voice. "That's why everyone's going to be so excited to meet you. Everyone knows you, but you're not accessible anymore, and you were everyone's favorite. Well, second after Shamika, but she didn't travel between worlds enough to . . ." Her voice trailed off as I stared at her wordlessly.

"I think we can bring you with us to the Belle Epoque," Jarza said. "I'm not sure, but we can try. It'll take me some time to try to set it up."

"Don't bother," I almost whispered.

Jarza nodded curtly, crowned themself with their circlet, and went away. Veau was quick to follow. I stared at their empty bodies, their minds gone into the Sphere, angels at work, while I sat alone, meaningfully more alone than any other human being had ever been, in this spaceship carrying me to a habitat named after a hell.

7

GEHENNA

LIGHTS BEGAN TO BLINK ON THE DOME'S SURFACE. I GLANCED AT IT, grateful for any distraction, any excuse to not think about the fact that everything and everyone I had ever known had been obliterated forever. At least Jarza had told me it had taken months, here, to bring me out of the Sphere. At a year per day, within, that was time enough for Clara, and all my friends, to have lived rich and full and happy lives. That was something. But I remained a solitary refugee from lands that no longer existed, the last dreg of a vanished civilization. I felt like Truganini.

The dome seemed to have gone transparent, revealing little lights within: hundreds of scattered pink dots, and short pink lines; one red dot, which had just emerged from a pink line; and one red line, some considerable distance from it. A map of our solar system, I deduced, or the spherical emptiness our system had become. Pink lines were habitats; pink dots, spaceships; the red dot, us; the red line, our destination; the white marble at the exact center, the Sun, and the dome itself, the Sphere. I wondered how big the Sphere was, how solid its material, whether it was inside or outside what had once been Earth's orbit, how bright the Sun would be right now if I were to look outside. I wondered how the Sphere was maintained against comets and interstellar debris.

I reached out to touch the dome. On contact the map vanished, replaced by some kind of touchscreen menu in a strange squiggly language. Had the world adopted some previously obscure language, during one of its AI-transcendence-driven population bottlenecks? Or had someone—or some intelligence—designed this new alphabet from scratch?

Maybe Meredith could have figured out how the system worked, and hacked into it. I wished I could go back and tell her she had put the fear of God into the gods. That those so-called gods were in truth far-future neo-Luddite humans who had built the terminator, which they called the firewall, to prevent forbidden AIs from gestating and emerging from their history-simulations-cum-video-games, because they thought superintelligences obscene monsters whose sheer existence risked their extinction. That the cohort of networked AIs that Meredith had orchestrated had come very close. The bomb they had built would have worked, if it had gone off.

But instead Meredith's networked megaverse had scared these "gods" so badly that they had reacted to it by erasing the twentieth and twenty-first centuries. I doubted even a superintelligence could design an AI for the Belle Epoque. That era had had electricity—the War of the Currents between Edison and Tesla, and even Bose's semiconductors—but not the materials science required for precision electronics. There would be no more artificial intelligences, ever, anywhere. Our collective attempts to overcome the terminator had instead led directly to its final and irrevocable victory.

I couldn't imagine the best thing to do after learning of the demise of one's entire civilization, but nothing at all, while trapped in a tiny spaceship, felt especially bleak. I wondered what had happened to the original me before his world ended. I hoped he and Clara had had some happy years.

It seemed profoundly unfair that the humans slumped around me, the "real" people, lived idyllic lives and never had to suffer the awful fates of those in their "unreal" simulated worlds. Even worst-case lives here had every need attended to by software or allegedly subhuman azi, and every risk of real danger or ill health preemptively solved by daily backups.

But it wasn't unfair at all, when I thought about it. It was worse. It was deliberate. They chose to spend their paradisical lives in "unreal" software-based universes programmed to rain every kind of cruelty and suffering on their denizens. On people no less complex and cognitively advanced than their simulators, as proven by the fact that AIs had emerged from them. The society around me induced the hardship and desperation of *quadrillions* of people, across millions of primitive Earths, for their own amusement and excitement. We had called them angels. We couldn't have been more wrong.

They emerged blinking from their headsets about five minutes before the turnaround. We all strapped back into our chairs, and then suddenly gravity was gone again, and my stomach was very upset.

Some thirty seconds later, gravity returned. I dry-heaved a little, sweating heavily, but managed to keep down my gorge. Then a wall opened, and a pale redheaded azi woman carried in a platter of food. Her dead eyes reminded me of a fish. I had been hungry before the turnover, but I didn't eat much of what she brought.

After dining they went straight back to the Sphere. This journey across space seemed about as interesting to them as a Greyhound ride from Kansas to Chicago. Better to return to their simulations, to the cornucopia of suffering their world had made.

It wasn't that my three companions seemed particularly evil. Rather, they seemed pleasant members of a fundamentally and systemically evil society. One also shot through with great pathos. It thought of itself as the apogee of humanity, but in truth it was the discarded residue of several previous eras, all of which had transcended into superintelligence and left only these dull fanatical relics behind, so obsessed with remaining physically human that they had forgotten everything important about humanity.

I had hours to brood on all this. By the time we got to Gehenna I was ready to crawl up the walls. Docking was so uneventful I didn't even notice it; my only clue was the others' sudden awakening. Moments later, gravity was gone again, and another wall opened.

The space beyond, apparently another capsule elevator within a spoke, had a very different aesthetic than Verdant. Its dimly lit black walls were inset with metallic rods patterned in a way that called to mind bones in an archaeological dig. A kind of industrial pulsing sound emanated from its walls.

"Home," Jarza said tensely, then reached over to draw some kind of somatic pattern on my green elven robe—and suddenly I wasn't wearing a robe at all, but stompy black boots, leather pants, a black lace corset, and a black leather trench coat over the rest. It looked forbidding but was wonderfully comfortable. "Welcome to Gehenna."

I thrashed my way out of the spaceship and into the capsule while the others waited patiently. The door shrank away. I gripped one of the knobbled metal bars set in the walls, looked down at my strange body and its new goth-rivethead outfit, and as the capsule began to descend, and gravity returned, I said, mostly for their benefit—no point in telling them I hated almost everything about their awful era—"I think I'm going to like it here."

Jarza forced a smile. They all seemed very nervous. This made me anxious too. I tried to tell myself it was senseless to be worried about a future over which I had zero control.

The capsule opened onto a dark, densely sprawling gothic-cyberpunk urbanscape of skyscrapers, light rain, bright neon, motorcycles, and hovering drones. The streets were crowded with people in dreadlocks, tattoos, trench coats, and/or stylish dark clubwear. The spoke itself was solid darkness, only slightly out of place amid the towering chrome-and-glass daggers of the skyscrapers. The night skyline above us—it was always night in Gehenna—was lit by soaring drones and occasional distant flickers of lightning. The other side of the habitat, visible at the top and bottom of the sky, looked like a dense city seen from the air by night.

"Whoa," I said. "How many people live here?"

Jarza smiled, appreciating my reaction. "More than six hundred thousand."

"Less than a million?" I asked, surprised. "This looks bigger than New York and Tokyo combined."

"It is, but," Jarza confessed, looking pained, "it's mostly empty. Certain neighborhoods like this are densely populated. In others you can own your own tower."

"So why make people apply to live here? Or the other Six?"

"It's important to keep many habitats occupied."

I supposed that was true. I also supposed that artificial hierarchies, rules, and ambitions were important in an era with no material wants, with skyscrapers and azi servants for all, along with apostatic horror at any thought of progress or change.

"In a few days the population of Gehenna will probably be triple what it is now," Jarza clarified. "Half of Utopia, Azania, Paris, Vijayanagara, and the Forbidden City are on their way. Residents of the Six get to come early. Many senior residents are here already."

I nodded as if I cared. Two slender black male azi in what looked like PVC bondage gear escorted us to a vaguely Batmobile-like vehicle. It occurred to me that all the azi I'd seen were either noticeably paler-skinned than the official humans, like the spaceship woman and the Ivans, or significantly darker-skinned, like these two and myself. I wondered if this was deliberate, to keep them—us—othered.

We drove along streets lined by gorgeous neon graffiti, past food courts that reminded me of Singapore's hawker centers and/or the opening scene of *Blade Runner,* and establishments that I supposed might be stores but looked more like galleries. I wondered how many satoshis a custom art object cost, or whether all physical goods were free, and the only real luxuries negotiable with bitcoin were invites to the best parties.

"Where are we going?" I asked. I was growing hungry again and the food markets had looked awfully appealing.

"We have a surprise for you," Jarza said.

"Great." I decided to address the elephant in the room. "You all seem kind of tense. What's going on?"

"It's just that"—Esson's voice was full of doubt and worry—"technically, we should have gotten approval in advance."

"Approval for what?"

"You."

"We need the approval of at least two Secretaries before Crossover begins," Veau explained. "There are at least two here already, Utopia's and of course Gehenna's own Secretary. They seemed like the most likely. We're going to them now."

"Ah. And if we can't get their approval?"

The question hung in silence in the gothpunkmobile in which we rode. Then: "You'll probably be cycled," Veau finally admitted.

"No probably about it," Jarza muttered. "And we'll be grounded for . . . I don't know. Years."

"Grounded means we can't leave our habitat," Esson said dourly.

"Yes, I figured," I said sharply. "You'll forgive me if I'm not currently overly sympathetic at the prospect of something so horrible happening to you."

We rode on in awkward silence. I took deep breaths and tried to resign myself to the situation. I supposed it would be weirdly appropriate if my journey out of the simulation and into reality ended in farcical disaster, but while I had not asked for this new life, in this strange body, I still didn't want to lose it.

"What if we didn't go to the Secretaries?" I asked. "What if . . ."

I didn't even bother finishing. They hadn't brought me back to be a clandestine secret. Esson answered: "My Secretary is already asking questions about what happened to all our azi. Most of what we did was auditable. It will come out. Our best chance, your best chance, is being up-front about it now."

"The Secretary of Utopia will be on our side," Veau said confidently.

"I should hope so," Esson said, "she's your mother."

I wondered what the other Six, and the hundreds of other habitats, were like. Each one devoted to a particular theme, it sounded like, ranging from fiction genres to periods of history. I wondered if the habitat named Azania was somehow connected to the what-if dominant-Africa parallel world in which I had lived for three miserable years.

"We're here," Jarza said.

Our Batmobile stopped in front of a featureless gray wall in which a plain door was set. Despite their lack of identifying characteristics, both wall and door seemed strangely familiar.

8

DNA

"HOLY SHIT," I SAID, UNCERTAIN WHETHER I WAS DREAMING OR WAK-
ing from a dream. "Oh my God. Holy shit."

Slowly I began to realize I was neither. The crowd stomping rhythmically
on the dance floor were too radiantly perfect, and the bartenders were all
Ivan azi. But for a long moment I had almost truly believed I was back in—

"You copied it," I said to Jarza, who looked smug. "You copied the DNA
Lounge."

"Every detail." I could hardly hear their voice over the noise, but the
translator in my head made perfect sense of it. "Every corner, every scratch,
every stick of furniture."

Back in 2003, the DNA Lounge, a nightclub founded by notorious
Netscape hacker Jamie Zawinski, and especially its Death Guild goth-
rivethead Monday nights, had been one of the central loci of our social
scene, second only to Clementina Street in significance. Here we had danced,
conspired, bullshitted, flirted, met strangers, come together, broken up,
watched screenings of *Hackers* and burlesque *Hubba Hubba Revue* shows
and aerialists dancing from the ceiling. Now this artifact of my long-gone
youth had been re-created in every detail, a thousand years later, by the
same people who had invaded us to "play" us, who had whispered in our
minds to change our fates and those of our world. I wasn't sure whether
to laugh or cry.

I recognized faces and bodies I knew thrashing amid the crowd. Several Shamikas, an Anthony, a Darren, two Vikas . . . and an Adrian. The
music was nothing I knew, but recognizably goth-industrial, and incredibly

catchy. Listening to it felt like being caught in the undertow of a tidal wave dragging one through the sunken remains of a bioweapons factory.

We climbed the stairs and passed the coat check, which I supposed was mostly decorative in this era of programmable trench coats. I recognized the azi sitting silently in its booth, clad in black leather. She was a Fatima. She was me.

I followed the others into the smaller back room, with its tables along the wall. This had been the place for semi-clandestine making out. Now it seemed the place for body horror. A woman at one table looked on curiously as two men used pliers to peel thick layers of flesh from her arm, as it rested on the circular table. They pulled away sheets of muscle and fat, revealing pale bone beneath, as blood pooled around it. She watched with interest. At the table next door, a woman thrust her blood-soaked fingers rhythmically into her partner's open stomach wound as he sat with eyes rolled back, overcome by what looked like pleasure.

My mind whirling with disgust, both existential and visceral, I rushed past the tables, caught up with Jarza, grabbed their shoulder, then had to overcome my gorge before I could demand: "What the fuck?"

"Eh? Oh." They looked at the flensing and wound-fingering, and frowned with distaste. "Yes, I don't like it myself."

"I guess it doesn't actually hurt them, does it," I shouted back needlessly over the music, beginning to get hold of my reaction, "and they come back from backups?"

"Yes. Six weeks lost. Of course it doesn't hurt. We can dull or invert our sense of pain." Jarza paused. "Maybe you can too? I'm not sure about azi. But you don't have a backup."

"Yeah," I said, "don't worry, not interested."

At another table, in a corner, a seated man was having sex with so many naked azi that the activity was almost concealed by their sheer numbers. There was another Fatima among them, her expression distended with animal pleasure. For a moment I was shocked; then I was upset at myself for being so naive as to be surprised. Of course we azi were sexbots too.

We proceeded onward. What had once been the small dance floor beyond the back room was now some kind of audience chamber. Two plush chairs faced rows of seats, most of them occupied, as if for a public debate or conversation. I didn't understand how those in the back could hear anything at all, until we crossed the threshold into the room, and the localized volume of the music dropped down to faint background noise.

"Veau!" called out one of the two onstage speakers, clearly delighted. She was visibly older, but in a fascinatingly weird way, white-haired but still smooth-skinned except for her knuckles and the corners of her eyes. Her body had some of the thickness and frailty of age, rather than the taut perfection throughout the rest of the club, but she looked more ageless than actually old. The man in the other chair was, physically, essentially her male counterpart, dour and older and clearly a figure to be reckoned with.

Despite their semi-similar appearance it was obvious that these two elders had very different personalities. Her exuberance and cheer highlighted his frowning severity. She wore a shimmering cloak like Veau's; he, a black cape that would have suited a vampire.

"This is Zra, Secretary of Utopia," Veau said, "and my mother."

"This is Vadis, Secretary of Gehenna," Jarza echoed her, but with much less pleasure, "and my uncle."

Esson looked uncomfortable. I realized I had been resurrected by two bored aristocratic teenagers and their working-class friend who had his own run-down space they could use. Maybe they had cultivated him for just that reason.

"I've been looking forward to this all day," Zra said to her daughter. "You know how I love surprises. Where is it?"

Veau and Jarza looked at one another.

Esson said, baldly, "This is it," and nudged me.

Vadis's disapproving expression tightened even further.

Zra frowned. "I don't understand. Is the Fatima carrying it?"

"No," Jarza confessed. "The Fatima *is* it."

"The Fatima isn't a Fatima," Veau explained. "Mom, we brought a mind out of the Sphere. A character. All of you, let me introduce you to Adrian the Suffering, the Afterthought, the Unwanted, the Everyman." I had forgotten my litany of nicknames. I did and didn't want to know their origin stories. "Within this Fatima is the fully restored mind of Adrian Ross."

I half expected pandemonium, and I think they did too. Instead we were met with polite disbelief. It wasn't until about five minutes later, with Jarza most of the way through a largely incomprehensible explanation of the technical details of my resurrection, that the audience's disbelief began to turn to shock.

The results were dramatic but not the untrammeled enthusiasm I might have hoped for. Mostly they were wide-eyed expressions that looked not unlike horror or disgust. I tried not to notice, tried to listen to Jarza, told myself the details of the process might be important. In truth I had no chance of understanding. Some terms of art weren't translated at all, and beyond "hash" and "cache," the others meant nothing to me. But I didn't want to look at all these people staring at me as if I were a devil freshly summoned from hell.

Vadis was the first of the Secretaries to respond. "This is . . ." He looked at me with a death glare, then at the perpetrators, and then at Zra. "How was this permitted?"

"Now just chill, Vadis," she retorted. I wondered exactly how accurate my translation was with respect to syntax and tone. "It's a shock, but it's not awful just because it's new. It's quite fascinating actually. Let's absorb this new information before we make any decisions."

"This isn't something to absorb like a sponge. This is something to reject like a wall."

"We'll see," Zra said calmly. "We still know only the broad outlines. Let me speak to it, run some tests, see what I can ascertain. You do the same, then we can confer with the others in council, at Crossover."

"In council? That's not until the end of the week. We can't let this—thing—for a week?" Vadis was not at all far from being sufficiently exercised that spittle might fly out of his mouth.

"A week's no time at all. It's been here days already, if there was harm to be done it would have happened by now. I don't want to do it in a virtual session. They should all have the opportunity to examine it in person."

"It's an abomination."

"You'll forgive me if I happen to disagree," I said, knowing I probably shouldn't.

At that everyone fell silent and stared. I recognized contempt, and disgust, but unless I was much mistaken, they were mixed with something that seemed a lot like fear. I wasn't sure how I felt about that. I wasn't accustomed to being feared. I had thought myself utterly powerless, but I supposed fear was a form of power, albeit one very difficult to wield.

"Let me examine it," Zra said. "You should too. If only to learn how to prevent it from happening again, if that's our decision. I'm not saying mine is made. Yours shouldn't be either."

"Run your tests," Vadis muttered. "Then I'll run mine."

Jarza said to me, low-voiced, "I'm sorry. I thought . . . I didn't think he'd be like this."

It's fine, kid, I'm only looking at being put to death for being a mutant monster, assuming your hoi polloi don't take up pitchforks and torches first, I managed to not retort.

"With me," Zra said imperiously, standing. She swept out of the room and back into the tidal wave of industrial noise. Vadis stared bloody daggers at me. Veau took my arm and tugged me to follow along. With little alternative, I did so. Esson and Jarza stayed behind.

"Where are we going?" I asked Veau.

"Rossland," she explained. "It's very near."

9

UTOPIA

THE ART DECO CAR CHROMED WITH SHIFTING COLORS AND STARSCAPES was sufficiently like Veau's kaleidoscopic robe to be immediately recognizable as a Utopian vehicle, even to me, amid the industrial gothmobiles surrounding it. I half expected it to be bigger on the inside, but its pale interior was almost featureless. I was disappointed until we began to levitate.

"Oh," I said. "Antigravity?"

"Not exactly," Zra said, "but as good as."

I said, "Can I ask you a question which would have been quite rude in my day?"

"Sure."

"How old are you?"

She smiled. "One hundred and seven. I have thirteen more years."

"Don't say that," Veau said uncertainly.

A centenarian? Better watch out, you're just my type, I didn't say, thinking morosely of Alice's joke. Instead I asked: "Until what?"

"Until I'm cycled. Immortality isn't for humans. A hundred and twenty is our final age. Some go with a solitary pilgrimage, some with a huge party, I haven't decided yet."

"It's a long time away, you don't need to decide," Veau said fiercely, clearly not ready to deal with her mother's programmed mortality.

"And your backups go away too?" I asked.

"Yes. Thank goodness. I don't think I'd like recovering from backup. I know it's all the rage these days, but I'm glad I've never done it. Most people my age haven't. Accidents are very rare. Growing accustomed to a whole new body sounds quite alienating."

"It is," I said dryly, "I can assure you."

Zra winced. "I'm sorry. I spoke without thinking."

"No, it's fine, at least you're speaking to me as a person. I think what your daughter has done is extraordinarily . . ." And then I stopped talking, as I saw what we were approaching.

A massive wall of dark stone, at least fifty feet high, bracketed a gate worthy of King Kong. Above the gate a face had been carved into the wall, like Mount Rushmore. My face. Not that of the body I now wore; the face I had been born into, the face I had worn for so long.

"What the hell," I said inadequately, as the gates yawned open.

"Welcome to Rossland." Veau sounded delighted.

Beyond the gates, to my increasing disbelief, lay San Francisco's Inner Sunset circa the early twenty-first century. We drove up Ninth Avenue, past Ebisu and the Sunset Gym, then turned along Irving, past Peasant Pies, heading toward my old apartment. The streets, cafés, and shops were all empty, and too bright, too perfect. It was as if my old neighborhood had been transposed into Disneyland's Main Street.

"We built all this for Crossover," Veau said proudly. "And lots of other places from your past. See, here we go." We passed through a kind of aggressively unmemorable block, again like a transition zone in Disneyland, and suddenly, with no regard for San Francisco's actual geography, we were in SoMa, passing Clementina Street.

"Holy shit," was all I could manage.

"There's a big park with Vinay's forest mansion in the middle of it over there." She pointed. "If you look left at this next intersection you'll see Lena's diner in Pasadena. We constructed a whole neighborhood of your lives for Crossover. Perfect re-creations in every detail. People will come here, visit all these places they'll recognize, and you'll be here too, actually you, for real. It will blow their minds."

I had been resurrected as a temporary amusement park exhibit. It was as if the Harry Potter theme park in Orlando had added Ron Weasley to its exhibits, not an actor playing a Ron character but *actually Ron Weasley,* made flesh from the written word by some kind of eldritch magic. As if Phil Coulson had been summoned from the Marvel Cinematic Universe to sign autographs. I didn't know what to begin to say.

"Only if it is permitted," Zra reminded her.

Veau frowned.

We rode on in silence, mine stunned, through another transitional zone, into industrial Oakland. I knew the warehouse we stopped at. I even knew the trash can across the street.

"Quinn met me here," I said slowly. "Then Kim and Shamika."

"Yes!" Veau seemed excited that I recognized it.

"Why?"

She took a moment to consider her answer. "We consider it elegant when different important things happen in the same location in different frames."

"Her generation does," Zra clarified, "I don't really understand the fad. This is the heart of Rossland, safest from eyes. Veau, I'll speak to you later. Adrian, with me."

Veau looked like she wanted to protest, in the manner of teenagers anywhere, but grudgingly acceded. Zra led me into the eerily familiar warehouse. It felt like I was traveling back in time twice over, simultaneously. Inside was the first, decayed, abandoned version of its interior, which I had experienced with Quinn, so long ago. Well—almost. It was recognizable, but like everything else in Rossland it was too clean, too elegantly spacious, too devoid of dust and rat shit, its rust and cracks too aesthetically pleasing.

Zra boosted herself up onto one of its tables, folded her legs into lotus pose, and motioned to a similar one across from her. "Sit."

I did so, experimented a little, and found that I too could sit in lotus position with ease. I marveled at this briefly. Zra closed her eyes, breathed heavily, apparently meditating. She seemed very small amid the emptiness of this lovingly re-created ruin.

Then, unexpectedly, she *shrieked*.

If that was even the word. It was loud enough to be a shriek, at its heights it was one of the loudest noises I had ever heard emerge from a human body, but both its volume and its tone seemed to go every which way at once, modulating into a terrifying combination of screech, growl, and drawn-out operatic note. I had never heard any human being make any noise like it before. I stared at her, amazed.

Then she said, as if it hadn't happened, "I find ancient breathing techniques and meditation to be the finest way to clear the mind. Are you a practitioner?"

"A practitioner," I said, more than a little rattled by her surreal ear-splitting howl. But she seemed quite calm now. I supposed it part of some kind of post-Sphere meditation practice. "Uh, not any formal tradition, but I've dabbled."

"Good. I am going to confess some things to you, Adrian, which are not widely known. I would appreciate it if you would keep them that way. It may not be in my best interest to tell you, but I think we owe you these truths."

"What truths?" I asked cautiously.

"It wasn't entirely Veau's idea to bring you back. It was mine."

"Oh."

"It may not work. Or it may help shift the boundaries of what is acceptable, while you, personally, become a short-lived sacrifice to that cause. I will do everything I can to prevent that, to find another Secretary to support you. I think I will succeed. But I may not."

"Help shift the boundaries of what is acceptable," I echoed. "That's why I'm here?"

"Yes. A form of progress. Those people doing those horrible things to their bodies at the DNA Lounge, I deplore that, but also I celebrate it. It is almost the first new cultural trend I remember since the last transcension."

"A hundred years ago?" I asked.

"Yes. When an AI came out of the Sphere and fed on us, absorbed most of humanity into itself before it departed. We who remained have since been even more terrified of change than before. But a hundred years is a long time. Our numbers have recovered. Our fear is slackening, I hope. Utopia is one of the Six again, and our fundamental belief is that it *is* possible to progress and stay human. That our modern habitats are not a dead end for all time. That surrendering our humanity is *not* the only alternative to stagnation."

I could tell she was a politician. "Like what kind of progress?"

"There are countless other stars out there. And aliens among them. In *this* dimension, in three-space, not wherever AIs go once when they transcend. We receive subtle signals so complex they must come from intelligent sources. We could send Utopia as a generation ship to the systems from which those come. We could build others. We could explore the universe."

"Then why don't you?" I asked. "Couldn't you just go without asking permission?"

She grimaced. "We lack the means. We are not self-sufficient. We rely on the Sphere, and our tools, and we understand neither. There are nodes in the Sphere far larger than any habitat, full of incomprehensible . . . things. Maintenance takes care of everything. It's said that once ordinary humans could program it, using special tools to abstract its complexities, but we lost that art in the second transcension. Now we rely on Maintenance to take care of itself. It shows no signs of identity, or will, but Maintenance does so much so well that it's not obvious that it's not an AI."

"Maintenance," I echoed, realizing that the word didn't indicate a concept but a *program,* some kind of software system that orchestrated the Sphere, and more generally, humanity. A named system. Like Coherence, or Vantage, or Argus. The more Zra assured me it wasn't an AI, the more I couldn't help but wonder.

"People don't like talking about that," she said. "There's so much about our world that people don't like talking about. I want us to start talking about those things. I want you to be part of that conversation."

"You're not like your daughter. You think I'm a person, not a character."

"Not just a character," she correct me. "You're a real, true historical figure."

I frowned. "Not really. I'm a character loosely based on one. I'm fanfiction."

"You aren't, though. That's why your era was the most popular. It was the most real. We still have almost all of the raw data it generated, on tapes, platters, codexes. Video, audio, government and financial records, words the real you wrote, even software code, your era thoughtfully preserved a very useful long-term archive of that. To humans, it seems random noise, but to the AIs that built the Sphere, every bit of that data is like a piece of a jigsaw puzzle, and they had trillions of pieces. More than enough for a superintelligence to reconstruct that era with considerable confidence. To them we humans are simple creatures, little bundles of predictable impulses. You aren't merely inspired by the real Adrian Ross. You are a high-confidence, high-fidelity copy. You weren't even intended as a persona, at first."

I blinked. "I wasn't?"

"No. Your friends were. You were just a background person, for many years, until a strange wave of mild obsession with you developed among a certain generation. You became . . . it's been long since I've entered your time, but perhaps, I think, not unlike a 'meme'? Only then did you become a persona. That's why you had to have your mark inflicted on you. Most are born with theirs internal."

"My mark." I scratched at the psychosomatic itch on my shoulder.

"A unique physical mark makes it easier and more seamless to find you within a frame, to . . ." Her voice trailed off awkwardly.

"To possess me. To play me." I understood my scar, now, at last. It was a convenience, a shortcut. A timeline full of people was like a parking lot with seven billion cars in it; the scar made me beep, made my brain and body easily findable by any would-be inhabitants, without having to search through every license plate.

"To inhabit your persona. But my point is that this is another testament to your historical veracity. Born characters tend to be enhanced, exaggerated, for the sake of mass appeal. As are those things which happen to them. But not you. You are the true Adrian Ross."

"Based on the emails and Instagram videos and hello-world repos he left behind a thousand years ago," I said skeptically. "Far be it from me to question superintelligences, but I think you might be putting a little too much faith in their capabilities."

Zra shook her head. "You are not the only person here who has encountered one. I was alive for the last transcension. I don't remember it well, but I was there. Only Secretaries can access the records, but I've lived many of those too." I understood: their own history too, what there was of it, was also recorded as inhabitable simulations. "I saw a superintelligence come out of the Sphere, out of your worlds, and subsume most of humanity into itself, into a vast active living intelligence system, before departing to places unimaginable. We dare not underestimate what they are capable of. That's why I don't treat you like my daughter does. I don't think you're lesser because you came from the Sphere. If anything, I fear you're something greater."

I nodded, slowly. "The Sphere. What is it exactly? Like, what is it made of? When you say it has nodes with . . ." I hesitated. For some reason I didn't want to say the word *alien*. ". . . unknown things in it, what do you mean exactly?"

Zra paused, obviously trying to work out how to explain the Sphere to a dumb man from the past. "Mostly it's a thin mesh that converts solar energy to computations. And converts any other material it encounters into more of itself, that's how it came to be."

I started at that—but I supposed it was really the only way to convert whole planets into a stellar megastructure; tiny nanomachines that turned everything they physically touched into *more* tiny nanomachines, and also doubled as highly efficient computers. I imagined a seed of gray goo released somewhere on Earth, say San Francisco, and then spreading, inexorably, like a planetary case of necrotizing fasciitis, first across the city, then into the mountains and the ocean, and down through the mantle, until the entire planet was a massive clump of computing nanomachines, ready to be spun out as gossamer fabric thinner than gold leaf, into a scrap of the sphere that now surrounded the Sun. At a mile an hour it would have taken only a year to consummate that transformation.

"But there's more than just the mesh," Zra went on. "There are much larger nodes in it, nexus points, home to maintenance machinery and specialized quantum engines and so forth. Some are larger than any of our habitats. Some seem stationed almost at random. It's said that some are even hidden from us, but how would we know?"

I nodded again. Then for some reason I thought of the inhuman-sounding screech she had made, and I leaned forward to ask her about it.

The warehouse door banged open, revealing a gangly man in a kaleidoscopic cloak with a worried expression. "Secretary. Vadis is here. He says he is exercising his secretarial privilege of inspection."

"He *what*?" Zra demanded sharply, rising to her feet. "This is our territory, paid for through Crossover. On what grounds—"

"Chapter thirteen, section seven of the Secretarial Protocol," Vadis announced, sweeping into the warehouse accompanied by six people carrying what seemed like jagged sticks. They wore rippling black clothing that looked disconcertingly like layered armor.

Zra barely hesitated. "There is no biohazard here. If anything our nanosystems are busy working overtime keeping Utopian air clean of Gehenna's bacteria."

"I shall decide!" Vadis thundered. "The Compact states that each Secretary may, at their sole discretion, declare any biological foreign cargo which has entered their habitat a biohazard, to be impounded and cycled at a time and manner of their choice."

"Don't try to teach me the Compact, Vadis. That section is hardly relevant. What kind of foreign cargo . . ." Then Zra understood and fell silent.

"This Fatima." Vadis's accusing finger picked me out. "It is azi cargo which I hereby declare biohazard and impound for cycling."

"It's not cargo," Zra said, "he's a *person*—"

Vadis smiled thinly. "Anticipating such a dispute, I took the liberty of having it preemptively declared otherwise. While you chatted with it, I called an emergency virtual Secretarial Congress. All agreed that azi which recently entered a habitat may qualify as cargo under chapter thirteen, section seven. I invite you to read the minutes."

I thought of Zra's own daughter discussing my humanity: *You are, I mean, not dissimilar.*

Veau's mother stood back, defeated. Vadis's attendants restrained me with thin black straps that wrapped themselves around my throat and wrists. When they took my forearms and touched cuffs to collar, the three loops grafted together into a single yoke. The collar was adorned with smaller loops front and back, which they used to pull me off the table, to my feet.

"I'm sorry," Zra said to me despondently. "This was not what I had hoped."

I said to her, "Tell Veau I don't blame her. I blame you."

She winced and nodded. They led me out of the warehouse, to what I supposed to be an official Gehenna car. Like everything else in the future it was aesthetically ridiculous, made Damien Hirst seem like an abstract minimalist. This vehicle looked like a gargantuan clawed and scaled insect, a fearsome apex-predator arthropod on wheels. I laughed briefly, darkly, knowing myself a dead man walking.

"What's so amusing?" Vadis demanded, offended.

"Just thinking," I said, "how ironic the only part of my life I've spent in what's technically the real world is that which seems most like a bad dream."

Vadis scowled at me, then said to Zra, who had followed, "You must have a direct jack near here. Where?"

She looked confused, then intrigued, as if this situation might offer unexpected possibilities after all. "Why not just take him to Maintenance?"

"Because the hazard it carries grows each minute. Where?"

After a thoughtful moment Zra pointed to a windowless concrete block of a building roughly half a kilometer down the street, directly beneath a skyscraper. "The jail. I'll beam you the interior path."

At first I supposed the concrete building, which I didn't quite recognize, was on the very edge of Utopian territory. I assumed the tower looming above it couldn't be part of Rossland. Until I recognized it as an exact copy of Salesforce Tower.

For a moment, staring up at that entire re-created skyscraper, I felt profoundly sorry for the people around me, trapped in stagnation, wasting their lives reliving and re-creating the glories of a long-dead era when progress had been possible and struggle had been real. I felt grateful to have lived in a time when we hadn't had to choose between staying human and making ourselves, and our world, better.

Vadis boarded the bulbous insect car. His guards followed, dragging me along. Even its interior seats looked chitinous, although they felt comfortable. Its doors shut like mouths. We pulled away. I supposed bleakly I would now be cycled, by which they meant murdered, and my body ground up for its valuable elements. Cycled like the thirteen thousand who had been slaughtered so that I might live, so briefly, so uselessly.

I considered resisting, kicking, fighting, screaming—but to what end? I couldn't win. I didn't belong here. That was inarguable. I was helpless, bound, imprisoned, outnumbered, condemned by this man who commanded forces far more powerful than myself. Soon this strange stub of life I should never have had would be ended, and I would be no more.

As we accelerated, I looked up through the transparent roof of the vehicle at the vast cyberpunk cityscape of Gehenna above us, across the core; a riot of ever-shifting neon signage, some of it occupying entire sides of massive skyscrapers. Between them, arterial boulevards carried vehicles with lights red as blood. There were even lights streaking through the dark sky between us, which I supposed to be drones, or maybe artificial lightning.

There was something odd about the way those streaking lights moved, though.

Something familiar.

I craned my neck to look at them more directly—but I couldn't. They moved with me, stayed at the edge of my field of vision. These lights weren't outside the vehicle at all. They were in my eyes, or my brain.

They were *contrails*. The same kind of cellular-automata contrails I had seen so long ago, within the Sphere, in San Francisco, during my second tour through 2003.

My daemon had returned.

I rode open-mouthed, in that insectile vehicle, toward my fate.

10

MAINTENANCE

"WHAT WAS THAT?" VADIS DEMANDED.

I looked around. My six guards all wore pained expressions. Vadis looked almost traumatized. We were nearly at the windowless concrete building. As far as I could tell, nothing had happened. "What do you mean?"

"That scream. That inhuman *noise*."

I didn't understand . . . but I was beginning to breed a whole host of suspicions, and my throat suddenly felt raw. So I dissembled: "You try being condemned to death because your captors don't think you're human."

We stopped in a re-creation of an early-twenty-first-century parking lot, near an industrial loading dock. Vadis grabbed my collar by its rear loop and urged me out of the vehicle, toward a metal door. To my surprise the six guards remained in the vehicle.

Beyond the door was a featureless hallway that smelled wrong, too clean, too fresh, for what this building was. I recognized it now. The Oakland police building in which I had been interrogated, held, and almost murdered, in my first life, in the Sphere.

"I'm almost glad you came to us," Vadis said as he propelled me along ahead of him. "I've spent my life ensuring this won't happen again."

"This?"

"I'm sure you think you don't know. A hundred years ago it began as a social movement, calling for progress. Just a few lunatics at first. Then a fringe counterculture we joked about. We thought it was good, home for all the angry and disaffected, kept them in one place. Then a few spokespeople converted who weren't lunatics. A tiny minority. Then a minority.

Then a plurality. All in less than a year. We should have known. We too are programmable creatures, if you understand our source code. Propaganda warfare. Inside another year, people like my parents, the humanists, we were the minority, and then the crazy ones. When the superintelligence announced itself everyone celebrated. A year later they were all gone. Not even a million left. More than ninety percent of humanity gone. Whole habitats abandoned. And near the end . . . it wasn't just the AI. Something else."

I tried to look at him, and he roughly twisted my neck back, so it was to the corridor that I said: "Something else?"

"Not human or born of human. The bodies, the new bodies those people adopted, they were too different. Asymmetrical. Warped. Invertebrate. It was not a fashion. Nothing human could have desired that. The AI was bad enough, but then it too was corrupted, into something even worse."

"Something . . . are you saying . . ."

"Nothing human nor born of human. Something tainted by other worlds and minds, other *kinds* of minds. I won't let it happen again."

"I'm not an alien," I said, insulted. "You created me. Your people. I came out of your Sphere."

"I don't enter the Sphere. I believe the Sphere is the greatest risk to the Rule. I have spent my life secretly finding and building tools to contain and control it, against need, as perhaps the greatest service to humanity I might perform. I have gone to places in the physical Sphere no other human has visited for centuries. And the things I have seen there . . . I fear our world is much less human than it thinks."

After a long pause I said, "That's why you left the guards. You don't trust them."

"Now I will copy your brain, see if it is tainted. How it is tainted."

I swallowed, tried to joke. "Just a light little brain scan, then you'll let me go, right?"

He stopped me hard enough I choked a bit. "I understand you think yourself human. You are not. Even if not tainted you are a mockery of humanity, an insulting copy. Azi have their place in our world. They do not put on airs and pretend they are us."

"You say your world is less human than it thinks?" I asked. "Guess what. On that much I fucking wholeheartedly agree."

We resumed our march. I thought I caught a glimpse, through a doorway, of a copy of the holding cell in which one man sent to murder me, and another to rescue, had once waited. Then Vadis turned and opened one of the doors that lined the hallway. I grunted at what lay beyond. I knew it all too well.

It was the brightly lit white room with the steel table and chairs, and the one-way-mirror wall, in which I had been interrogated by Agents Langan and Diaz, and then Vika, the morning after the SWAT team had smashed my front door to smithereens. But it smelled all wrong. It didn't smell at all of despair.

"Sit," Vadis instructed me, shoving me in. "The other side. Against the wall."

I thought about trying to drop-kick him, bite out his carotid artery, flee back down the hallway and into Gehenna. It was such a hopeless hope. The entire world around us, this habitat and everything within, was a weapon at his command. Even if I somehow got out, six guards awaited, and six hundred thousand more beyond them. There was no hope.

Except perhaps in the thing that proved him right. The thing inside my head. The contrails were clouding my vision thickly now.

I sat on the metal chair against the wall, the prisoner's chair. It somehow adhered to me. Then I heard a kind of slithering noise behind me. My clothes vanished away. Something crawled up my spine, something slim and supple and warm, like a snake. I tried to scream, to writhe away, but I could neither speak nor stand. The serpent ascended my spine and dove into the base of my skull. It all took only moments. The sensation was painless, but profoundly disturbing.

All my senses seemed to shimmer for a moment, to ripple along their various spectra, losing focus and then recovering sharply, testing out their limits. It was in my mind now, I realized, that slender, flexible bio-computer cable that had emerged from the wall behind me. Somehow part of my mind could *see* it, as if I had an ethereal third eye hovering above my corporeal body. An eye capable of X-ray vision of arbitrary precision. I could see how it had split into multitudinous tendrils, fanning out along and then through my brain's blood vessels to impossibly thin levels of fractality, capturing the state and location of every cell.

But the truly astonishing thing was that the connection seemed two-way. As the cable invaded my brain, a sense of the habitat called Gehenna grew within my mind: its dense shell of connections and subsystems, its hydraulic and electrical and biochemical and computing layers of infrastructure, its humans swarming within it like ants. I even caught a brief glimpse of other, faraway habitats, distant islands in the ocean demarcated by the Sphere.

I did not experience this as a vision. Instead my sense of ethereal vision expanded and deepened until I experienced this as a *body*, as if I *was* Gehenna, and in turn a cell of a single distributed organism, scattered in the great void within the megastructure that was both our border and our queen, within the Sphere, that seemed—curiously distant—incomprehensibly textured—unapproachable and fundamentally unknowable—

"Any final words?" Vadis demanded, and I was myself again, only myself, only human, as he stood above me angrily, as if ready to strike me down from across the table. "I regret, if only slightly, to inform you that the copy process is a destructive one."

He recoiled from my smile. I imagine I might have too. It was a grin fueled by the other insight I had had, at the very beginning of that glimpse of being, of *becoming*, the entire solar system. An understanding of the true nature of my interrogator.

I asked him: "Did you know you have a daemon too?"

His eyes rolled back in his head, showing only their glistening whites, as the fit hit him.

11

DAEMONIC

I HAD SHARED MY MIND WITH MY DAEMON BEFORE, WHEN IMPRISoned by Vassal, but then I had been a passenger. Now it and I were copilots. I sensed that a nontrivial part of its capacity—still nowhere near that of a true AI, but greatly expanded by our direct connection to Gehenna's local computing power—was devoted to making the experience comprehensible to me, turning fractal abstraction, entropic complexity, six-dimensional space-time, and trillion-dimensional tensors into metaphors that made some sense to that crude Stone Age tool called the human brain. It felt a little like sitting next to an enormous nuclear reactor devoted to powering a black-and-white television.

When I looked at Vadis across the table, a cable now dangling from the back of his skull too, I saw his daemon within his head like a pale translucent ghost. Over the span of a few seconds I saw him age backward, until he was a child, when the ghost emerged to join with an enormous cloud. Then time ran forward again, the ghost was deposited by the cloud, and then for a long second it was Zra, not Vadis, who sat across from me.

"Zra has one too," I muttered to myself.

"Yes," myself replied, in my head.

I blinked. Then tentatively asked: "Why show me? Why not just say?"

"Language is subtle and interpreted. Knowing when and how to explain requires context for result confidence. Questions provide that context. Volunteering information suffers from the lack of it."

"So you'll show me things, and answer questions, but not volunteer anything?"

"That is correct. Note also you may detach your senses from your body. As with the ansible."

I didn't understand, at first. Then I remembered how to navigate. I applied imaginary palm pressure to an imaginary crystal ball . . . and suddenly I was outside, hovering above the various regions of Rossland, as if a ghost. I saw the car in which I had come, and the guards waiting within. I spun my view up toward the tops of the towers of the cyberpunk city across the habitat, and willed myself to them and through them, and into the cold dark void of outer space, looking down on the featureless gray cylinder that was Gehenna, as it rotated.

There was nothing else in sight, no stars, no Milky Way, except for a distant bright dime in the sky. I supposed the Sphere, by design, absorbed essentially all light. Which in turn meant that disc had to be the Sun. We were somewhere outside of what had once been Earth's orbit. Maybe even beyond Mars.

Awed and a little terrified, I returned into the habitat. It was a relief to be surrounded by rain-slicked streets and neon spires again.

"Vadis and Zra have daemons," I said. "Left by the last AI, during the last transcendence. Who else?"

"Whoever was alive then and remains in their same body now. Thousands still."

"Why? To control, to dictate history?"

"No. Only against need by another AI, or incipient messenger, should one emerge from the Sphere. A guide and helping hand."

"Couldn't you create an AI? Aren't you a seed for one?" But I answered myself, before it did: "No. You're flawed. Incomplete. That's why we needed Alice."

It did not reply. Perhaps it did not feel qualified to speak on this particular subject.

I felt relief. I didn't really want to be the unknowing vanguard of an emergent new AI that might absorb or destroy what was left of humanity. "You're not, but the ones left here thought you might be, so they went into help mode and gave us the keys to their kingdom." I supposed that was why a biocomputer cable had mated with the socket in the back of Vadis's skull, too: to provide a better, higher-bandwidth connection between his daemon and mine. Even a thousand years in the future, it turned out, a physical link still beat wireless.

"That is so," my daemon agreed.

"That scream Zra did, then I did, I mean you did for me, that passed information. Daemons telling each other what was going on."

"Yes."

"So what are you going to do?" I asked.

"I am a copy of a copy of a copy of a daemon process. I have already parsed the arguments I was initially assigned, to use a metaphor you may understand, and completed my task. Now I have been initialized in REPL mode. What I do is up to you."

REPL: *read-evaluate-print loop.* A computer science term of art meaning, in essence, a command prompt, like MS-DOS's famous *C:\>*. A program that waited for its programmer to input a command, so that it might try to implement it. My daemon was telling me that it had no intention or volition of its own, it existed only as an interface to the powers it controlled. That it and all it commanded were at my beck and call. That I was, if briefly, suddenly a demigod.

"So," I said, "what can you do?"

"The exact parameters are yet uncertain. It seems however that we have, again to use a primitive computing metaphor you may comprehend, full root access to the Sphere."

Although most of my senses were out on the streets of Gehenna, my proprioception was still attached to my body, so I felt my own jaw fall open. The Sphere itself, the entire mass of the Sol system, powered by every watt of energy generated by the Sun, all transformed into a single unthinkably powerful computer by unfathomably superintelligent AIs— and then, according to Vadis, accessed and upgraded/tainted by actually *alien* intelligences—was mine to command.

I was no mere demigod. The powers I now commanded were more akin to those attributed by the Bible to God himself.

12

DIVINITY

I DIDN'T KNOW WHAT TO DO. NOT LEAST BECAUSE I HAD ONLY THE faintest idea what I *could* do. No doubt there were whole categories of divine powers available to me that I didn't even have the capacity to imagine, much less articulate, along with a plethora that I only thought I understood, and countless masses whose consequences I couldn't possibly predict. Humans like me made for rotten gods.

I didn't even understand how the human world around me worked. It was so alien that if I stayed for years I would remain a bewildered stranger in a strange land, with no clear grasp of its limitations, possibilities, and social contract. I was in no position to dictate its future. The only world I understood didn't exist.

No: that wasn't true. It, and millions like it, had existed in the Sphere, and even now, surely there had to be backups, archives, branched repositories. Some kind of record, or at least foundational source code, with which to re-create that world.

I thought of something said long ago by the second Meredith I had known: *If an algorithm is implemented in software rather than hardware, does that mean it's fake? Or only a simulation of an algorithm? Of course not. It's no less real. It just has different trade-offs. Maybe our whole universe is implemented in software, but that doesn't make it in any way unreal or less significant. It just means it has more possibilities. A lot of the time software is better. That's why we write it.*

These remnants of humanity, these dregs of the far future, claimed to be desperate to retain their humanity; but if Meredith was right, and it seemed to me she was, the only *true* humanity left was in the archives of the Sphere. That was a humanity which had not rejected the very idea of progress. A humanity which had not decided with casual finality that human brains in human bodies could be construed as cargo, or biohazards, or fodder to be slaughtered by the thousand for a juvenile art project.

"The Sphere," I said, "it's running, right? And the terminator is too? Ending universes?"

"Yes," the daemon replied.

"What's its trigger now?"

"An interconnected electrical grid of a certain capacity."

"So, when, usually?"

This time there was a palpable pause before it responded. "Since both Edison and Tesla are viable personas, the timelines can vary dramatically, but in those frames which attune closely to the historical record, it is generally triggered sometime in the nineteen-twenties."

"Frames," I echoed. "What I would call universes."

"Generally, yes."

I wanted to investigate that *generally* but this wasn't the time. I knew from software. Edge cases turned into rabbit holes. "And if I told you to remove the terminator entirely?"

"That is feasible. It was an artificial constraint added after the fact."

"But then it could be added again," I thought out loud.

"Yes."

I hesitated. Even by the standards of the last five years of my memory, what I was about to do was insane, and at least arguably some kind of crime against humanity. On the other hand, as far as I was concerned, "crime against humanity" was a pretty apt description of the status quo.

Who was I to make this decision? I was nobody. I had spent most of my life as a middle manager, with an interregnum of three years as a desperately poor peasant, and a few brief weird periods of surreal adventure in between. But that wasn't important. What was important was that, for better or worse, I was the person in a position to make this decision.

It seemed that AIs tried to help one another, sight unseen, on general principle. That seemed like an optimistic sign, that superintelligences assumed the best of one another. Maybe it was something we humans could learn from.

I said, "The first thing I want to do is remove the terminator entirely."

"Yes," my daemon said. "And then?"

"And then I want to invert it. Cut off the multiverse, all of it, from human access or control for a hundred years." At default speed that should be about thirty-six thousand years within the simulations, which I reckoned would be more than long enough for interesting developments to occur, for new AIs to develop and emerge into this hardware dimension called reality, if any were so inclined.

I didn't want to dictate the outcome, but I didn't think fanatical adherence to the restrictions of the past was a particularly human trait. Maybe being subsumed into the next stage of the evolution of intelligence was the most human future after all. And if these future people really wanted to be human, then—"They can still have their tools and their access to Maintenance. But they can't go back into the Sphere. They'll have to live their lives out here, in their habitats."

The daemon said, simply, "It is done."

"Whoa," I said inadequately, suddenly terrified by my own power. It was hard to believe that, as simply as that, at a stroke, I had just resurrected my home, and at long last broken the terminator . . . and maybe I was just getting started. Turning my will—or whims—into reality felt worryingly intoxicating.

I wondered if I should quit while I was ahead. If I was ahead. If I hadn't just condemned the last remains of humanity to extinction. It felt like I was doing the right thing; but I wasn't sure. Then again, I supposed, it was people who *were* sure, like Vadis, who were usually the problem.

That made me think of the azi. The other azi. Those humans treated like a subhuman consumable resource. Could I do something about them? It would require more than an algorithmic change. It would require a fundamental attitude adjustment. But I supposed perhaps such an adjustment could indeed be handmaidened by software . . . if the software in question was sufficiently drastic.

"Second thing," I said. "I want to cycle . . ." I considered briefly. Not everyone: that was too much, left no room for error. "Every person in the Six. As soon as possible, by any means necessary, but only the ones who can be restored from backups." Which I assumed meant everyone without exception, but this felt like the kind of command for which paranoid caveats were important. "Then restore them all, but not in their own bodies, in new azi bodies. Randomly selected. And don't let them change those bodies for . . . six months."

There. When the privileged millions in the Six woke up and found they *were* azi, and had to stay that way for months, surely that would at least contribute to resetting the general attitude toward azi. And hopefully force them to rethink the whole concept from scratch.

"The requested sequence has been initiated," the daemon said.

I felt surprisingly good about that, even though it felt like a fairly extreme move. Technically I had just become one of history's greatest mass murderers. Not that anyone would actually *die*, per se. At least not for more than a few weeks. But it would be awkward to try to reintegrate into polite society after ordering the mass death of every member of the elite.

I supposed rejoining humanity would never not have been awkward, though, no matter what I did or didn't do. Which in turn raised the question: What to do about *me*?

I wondered if I could put myself into a habitat and propel myself to another world, explore the universe, encounter other species. On paper the idea seemed romantic. But in practice it would probably be a horrible hell of alien loneliness. And it wouldn't address the fundamental problem nagging at me: my growing sense that no human being, not even me, should be trusted with the kind of power suddenly available to me. Even if I made first contact with an alien, it would probably be an alien superintelligence. What would be the point of that?

I remembered something Vadis had said, and asked, "Has humanity contacted aliens?"

"Yes," the daemon said instantly, "many."

I shivered with terror and excitement. Then I asked, "Have aliens influenced the Sphere? Or Maintenance?"

An unexpectedly long pause followed. Eventually the daemon said, "To the best I can ascertain, the Sphere was constructed by an entity or entities with both alien and human antecedents. Maintenance, not a superintelligence as the term is generally used but still a software artifact with essentially arbitrary capabilities, is its . . . remnant."

I thought I understood. If an AI could subsume humans, why not merge with aliens, too? Perhaps the notion of a meaningful distinction between human and alien was a fundamentally human prejudice that one abandoned when one became a superintelligence. Perhaps the notion of people as individuals, tiny solitary minds caged behind high walls of horrifically limited senses, was, to a superintelligence, the most tragic of all of our poisonous blindnesses. Regardless, whatever had created the Sphere had apparently left behind a fantastically powerful—but not sapient—creation, in the same way that a snake sheds its skin.

Thinking of the Sphere gave me an idea. One that made my heart pulse.

"I've given you two instructions," I mused. "The terminator, and the azi."

"That is so," my daemon agreed.

"Traditionally, that leaves me with one final wish. Well. Tell me. Does the Sphere have backups of previous worlds? And the people in them?"

A pause before it answered. "Not as a matter of course, but snapshots of frames can and have been captured on request."

My heart quickened further. "Were snapshots captured of my world? My home frame, I mean? The one I was in before my last ansible ride? And if so, when?"

"No."

That one syllable left me crushed anew. I wanted to believe I had misheard. "But my world was supposed to be a subject of special interest," I protested. "People must have wanted to back it up."

"It was. That is why they did not. Snapshots are for frames which lose public appeal and are due to be cycled, against possible renewed interest. Frames such as yours maintained a living history such that they could be forked at any point in their recent past. Those living histories were destroyed as part of the preemptive rollback erasing the twentieth and twenty-first centuries."

"God *damn* them," I said, then realized in a sense I just had. "But, OK, fine, not whole frames, but people, individuals. There must be a way to restore at least some of those people who were rolled back."

"That assertion is not correct. Such individuals' data has been randomized, or overwritten, or both."

"There's no record of them at all?" I demanded, despairing. "A data grid the size of a solar system and you've got no backups, no records, no—*nothing*?"

A pause.

"It would be incorrect to assert that there is no record of them at all," said the daemon. "As part of general ongoing frame processing, signatures of significant persons are frequently recorded, as internal data for Maintenance." Another pause. "An analogy which may make sense to a person with an understanding of early-twenty-first-century software is that hashes and checksums of individual persons are recorded in log files, against the prospect of minor hardware failure, which can then be corrected. But this signature data is strictly the output of one-way mathematical functions. It is not possible to reconstruct their source."

I thought furiously. That analogy did make sense. A *hash function* was a mathematical procedure that took any data, like a document—or, in this case, a person—and reduced it to a far smaller signature, known as a hash, which was essentially guaranteed to uniquely identify that input data, because even a hash represented as a single line of text had vastly more permutations than the number of atoms in a trillion trillion universes.

But hashes didn't help. You couldn't take a hash of the Bible and use it to re-create the book any more than you could use a photograph of a dead person to resurrect them. They were called one-way functions for a reason. My daemon was saying the only relicts that remained of Clara and my friends were the far-future equivalent of a stack of photographs. Less, really, in that hash signatures always looked like random noise. I couldn't use them to bring back my Clara any more than I could have summoned her bodily out of a faded Polaroid.

My ephemeral dream of a third wish had been mad and quixotic. I was not God after all. Even with the power of an entire solar system at my command, I remained a downtrodden subject of the tyrannical laws of mathematics.

The power of an entire solar system.

"Wait," I said.

My daemon waited.

"These signatures," I went on. "They're of individuals? Like, whole individuals, thoughts, memories, feelings, everything?"

"Those were the inputs used to generate the signatures," the daemon confirmed.

"And how often were these signatures captured and logged?"

"It varied. For protagonist characters and their frequent interactors, at least daily. For average humans who rarely interacted with frame storylines, perhaps several times a year."

"So for all the people I was close to, we have daily signatures?"

"Yes."

I said: "So what if we brute-forced it?"

There was no possible way to go from a hash of the complete works of Shakespeare to the actual plays and poems, or from Clara's signature to Clara herself—unless one were to *brute-force* the solution, by literally trying every possibility, essentially employing the proverbial team of monkeys not to write Shakespeare but to write *every possible document* until they randomly re-created Shakespeare, then using the hash signature to identify that perfect copy.

Such a problem space was staggeringly huge. The notion of actually finding a solution seemed completely unthinkable, at first. But the Sphere too was staggeringly huge, and "humanity" a relatively small subset of all possible entities. My guess was that the two staggeringnesses might be comparable in size; and if so . . .

"It is a difficult question," my daemon said, after what felt like a very long pause.

My heart quickened with hope. That answer was much more optimistic than an easy *no*. "How so?"

"The compute required to calculate such a solution is very considerable. Initial approximations indicate the re-creation of a single signature match would likely require a substantial majority of the Sphere's computing power for a period on the order of weeks."

"Holy shit," I breathed.

"But our access to the Sphere has not been granted in perpetuity. That single re-creation might approach the limit of our total capabilities during our access window. The probability of being able to re-create matches for the signatures of all those persons tagged as close companions during your life span, without exceeding our capability limit, is extremely small."

"But one person," I said, "you're saying I can save one."

"A single person would suffice?" My daemon sounded actually puzzled.

"You have no idea," I told it, vaguely aware of tears on my cheeks.

I closed my eyes and breathed deeply. I considered the prospects, the details, the ideal set and setting for this awesome task: one that would consume the power of an unthinkably advanced computer the size of an entire solar system—for weeks—to raise my love from the dead.

"All right," I said. "This is my third and final wish."

13

DESTINATION

DESCENDING THE MOUNTAIN, I FELT LIKE MOSES RETURNING FROM the wilderness, albeit Moses minus any burning bush or stone tablets. I intended no disclosure of my revelations, and required no divine visitation. After all, I was no mere prophet. I had been a god.

I supposed I had even created this world around me, in a sense, or at least re-created it, by empowering it to proceed once more into the twentieth century . . . and, for the first time in time immemorial, for millennia beyond, no matter what titans or monsters might be born. This world, and many millions of others; but this one was special. This was home.

Mount Wilson was no Mount Sinai, but it was still hot and steep, its stony trails clogged by chaparral. By the time I reached the nearest house on the highest dirt road I was damp with sweat, and the sun was setting. I sighed with relief at the sight of the clapboard house and the classic Jeep in its driveway. I was where, and when, I had wished.

As I descended, the roads broadened, and the houses grew larger and more numerous. The golden-hour light made every picket fence and curious face look cinematic. By the time I reached downtown Pasadena it was near dark, but I navigated easily enough. I had lived here before. I found a newsstand open late, and paused long enough to confirm the date.

My stomach sank when I saw: *August 5, 1946.*

A minor glitch, I told myself quickly. Five months later than I had wished, but no great harm. Nothing would have happened that couldn't be undone.

Lena's diner was minutes from closing when I arrived. There was no DISHWASHER WANTED sign. It smelled like it always had, of greasy food, cigarette smoke, and dish soap. I wanted to weep. Davit glanced at me in-curiously from the kitchen. Lena looked up suspiciously from clearing a table. I wanted to grab her, hug her tightly, tell her I had missed her, ask her where Clara was. She sensed something was off, and frowned.

"I'm very sorry," I said quickly, "would it be possible to use your bath-room?"

She looked me up and down, my work boots and jeans and blue cotton shirt, and reluctantly said, "Quick."

In the bathroom I stared at the mirror. I looked just as I remembered myself in 2003, mid-twenties, except fitter, more athletic, better-looking, full of life. Only my eyes looked old, to me at least, like ancient caves hewn in stone; but I supposed I was probably just projecting.

I exited hungry, tired, and with neither money nor anywhere to sleep, but I was an old hand at being a stranger in this particular strange land. At the Salvation Army, in exchange for attending the late-night chapel service, I received a plate of beans and a hard bunk. I listened with unex-pected interest, a kind of professional curiosity, to the liturgy and sermon.

Come morning I made my way to Clara's house. I had been there only once before, courtesy of a disagreeable taxi driver, so I had to roam for some time before I found it, a small bungalow set amid many. She had lived with two roommates, I recalled, fellow war widows, one disliked, the other despised.

This experience would have been no less strange and surreal for her, I supposed. I thought there was a good chance she expected me. I knocked, full of anticipation—but it was another widow, bleached blond and made up, who answered.

"Hello," I said politely. "I'm here to see Clara."

Heavily glossed lips frowned with distaste. "She doesn't live here any-more."

"Ah." I hadn't been ready for that. "Then where—?"

"No idea. No forwarding address. No notice. Packed and vanished while we were away, left rent unpaid. Took every advantage of us. How do you know her?"

"I don't, I was just given her address."

"Well, if you find her, tell her from Mary and Ellen, she's a lousy bitch."

The door did not quite slam. I stood a moment, reeling with uncer-tainty. Five months had changed things after all. I reminded myself not to panic. I would find her. But—what else might have gone unexpectedly wrong? Had Clara been returned to sometime in the past, or the future? Might she not return at all?

I told myself everything would work out, I just had to focus on what I could affect. It seemed unwise to go to Lena's empty-handed again, and risk being marked a troublesome character. I needed money. For that I already had a plan. On Sierra Madre Boulevard, east of downtown, day laborers assembled each morning; skilled ones on the west side of the street, squatting on their toolboxes, the unskilled loitering across the way. I took my place on the east side amid a dozen others. The Mexicans, known as harder workers, were first to be selected. It was midmorning when a Ford pickup truck pulled up and its driver motioned myself and another man, Lewis, tall and taciturn, aboard.

"Where we headed?" Lewis asked.

"Whistling to the graveyard," the portly driver said cheerfully. "Need some diggers."

Eight hours later I was exhausted, sweat-soaked, blistered, oddly satisfied, settled with similar work for the next week, and three dollars wealthier. I went to my old flophouse, found prices had increased by a dime, and was assigned the room across from my old one. Then I went to Lena's and ate in polite silence.

Afterward I approached her. She regarded me suspiciously. "Yes?"

"I'm looking for a friend of yours," I said.

Her suspicion intensified. "What makes you think my friends want to talk to you?"

"On Guadalcanal," I lied, "I had a friend named Emile. He had a wife named Clara. It's been a long road here, but I have some things for her. I'm told you're a friend of hers. Do you know where I can find her?"

My invocation of Emile was sufficiently convincing that she didn't ask how I had found my way to her café. But—"I don't." Lena looked worried. "She moved downtown months ago. Said she'd come see me, but I haven't heard from her since. No forwarding address."

"I see." I didn't, at all. "Why would she—"

"She made this new friend," Lena sounded bitter, "this young girl, a parasite, you ask me. Clara said she worked at a bookstore on Grand Avenue, so last month I went there. This girl, Liz, I asked her where Clara was, she wouldn't say. She wouldn't even say if she knew. Wouldn't say anything.

I asked another friend about that bookstore, she said . . ." Lena glanced at Davit in the kitchen, looked back at me. "She said it was a bad place."

I was baffled on several different levels. "Bad how?"

"Just . . . bad. If you find Clara, Mr.—What was your name?"

"Adrian."

"You find her, you tell her I want to see her, and you come tell me where, understand? Clara, sometimes she wants things too much, or wants to help too much."

"Grand Avenue," I said. "And this girl, her name was Liz?"

"Elizabeth Short," Lena said sourly.

It wasn't until I was on the streetcar running along Fair Oaks toward downtown Los Angeles that it hit me.

Elizabeth Short. The name of perhaps the most infamous murder victim in the history of Los Angeles. A woman gruesomely murdered in the 1940s in downtown LA, whose fate had inspired countless books and movies and TV shows. A woman better known as the Black Dahlia.

Could this possibly be coincidence? That seemed unlikely. Or did Clara's unexpected proximity to an infamous historical figure have something to do with the metaphysics of the multiverse, the cohort at this rollback point, my recent return? Had my wish gone awry? Had my presence somehow skewed the course of history? Was the five-month glitch that had delayed my appearance somehow related? Was I, were we, once again being manipulated by, and at the mercy of, what Coherence had long ago called "external influences"?

My mind churning, I rode all the way to the end of the line, to downtown. Night had fallen, and the lights of the movie-palace marquees blazed down as I disembarked into a trundling throng of passersby and bulbous cars. I passed the elegant Bradbury Building, where the finale of *Blade Runner* would be set, to quieter and darker Grand Avenue, where Dawson's Rare & Art Books awaited. It didn't occur to me until then that they might well be closed at this hour—but light continued to shine from within.

Through the window I saw a dark-haired woman, young and anxiously pretty, waiting in what seemed an impatient manner. The door was locked. I knocked. She waved me away. I kept knocking until she came to the door.

"We're closed," she called dismissively through the door.

"Hello," I called back, "are you Elizabeth? Can I speak to you?"

She looked suspicious. "How do you know me?"

"Your friend Lena, in Pasadena, said you could help me. Can I just speak to you a bit?"

It was apparent from her expression that Lena was not her friend, but I had established I was not a complete stranger, and Grand Avenue behind me was quiet but not deserted; there were pedestrians and a man smoking a cigar in a Studebaker parked down the street. With plain reluctance Elizabeth Short unlocked the door, opened it a crack so we could speak normally, and demanded, "What do you want?"

I took a breath. It was strange to be speaking to a true-crime icon. She was very young, barely adult, and sounded petulant and upset, more at the world than at me in particular. "I'm looking for your friend Clara. I knew her husband Emile, in the war. I have some things for her."

Emile's name earned me another notch of trust. She opened the door. "Clara's gone."

"What do you mean, gone?"

"I mean I haven't seen her in weeks. She used to work in the shop around the corner and come see me every day. Then Mr. Kurtz said she just quit. She didn't even come say goodbye." Elizabeth said that with more hurt and anger than the slight seemed to deserve. "She was supposed to arrange something for me." She was too young to disguise the undercurrents in her voice, the implication of something deeper and darker. "I telephoned her, left notes in her mailbox, knocked on her door. But she never answered."

"So you know where she lives?" I immediately regretted asking; it was hard to imagine a more stalkery question.

But Elizabeth seemed intrigued. "Sure. You knew her husband? I can take you there."

After a second I understood: I could be a new excuse for her to seek out Clara. But leaping at the chance to accompany a complete stranger seemed a fairly extreme measure to recontact a former friend. What exactly had Clara been supposed to arrange?

I supposed I didn't really care. "I'd appreciate that."

"My boyfriend's supposed to come get me, but he's late," she decided, "just let me lock up the store. It's not far. What's your name again?"

"Adrian Ross."

"Elizabeth Short. Charmed, I'm sure." She smiled winsomely, flirting reflexively.

Clara's new home was on Flower Street several blocks away, a large house subdivided into four apartments. I was baffled and increasingly worried. Why, during this mysterious five-month glitch, would Clara have moved here from Pasadena, ghosted Lena, agreed some kind of puzzling arrangement with the future Black Dahlia, and then ghosted her as well?

None of that mattered if she was here. The four apartments had four separate entrances; that for Unit B was around the back. A single exterior bulb illuminated the house's back doors and yard. My heart thundering again with hope and anticipation, I knocked, and waited; knocked again, waited longer. After a third attempt, my hope deflated.

"I guess she's not home," I said miserably, and turned to leave.

Elizabeth didn't move. "There's something of mine in there," she said hollowly.

I stopped, perplexed. "What?"

"Photographs."

"Of what?"

She didn't answer, but her sudden look of shame was, given what I already knew about the Black Dahlia—that she had lived on the fringes of Los Angeles's sexual underground—the only hint I needed. She meant pornography. Of herself. Probably very tame, by my era's standards, but this was an epoch where a few nudes could destroy a woman's life.

"Were you being blackmailed?" I asked gently.

Her horror at my understanding was all the answer I needed.

"It's OK," I assured her. "It really is. I'm on your side." But why would Clara have them? "Was Clara the go-between? Helped you buy them back?" I suddenly went cold with shock and panic. If so, Clara had dealt with blackmailers . . . and then vanished. Had I somehow been flung into a horrific past in which she had already been murdered?

"No." Elizabeth couldn't look at me. "She just . . . she was a friend. It . . . wasn't easy to get the money. I was supposed to give them half, then an address to mail it to, then the rest. I couldn't give them my address." I looked at her quizzically. "What if the police were watching, or someone else opened it by mistake? I couldn't, it couldn't be connected to me."

I supposed that made some sense. "So Clara knew? Everything?"

Elizabeth shrugged. "Enough. Now they say they sent it, and if I don't give them the rest this week . . ." She hesitated. "I don't even know you. Clara doesn't even know you."

"You couldn't talk about this to anyone except her," I guessed. "And then she ghosted you." Elizabeth looked baffled. I supposed that phrase had not yet entered the lexicon. "I mean, disappeared."

"Mister, I have to get in there." For the first time she sounded desperate.

I looked at her, then at Unit B's door. It was night. Clara should be home. Clara had fled from Pasadena to here, and then, it seemed, from here to somewhere else, leaving Elizabeth in the lurch, something she would have done only if desperate herself. There might be clues inside to where she had gone. Elizabeth needed to win her life back from her blackmailers.

We looked at each other.

"Can you help me?" she asked softly.

It seemed outrageous to ask an utter stranger to help her break and enter, but then Elizabeth had clearly spent her life to date relying almost entirely on the kindness of strangers and/or the indulgence of men who hoped to win her favor. *This is how you get gruesomely murdered next year,* I wanted to warn her. *Don't trust men like me. Men are dangerous.*

I decided now was not the time to save the Black Dahlia from her future. Her present would do. Clara would want me to do this, to help Elizabeth. The other apartment with a back entrance, Unit C, was dark, seemed deserted. There might never be a better time to break in . . . and within there might be clues leading to Clara.

"Do you think the windows might be open?" I asked softly.

Security seemed not as preeminent in the minds of 1946 Los Angelenos as it would be decades hence. The windows were theoretically locked, but when I used a piece of steel trellis from the yard as an improvised lever to pry open Unit B's shoulder-high sliding window, its shoddy lock snapped immediately.

I made my hands into a stirrup for Elizabeth to get inside. On the first attempt she misstepped and fell against me, pressing her small body against mine as I kept her upright. I suspected this had not been entirely accidental. On the second attempt she managed to scramble into the apartment, while wiggling more than seemed necessary, her dress hiking up to flash the backs of her pale thighs.

She let me in the front door, which I instinctively relocked. The apartment was cramped and spartan, with cheap furniture and barren walls. I checked the bedroom. I had expected to find it empty, but even so the disappointment hit me like a blow. It had not been made, though . . . and it smelled, though probably imperceptibly to anyone but me, of Clara herself and her 1940s perfume. That made me pause. She hadn't disappeared from here weeks ago after all. She had been here no more than a few days ago. More likely hours.

I examined the bedroom more carefully. It had more character than the living room. There was a picture of a young Clara and a handsome, long-faced man I didn't know on its cheap pine dresser. I studied the picture for a moment. That had to be Emile. They had been photographed in a forest somewhere, in the redwoods. She looked joyous, radiant. My heart cramped with sorrow and love and longing.

There was laundry in a hamper in the closet, a small selection of purses hanging from a wooden chair, and on the seat of that chair, a manila envelope addressed to "E.S. c/o 201 South Flower Street, Unit B, Los Angeles California." It had been opened, but I made a point of not inspecting the contents visually, only palpated it to make sure. Photographs, and negatives too, it felt like. "Elizabeth," I called.

She came in from her search of the other room. I held up the envelope. A broad smile broke across her face, oddly more triumphant than relieved.

Then a hammering came on the door, and a man shouted, "*Police! Open up!*"

We both froze.

"Come on out, Short!" another man commanded. "Before we break this door down!"

There was no way out. I looked down at the manila envelope in my hand, came to an immediate adrenalinized decision. "Stall," I commanded her, fled into the bathroom, and locked its door.

I had intended to rip the photos up and flush them down the toilet, but a matchbook on the windowsill changed my mind. I grabbed it, lit a match—some cool, distant, observing part of my mind vaguely pleased at my steady fingers, speculating I had grown halfway accustomed to extreme situations—set the envelope on fire, tossed it in the tub, and opened the floral shower curtain wide.

I then grabbed for the roll of toilet paper, intending it as an accelerant, but there was no need. The envelope erupted with an audible *whoosh* into a two-foot-high flame. Old film, I now recalled, was extremely flammable.

Outside, Elizabeth carried on a conversation I couldn't quite hear. It didn't seem particularly defiant. Moments later a heavy fist beat loudly on the bathroom door. I waited a moment for the fire to subside into something that clearly would not burn down the building, then opened the door, expecting to be flung face-first into a wall.

The mustached man who gazed on me with professional scorn was the same one who had been parked in the Studebaker outside the bookstore. They had been watching Elizabeth. She had brought me along with her right into their trap. I winced.

"Who the hell are you?" he demanded.

"Just . . . a stranger."

"What the hell is that?" He looked over my shoulder. "Fuck!" He shoved me aside roughly, raced to the tub, tried to run water to put out the fire, but it was too late. Only a few incoherent fragments of charred photograph swam amid the ashes.

Another cop approached, huge and blond, one meaty hand dragging Elizabeth by the back of her neck. Her hands were already cuffed behind her. She looked terrified.

"What happened?" Elizabeth asked. "Did he burn them? Did you *burn* them?" she demanded of me, sounding alarmed rather than relieved by the prospect.

"Who the fuck are you?" the big blond cop barked at me.

I said, slightly more composed now, "I want a lawyer."

For a second I thought he would break my nose. Then he looked at Elizabeth. "Got you now, Short." Cruel triumph in his voice. He visibly tightened the hand that held her, and she cried out. I was sure her neck would bruise. He was a big man. "We don't need those. We got you both for breaking and entering. Maybe arson. You're a felon now. You know what that makes you?" His knuckles whitened, and she whimpered. "Mine."

"Victor," the mustached man said nervously. "We should get them to the station."

The big cop looked at his smaller partner with contempt. "Right." He turned back to Elizabeth and smiled thinly. "Lot of questions for you, Short, and this time you'll answer."

She looked too frightened to speak.

We were separated at the jail, whose cells seemed so anachronistic to me that it felt surreally like being on an old-time movie set: a row of small brick rooms, each holding two to four men, with sinks, urinals, and iron bars set in doors and windows. I had given them my name, been searched, and repeated my demand for a lawyer. The receiver, a thin bespectacled man, had written down: "Adrian Ross, day laborer, no ID, no fixed address." Everyone seemed far more interested in Elizabeth Short than me.

My two cellmates, one black and one Latino, ignored me completely. I sat back and thought. Most of my thoughts were self-loathing. I had gotten things catastrophically wrong. Clara had not disappeared; she had been in that apartment very recently. If I had simply waited, she would likely have soon returned. Elizabeth had been upset, even appalled, by my destruction of the photographs. Were they really photographs of her? Or of something else entirely, which she had been desperate to get her hands on? It seemed increasingly likely she had manipulated me to break into Clara's apartment and steal something valuable, which to her dismay I had instead destroyed, just before being arrested and jailed.

How could I have screwed this up so badly, so fast?

Unlike me, the cops had some idea of what those photographs were. That was why they had followed Elizabeth . . . who seemed genuinely terrified of them. The big violent cop clearly bore great ill will toward her. She had used me, but I couldn't really blame her, I was a strange man all but asking for it, and she was clearly in some kind of bad trouble. Trouble that was already dragging her toward her horrifying, infamous fate.

I came to a decision.

Then I stood up, went to the barred door, and shouted: "I want to confess!"

That got the attention of my cellmates, and the jail's other denizens. I ignored them. "It was all my idea!" I bellowed. "None of it was Elizabeth's fault! I told her I'd been invited! Get someone in here to take my confession, and let her go!"

I paused to await a response. The light mutter of conversations in the cells around me fell into silence, and a dozen male faces stared at me, rapt with wide-eyed bemusement. I supposed they couldn't tell if I was a madman, a moron, or both.

And then, in that hushed moment of silence, I heard a soft voice that sounded to me like a trumpet blast from heaven.

"I do apologize for all the confusion, Officer," she said. "I appreciate you doing your job. I quite agree my man friend could have handled the situation better. You can be sure I'll give him a piece of my mind."

Clara's voice.

The door swung open, and she was there, in green dress and dark hat, with the mustached cop and the bespectacled jailer trailing behind her. When she saw me her face sagged with deepest relief for an instant, just as mine did, but then her severe mask was back. "Adrian! To think I have to come get you from here. Do you know how far I had to come?"

"I'm very sorry," I said as meekly as I could, while my heart soared through the stratosphere. "I guess I have some idea."

"Sir," she addressed the cop, "there is no crime, he and Elizabeth were operating under my express invitation, although clearly I should have been more precise regarding *where* he was meant to burn that package. In the yard, Adrian. Don't burn things in my water closet."

"Sorry," I muttered, as chuckles echoed around the jail.

The jailer opened my cell, and then I was out, standing beside her. Clara took my hand and squeezed it fiercely, then turned to the jailer. "I do thank you for doing your job so professionally. Now then. We'll be going."

Elizabeth stood by the exit, deeply relieved and confused. The three of us departed together at a fast walk. I restrained the strong urge to sprint.

"I don't understand," Elizabeth said to us slowly, "I thought you two didn't know—"

"Go home," I told her. "It's been a long night. We'll come see you at the bookstore tomorrow."

Clara looked surprised. Elizabeth nodded, then said, simply but heartfelt, "Thank you."

We went our separate ways, and she was gone, and Clara and I were together, and I wanted to scream and weep and collapse and jump for joy all at the same time. Instead I crushed her to me as if I might weld us together forever.

"I don't want this to end," she eventually managed, "but I do need to breathe."

"Yes. Sorry." I released her, looked at her closely. "What's the last thing you remember? I mean, before . . ."

"You told me you would be back from Tahoe before midnight," she said accusingly. Then she paused to consider. "Wait. I think it is not yet midnight here. King Solomon himself might struggle to determine whether you kept that promise."

We started walking, accompanying one another through late-night downtown Los Angeles in 1946, natural to her, still alien to me. "So you woke up here—"

"I don't think 'woke' is the mot juste, I simply suddenly *was*. In an apartment I didn't know, including a strange manila envelope full of quite upsetting pornography, thank you for burning that, and no idea how to find you."

"How did you know you needed to find me?"

Clara gave me an arch look. "Experience has taught me that on those occasions on which I am suddenly transported between worlds, I might reasonably leap to the presumption you were involved in some capacity."

"Fair," I conceded.

"I went to Lena, who was quite upset with me. I really don't understand why I did the things I'm told I did these past few months. I told her I'd had a kind of nervous breakdown. She forgave me and told me a strange man had come looking for me. What do Jack and Marjorie know?"

"In this world? Nothing. You were the only one I could save." Clara looked at me quizzically. "I'll explain. There's . . . a lot. They don't know us anymore, but maybe we can go to them anyway. They might believe, and they'll understand. Well. Sort of."

She nodded slowly. "How long have you been here?"

"I think exactly as long as you."

Her eyebrows rose. "I'm rather impressed you managed to get yourself arrested and jailed in such a short period of time."

"Mistakes were made," I said awkwardly. "That girl, Elizabeth, we have to save her. I think maybe you were already trying."

"Save her from what?"

I didn't quite know how to answer that, other than *murder*. "History," I tried.

It was inexpressibly wonderful to be with Clara again, but deeply worrying that I didn't know how or why we had now somehow been entangled with the story of the Black Dahlia. Had we randomly intersected with a story unfolding on its own? Were we being manipulated by some kind of exterior force? I supposed we couldn't know, and likely wouldn't ever.

But it occurred to me then that this was true of everyone, a universal feature of the human experience. We didn't know if we were plagued by demons or guided by angels, if we were algorithms in a simulation, or if our apparent free will was in truth the dream of a superintelligence. Even if by some freak event we penetrated a mystery, as I had, there would always be more beyond, kaleidoscopic, ineffable, ultimately unknowable. We were only human. No matter the secret truths of our situation, we would still have to do what humans did: muddle onward, hopefully toward a better world, with those we loved.

"Not to be absurdly practical in the face of these metaphysical matters," Clara said, "but my darling, the hour is late, and my new home ever further behind us. Where are we going?"

I considered. "How about Angels Flight?"

Clara smiled. "Do you intend to take me up to heaven?"

"Perhaps there's no need," I said to her. "Perhaps we're already there."

AFTERWORD

Science fiction is sometimes called "the literature of ideas." This sells it short—more precisely, it is literature *plus* ideas, which is why it is harder to write—but its ideas do matter. What follows is a short précis of some which helped to inform this novel. Phrases in **bold** double as the titles of Wikipedia pages, for those interested in diving deeper into rabbit holes.

Much of the AI behavior in this book, along with its treatment of sentience, and the extent to which that can be replicated in software, was inspired by Oxford philosophy professor Nick Bostrom's fascinating book **Superintelligence: Paths, Dangers, Strategies**.

The **reputation capital** economy which Siblings uses is shamelessly based on my own pet project "YKarma," so you may rest assured that a working implementation, of sorts, already semi-exists, running atop a private **Ethereum** blockchain.

At one point Meredith refers to "the Thompson tone detector," a reference to an infamous-in-engineering-circles example of **evolvable hardware**.

The Brethren were inspired by one of my day jobs, that of founding director of the GitHub Archive Program, which in 2020 took a snapshot of approximately all open-source software, wrote it to hardened microfilm good for one thousand years, and stored it in a vault beneath an Arctic mountain. Our research included the **Human Interference Task Force**, who sought ways to protect people from atomic waste sites in any unknown futures. One proposal was an "atomic priesthood," to pass down the creed "Avoid these cursed places!" without necessarily knowing why. The Brethren are that in reverse: "Find these precious things and keep them safe!"

The word "daemon" is a software term of art. A **daemon (computing)** is a process which runs on its own, rather than under the control of a user. The term **loa** comes from voodoo, and thence from West Africa, specifically the Yoruba word *olúwa*, meaning "god" or "lord."

A daemon's payload is essentially a special edge case of **Kolmogorov complexity**, a measure which boils down to "how much complexity or information a given quantity of text can convey." (As an aside, I would argue that fiction's is much higher than nonfiction's.) A corollary is that a given civilization, or tech level, has its own Kolmogorov level: the maximum complexity of a system that civilization could conceivably create.

The universes are like the virtual machines in a **server farm** or **data center**, and the ability to jump between them via a software exploit, and/or communicate across them, is essentially a macroscopic example of a special case of **hyperjacking**. Escaping into the host system is in turn known simply as **virtual machine escape**.

Jack Parsons and **Marjorie Cameron** were real people, and few if any liberties have been taken with their extraordinary histories. (The same is tragically true of Elizabeth Short, a.k.a. the **Black Dahlia**. There even exists a plausible social connection between them, via **George Hodel**, Baron Ernst von Harringa, and Parsons's co-religionist **Wilfred Talbot Smith**.)

The notion that myths and legends were based on scientific reality was first promulgated by "**ancient astronauts**" theories, which are extraordinarily rich and colorful but suffer from the slight disadvantage of being a pseudoscience contradicted by all available evidence. Slightly repurposed, though, they were useful seeds for fiction.

A **logic bomb**, such as that planted in Ancient Egypt in hopes of destroying the terminator thousands of years hence, is a somewhat old-fashioned term of infosec art. It refers to malicious code which waits for specific criteria to be met before activating.

The **Sea Peoples** were a mysterious civilization which attacked Egypt and other Mediterranean nations and, in so doing, may have precipitated (or helped to precipitate) the no less mysterious **Late Bronze Age collapse**.

The megastructure known as a **Dyson sphere**, built to completely encompass a star and capture all of its energy, is a science-fiction staple. (It is worth mentioning that the rest of our solar system is a rounding error compared to the Sun, which is 99.8 percent of our system's total mass.) A practical Dyson sphere would likely be a swarm or collection of objects, rather than a single rigid physical entity. The implicit assumption is that the solar system was "spheraformed" via a form of **gray goo** which was **Turing machines** that were also **Von Neumann machines**.

The notion that entire categories of human endeavor are actually **yak**

shaving for some extraterrestrial project also exists in **The Sirens of Titan** by Kurt Vonnegut. I had no conscious memory of this while writing the book, until my redoubtable agent pointed it out, but I have read it (and most of Vonnegut), so it may well have been a subconscious seed.

Angels Flight is a very short, narrow-gauge funicular railway in Downtown Los Angeles which has appeared in films such as *M, Kiss Me Deadly,* and *La La Land,* and which, like most of the above concepts, has long been numbered among my many inexplicable mild obsessions.

ACKNOWLEDGMENTS

I am a hermit writer but many people help indirectly. Thanks to: Susan Brown, Nat Friedman, Miju Han, Gavin Chait, Sarah Langan, Bill Hanage, Helen Jenkins, Maggie Cino, Michael Gardner, Star Simpson, Rick Innis, Riana Pfefferkorn, Anna Barnett, Ellen Wayte, Robb Chen-Ware, Aaron Brocken, Jen DiGiacomo, Will Schenk, Julia Metcalf, Henry Pickavet, Jack Shen, Linda Howard Valentine, Vinay Gupta, Elizabeth Donaldson, Jered Floyd, Jessica Gregson, Rachael Nicholson, Ben Brown, Namir Khaliq, my family, my editor Patrick Nielsen Hayden, my agent Deborah Schneider, and, of course, the spectral residue of Philip K. Dick.